Wooden Spoon Wars

K. Minko

oddopus

Wooden Spoon Wars
Author: K. Minko
Copyright © 2025 by Alexander Kremer
Published by Oddopus

ISBN   978-1-0684114-3-4

Fig. 1. Fragments excavated from the ruins of the Temple of Archilochus on Reumatonese. c. 450 – 200 BCE. Akademie Museum, Berlin.

Please cut out and paste these *Home Redaction Strips*™ over any words or phrases which offend or trigger you
(e.g. ***crap, wank, bum-bandit***).
Thank you.

PROBLEMATIC-PROBLEMATIC-PROBLEMATIC-PROBLEMATIC
PROBLEMATIC-PROBLEMATIC-PROBLEMATIC-PROBLEMATIC
PROBLEMATIC-PROBLEMATIC-PROBLEMATIC-PROBLEMATIC
PROBLEMATIC-PROBLEMATIC-PROBLEMATIC-PROBLEMATIC
PROBLEMATIC-PROBLEMATIC-PROBLEMATIC-PROBLEMATIC
PROBLEMATIC-PROBLEMATIC-PROBLEMATIC-PROBLEMATIC
PROBLEMATIC-PROBLEMATIC-PROBLEMATIC-PROBLEMATIC
PROBLEMATIC-PROBLEMATIC-PROBLEMATIC-PROBLEMATIC
PROBLEMATIC-PROBLEMATIC-PROBLEMATIC-PROBLEMATIC
PROBLEMATIC-PROBLEMATIC-PROBLEMATIC-PROBLEMATIC
PROBLEMATIC-PROBLEMATIC-PROBLEMATIC-PROBLEMATIC
PROBLEMATIC-PROBLEMATIC-PROBLEMATIC-PROBLEMATIC
PROBLEMATIC-PROBLEMATIC-PROBLEMATIC-PROBLEMATIC
PROBLEMATIC-PROBLEMATIC-PROBLEMATIC-PROBLEMATIC
PROBLEMATIC-PROBLEMATIC-PROBLEMATIC-PROBLEMATIC
PROBLEMATIC-PROBLEMATIC-PROBLEMATIC-PROBLEMATIC
PROBLEMATIC-PROBLEMATIC-PROBLEMATIC-PROBLEMATIC
PROBLEMATIC-PROBLEMATIC-PROBLEMATIC-PROBLEMATIC
PROBLEMATIC-PROBLEMATIC-PROBLEMATIC-PROBLEMATIC
PROBLEMATIC-PROBLEMATIC-PROBLEMATIC-PROBLEMATIC
PROBLEMATIC-PROBLEMATIC-PROBLEMATIC-PROBLEMATIC
PROBLEMATIC-PROBLEMATIC-PROBLEMATIC-PROBLEMATIC

"Давайте!" my President calls. The flashes of a hundred cameras ricochet off the rococo mirrors and gilt pilasters. The President of the Russian Federation, standing tall in his raised shoes, pins FSB medal number 415 to my left tit. I'm a blonde Siberian babe with a medal - propaganda in 9 cm heels.

My President pulls me closer. "I speak to you as one spy to another, Anastasiya Kirillovna," he whispers. His breath smells of cologne and bacon. "Can you keep a secret?"

"That's my job, Excellency," I said. "But please call me Nastya."

"Ah, I see that you've adopted the overfamiliar ways of the West. But that's no surprise, given your specialty. You know what, Nastya? Our whole frigging Russian army is on the Ukrainian border. Maneuvers my arse! Next Tuesday - we're in Kiev. No shit. Thursday tops. And we will owe our victory to you. Russia salutes you."

Chapter 1 - In the Agora, Athens, 7th of Boedromion, 378 BC

I am Diogenes of Sinope. I live in a barrel. I am about to be kidnapped and enslaved. Worst of all, I am not the main character in this story, so I might die at any time.

Obviously, when you live in a barrel, the first thing you want in the morning is a good stretch, and the second is a good crap. Stretch up and crouch down. So, I, Diogenes of Sinope, stretch my arms up to the scorching Hellenic sky and begin the daily hunt for a place to crouch down. And, as usual, there's a line of out-of-town tourists outside my barrel. These trippers are waiting to see me, Diogenes of Sinope, the Stunt Philosopher, take one of my celebrated dumps. Or, if they're lucky, a quick-fire performative wank.

This crapping routine has become unnecessarily complicated. Vexatious. It all started - by the Dog, I can't even remember the year - when I was returning from a typically unprofitable day at the poultry market, just minding my own affairs and whistling a carefree - but nonetheless poignant - melody. The downside was, the night before, finding myself temporarily lacking the requisite drachmas for clean food, I'd eaten one of my own putrid chickens, and now the Promethean pangs came on so suddenly that I couldn't make it to the cypress grove in time. I just had to let rip there and then, half-way across the Agora, before the astonished eyes of the attendant riffraff, piss-artists and tosspots. No sooner is the business done, and I am looking around in some embarrassment for the nearest smooth stone, than this beardless ponce flounces out of the crowd and points triumphantly at the fruit of my exertions.

"People of Athens, behold!" he cries. I recognise him straight off - Phocion. One of those rich teeny-boys who hang out with that pseudo-philosopher-bum-bandit, Plato. Phocion's already caught that smartarse lingo from his so-called mentor. *Plato-patter*, I call it.

[In parentheses, if the phrase 'bum-bandit' trigger thee, recall that this was 378 BC and that I was speaking Attic Greek. Anyway, nobody cared about words until that snowflake Plato came along. Before Plato, words were just noises. You could call any random Macedonian in the Agora a hairy-toed, fascist sheep-shagger and he would just smile and say, "Sticks and stones may break my bones, but conventionalist labels will never hurt me." Happy days!]

Why do I so loathe Plato? Let me count the ways.

(1) Mostly on commercial grounds. In the stunt
philosophy   trade,   Plato's   the   effing

competition. He's cornered the upper-class hipster market segment, raking in juicy tuition fees from the olive-oil-glistened curly-locked sons of the Athenian aristocracy, and leaving me to collect a few obols for performing my crap-wank show to low-budget trippers.

(2) Plato petitioned the Council of Five Hundred to have me banned from the Agora. Apparently, my crap-wank show was debasing philosophy.

(3) Plato's philosophy is bollocks. Just words.

"Behold a true man, people of Athens!" Phocion declaims.

As you may imagine, I'm more than a little uneasy now. Not only have I pulled a Number Two in the agora, the throbbing heart of the city which is supposedly the epicentre, the very belly-button of Greek so-called civilisation, not only am I crouched and crawling crab-like towards a tantalisingly distant flat stone, not only is there an imminent risk of wardrobe malfunction, owing to my horny big toenails getting hooked in the fringe of my chiton, but now I have the malodorous riff-raff of Athens streaming in from every corner of the Agora to gawp, and a pretty philosophy student perorating Demosthenes-style over my doo-doo.

Phocion adopts the philosopher stance (weight on the back foot, front knee slightly bent, eyebrows raised, palms upturned, gaze on the horizon). Then he points at the end of my nose.

"Observe how the True Man shakes off all the superfluities of custom. Observe how the True Man strips away superficial appearances. Observe how the True Man disdains to conform with the artificial *nomos*. Observe how he instead embraces the *physis* of humanity, the essence of what it is to be a person, defecating in the open without artifice or ceremony. Yea, we are born, we eat, we defecate, we copulate ... and then we die. What then indeed is thy purpose, O True Man?"

I wasn't quite sure how to reply. Somehow, "I ate rancid poultry" didn't seem to cut it. Anyway, I needn't have worried. Being a disciple of that corporeal fart Plato, Phocion was more interested in the sound of his own questions than waiting for answers.

"What is thy name, O True Man?" says Phocion.

"Sophocles," say I, continuing my crab-like shuffle. If in doubt, give a false name. That's what Dad taught me, before we both got nicked for debasing the Sinopean drachma. But more of that later.

"That's not Sophocles," brays a fruity voice from the crowd. "That's Diogenes. I know him. He sold my

Mum a featherless chicken." The nouveau riche accent and petulant tone are vaguely familiar.

"Ah, Diogenes, Diogenes," says Phocion, rolling my name around in his mouth like a Cretan merchant sampling an olive. "Tell us, O Diogenes, why didst thou claim to be called Sophocles?"

Making a run for it was no longer a viable option. By now the crowd around me was at least six deep and growing. The unwashed of Athens were gazing at me in fish-like silence, gawping like the holy mackerel of the Temple of Triton.

"It's none of your bloody business what I'm called, O Phocion. I could be Sophocles or Helen of Troy and it's all the effing same to you."

My words appeared to have the opposite effect from that intended. Phocion raises both hands to the skies. "Hail the True Philosopher!" he cries. "He sees through the flimsy translucent trappings in which we dress reality. Like a man who pulls a curtain aside, he has discovered the essence. He knows that a name is just an arbitrary string of sounds with which we veil the fundamental reality. The name is not the thing. The name is temporal and human-caused *nomos*. The thing is its own eternal virtue. He knows that he is neither Diogenes nor Sophocles." And then, triumphantly, syllable by syllable: "He Knows That He Is What He Is."

Between you and me and the Bronze Nob of the Colossus of Rhodes, what exactly the fuck was that supposed to mean, honestly?

A murmur of awe emanated from the cretinous assembly. The enterprising bluebottles on the turd were apparently the only rational and purpose-driven creatures in the Agora at this moment in time.

"Wherefrom hailst thou, O True Man?" calls Phocion, with an upward inflection at the end of the question that was probably meant to sound Themistoclean but came out like the shriek of a constipated gannet. If I were a cynic, I would say that Phocion was getting his kicks more from the attention of the *hoi polloi* than from the pursuit of Essential Truth. Narcissism, to coin a word.

Well, no way was I going to reveal to these cretins where I came from. (i) Like Dad said, that dismal day we got off the boat from Sinope, when you're up against it, son, shtum never fails. (ii) These Athenians, they've never accepted us Ionian immigrants. In their eyes we're practically Persian wogs, especially since Spartexit from the confederation of the Hellenes. (iii) Dad and I once had that little trouble with the law back in Sinope. It's all ancient history now, but I ran the city mint, and the local magistrates somehow got the impression that I was exercising a little too much artistic licence regarding the copper-silver ratio. I called it productivity. They called it debasing the currency. Potayto potahto. Just to rub it in, they collected in all my coins and smashed them with a chisel. Not the kind of story you want to advertise when you're trying to make a fresh start in the poultry racket, and (iv) I come from a place which theoretically doesn't exist, Ionia having become part of Sparta at the end of the Corinthian War.

"Wherefrom hailst thou?", repeats Phocion, and I can see the sinews in his crimson neck straining so hard that it looks like his turn to drop a steamer. "See how the True Man hesitates to reply. For does the origin of a man determine his *physis*? Can you put a Corinthian next to a Theban in the Agora and distinguish their essence? Is the indivisible quality of a man in any way modified by the place of his birth?" Another breathy sigh of appreciation from the crowd. Now they're having to stand on tippy toes at the back to admire the spectacle of yours truly squatting in the sand.

"Tell us, O True Man: art thou a citizen of the world: a COS-MO-POL-IT-AN?" Phocion surveyed the crowd smugly like a lyrist who's just pulled off a tricky riff and is waiting for the applause from the stone benches.

How do you answer that one? "Art thou a citizen of the world?" Best just to go along with it. "Well, I suppose we're all citizens of the world, if you put it like that."

Phocion surveyed his audience, smiling and nodding. "We're all citizens of the world," he whispered slowly. Then he just stood there, rubbing his hairless chin, letting his words hang in the air like chalk dust. Ten seconds passed. Twenty. The onlookers began to look at each other. Matters seemed to have reached a natural conclusion. Time for yours truly, Diogenes of Sinope, to slide inconspicuously away towards the beckoning cypresses, the appropriate moment for the smooth stone having already passed, as it were.

No such luck.

"What about my Mum's featherless chicken?" boomed the fruity nouveau riche voice from the crowd.

"Who speaks?" called Phocion.

"It is I, Plato of Athens, philosopher, seeker of the Truth, disciple of the thrice-worthy Socrates." Dramatic pause. "This man sold my Mum a featherless chicken and I want my money back." The crowd parts and some bloke with a craggy face and curly beard steps out. He stands next to Phocion, legs apart like the whole bleeding Agora belongs to his pappa.

As I said earlier, those who haven't actually visited Athens tend to get the wrong idea: they believe that this whole city is a den of tarts, bum-bandits, goat-shagging politicians, barrack-room lawyers, preening actors, luvvy playwrights, stoner oracles and narcissistic gymnasts slathered in olive oil. Cultural ferment my arse. You can suck my dialectic. The fact is, dear citizens of Macedonia, Corinth, Thebes and Sparta, that Athens is just as dull as your hometown. I mean, clearly the Athenians' life is short on thrills if they're prepared to sit on an arse-flattening stone bench for five hours listening to some blind dude in a mask moaning about how he 'accidentally' rogered his mom. In fact, with all due respect to Herodotus, the entire Athenian Empire is as disappointing as one's first time shagging a sheep - with the honorable exception of Lesbos, of course. And more about Lesbos later.

So, when some bloke says in the middle of the Agora, "This man sold my Mum a featherless chicken and where's my money back?" it's naturally a crowd-puller. Everyone's looking at me with big, round, expectant eyes, like they're thinking, "How're you gonna get out of that one, smarty-pants?"

Which is exactly what I'm thinking too.

You see, if Dad and I had known better, we'd never have gone in for poultry. When they booted us so heartlessly out of Sinope, on account of that difference of opinion on the role of the private sector in quantitative easing, which the municipal gerontocracy misconstrued as counterfeiting, and when we pitched up in Athens with nothing but the lash-scars on our backs, we hadn't researched the market. That is to say: we didn't realise what a moaning, whingeing, chiselling, nose-curling, drachma-pinching piece of meanness is your average Athenian consumer. Any bird you showed them was either too skinny or too flabby, too dark or too pale, too old or too young - anything to knock a couple of obols off the price. And if you told these people about the effect of the Corinthian Wars upon the price of chickenfeed, I'm telling you, they just didn't want to hear. When I thought that I could still be knocking out the old alloy in Sinope, it made me weep bitter tears into my taramasalata.

So obviously, when an ἐπίδημιά of chicken lice struck our flock and all their feathers fell out, we just had to make the most of it. "Oven-ready chickens", we called them. To give the Athenian *hoi polloi* due credit, not many of them fell for it, but obviously Plato's Mum did. Which makes one question the *nous* in that particular bloodline.

But, to return to the existential crisis currently unfolding in the Agora, there's me down on my haunches, and the crowd getting restless and clearly anticipating the pleasure of kicking the shite out of yours truly. There's Phocion stretching both arms out towards me like he's a Piraeus pimp displaying his menu du jour. And there's the great Philosopher Plato glaring disdainfully downwards and, if I'm not mistaken, dealing Phocion's bum a surreptitious fumble. Considering that Plato's mentor Socrates was hemlocked for 'corrupting the youth', the philosophical profession as a whole seemed to be having trouble reconciling the duality of the temporal flesh and the eternal spirit.

"This man sold my Mum a featherless chicken, and where's my money back?" snarls Plato.

Then my refugee smarts kick in. Say what you like about stereotypes, we Ionian wop dago spick wog greaseball immigrants know how to talk our way out of a tight spot.

"O noble Phocion, O fellow Athenians. 'Where's my money back?' I shall answer this question of the great Philosopher Plato after the manner of the renowned Socrates. To wit, I shall answer the question with questions."

A rustle of moronic excitement from the crowd.

"O triply-wise Plato of Athens," I proceed, "dost thou distinguish between the price of a chicken and its intrinsic value?"

"O Diogenes, indeed, one must distinguish between the price of a chicken, which is a transient human deal-i-o, and its intrinsic value, which is eternal unvarying truth."

The old dualism one-two. *Physis* and *nomos*. I knew he'd fall for it.

"Tell me, therefore, O many-witted Athenian, which has more intrinsic value, a man or a chicken?"

Plato cleared his throat ostentatiously. "Clearly, O Diogenes of Sinope, a man has more value than a chicken, for a man alone is blessed with intelligence and the divine spirit." The crowd nodded approvingly.

"So, O Plato, if, on the one hand, the price of a chicken, its transient *nomos*, were greater than its value, the eternal *physis*, would this not be a rip-off?"

"It would indeed be a total scam, O Diogenes."

"But if, on the other hand, the eternal *physis* were greater than the transient *nomos*, would this be a bargain?"

"It would indeed be a cracking deal, O Diogenes."

"So then, O noble and wise Plato, canst thou tell me, would not thy mum have received a cracking deal if, having paid the price of a chicken, she received instead a man?"

"She would indeed have received a corker of a deal, O Diogenes of Sinope, if she received the eternal unvarying value of a man blessed with divine spirit for the transient price of a chicken."

Dear Reader, I am aware that the line of reasoning which now follows is not exactly kosher, to borrow the lingo of the cedarwood merchants from down South who occasionally pitched up in Sinope. However, sometimes necessity has its own logic. Let's just call it "My Truth" and move on.

"Tell me, O handsome Plato, is a man a biped?" say I. The crowd was lapping this up, clearly forgetting that it was practically yesterday that they'd executed Socrates basically for being a clever dick.

"A man goes on two legs and is therefore a biped," replies Plato.

"Does a man have feathers, O Plato?

"A man is featherless, O Diogenes of Sinope."

"Aha!" I cry, turning slowly around for dramatic effect. Total silence from the crowd. You can hear the wind. "A man is a featherless biped. I sold your Mum a featherless biped. Therefore – O triply-wise philosopher - I sold your Mum a man. Ergo, your Mum received a corker of a deal by receiving a man, endowed with divine spirit, for the price of a chicken. Ask not therefore, O Philosopher Plato, when you are going to get your money back! I ask thee, O Plato, when willst thou pay me the just price of a man which <u>thou</u> owest <u>me</u>?"

A low gasp from the crowd.

Plato's looking sheepish now and mumbling something about syllogisms and fingernails but nobody's listening. The crowd's with me.

"Yo, Plato!" shouts a bloke with a hammer, an apron and the physique of a meatloaf. "When yer gonna give Diogenes his cashback?"

"The Pathetic Fallacy ..." Plato begins, but the plebs can't hear him. They're all shouting at the same time: "Diogenes the True Man!" "Diogenes the essence of humanity!" "Diogenes sees through the name to the reality." "Diogenes is a cosmopolitan citizen of the world." "Diogenes knows that he is what he is!" "Diogenes separates fundamental truth from custom; he craps in the Agora."

And the next thing I know they're showering me with cash. Drachmas, obols, even a Nubian shat, silver coins flying through the air faster than I can pick them up. Even Plato eventually knows when he's beaten and grudgingly drops a stonking gold stater onto the sand before slinking off.

So that was when I threw over the poultry and went in for the philosophy racket.

I shacked up in a barrel in the Agora. Whenever I needed cash, I'd light up my lantern in daytime and wander around saying I was searching for an honest man. Of course, with a virtue-signalling gimmick like that, I was getting obols thrown at me wherever I went. I would defecate and masturbate in the agora, and the rich, fat sightseers, oil merchants from Thebes and panders from Corinth, would toss tips at me - from a hygienic distance. I was a Tourist Attraction, a Stunt Philosopher. Occasionally I had to pull a cheap trick like eating a gyros kebab in Plato's Academy, but it surely beat shoveling chicken shit for a living.

The only downside, as I said at the beginning, was finding somewhere to have a crap in peace. So, we return to today, as I stride out into the sunshine with a gaggle of Boeotian tourists tagging along behind, the gnostic joy of the clever dick in my soul somewhat alloyed by the earthly discomfort lower down.

But if I'd known how today's crap was going to turn out, frankly I'd have stayed in my barrel and clenched my sphincter.

Chapter 2 - Croydon, 2019 A.D.

Mikhail needed to find his father.

I don't mean that there was something missing from Mikhail's life. There wasn't an emotional gap after thirty-nine years of dadlessness. No feeling of incompleteness for Mikhail. In fact, right at this moment, at 11.59 a.m., the first of December 2019, standing at the counter of the Home Office, 11th floor, Lunar House, 40 Wellesley Road, Croydon CR9 2BY, Mikhail was about to miss his Dad for the first time ever.

"It's Christmas time in Texas

And the feeling is infectious", sang the loudspeaker.

"Texas-infectious", thought Mikhail. "Nice rhyme."

It was the best of times. It was the worst of times. On the west side of the Atlantic Ocean there was a fat, red-faced ginger-headed president. On the east side of the Atlantic Ocean there was a fat, red-faced straw-headed prime minister.

Mikhail turned his attention back to Jacqui, who was saying, "You understand we have to go by the rules, sir." Jacqui was the girl behind the sign that said 'Jacqui Perkins.' But why not Jackie? Well, presumably her real name was Jacqueline, so Jacqui was closer to the original in spelling than Jackie, which makes it OK. But, on the other hand, was it OK for somebody who works in the very place which makes your identity, the Home Office, the Ground Zero of authentication, to use a made-up name? No, it didn't fit. It was wrong. Cognitive dissonance. Ouch!

As a Mikhail, Mikhail had plenty of options for going rogue. He could have called himself Mike, Mick, Micky or even Mikey. His Mum had called him Misha, of course, because Misha (the name, not the person), that was what they used in Russia where she came from. Or the Soviet Union. Or the Soviet Republic of Moldavia, where he was born. Or Moldova, as they called it now. Or Pridnestrovie, the unrecognized state within Moldova which was his birthplace. Or Transnistria, as the world now called it.

"You understand we have to go by the rules, sir."

"Yes, rules are rules," Mikhail replied, looking over Jacqui's shoulder at the clock, whose minute and hour hands clicked with satisfying simultaneity into the vertical position. This only happened once every 12 hours. What good luck that he hadn't missed it.

"As you may have noticed," Mikhail continued, still looking past Jacqui at the clock, but watching now for the first sign of a divergence between its two hands, "I am on the Hesburger's spectrum. This means that I am fully functional, and I have a good understanding of rules. It isn't an illness - just a difference."

Jacqui smiled for some reason. "That's all right, sir. The Home Office has a diversity policy, which covers neurodiversity." She looked at her watch. The strap had a little silver heart on a chain dangling from it. It was £9.99 in Argos, Mikhail knew. He'd read the catalogue. "I am afraid that your leave to remain in the UK will expire on December 31st unless you can establish by that time that you have British citizenship by descent. It says in your file that your mother claimed political asylum in the UK, but never took citizenship. Since your mother was a Russian citizen only, the claim to British citizenship by descent would have to come from your father. Basically, everything depends on where you're from, and where you're from – in this case - is where your father is from."

"My mother disappeared presumed dead in 1989," Mikhail said, "so she was not a Russian citizen. She lived and died a citizen of the Soviet Union. I was born on the twenty-fifth of September 1982. So, I was a citizen of the Soviet Union for seven years and two months exactly and am now a citizen of a country which no longer exists. I have lived for thirty-seven years in a country which exists, but which sent me a letter that my identity doesn't exist anymore, so I have to leave."

Jacqui smiled again for some reason. "The thing is that you need to establish the identity of your father, and that he had British citizenship."

"But if I can't live in Britain, where will I go?"

"You would have Russian citizenship from your mother."

"Grandma Krutova is from Tiraspol, which is not in Russia now. It's in Moldova, where they speak Romanian. But actually, Tiraspol is in a part of Moldova called Transnistria, which is on the east side of the River Dniester or Nistru and Transnistria thinks it is a country but officially it isn't a country, even though it has its own government and money and postage stamps. And in Tiraspol they speak Russian, not Romanian. Anyway, I don't speak Russian or Romanian, so it would be very difficult to live either in Russia or in Moldova, or in Transnistria, where one hundred percent of the population speaks Russian."

"I am very sorry, sir. My advice, sir, would be for you to follow the instructions in our letter. We have to go by the rules."

"There must be rules," Mikhail agreed. "The rules define a line, with those entitled on the good side of the line and everybody else on the bad side. Then of course there are people who end up on the bad side but very close to the good side and the bishops say how unfair it is for them not to be allowed to land their dinghies in Dover and the bishops say that the government should move the line a little bit to let them into the good side. This is the Continuum Fallacy. Do you know the Continuum Fallacy, Jacqui? Then if the government moves the line a little bit to allow the dinghies, then other people on the bad side will now be very close to the good side and the bishops will now say it's unfair. In America they check immigrants' teeth to see which side of the line they are on but in England they stopped checking immigrants' teeth in 2016 when some bishops complained." Jacqui smiled and shrugged.

Mikhail left with his papers in a brown envelope without a stamp on it. The revolving door turned 120 degrees on his way out. The weather felt about three degrees Celsius colder than when he had gone in.

I should explain at this point that I am Mikhail or, more definitively, Mikhail is me. If you are telling a story, you must tell it from somebody's point of view. If you use the first-person viewpoint, you can't write as though you are certain what's going on in other people's heads. That's the rule of writing in the first person. But the thing about being on the Hesburger's Spectrum like me is that it's really hard to know what's going on in other people's heads anyway. So, if I say 'Mikhail' in this story instead of 'I', then I am allowed to guess what other people are thinking and it's not breaking the rules to put my guesses into their heads. That makes sense.

Anyway, Mikhail needed to find his father, so that he could continue to:

a. speak English among the English;

b. live in Streatham, among the Nigerian nail bars and Turkish kebab houses;

c. work on the IT helpdesk at Imperial College, changing trains at Clapham Junction in both directions i.e. from and to Streatham;

d. attend Imperial College's philosophy lectures free of charge, learning about popular follies like the Pathetic Fallacy and the Continuum Fallacy (sitting at the back);

e. not to have to give away Humpty the parrot - or have the vet put him down.

Mikhail explained this Predicament to the lady at the Citizen's Advice Bureau. Her badge said, "I'm Pabsy – I speak Tagalog." Pabsy said that there was an element of subjectivity in the decisions of the UK Visas and Immigration department. "They'll always tell you they're just following the rules, Mikhail, but when all's said and done these decisions are all taken by a flesh and blood human being is the bottom line. My advice to you is to write down the whole background story, how you came to be in this situation and why you need UK residence. Send it to the Home Office. And your MP too. Where do you live?"

"Streatham."

"Labour. Pity."

"The political situation in Streatham is ambiguous," Mikhail replied. "Chuka Umunna, representing the Labour Party, was elected in 2016 with 68.5 percent of the vote, but he defected to the Liberal Democrats in February 2019 because he wanted a second Brexit referendum."

"Brexit. Brexit. I swear it's half my work, love. Everyone's worried about their status. People who thought for decades they knew who they were and then poof they don't even know what to call themselves. Bewildered. Like someone who sat down, and the chair wasn't there. What I learned, love: we just don't realise how flitty-bitty our identity is until it's gone. The stories I could tell you. Honestly, I feel like the Britain I came to doesn't exist anymore, and not just me. Anyway, no harm in trying Chuka. Just the price of a stamp. And you said you worked at Imperial College. Rope them in too. They'll love a campaign."

So Mikhail wrote down that his Dad disappeared and how then his Mum disappeared too, possibly dead. But possibly not dead too, because we don't know anything for sure until the opposite is disproven i.e. Karl Popper's Empirical Falsification. Unless the body of Mikhail's mother is found, it is not proved that she is not alive, and I am therefore not certain that she is dead.

I hope that Mikhail's mother is alive.

As instructed by Jacqui and Pabsy, Mikhail took out his Imperial College laptop on the train from Croydon and began to write:

My mother, Anna Dmitrievna Krutova was born in Tiraspol, in the Moldavian Soviet Socialist Republic, in 1966. Anna's mother was a doctoral candidate in Art History writing her dissertation on brutalist architecture in the post-war reconstruction of Moldavia. Anna's father was an engineering student. Mama was first in her class to be enrolled into the Young Pioneers. As soon as she turned fourteen the principal of her Gymnasium recommended her for the Confederation of Soviet Youth. Although Anna was top in maths and physics, though, it was her chess skills that mattered most in the end.

Chapter 3 - New Holland, St. Petersburg, at approximately the same time

Привет, dear reader! Hi! I'm a troll. Троллъ. I earn a splendid living by posting on Фейсбук (Facebook), Твиттер (Twitter) and Снапчат (Snapchat). I am worth every kopek they pay me. On the last Wednesday of every month, I send a portfolio of my work to a Gleb in Moscow, whom I have never seen, and on the first Wednesday of every month the Gleb transfers a USD deposit into my Sberbank account and uploads my playbook for the month to come. It's the most skilful job in the world.

What's my name?

I'm Vindaloo_Ken, the fat git from Swindon, UK, *whos just a joiner trying to make an honnest living. But those Polish scum I know there game there benefit scams there cash discounts no VAT there complete disregard for health and safety and Im not racist but how can a proper English tradesman make a living when all thats going on undercutting our prices but these politicians dont give a toss only Boris does.*

I'm V4Victory1945 the pensioner from Bishops Stortford who says *its absolute madness actually paying for more pakistanis to come to England so they can stab us on Westminster Bridge when wev got 1000s of wounded servicemen even you see them on the streets sleeping in shop doorways. i met this squaddie down the pub lost his leg in Bagram Afganistan and when he got back they gave his job to a romanian gippo and cut his bennefits talk about adding insult to injury.*

I'm texasranger327 who says *isn't it funny the way the libtards are always jerking off about racial profiling but all the time the worst racial profiling is done by the muslims because the only people letting off bombs have got muslim profiles but you say that and of course they call you racist like theres nothing else they can say.*

But I'm also tacogirl513, the bisexual mulatta Honduran with three kids from three fathers, a doctorate in Gender Studies and a tenure track professorship from Uncle George Soros. And a blog on intersectionality where I can expound the crazy libtard theories that give texasranger327 his daily boner. At some point next year, I will be forced to admit that I'm not a biracial Honduran after all but a pureblooded pedigree Jew from New York. To maximise its impact, tacogirl513 is saving up her big reveal for the bit of the

2020 Presidential Campaign when it all gets repetitive and self-referential.

I'm Kaboomshka69, the twenty-five year-old Siberian babe with a green card and a degree in journalism from Irkutsk. And an apartment in Washington DC. And tits as lively as June squirrels. Kaboomshka is looking for *"A real man who believes in freedom. A real man who's gonna treat me like real woman - and then beat me like a real woman."*

I'm orneryjoe18. I've got a Big Mac in my hands. I've got grease on my jeans. I've got the Stars and Stripes flapping from my mailbox but it's looking tattered these days. I might be your plumber. I might be the guy who fixes your car. I might be the guy you see wearing camo in the bait section of the filling station on Maryland Route 355. *I'm sick of all these politicians. Democrats, Republicans. They all make me wanna puke. If you ain't a hairy lesbian liberal or a psycho gun-nut conservative, they plain don't care. Just give me one straight-up guy who understands ordinary Americans, and he gets my vote any day of the week.*

Have you heard of Ragebombs? No? Excellent! That means they're working. Ragebombs are my main product line these days. My tweets are the cluster Ragebombs: they're tiny but they spread everywhere and they're impossible to clean up. But when an FSB agent introduced Harry to Meghan, that was the bouncing Ragebomb: old-fashioned, spinning and elegantly positioned. But what *everyone* is seeking, what *I want*, is the thousand-megaton thermonuclear Ragebomb, the Ragebomb to wipe out Western civilisation.

Can you imagine me trolling, dear reader? Sitting at 3am in my parents' spare room, crumpled Man U duvet cover, two days' black stubble on my sickly skin, an Iron Maiden tee shirt and jizzy boxer shorts, tin of Red Bull on my nightstand, face blue in the glow of my laptop? Can you see me now?

WRONG!!!!

My name is Anastasia, but you can call me Nastya.

Or Allie, which was once short for Alice. Allie would be from a suburban cul-de-sac in the San Francisco Bay Area. She's got that straight-up, farmer's daughter look of Allie McGraw in 'Love Story' Except she's blonde and freckled. She just doesn't care about a damn thing and her cute little ass in her cutaway Levis wriggles when she walks and she smokes pot on the beach and watches the sun go down, listening to the surf and the seagulls.

Under the boardwalk
Down by the sea-he-he-heee
On a blanket with my baby

32

That's where I'll be.

Because *Allie* is *Alice*, and I am Alice in Wonderland, and Humpty Dumpty is my spirit animal. The egg-shaped gentleman has been my hero, my oval pin-up, ever since I saw *'Alisa v Stranye Chudes'* on TV. And here's why:

`When I use a word,' Humpty Dumpty said, in rather a scornful tone, `it means just what I choose it to mean -- neither more nor less.'*

`The question is,' said Alice, `whether you can make words mean so many different things.'*

`The question is,' said Humpty Dumpty, `which is to be master -- that's all.'*

Well, I am the master, and I choose the meaning of my words. So Alice. Allie.

But back to Nastya. This year Nastya/me had her third vacation in Italy. And next year I am renovating my apartment instead of a vacation.

Free. Single. Suntanned. Not a virgin but near enough. Pretty damn good for a Philology Graduate from the Minsk State University. Let that sink in. A philology degree, aka the one-way ticket to graduate poverty and a premature visit to the Office for Matrimonial Acts. All my girlfriends from class are pulling down five hundred dollars a month if they're lucky, probably married to some piss-artist friend of their brother's, or else shagging their boss for want of anything better. But I am free. Living off my wits, master of my words.

Actors have it easy. They play one role at a time. I, however, have got more than a hundred logins and I might inhabit a dozen characters in an afternoon. Actors have an author. I, however, write my own scripts in real time as I perform them. I'm like Spiderman, spinning my web and swinging from it at the same time, nothing holding me up but my own creations. One word out of place and I'd crash. For example, when I was starting out, @countrygurll from Mechanicsville VA spelt 'colour' the British way, with a 'u', so she was exposed, and I had to kill her off. Cancer of the spleen, because the spleen's quick but still gives you a few days to rage about Obamacare. Pity about @countrygurll. She had a rockin' good line in salty homespun truths. *"When they drained the swamp in Washington, hell, they found another swamp under the swamp."* RIP @countrygurl. Missin' ya, hon.

I am worth everything that the Federal Security Service pays me. But most of all I am worth my apartment. New Holland, St Petersburg. (aka Leningrad, aka Petrograd, aka St. Petersburg again.) Double glazing. View onto the Admiralteiskiy Kanal. Mama's portrait in oils on one wall of the living room. Bang and Olufsen on the other. One bedroom. One big bed waiting. But who's in a hurry?

34

And no Red Bull, please. Japanese Sencha in a celadon ware cup.

So, let's bin this idea that salaried trolls are geeky boys in tee-shirts. Maybe they're mixing up trolls and hackers. Trolling is a woman's job. It stands to reason. First, you need to speak English. Stand outside the Linguistic University at knocking-off time and tell me how many boys you see. Not a lot, right? They're all at the State Engineering Institute. Second, you've got to get into the skin of your characters. You've got to see the world through their eyes. You've got to BE the zeitgeist. You've got to hate the Poles, Romanians, Nigerians, Somalians and Pakis as much as they do. You've got to *yearn* to smash their faces in.

Empathy. It's a female quality.

And don't pretend to be so shocked at my gender stereotypes, my dear Western readers. I've got one foot in St. Petersburg and the other foot in SoCal. So I can be woke when I want, but I can also go blonde, red-lipped and misty eyed for the Russian tricolor when I want. I can be Katyusha, moping on the riverbank amidst the mists and pear-blossom, imploring the mighty eagle to carry my love-song to the distant front, where my darling defends the Motherland from fascism.

Мы любим страдать. (We love to suffer.) Time to put Lyube on the Bang and Olufsen.

Don't be an idiot, America!

Here's your woolly boots.

What are Siberia and Alaska?

Two shores of the same ocean.

Sauna, vodka, accordion and salmon!

You liberal babes of London, Washington & SoCal, you think you're liberated. But you're indentured pantry maids compared with Nastya, free-flying Nastya who can be a man, a woman, a Californian, a Texan, a Londoner, a fascist and a libtard. You're hunched over your sweatshopped i-Phone, toi hypocrite lectrice, ma semblable, ma soeur, agonising about whether you just said something 'problematic' about Princess Kate's shoes, waiting every minute for the tap on the shoulders that says you've been woke-shamed. Yes, I read your Facebook feeds, I know the phrase 'virtue signalling' and I know what it means, 'cause I do it for a living. Suckerrrrs!

You've lost your minds, my dear Western babes and bros. The only art and literature you have left is made from irony, because irony's all that's safe enough for you. The only views you have are views on other people's views.

Mikhail Krutoy, I sent thee a friend request. Please be my friend. I shall exalt thee to a great height. I shall take thee to a very high mountain, as Beelzebub elevated our Saviour, so that you shall see all the

36

kingdoms of the world and their splendour. Yea, Mikhail Krutoy of Streatham, I shall put thee on the cover of Time and Newsweek and people of all nations shall tweet your name and yea, they shall invoke thee in their virtue-signalling. Then, Mikhail Krutoy, I shall cast thee down into the bottomless pit of fiery sulfur, where there is woke-shaming and gnashing of teeth and thy name shall be curst and reviled, even unto the fortieth retweet.

Chapter 4 – Application from Mikhail Krutoy to the Secretary of State for Home Affairs for indefinite leave to remain in the United Kingdom, ref. ILR/2019/AK/034

<u>Attachment 6. Statement from the applicant</u>

Although my mother was top of her class in maths and physics, it was her chess skills that mattered in the end.

My mother, Anna Dmitrievna Krutova, disappeared when I was seven. I knew her long enough then to miss her now. She didn't tell me her story. I suppose she was saving it up - for a day that never came. Julius and Pearl Litvak didn't tell me much either after they fostered me. I must have asked them questions: "Did Mum leave any messages before she disappeared? Did the police find any clues? Were there detectives? Was it on Crimewatch UK? Was it on Police Five? Was it on Britain's Most Wanted?" Probably Julius and Pearl Litvak changed the subject or said they didn't know. That was their way. By the time I was eleven, I must have realised, in my abrupt Hesburger's way, that my questions were disturbing them. So then I stopped asking. And now the Litvaks aren't around either.

Instead, I assembled disconnected clues. The biscuit tin (Walker's all-butter shortbread) containing my mother's belongings that the Litvaks gave me on my sixteenth birthday. Two cuttings from the Oxford Evening Post. A police report. Twenty-five quid for an online search of the National Registry Office, which knew me as *father unknown.*

These fragments I have shored against my ruins:

From an expired Soviet passport: I know that my mother was born in 1966 in Tiraspol in the Moldavian Soviet Socialist Republic; I know that she made a short visit to the UK in January 1983 i.e. nine months before my birth.

From a team photograph: I know that my mother was in the USSR team at the January 1983 world under-18 chess championship in Oxford, England.

From the same passport: I know that she returned from Moscow to the UK in April 1983, when perhaps the foetal me was becoming apparent.

From my birth certificate: I know that I took the masculine form of my mother's surname; her Krutova became my Krutoy. She must have refused to reveal my father's identity.

From a single unsigned sheet of St. John's College notepaper:

3/27/1983

Dear Anna,

In response to your long epistle, as I said, it all comes down to the Continuum Fallacy - color and age. There is a point at which small differences become impossibly big. I will not take responsibility for a child, which, for all I know, is not mine. I have nothing more to say to you.

From the letterhead I know that my father was one of several hundred members of St. John's College, Oxford in 1983.

From the rhyme that my mother taught me in case I got lost, I know that we lived at:

Twenty-five

Cowslip Drive

Cowley, OX3.

From a letter headed Oxfordshire County Council Educational Psychology Service: I know that I am on the Hesburger's Spectrum, that it is a difference, not an illness, and that I am fully functional.

(Note, with threefold appropriateness, the use of the Oxford comma in the preceding sentence.)

From the Oxford Evening Post, December 1990: I know that one Wednesday afternoon my mother didn't pick me up from school. That, when my teacher took me to Cowslip Drive, the house was dark, locked and empty. That the new in-store bakery at Marks and Spencers, where my mother worked, said that she had gone out for her lunch break and never returned. That I was taken into care.

From the Oxford Evening Post a month later: I know that a Leeds insurance broker returning from a ski trip to Courchevel found her clothes and handbag in his garden shed. That the Litvaks, refusenik Jews from Kiev/Kyiv, had *"read about young Misha's plight and immediately knew that they had to offer the poor child a foster home"*.

From the police report: that a forensic examination of the garden shed in Leeds found no sign of assault, sexual or otherwise. That my mother's keys and debit card were in the handbag but there was no cash. No body. No proven death. No coroner. No verdict.

Beside her body they found a shopping bag containing a pale blue teapot in the shape of a clock, a teddy bear, and the remains of a peanut butter sandwich.

From the photographs in the biscuit tin: I know that my mother used to take me to the museums in London and to an unspecified beach. That there were no other adults present when we celebrated Christmas or my birthday. That my mother loved me. That she

41

would never have chosen to leave me of her own free will.

From the pale blue teapot in the shape of a stopwatch, who knows?

From the Home Office's letter of December 2019: I know that I must now prove who I am, who my father is and where he is from. That otherwise I must go to another country that I have never seen and where I cannot communicate.

How can I find my father from so many hundreds of students at St. John's in 1983? Just one word in my father's letter to my mother narrowed it down to two candidates. Can you see how?

Attachment 7: statement from the applicant's employer, received 4 December, 2019

Referee's name, job title, employer: Jeena Bhatt, Registrar, Imperial College, University of London

Referee's email address: jbhatt3@imperial.ac.uk

Referee's phone number: +44 (0) 79 XX XX XX 52

Applicant's name, job title, employer: **Mikhail Krutoy, IT Support Specialist, Imperial College, University of London**

What scarce skills does the applicant have that the Secretary of State could take into account when making a determination? (maximum 1000 characters) :

(i) Mikhail Krutoy has been in his current IT Support position with Imperial for 13 years. His long experience and in-depth knowledge of the College's network architecture and system patches make him the indispensable "institutional memory" of the department. Were he to become unavailable for employment in the UK, this would have severe implications for Imperial's ongoing systems maintenance, for data integrity and for the implementation of the College's 2020-25 platform migration project.

(ii) In addition to the above, Mikhail has volunteered to work in his free time for the college's Department of Neuroscience and Mental Health. He is contributing as a programmer to the

43

department's 'Diogenes Project', which aims to provide a therapeutic virtual reality environment for people with Autism Spectrum Disorder (ASD), including Asperger's and Archilochus-Hesburger Syndromes. The application is currently in beta-testing, and it is therefore vital for this project that Mikhail should remain eligible to work in the UK.

Chapter 5 - St. John's College, Oxford, January 1983

Although Mikhail's mother, Anna Krutova, was top of her class in maths and physics, it was her chess skills that mattered in the end.

I imagine a drizzly Monday morning on the pedestrianised Cornmarket. A foot sticking out of the pile of blankets and cardboard boxes in the doorway of Carphone Warehouse. A Rastafarian with a barrow and an orange Hi-Viz jacket sweeping up the styrofoam burger boxes outside Wetherspoons, flicking his broom with casual artistry around the pancakes of vomit. Pigeons pecking daintily at dropped fries from Burger King. The sounds of an awakening city: behind you, a Routemaster bus growls across Carfax; ahead of you, the shutters of Kentucky Fried Chicken rattle up for the morning crowd.

A skinny girl of sixteen is running unevenly towards St. Giles. (Could she have a hangover?) She doesn't know her way. When she stops to unfold her free tourist map, it is crumpled and damp from the rain. She breathes quickly; she is terrified. She looks at her watch. Although she is panting, her face is pale.

She's not from round here: high black PVC boots, too big for her, a long loose thread coming out of the top of one, laddered brown middle-aged stockings, a knee-length lilac-coloured quilted coat with purple fake-fur trim, too warm for the clammy English winter. No make-up. An old-fashioned crimson felt hat with a ribbon and a feather. Undyed mousey hair. Small white hands clutching the map. Her wide eyes cast around for name signs on the walls. The sweeper observes her fear. When he comes to offer help, she freezes for a second and then suddenly turns and dashes away down Ship Street. Her map flaps behind her, torn along the crease.

Anna Krutova runs through the gate of Exeter College. She looks at her watch. 7.55. The college porter thinks, "She must be one of the Russki birds come for the chess tournament. She's in for the high-jump."

Q Staircase. Anna runs up the stairs three at a time. Maybe the girls' chaperone hasn't noticed that Anna is missing. Maybe the girl's chaperone overslept. Maybe the girls' chaperone spent the night with the boys' chaperone, just like the girls all whispered. Maybe she had jet lag and went for a walk. Maybe she died in the night.

The girls' chaperone was standing in front of Anna's door, fully dressed, arms folded.

"Tatiana Mikhailovna, I'm sorry. Please, please, please..."

"You know what this means, Anna."

"I know, Tatiana Mikhailovna. But, please, please, I beg you ...

"Follow me, Anna." Tatiana Mikhailovna led Anna up another flight of steps into room Q7. She locked the door from the inside and pointed Anna to the wooden chair next to the bureau. The student room smelled of cigarettes and man-sweat. On the wall, to the chaperone's left, was the Athena poster of the tennis girl rubbing her bum. To her right were a washbasin, a plastic cup and two toothbrushes.

"Who was the boy?" the chaperone whispered.

Anna looked at her boots.

"Yes, it matters," hissed the chaperone. "Names always matter. In this case, the name may decide what becomes of you."

Chapter 6 - the New Tretyakov Gallery, Moscow, December 2019

Nastya here again. So here I am, waiting for my Mama under the concrete vault of this temple of the post-Soviet soul. In the ticket queue, pink rain-capes and mauve backpacks are dripping onto marble tiles. The cleaning-lady skirmishes around the Chinese pensioners, flicking her mop between their feet with casual artistry as though they were traffic cones rather than people.

Mama. She called yesterday. For five months she doesn't contact me, so I know something's up when she does:

"And, *finally*, you answer the phone, Nastya. Remember me? I'm your mother." As usual, as soon as Mama's voice gimlets its way into my auditory cortex, my synapses blaze, and her bulging eyes and cheeks lurch into my mind's eye. I say a silent prayer of thanks to the genetic lottery. I got my ballerina looks from my father, whoever he is.

"So - how's things, Mama?"

"Dreadful."

"And how are you, Nastya?"

"Fine, Mama."

"Nastyenka, daughter mine, don't lie to me, saying you're fine. You're not an American. What's the first rule of being Russian, daughter mine?"

"Say life's shit when it's shit, Mama."

"So, how are things, daughter mine?"

"Shitty."

It's 2019, for God's sake. You can buy dried borsch in packets by Knorr. There's actual Italian buffalo mozzarella from actual Italian buffalos in Magnit supermarkets. You'd think that by now our parents' generation might occasionally venture out of their Soviet dreamworld. But no. It's got to be crap salami, black tea, Alla Pugacheva on the radio (always in bloody A minor), and a dumb refusal to admit that anything might ever get better.

"Right, Nastya. Now listen. Tomorrow at three in the afternoon you and I shall meet in the lobby of the New Tretyakov. You understand? And don't pretend you can't come because you have a job. I don't know what the hell they pay you for, but sure as hell it isn't work."

"I know what you think of my job, Mama. Let's talk about something else."

"Just take the overnight train, Nastya."

"Mama, I told you before. Everyone flies. But what's the hurry?"

"I need to show you something in the New Tretyakov. The New Tretyakov, Nastenka. Nowhere else. It's urgent."

"You want to show me a painting in an art gallery, Mama?"

"You could say that. Don't be late, Nastya. I'm having my hair done at five. It might be my last chance."

"Oh, Mama, for heaven's sake. Don't be such a *prima donna*."

"Three p.m., Nastya."

So, I burn some airmiles in Business Class on the S7 shuttle down from Pulkovo Airport. And now I'm in Moscow, scrolling through my Snapchat in a gallery of Twentieth Century art, as though I didn't have two dozen internet ghosts to bring to life and the Armageddon of cultures to oversee.

Yeah, yeah, yeah. And there's my mother in the glass revolving door, like a fly in a jam-jar. On the doormat she shakes her black umbrella dry with a couple of practiced twirls - like the well-trained Soviet citizen that she once was. She scuttles towards me across the shiny floor, a busy black speck in this vast socialist cuboid of concrete and marble. As usual, I am surprised at how small she has become.

"Hello, Mama. How are things? Still dreadful?"

Mama raised one eyebrow and gave me one of her martyred sighs. "What month is it, daughter mine?"

"December, mama."

"Early or late December?"

"Mid-December."

"You see!" she snaps. "It's raining in mid-December." She shakes her umbrella at me. "This is exactly what I'm talking about. The decline of Russia. In the Soviet times, it was snow from November to April. Crisp, glistening snow. And now it's this ... dirty grey western European north Atlantic pizzle-drizzle. Rain in December. We've lost our identity as a nation."

"It's global warming, mama."

My mother sighed as though she were talking to an idiot. "Our today's agenda, Anastasia Kirillovna, is in four parts: first we shall drink tea; second, I shall show you something; third, I shall tell you my secret; fourth, and finally, I shall tell you some bad news. After that I will take my taxi and go to the salon to get my hair done at 5 pm. And you will take your taxi in the opposite direction to Domodedovo airport and decide whether you want to help me. And that might be the last time we see each other."

"Mama, don't be a drama queen. Just tell me what you want to say."

But Mama doesn't reply. She isn't facing me now. She has turned to watch the gaggle of Chinese

51

tourists who have bought their tickets and are now deciding which sign to follow. They revolve in synch like a murmuration of starlings, and head for the museum gift shop.

"I thought so," says Mama. She turns back to her only daughter: "Now, Nastya, buy me a cup of tea."

In the museum cafe I order Mama her usual black tea with no milk, and a soy flat white for myself. While I wait for my coffee, I watch Mama wipe the table and seat with a serviette.

We sit opposite each other and sip in silence.

Soon it is too much for me. "What are we doing here?" I ask. But when I hear my voice, it is the squeak of an angry eight year-old.

"I told you. We are drinking tea," says Mama. She takes another sip, staring across the rim of her teacup. I look carefully into her eyes. Pouched in wrinkles, they have no humour in them and no cruelty. She is not playing with me. She is not putting on a performance. She is just drinking black tea and looking past me, through a glass façade, to the museum gardens, where a post-modern autumn rainstorm is lashing the statues of Brotherhood and Labour. We do not speak.

At length, she carefully rests her cup on its saucer and dabs her mouth with a clean serviette. She folds the serviette to hide the crimson lipstick marks and looks into my eyes.

"Item one on the agenda, Nastya: I have shown you what it is simply to drink of a cup of tea," she said. "Just me and the tea. No selfies. No irony. No signifiers. No subtexts and metatexts. Just physiology: the relief of thirst and the ingestion of a mild stimulant. Why can you not be so simple? I am asking you for your own good. Why do you have to live through the looking-glass when you could live in the real world?

"Nastya, Karl Marx was two-thirds right, but now you're trapped in the final third. *All human history hitherto is the story of control over the means of production.* When the world fed itself by coaxing rye and beets out of the unyielding earth, Nastya, we killed each other for the ownership of land. Marx got that right. When the world clothed and furnished itself by power-looms and foundries, we butchered each other for the ownership of coal and steel and trade routes. Marx got that right."

"Mama," I whined, "Spare me the Sovok lecture. I'm not a Young Pioneer. Please, let's go and see the picture."

Mama reached across the table and put her liver-spotted hand around mine. "This is serious," she said. "Now we are in the third third. And now that we are fed and clothed and furnished, Marx thought we would be

53

at peace. He thought that there'd be nothing left to fight over once our bellies are full and our toes are warm. He was wrong. Now that we are entertaining ourselves with tweets and hashtags, my Nastya, we are killing each other for the ownership of words." She sat back.

"This is what Marx got wrong, Nastyenka. He thought that once we were all fed, clothed and furnished, we could stop fighting. But now we fight over words. In America they are tearing society apart over the meaning of the word 'American.' In England they are sacking people for the way they define 'woman'. In Donbass they are spilling blood over who gets to speak Russian. In Moldova they are tearing themselves apart over whether a kebab is called a shashlik or a frigarui.

"And every day you, Nastya, you sit down in front of your computer and fill people with hate. Words are just illusions, Nastya. They are just empty noises. Just weightless shadows. And when everybody realises that words are just empty shadows there will be peace. But you are turning words into weapons. You are imbuing words with anger and fear, which solidifies them into cold steel.

"You have only one life, Nastya," Mama says. "Use it for good."

By the way Mama purses her lips I know what's coming next. Hospital Number 4, Kishinev, June 1986.

By now you are probably wondering how I am feeling. Am I hurt and angry inside because I've never known my father, and all my life I've been secretly yearning for my mother's approval? Not really. You see, I've been getting these twice-yearly monologues ever since my first period rocked up and the sight of my tampons flicked on some kind of anxiety switch in Mum's head. Maybe they reminded her of the transience of life or something she once had and lost. So I listen to her. I play the character of Anastasia, the daughter. Not hurt. Just wondering: why now?

"I'll never forget those brave boys," Mama begins.

Dear Reader, the real hardcore Sovoks, the ones who think the sun shone out of the USSR's ass, nine times out of ten they were the teacher's pet at school. 5/5 in every test. Homework in on time. Follow the rules. Snitch on classmates. First batch into the Young Pioneers. First batch into the Konsomol. Party card. Well, that was Mama. Top in her class in maths. Top in her class in physics. Even made the national youth chess team, she says (though I'm not totally sure about that, because she says she lost all her trophies. I mean: who loses the only proof that their life was significant?)

So naturally, when Chernobyl blew up, Mama was a head of department in the Radiological Research Institute of Minsk State University.

"I'll never forget those brave boys. I had to record the radiation coming out of their bodies. They were metamorphosing from people into laboratory samples. So, I held the Geiger counters above their bellies, and I measured the radiation which was flowing out of their guts and flowing into me. They didn't know what change was growing inside them. You could see the bewilderment on their faces. The skin on their faces was boiling from the inside out. So they just looked quietly at the ceiling, waiting to die. Lying in rows, waiting patiently to melt internally, with no promise of a heaven to receive them, and no sins to be paid off by their selflessness. No hope for fame. They only knew that they had done their duty. That they had helped their fellow man. And I was doing my duty in a smaller way, and my body soaked up the neutrons from their bodies. Theirs was a real job, Nastya. An action you can see with a result you can touch."

You only had to read that sermon once. Count yourself lucky. I've been hearing how Mama saved the world from caesium-137 since forever.

She tapped her teaspoon on the side of her cup. "Now to the next item on the agenda. I want to show you something." So she pushes back her chair and strikes out across the atrium. I traipse behind her like the sulky schoolgirl I have become.

Always full of surprises, my Mama. Just as we reach the wide concrete steps that lead to the galleries, she veers right into the gift shop. She heads for the rack of framed reproductions. You know the deal – they photograph a painting from the museum collection, LaserJet it onto canvas, slap it into a passepartout and price it at a hundred and fifty bucks.

Mama knows exactly what she's looking for. With a frown of concentration, she rifles briskly through the reproductions and pulls one out. Then she thrusts it towards me with both arms like a priest showing an icon to the congregation.

"See this, Nastya!" Shoppers turn to look at her and then they look at the picture and then they look at me. Maybe you're wondering whether I'm embarrassed. No, I'm not embarrassed. I'm playing the character of Anastasia, the daughter, remember.

The painting shows a blonde, blue-eyed Soviet mama in a white gym outfit with red trimmings. She's got practically no tits but in recompense her thighs are like a stupendous, splendiferous pair of tree-trunks. On her shoulder she carries her smiling cherubic daughter, who wears cute red sandals and waves a red flag. "Do Physical Education!" says the poster. I'm thinking that mama's done plenty of physical education.

"How can this be for sale?" Mama cries, shaking the picture up and down. "These pictures are not ornaments. They are not jokes. They are not experiments in graphic design. They are not post-modern ironic decorations for a toilet in a Manhattan apartment. They are real messages from real people to real people about how to improve their real lives."

Mama turns to the poor boy at the till. He's got a beard and a man-bun. She says in her small grandma voice, not angry, just imploring: "I am simply asking: please tell me - how can this be for sale?"

The boy blushes behind his beard. He looks around at the crowd. "The tourists like socialist realism," he stammers sotto voce. "They want to go home with a piece of our history."

My mother smiles in triumph and draws herself up to her full shortness. "Young person," she says - maladoy chelovyek, the proper Soviet appellation for a proletarian behind a counter. She points at the tourists. "They want to go home with a piece of our history. So you're saying that I am history, is it? And if, so when exactly did I turn from a citizen of the USSR into history? Yes, I'm asking you: when did the life of Anna Vladimirovna Krutova turn into history? And Chernobyl, eh? Come on. Let's talk about Chernobyl. Why not? When did all those liquidized abdomens and those grilled faces turn into history? How can it be history if I can still see those scorched, raw lips when I try to fall asleep? When did we turn from a life being lived into an object to be watched? Can you name the date and the year? Was it when the Americans turned Chernobyl into a TV series? Was it the day that the Chernobyl tours were posted on Tripadvisor? Was that the precise moment in time that capitalism made an object of me?"

Mama nods with satisfaction and puts the picture back into the rack. She gives it a little pat on the head, and says to the picture, "That's you put in your place, my little friend. Your sincerity just turned into history. Your realism just became a knick-knack. You're a paradox now."

Mama turns back to the crowd of shoppers. Two tourists are filming her with their cellphones. "Meme me into a meme!" she cries. And she is smiling, her raisin eyes sparkling gloriously out of her wrinkles. She gives her audience the thumbs-up before grabbing me by the elbow and hustling me out of the gift shop.

"Now I give you my secret and after that the bad news," she says. "But first I need to go to the toilet."

Chapter 7 - Kensington and Streatham

Mikhail stands outside the Russian Embassy on Kensington Palace Gardens with his new apple-red passport in his hand. Pedestrians and cars and buses and taxis continue their journeys as though everything is normal. They don't realise that an alchemical transformation just took place in 6-7 Kensington Palace Gardens. It's as though a Pacific atoll just acquired its first ever name and became an island on a map. Mikhail had his first ever passport. He has an identity.

Mikhail thinks, "It turns out that I have been a Russian all my life."

Mikhail is going to America. Did you work out why? Think carefully. Mikhail showed you two clues. OK. Let's try again and see whether you can spot at least one of them this time. Mikhail is on the Hesburger's spectrum. It helps him to notice such details. It's a difference, not an illness.

3/27/1983

Dear Anna,

In response to your long epistle, as I said, it all comes down to the Continuum Fallacy - color and age.

There is a point at which small differences become impossibly big. I will not take responsibility for a child, which, for all I know, is not mine. I have nothing more to say to you.

There you have it. "Color", not "Colour". Without a "U". And the month comes before the day: "2/27/1983", not "27/2/1983", (which would be more logical because "27/2/1983" goes consistently from smaller to larger divisions of time). So the man who wrote this letter, whom Mikhail assumes to be his father, is an American (or Canadian) who was attending St. John's College, Oxford in March 1983.

Mikhail emailed his enquiry to the St. John's College archivist. He received the following day the information that two male U.S. citizens were studying at St. John's in the 1982/3 academic year. Both held Rhodes Scholarships. Both were reading PPE: Politics, Philosophy and Economics. Both were born in 1958 and were now 60 years old. They were Brent Lundscum from Yale, and Shaun Shaughnessy from Berkeley. All Mikhail had to do now was to fly to America and find out which of them was his father. The easiest would be for one of them to confess.

Mikhail emailed the archivist for Brent and Shaun's contact details so that he could tell them he was coming. The archivist said that he couldn't share their contact details because of the Data Protection Act of 2018. So, Mikhail googled their names instead. It turned out that both men had made successful political careers. Brent Lundscum was the Governor of Arizona and was running in the Republican primaries for the 2020 Presidential Election. Shaun Shaughnessy was a Senator for New Jersey, running in the Democratic primaries. They both had good hair. Mikhail thought it logical that both the candidates for his father were also candidates for President of the USA. It was logical because it was symmetrical. It was also convenient, because if Brent and Shaun both frequented Washington DC it would mean less travel for Mikhail.

On the bus back to Streatham, Mikhail took out his cellphone and reviewed his action plan in Google Sheets.

Plan of Response to Home Office Letter
1. Obtain Russian passport (done).
2. Book air ticket from London to Washington (WAS), NB for a Wednesday so as to benefit from the statistically proven lower fare, and allowing 5 weeks to obtain a visa.
3. Book a hotel in Washington as close as possible to the Capitol while remaining within my $131/night budget, which is equivalent to a

hundred pounds, also taking account of commuting costs.

4. Obtain US Visa, using the Expedited Visa Appointment option, on the grounds that I have until the 31st of December to find a father or else be deported to Russia.

5. Put Humpty in boarding at VIP(Very Important Parrots)

6. Fly to Washington.

7. Ask to meet Brent Lundscum and Sean Shaughnessy. The meetings would be one after another rather than simultaneous, because the probability of finding a time convenient for both of them together would be the product of the fractional probabilities of finding a time for meeting each of them separately.

8. Ask Brent Lundscum and Sean Shaughnessy which of them made my mother pregnant.

9. Obtain affidavit (original and notarized copies).

10. Obtain US passport.

11. Obtain IT job in America.

12. Quit job at Imperial College, but request to continue working on the Diogenes Project remotely.

All unidirectional, logical and sequential, Mikhail thought, except for one thing. Was it possible to find a hotel in Washington D.C. for less than $131 per night? He checked on Hotel.com. It was possible. So, everything was in order. Which reminded him: he had to buy his cornflakes and washing powder on the way home.

However, when Mikhail opens the door of Manor Court, Streatham, the lobby is crowded. Mikhail sees Dumitru and Stela Munteanu, the Romanian couple from flat number 3, Mr. and Mrs. Khan from flat number 4 and Ruby Kufuor from number 5. Then he sees the policeman and policewoman in uniform. All Mikhail's neighbours rotate towards Mikhail as though they have been waiting for him to come home. Then everyone turns back to the police officers to see what they will do. This makes Mikhail feel uncomfortable, what with his big boxes of cereal and detergent, so he walks through the crowd and begins to climb the stairs.

"Excuse me, sir," says the policeman. "Would you mind if we had a quick word?"

Mikhail steps slowly back down the stairs. His heart is pounding, and his stomach feels heavy. Have they come to deport him? "They said until the end of December," Mikhail stammers. "I've still got two months and several days."

The police officers look at each other. "Are you Mikhail Krutoy, from flat number 2?" Mikhail nods. "I'm PC Fields and this is PC Cook. We're here because there's been a report of hate speech," says the

64

policewoman (PC Cook, the one with the northern accent). "One of the occupants of this stairwell found this offensive note taped to the mailboxes. Do you know anything about this offensive note?" Mikhail looks at the mailboxes. A sheet of A4 is taped untidily to flat number 3's letterbox - the Munteanus' letterbox.

"I don't know," Mikhail replies. Dimitru Munteanu gives an "I told you so" nod to the police officers.

"What do you mean you don't know? Either you've seen the note or you haven't," says the policeman.

"I have seen it. What I don't know is whether it is offensive or not. Please let me read it," Mikhail replies, "and then I will know. Maybe." Mikhail sets his two boxes on the floor and approaches the letterboxes. The note is printed in a heavy, bold font in the streaky characters of a clapped-out inkjet.

BREXIT IS COMING

AS WE ARE FINALLY GETTING OUR COUNTRY BACK WE FEEL THERE IS ONE RULE TO THAT NEEDS TO BE MADE CLEAR TO RESIDENTS OF MANOR COURT.

WE DO NOT TOLARATE PEOPLE SPEAKING OTHER LANGUAGES THAN ENGLISH IN THE FLATS.

WE ARE NOW OUR OWN COUNTRY AGAIN AND THE QUEENS ENGLISH IS THE SPOKEN TONGUE HERE.

IF YOU DO WANT TO SPEAK WHATEVER IS THE MOTHER TONGUE OF WHATEVER COUNTRY YOU CAME FROM THEN WE SUGGEST THAT YOU RETURN TO THAT PLACE AND RETURN YOUR FLAT TO THE COUNCIL SO THAT THEY CAN LET BRITISH PEOPLE LIVE HERE AND WE CAN RETURN TO WHAT WAS NORMALITY BEFORE YOU INFECTED THIS ONCE GREAT ISLAND.

IT'S A SIMPLE CHOICE OBEY THE RULE OF THE MAJORITY OR LEAVE.

YOU WON'T HAVE LONG TILL OUR GOVERNMENT WILL IMPLEMENT RULES THAT WILL PUT BRITISH FIRST. SO, BEST AVOLVE OR GO BACK HOME.

GOD SAVE QUEEN ELIZABETH, HER GOVERMENT AND ALL TRUE PATRIOTS.

"I still don't know whether it is offensive or not," Mikhail says. "Dumitru, is it offensive?"

"Very offensive," Dumitru snaps.

"OK, there's your answer," Mikhail tells the police officers. "If it has offended Mr. Dumitru, then it must be offensive. A fart in a lift would offend someone if there were someone in the lift to smell it other than the farter. So even if the farter is alone, we can deduce that the fart is offensive. Now if you said to me, "Mr. Krutoy, is this note inappropriate?" or "Mr. Krutoy, is this note racist?" then that would be a more difficult question, because there is no nose to smell inappropriateness or racism."

Mikhail turns to PC Cook. "Are you from Yorkshire or Lancashire?"

"Cumbria actually."

"I was asking because of your accent. Sorry if my question was offensive. Was it offensive? Was it offensive to you?"

PC Cook raised her pencilled eyebrows. "Not really, sir. "But in your opinion, Mr. Krutoy, is this note hate speech ? Just 'yes' or 'no', please, sir."

"Uh?" Mikhail hadn't been listening to PC Cook. He had been distracted by the shape of her depicted eyebrows. Each one had three distinct sides: a short vertical edge adjacent to the nose, and two curves sweeping up to meet in an acute angle beside the temple. And although the shape bothered him in its entirety, it was the vertical edge which bothered him the most. It was too straight for nature. So why paint an imitation eyebrow on your face and not make it an imitation of an eyebrow? An eyebrow has no geometry, it has no distinctness, no form and no boundaries. So why make an imitation eyebrow which lacks the characteristics that make it an eyebrow? Those ochre triangles on PC Cook's forehead, they weren't eyebrows at all. They were geometry.

Mikhail was therefore not surprised when PC Cook's face did that thing that faces often do, especially faces on television, or on flat advertisements on the sides of bus stops, or on curved advertisements on the Tube. PC Cook's face stopped being a face on the front of a person and became an assemblage of shapes. Mikhail knew the drill. You had to stop looking at the shapes. As the proverb says, 'A watched pot never boils." The longer you looked at those shapes, the harder it was to recover the fragile illusion that there was a person in there somewhere. Mikhail shut his eyes so that PC Cook would become a person again.

PC Cook was raising her voice. "I need you to answer a question for me, sir." It wasn't a shout, though it might yet become one, but it wasn't ordinary speech either. "I was asking: in your opinion, is this note hate speech? Yes or no?"

"Well, that's obvious, officer. It's not speech. It's words on paper."

PC Cook inhaled. "I'm just saying this in a friendly way. I am advising you not to mess around with me, sir."

"I'm not messing around with you," says Mikhail. "I have got Archilochus-Hesburger Syndrome. It's not a disability. It's a difference. Can I go now?"

68

"Not quite yet," says the policewoman. There are five flats and one way in. Only the residents of these five flats have keys to the front door. Obviously, the person who wrote this note is not an immigrant. So that rules out the residents of flats 3, 4 and 5, who are from other countries. That just leaves you and flat number 1. Except flat number 1 is on holiday in Tenerife, so that just leaves you. Basically, sir, we've got enough to take you in."

"But it can't be me who put up the note either," Mikhail says. "I'm black."

That's why I never read fiction. You read and you read and you know you're only getting one side of the story. There's all that stuff they're holding back. You spend £13.99 at Amazon and you're four hundred pages in and then suddenly on page 350 it's "Oh, by the way, we forgot to tell you. That guy, you know, David, the one Samantha's engaged to, well actually he's her biological half-brother. Basically, you could have skipped the first 350 pages, saving yourself 350/400 x £13.99 (i.e. £12.24), because those pages were a smokescreen designed to overcharge you. And, the thing is, if you've got Archilochus-Hesburger Syndrome, which is a difference and not a disability, you know that the coincidence is just words and that Samantha is just words, so you're not dazzled by the coincidence or concerned for Samantha, and all you're aware of is how you've been ripped off for £12.24.

But in this case it's even worse. We have been doubly perfidious. Not only did we withhold a key fact, but we've been unfairly letting you form your own mental image of Mikhail. You've been visualising his face, haven't you? You had to, because you don't have Hesburger's and you can't help yourself. You're always visualising and emphasizing and humanising and sympathising. What has Mikhail been looking like in your mind's eye, dear reader? IT guy pallor? IT guy stubble? IT guy haircut? Russian guy crewcut? Red-faced? Hollow-cheeked? Flabby-jowled? Clean-shaven?

Was he white? 'Cause it woz you made him white, sunshine, not I. Suckerrrr!

The only consolation is that this novel's only just begun, so it's not like this story was taking you for a mug all the way through to the final chapter and then, "Oh, by the way, Mikhail's black." You have only been cheated out of 13 percent of the story.

I won't call you a racist for making Mikhail white in your head. Calling you a racist would be unfair of me. You had to make him some colour, didn't you? You couldn't just have him coming home to Manor Court, Streatham as some kind of Invisible Man, with an empty space where his head ought to be and you seeing all the way through his empty collar to the Primark

70

label on the back of his shirt. Because making Mikhail invisible would have been the only way not to assume his colour in your mind's eye. And if 97 percent of tech employees in the UK are white, white's as good an assumption as any. No, I'm not going to accuse you of being racist. I'm just going to acknowledge that you're a human being without Archilochus-Hesburger Syndrome.

And by the way, now that you know that Mr. and Mrs. Khan live on the same landing as Mikhail and that it's dinnertime, are you imagining the smell too? It would make sense if you did. Garlic and fenugreek.

"Basically, sir," says the policewoman, 'we've got enough to take you in."

"But it can't be me who put up the note either," Mikhail says. "I'm black."

"Yeah, right!" says Dumitru. He puts his hand next to Mikhail's hand and nods at the police officers. "I'm not seeing any difference in skin tone," he says. Ruby Kufuor isn't saying anything - just observing.

Mikhail is feeling confused and stressed by the noise and the policewoman's impatient expression. "I really am black," he insists. "I would be a quadroon but that word is offensive, so I am therefore not a quadroon; I am black. I am black because I am not white. In fact, I am a human representation of the fallacy of the missing middle. Unwhite like Alexandre

Dumas, who wrote "The Three Musketeers" and unwhite like Archie Windsor who is seventh in line to the throne and unwhite like my compatriot Mikhail Pushkin, who wrote "Eugene Onegin". My mother is half black. I swear. Her father was a Mozabican engineering student at Tiraspol State University. And my father is a white American presidential candidate called either Brent Lundscum or Shaun Shaughnessy." The two police officers looked at each other silently, as if to say, "OK. Mental health."

"Oh, for the love of fuck," Dumitru cries out. He's waving his hands around. "You don't look black. You don't talk black. Your name isn't black. Nobody thinks you're black. If nobody can tell that you're black, then it doesn't count."

Mikhail asks, "Is Ruby black?"

"Yeah, obviously."

Mikhail's voice is exasperated, despairing. "So you're saying that somewhere between Ruby and me there's a cut-off point?"

"I guess."

"Where's the cut-off point?"

"Oh, come off it, mate," says Dumitru. "The point is, are you an immigrant, and the answer is no you're not, OK? So, it can only be you who put up the frigging note."

"I am an immigrant as of today," says Mikhail. He pulls his new passport out of his anorak pocket. "Thirteen days ago I was a local because I was born in England. Then the Home Office said I was nothing. And since half past twelve this afternoon I'm an immigrant like you. Look, I'm Russian today." Mikhail fishes inside his satchel and brings out an apple-red booklet. Proudly he shows the police officers the passport page with his photo on it. The policewoman sighs and puts away her notebook.

"So when did you leave Russia?" Ruby Kufuor is looking sceptical.

"Aren't you going to do anything?" said Dumitru, pointing at the note. "This is hate speech. It's deeply offensive. It can only be this guy."

"Yes, offensive," say Mr. and Mrs. Khan.

Mikhail throws his hands over his eyes. "But nobody's making sense! I'm an immigrant since this afternoon," he howls.

The policeman pulls his shoulders back to make himself tall. He raises an eyebrow as if to show that he understands everything. He looks sideways at his colleague. The policewoman says, "Er, I suggest you all go back to your flats. You've got my number. Give me a call if there's anything else to report. We don't tolerate hate speech."

"Yeah, right," says Dumitru.

"And you," says the policeman to Mikhail, "we're keeping our eyes on you."

Thank you," replies Mikhail. He's sweating with anxiety and he feels cold. He grabs his cereal and his washing powder and runs up the worn concrete stairs two at a time, leaving the police officers and his neighbours standing confused in the lobby. Mikhail needs to calm down. This was too much noise and chaos, too many emotions and too many non-sequiturs and fallacies. Too many accents and inexplicable facial expressions. He needs to be in his happy place, a place where people make sense. Only one thing will tranquilise Mikhail.

He slams his flat door behind him, drops his shopping in the bathroom and runs into the middle of his living room.

Humpty the African Grey parrot has been dreaming of the Congo rainforest but, when the door opens, he wakes up in Streatham. Now he's hopping from leg to leg on his perch, screeching, "Plato talks bollocks! Plato talks bollocks!" Mikhail opens the cage door and Humpty swaggers out onto the bookshelf. After scanning the room haughtily to show who's boss, Humpty dismisses Mikhail with an arrogant 'chuck' and sets to preening his feathers. With Humpty settled, Mikhail grabs the Virtual Reality goggles and headphones dangling from the ceiling, boots up and opens his eyes in classical Athens.

Chapter 8 - Still in the New Tretyakov Gallery, Moscow, December 2019

Mum bustles back from the toilet across the marble tiles of the lobby. She is wiping her tiny wrinkly monkey-hands on her corduroy shirt. Her eyes dart right and left. That's how I always remember her in our Stalinka apartment: looking for something out of place, a misaligned snow boot by the front door, or a dictionary where the chess books should be.

"Nastya!" She comes very close and peers up at me frowning. "Do you know why Chinese women take longer to piss than we do?"

"No, mamma," I sigh.

"Hmmm. Now then, Nastya, I have changed my mind. I am going to give you the bad news first and then the secret. Although the secret precedes the bad news chronologically, the bad news is logically precedent to the secret. Follow me."

We walk towards the broad concrete stairway at one end of the lobby. At the bottom step Mama stops and points down at her feet. "Do you see something, Nastya?"

"No, Mama."

Mama tut-tuts. "You don't see anything, daughter mine, because you are looking for what you expect. Look carefully, Nastya. Don't look with the expectation of what's important and what's not important. What do you see?"

"Your shoes, Mama."

"Good. And?"

"A step."

"Getting there. What kind of step, Nastya?"

"An ugly concrete step with a Sovietic mosaic effect."

"And?" She is peering up at me with that frown again.

"Mama! OK, Mama. And I see a gap between the steps."

"Good girl!" Now you're looking without expectations. You've seen a gap. An absence. A zero. Now, what's special about this nothing?"

"Please, Mama!" I wanted to tell her that people were staring, but nobody was taking any notice of us. We Russians know how to mind our own business. We learned our manners from the KGB.

I looked at the gap between the steps and then I looked at the whole staircase. Then I saw.

"Mama, do you mean that this gap is shorter than all the others?"

"Yes, Nastya! Molodtsa! This is the difference between our Soviet staircase and a Western staircase. The Westerners would divide the total height of the staircase by the number of steps and that was the height of each step. But we Soviets have a Soviet way of thinking. We had the regulated height of a step, which was dictated by the regulations from Gosstroi and by the regulated height of our Gosstroi-defined bricks. A step means a step and it is a step because it is exactly as tall as we say that a step should be.

"And you are Anastasia. You're not Alisa in Wonderland. You are what is written in your passport. Anastasia Krutova.

"So don't tell lies for a living, Anastasia. Don't play with words for a living. The Soviet Union was right in many ways. We knew that there was a standard. Hunger was a standard. Power was a standard. We didn't play with meanings.

And I was thinking ...

`The question is,' said Alice, `whether you can make words mean so many different things.'

`The question is,' said Humpty Dumpty, `which is to be master -- that's all.'

"And, Nastya, because the prescribed height of the step never divided exactly into the actual height of the storey, we would always have a remainder. And

78

that's why our Soviet top step or our Soviet bottom step is always shorter than the others." Mama looked at me with a proud smile as though she were waiting for me to break into applause.

"Why are you telling me this, Mama?"

"Because I want you to know that there was always a remainder during the Soviet Union, and that remainder was the person who didn't fit the standard. A person who had to be trimmed to size to fit the scheme. And there's nothing wrong with that, Nastya." Mama was talking softly now, reverently. "By cutting down the remainder to size you make the whole building fit the standard."

"Yeah, right," I scoffed. "That's easy to say, just so long as that remainder isn't you."

"That remainder is me," Mama said. "And now I myself am being trimmed." Mama took a deep breath and shrugged her shoulders. "I knew it would come sooner or later. I have pancreatic cancer, Nastya. It's the price for being the remainder at the foot of the staircase, for volunteering to work with those young men in the hospital, soaking up the neutrons from their bodies." She laughed. "To think that I actually requested the Chernobyl necklace. I asked them to take out my thyroid, because I thought it was the thyroid that would get me." She pointed at the V-shaped scar across her throat. "Nastya, I believe I will be dead in a couple of months. Oh, don't pretend to look sorry. It's too late for that, don't you think, and it doesn't suit you.

"You know, Nastya, I was thinking of not telling you at all. Then it would be as follows. You wouldn't bother to come down from Petersburg to see me, as usual. Then one day my phone wouldn't have answered. And you wouldn't have thought twice about it. Then after a few weeks of my phone not answering, you'd have taken the train to Moscow. It wouldn't have been just to see me of course. You'd have waited until you could combine me with a work meeting. No – not necessarily a work meeting. You might have combined me with a party. And you'd have told those friends of yours, "Sorry, guys. I might be 20 minutes late. Seeing my old mama while I'm in town." Then you'd have come up my apartment stairs, all seven floors, cursing because the lift's not working and you're in heels, and you don't want to break a sweat because of the make-up, and your dress is tight, because you want to show off your best aspects, I know, and that's fine. And you'd have cursed when you knocked and nobody answered, and you'd be muttering and pulling that golden pencil out of your handbag to write me a note when Semyon from next door (who by the way still lives with his mother) steps out of the lift. You say you're my daughter. Semyon shrugs, says he's got the keys and lets you in, Semyon assuming naturally that you already know that I'm dead, you being my daughter after all. Then you'd think it's a bit strange that Semyon has my keys (You notice Semyon's rough plumber's hands and inside you wince a bit.) But all the same you step inside and take your shoes off. Then you'd look around the apartment wide-eyed, taking in the dust on the books and the sheets over the furniture. You'd turn to face Semyon, who would suddenly realise that you didn't know. You'd see the embarrassment in Semyon's decent blue eyes and that would have been the exact moment that you'd learn of your mother's death from pancreatic cancer. All because I was the remainder who soaked up the neutrons in May 1986."

Mama shrugged again. "Well, Nastya, that's that." She raised her eyebrows expectantly. I'd have liked to react the way she wanted - but I didn't know what she wanted. I felt sorry for her because she was so shrunken, because she was so lost and diminished in the right-angular expanses of the Soviet Tretyakov.

"That was the news," Mama said. "And now the surprise."

Chapter 9 - Still in the Agora, Athens, 7th of Boedromion, 378 BC

So here I am, still recumbent in my barrel, little knowing that my happy existence as a discarded scrap of human detritus is about to end. There's a wet patch inside my left ear where Chorismos the dog has been dribbling all night. Now he's licking his balls, lucky little feller. Ah, Chorismos, may the God bless you, my one true pal. He's got it all worked out, that hound. He can stick his nose up his arse when it gets cold. He can scratch his ears with his toes. He can lick his own balls. He can smell if someone's lying.

That preening charlatan Plato tells his boys that *chorismos* is a gap between appearance and underlying forms. I call my dog Chorismos because he's proof that what you see is what you get i.e. Plato's talking bollocks. I am training Chorismos to hump Plato's leg.

Obviously, as I may have said already, when you live in a barrel, the first thing you want in the morning is a good stretch, and the second is a good crap. Beyond my lumpy knees, wrinkly like the tits of Tiresias, beyond my nine jagged toenails, pointing heavenwards like the craggy peaks of Olympos, through the sphincteresque aperture which constitutes my front door, I see a variety of human feet. Hairy feet. Knobbly feet. Expectant feet. Tourist feet, belonging to kosmopolitan trippers who have got up early to see the great Diogenes of Sinope take one of his celebrated poos in the Agora. A woman's voice, with those soupy, slutty Lesbian vowels, calls, "Hey, dawggie! Good dawggie!" Chorismos lifts one bald, scabby ear, reflects for a moment on the hopes and aspirations of homo sapiens, drops his ear again and then resumes his slow scratching. What an aristocrat! Good boy, Chorismos!

I know what you're wondering, and frankly it's a fair question: when Diogenes of Sinope is in his barrel, is he head-in and feet-out or feet-in and head-out? Well, I'm glad you asked, because it's an interesting discourse and there's something to be said for both approaches. When you're head-out, you have a greater awareness of your peripheral surroundings, which is handy when it comes to anticipating the pranks and japes of the Scythian Astynomian constabulary, such as pinching one's lamp or tipping a days-worth of scrapings from the gutters of the fish market into one's front porch. On the other hand, when you're head-in, you have a greater sense of peace and security. When you're head-in and your entire kosmos consists of an arc of barrel-staves scarcely a daktylos above your nose, you can kid yourself that Plato got it right. You can imagine that the kosmos is a perfectly arranged sphere. I have therefore developed a routine: start the night head-out and then after the midnight piss-break, go head-in until morning. You see, in fact Plato got that wrong too. There's no such thing as perfect. There's just fit-for-purpose.

I grab my lamp, so that nobody will nick it while I'm outside, and slide out feet-first into the caustic sunlight of the Athenian summer.

Tourists. There's about thirty of them, and that's just the ones who got up early to see me crap. They'll keep coming all day, to visit the renowned Diogenes of Sinope, the man who takes life-coaching from his dog Chorismos. The Cynic, which means the DogMan. Well, the tourists pay to see me. You've gotta eat.

Hunger and lust.

I am hungry. You don't know what that means, dear Reader. The very fact that you have the time and energy to listen to me means that your life has never been reduced to its bare elements: the desire to stay alive and the desire to procreate. Hunger and lust, dear Reader - the two constants of our lives. The moment you're well-fed you want a shag and as soon as you've had a shag you want to eat again. It's the wheel of life and we're strapped to it. That day when I jerked off in the Agora, that was to show the crowd how simple it is to relieve lust. When I crapped in the Agora, it was to show how what goes in must soon come out. And it was hunger and lust that are about to screw me over today. The sun is rising behind the Acropolis. By the time it hangs above my head, I will already be undone, and all because of hunger and lust.

I recognise their tour guide, a rosy-cheeked ephebe with an accent that says, "Bullshit-merchant of the Platonic School." Straight off I can spot the type: "Nouveau riche Daddy sent me to Plato's academy to learn how to bullshit properly like old money, only I lost all my money to Phocion at dice so now I'm a tour guide."

"Well?" I say. I act grumpy but in fact I'm ecstatic to see these tourists. Thanks to them I will be able to pay for my next meal. Like I said, hunger and lust. Chorismos also pricks up his ears at the sight of the tourists. He knows: if I eat, he eats.

"They've come to see you, O Diogenes of Sinope," said the guide.

"I think you mean they've come to see me crap in the middle of the Agora," I whine passive-aggressively. The guide blushed. "Have you got a name, or don't you have the courtesy at least to introduce yourself to an elemental man before watching him take a shite?"

"Aristotle." His ephebe voice cracked. "Aristotle of Stagira."

"Well, Aristotle of Stagira, I think you know the drill." Aristotle blushed again and nodded quickly. He whispered to his tourists, "Two tetartemoria per man, one tetartemorion per lady."

"Why are we women half-price?" asked the Lesbian bint. "Are you implying that women are half the value of men? That wouldn't go down on Lesbos."

"You're not half-price," I explained. "You're awarded the privilege of paying the True Price, as a token of my respect for you as another elemental human being. The men pay double."

Little Aristotle was beaming. "What a treat, all laid on for you!" he proclaimed to the tourists. "Harken how Diogenes of Sinope reminds us to distinguish between on the one hand the true value of a defecatory spectacle, which is hidden from us in the sphere of ideal concepts, and on the other hand the price determined on earth by the base laws of supply and demand."

With the benefit of hindsight, I now regret what I said to Sluttyvowels the Lesbian bint. I misspoke. 378 B.C. was a different time, and I didn't know then what I know now: that those words were inappropriate and unacceptable. I apologize to anyone I may have upset. What I should have said was, "Women are half-price because they are intellectually incapable of taking decisions for themselves." It has been a learning experience for me. I, Diogenes of Sinope, commit to educating myself about gender."

I took the coins from Aristotle and tied them in my snotrag. And, by the way, at least I'm woke enough to call her 'Sluttyvowels the Lesbian bint'. Obvs., I know it's totally unacceptable to use a woman's real name in public in pre-Hellenistic Athens. You can't label women with names. That would be objectification.

But, even if I can't tell you Sluttyvowels's real name, at least not yet, I can tell you what she looked like. She looked like a boy - a boy who is only just on the right side of puberty. In fact, if she hadn't said 'we women' I'd have had to ask her to whip off her clothes so as to know whether to use the masculine or feminine form of the adjective 'fortunate'. Flat chest. Hint of a little black moustache. Raspy voice. Utterly captivating.

You say 'stereotype'. I say 'Platonic ideal form.' Potayto potahto.

Chorismos and I parted our way through the crowd and strode manfully and dogfully to the geometrical centre of the agora, me holding my head up high because I wanted to look sexy for Sluttyvowels, and Chorismos holding his tail up high because he's a dog. Pride before a tragic fall - there ought to be a Greek word for it. Chorismos and I defecated *à deux* to the sound of polite applause. When the job was done, Chorismos kicked the dust backwards with his hind legs and then so did I.

I eat. I crap. They pay me. I buy food. It's the circle of life.

The task performed, Chorismos and I returned to our barrel. I leaned back against its warm, curvy, motherly flank, with my fingers curled around my lamp (so it wouldn't get nicked), and Chorismos curled up at my feet. We closed our eyes and began the day's lounging. But just as I was gliding away to my happy place, slipping through that land between waking and sleep where all Truth reveals itself to the inner eye, meaning that my inner eye was conjuring up a vision of Sluttyvowels's naked no-tits, a shadow fell across my face. Opening an outer eye, I observe an unwelcome addition to the crowd. Little Aristotle has been shunted to one side and now there is the Doric shadow of Plato, who is spraying rhetoric all over the tourists like the Castalian Springs of Delphi. "What's he doing here?" I wonder. Ever since I humiliated Plato over that matter of the featherless chicken, he's been out to get me and my share of the stunt philosophy market. Something is afoot. If Plato wasn't sniffing around after rich teenage boys, you knew he was up to no good.

"Look at this great crowd of human beings who have come to see you," says Plato.

"I can see a great crowd," I replied with cynical nonchalance, "but I can't see any human beings." I shut my eyes again. One-nil to me.

"I've come to do you a favour, O Diogenes of Sinope," he says.

"Well, if you want to do me a favour, you can get out of my sunshine," I reply. "You can't make the sun shine out of your arse, so don't stop it from shining on me. Therefore, kindly remove your shadow, Plato of Athens. Otherwise, you can piss off."

Plato stepped to the left. Two-nil. "I'm taking these tourists to see a statue-push," Plato said. "You should come with us. Now I think of it, Diogenes, you could be part of the show. Give Aristotle's tourists their money's worth. We could do some verbal sparring. A philosophers' rap-off." He raised his fists like a boxer. What a creep.

"Isn't it a bit early in the morning for a statue-push?"

"It's in the Piraeus."

"Two hours there and two hours back for a statue-push? In this weather? Well, then you can definitely piss off."

"Please yourself." Plato gave a theatrical shrug. "Of course, Diogenes, if you come along, there might be a drachma or two in it for you."

"Oh, yeah, and what would I have to do in return for my drachma or two?" I drawl, trying to hide my interest.

"You could masturbate in public."

"Oh, come on! Just because I live in a barrel, it doesn't mean ..."

"Don't be such a wimp, Diogenes. You've done it oft times before."

"Purely as a teaching aid. I was demonstrating the concept of satisfaction." As I spoke, I observed a pronounced flush arising upon Sluttvowels' cheeks. "It illustrated the parallel between lust and hunger. Action learning."

But we were suddenly interrupted by the unacceptable sound of a woman talking philosophy. Chorismos pricked up his ears in alarm. "Masturbation", said Sluttyvowels, "is a specific representation of a universal truth, namely that sensual pleasure is only the removal of desire."

"OK, Diogenes", says Plato. "Three drachmas for the statue-push. And no public masturbation - unless you want to, obviously."

I picked up my lamp. "Let's go," I said to Chorismos. "You can finish licking your balls in Piraeus."

Plato led the way, followed by Aristotle of Stagira the tour-guide, then a snaking file of tourists, then me, then the dog, and Sluttyvowels of Lesbos at the back, obviously, because she was a woman.

As everyone knows, the toppling of cherished monuments is a sacred tradition handed down to humankind by the Olympian Gods. You don't see any statues of the Giants around town, not since the Gods cast them down for being uppity. And you don't see any statues of Prometheus either, not since the Gods fed his liver to the eagle for giving fire to mortal men. Thus do we humans continue the eternal legacy of the Olympians, raising up statues of the people we admire and pushing them down again when we tire of their opinions.

Luckily all our statues in Athens look pretty much the same: alpha males with curly beards, mass-market togas, broken willies, and holes in their eyeballs. So, when we swap an old truth for a new one, we push our statues down, rub the old, despised names off the plinths with pumice stone, engrave the names of the new-beloved heroes in their place, and raise the statues back up. And, while we're pushing, we remember that what we now hold dear will certainly appall our descendants, so none of it really matters. And recycling monuments saves public money.

Today we were off to topple Alcibiades. We erected his statue in Piraeus when he was the golden boy of all Attica, a bender in whom we could all take pride, with a crush on baldy Socrates himself. To us Alcibiades represented everything we held dear in the Athenian character: lechery, deviousness, arrogance and perversion. Just hearing his girly lisping orations made us feel like Athens was the Ground Zero of name-calling, fake news, duplicity and alternative truth – indeed the very Cradle of Democracy. Alcibiades made us proud to be Athenian. And then, inevitably, credible sources reported that Alcibiades was prancing around Athens by moonlight knocking the pricks off all the statues of Hermes. This was an affront to our civic decency and family values, so we pushed his statue over. But pretty soon after that he was General Alcibiades, slicing up Spartans all over Sicily, and up went the statue again. Then, next thing we knew he had defected to farty Sparta, not to mention consorting with the oily, garlic-breathed woggy Persians, so down went the Alcibiades statue, because we Athenians have at least the self-respect to prize racial loyalty. But everyone likes a guy with style after all, so we invited Alcibiades back, gave him a parade, an army, and a front seat at the Eleusinian Mysteries, and up went the monument again. Then we just got bored of him, because we're fickle basically, and moreover democracy is the collective form of Attention-Deficit Disorder. Which is why now we're all going off to a statue-push in Piraeus. Like I said – recycling.

It's effing hot. Chorismos's tongue is hanging out and his breathing sounds like crackling twigs. Sluttyvowels turns around. "Come on, Diogenes of Sinope! You don't want to be left behind by a girl, do you?"

I don't reply.

"I'm Arete of Cyrene," she says.

"Cyrene? I thought you were from Lesbos."

"You assumed. Huh." She slows down so that I draw level with her. "Do you know why I came all the way from Cyrene to Athens?" Her voice is low, clear and bell-like.

I check that the other tourists are far enough ahead not to hear me talking with a woman in public. I may live in a barrel but that doesn't mean I don't know good manners.

"No," I whisper.

"Do you know how far it is from Cyrene to Athens? With the wind in our faces, it took us eight days. On the second day the sea was slopping in through the oar-holes. You could their terror; the sailors thought we were finished. But while they were sacrificing chickens and calling on Poseidon in all the tongues of Hellas, Asia and the Levant, all I could think of was Athens. The city of gold and marble. The city where syllogisms splinter and sparkle in the piercing Hellenic sun. I sailed across the perilous deep to talk with you, Diogenes of Sinope. And now I am standing next to you on the road to Piraeus and I have so many questions to ask."

I am looking at her huge feet and at the streaks of dust around the fringe of her chiton. "Why ask philosophical questions, O Arete of Cyrene?" I reply. "Either a question is answerable, in which case you can work out the answer for yourself, or the question is not answerable, in which case there is no point asking it. So be quiet."

Arete's laugh sounds like when you drop a handful of pebbles. "Maybe you don't know - I studied philosophy under Aristippus," she says.

"Aristippus of Cyrene. I think I've heard of him. Ah, yes. The only one of Socrates's students who charged his students for lessons. Couldn't hack it with the big swinging dicks of Plato's Academy and headed back to small-town Cyrene to teach the oiks and yokels. A mediocre intellect."

Arete laughs again. "Aristippus is my father," she proclaims. Her ringing confidence fills my heart with contempt and lust.

"Do you know why I wanted to talk with you, O Diogenes of Sinope?" she asks.

"No."

"I'll tell you why." She skips ahead, turns around to face me and raises her hands. I lift my eyes from the path to her eyes. She's smiling, and there is a gloss of sweat around her faint black moustache. I feel the desire rising inside my chiton. "Diogenes of Sinope," she proclaims. "I want to convert you!"

"You're in my way," I growl and stride past her. Chorismos wags his tail and trots after me, giving Arete a sideways glance.

But Arete quickens her pace until she is level with me again. "Why do you make everything so ugly?" she asks.

WHY DO YOU MAKE THE WORLD SO OFFENSIVE??? So that's it. She's not a Lesbian. She's a Cyreniac hedonist.

"I do not make the world offensive, Arete of Cyrene," say I. "I describe the ugliness of the world. You say, 'Offensive'. I say, 'Take all your clothes off so I can check you're a woman'. 'Offensive' is just a word. It is a vibration of the air. If I crap or masturbate in the Agora, it is only offensive because someone - let's call him Plato - is offended. And Plato has no reason to be offended. Plato could just as well be delighted, as he is delighted by the smell of thyme. Chorismos here finds the smell of thyme to be offensive and the smell of excrement to be as delightful as acacia honey. Does that mean that thyme is offensive, and shit is delightful? Yes, it does. If you put Plato and Chorismos together, does it mean that thyme and shit are both offensive and delightful at the same time? Yes, it does. Because 'offensive' and 'delightful' are just words, just vibrations in the air, and they can mean whatever you want them to mean. And because you can instruct words to mean anything, they mean nothing. So, I do not make the world offensive, Arete of Cyrene. You do. Your own mind itself puts offensiveness into the world.

"You have read Plato, Arete, and it shows", I continue. I am showing off because I am a man and she is a woman and I have fallen in love. I know that love between men and women is futile and empty (because there is no such thing as love), but I can't stop myself. "Arete, Plato the chicken-shagger taught you that there are ideal qualities hidden inside words and ideas, and you believed him. Don't believe Plato. Believe Chorismos the dog, because Chorismos knows that life consists of eating, sleeping, licking your own dick and causing harm to nobody. Look at Chorismos's tail. It's wagging. He owns nothing. He doesn't know where his next meal will come from. He can't remember the last time a bitch offered him her arse, but he is happy. He is happy because for him the world extends from five seconds ago to five seconds in the future, from ten yards to the left of him, to ten yards to the right of him. He is in the moment."

I kicked Chorismos spinning into the dust. He yelped. As I counted to five, Chorismos rolled onto his four feet, looked at me, shook his body so that his ears flapped, and began walking again, his tail wagging joyfully. "You see, Arete," I said. "For Chorismos it's already as though the kick never happened. This dog has more wisdom than a hundred of Plato's bum-ticklers. I have observed the bankers of Sinope and the chicken-wankers of Athens, I have built and lost two fortunes, and all I have concluded is that we should all live like dogs. That is my philosophy."

Arete didn't even pause. "But, O Diogenes of Sinope, I desire to convert you. Ever since my father taught me of your doggish philosophy, I knew I had to sail across the wine-dark sea to Athens to win you over."

"Why do you want to convert me?"

"Diogenes of Sinope, I want to convert you to the pursuit of pleasure. Having heard your reputation, wafted to Cyrene across the water by Eurus the east wind, I want to have sex with you, but preferably not in a barrel, and then marry you and live with you in Cyrene and keep having sex with you for as long as you are able. Your sperm is a precious commodity, because it can encapsulate your intelligence and pass it on to future generations. It is too valuable to be spilt on the sandy floor of the Agora for the salacious amusement of Boeotian tourists. I will therefore devote the rest of my life to harvesting your manly fluids. We will found an Academy and we will be known to history as the Cyrenaic hedonists. And if the Gods wish for us to have a child, we will call his Aristippus, after my Dad, and bring him up as a hedonist philosopher like ourselves."

I liked the sound of that.

"However," Arete continues, "all of this depends upon my persuading you of some fundamental philosophical truths."

I must admit I nearly dropped my lantern. I was getting into a sweat and not just because of the sun. When I saw the charming sheen of perspiration on Arete's downy moustache, I knew that I was destined to convert to Hedonism, the philosophy of pleasure. Hunger and horniness, as I may have mentioned earlier, are the downfalls of the philosopher.

"Arete of Cyrene," I declaim, "the lantern in my hand bears witness that I seek truth and honesty in the darkest recesses of this stinking latrine which we call the kosmos. Though our philosophies may differ, yet my mind is always open to fresh wisdom. Pray enlighten me."

Her no-tits heaving, Arete takes a series of deep breaths and looks into the distance like a student recalling a memorised text. "O Diogenes of Sinope, you and I share the same insight, but this insight has taken us to different conclusions. You and I both agree that there is no such thing as virtue. You and I both agree that Plato's ideals are just an invented fiction. We agree that words are empty; they don't represent eternal values. You and I agree that an axe is only called an axe because we call it an axe. We know that it is a lump of sharp metal on the end of a stick. We know that if you replace the metal and then replace the stick, the axe has not changed into another axe, because there never was any axe." She raises her voice. "You and I know that Plato is wrong about everything. Everything!"

Methought the lady did protest too much. I interrupt. "O Arete of Cyrene, did Plato ever shag you?"

"Never!"

"Did he even try?"

"Plato was interested in other things than women," she sneered bitterly.

"Aha! Carry on."

"Diogenes of Sinope, you know that all ideals are empty shells. You strip away all superfluous things. You disdain meat and wine. You live on lentils and discarded crusts. Scraps which even the crows refuse are your daily diet. You disdain fine clothes. You wear shit-stained rags."

"Actually, about the rags ..."

"You disdain the company of women and consort with a dog for your physical needs."

"Actually, that's not..."

She put her finger to her lips. "Don't deny it," she whispered. "A Hedonist welcomes all pleasures."

"I'm definitely bipedally inclined," I protested. "And, coming back to the stains on my tunic..."

"Hush, O Diogenes of Sinope, and harken to the words of Sappho of Lesbos, Sappho whose immortal

verse still gives voice to the liberated female spirit."
Arete inflated her no-tits chest, and declaimed:

> "There was a young goddess called Juno,
>
> Said, "There's one thing in life that I do know.
>
> With a man it's a pleasure,
>
> With a woman a treasure,
>
> But a sheepdog is NUMERO UNO.""

Her husky voice resonated from the rocks up to the shimmering Attic sky. And as her slutty vowels receded, as the poetry of the eternal feminine archetype soared to Olympus, leaving behind only the noonday screech of the cicadas and the crunch of the flints beneath our feet, I knew that I was hers.

Chapter 10 - In the grounds of the New Tretyakov, after the rainstorm

"My imminent death was the news," Mama said. "Now for the surprise. Oh, look! It's stopped raining. A respite from your western pizzle-drizzle. Let's get some fresh air." That's another thing about us Russians. Every spell of sunshine is the last time the sun will ever shine on earth. We enjoy it, all right, but deep inside we know that sunshine, ice creams and happiness are just a temporary deviation from the world's default condition: sleet outdoors, mildew indoors and pervasive misery.

For Allie, of course, it's the other way around. All the residents of Allie's San Francisco suburb have a right to 160 days per annum of clear skies, and that's not counting the carefree, sun-dappled happiness of cumulonimbus days.

So, in the geometric gardens of the New Tretyakov, it is the Fox's Wedding. Under a charcoal sky, the angular granite giants of Soviet labour glisten in the horizontal sunbeams. The statues of the workers still stand undaunted, legs monumentally apart in their cubist trousers. They rest their weary elbows on their sledgehammers and stare purposefully across puddles and shrubberies, weary but proud, and perhaps a little contemptuous. And why shouldn't they look down on us?

I could hear the hiss of distant traffic on wet roads, the crunch of rain-soaked gravel beneath our feet and, for the first time, when Mama inhaled, I noticed the crackle in her chest.

"Chess," Mama said. "You must have seen my trophies in the apartment. But naturally you never asked me about them.

"The trophies were just there, Mama. I was a child."

"Some daughters would have asked, Nastya," Mama said. She paused for a rather theatrical cough. "Some daughters might ask now. For example, some daughters might ask why they didn't have any brothers or sisters."

That was it. Suddenly Mama and I were in a place we'd never been. Now we had crossed into No-Man's Land.

"Why did you never ask me, Nastya? Never. Not when you were at the kindergarten seeing the other children being dropped off. Not when you went to birthday parties. Not when you were hanging out with your girlfriends. I was waiting every day for you to ask me why you were an only child, but you never did. Then I would have been able to tell you."

"Mama, you're not making sense. Many of us don't have fathers, let alone brothers or sisters. It's the great demographic disaster of the Soviet Union. Everyone knows about the Soviet woman's favourite operation."

"Well, you do have a sister, Nastya." She opened her handbag and pulled out a paper handkerchief with a number scrawled in red ballpoint. "Have you got your cellphone? I don't like carrying mine around with me. One never knows who's going to call. Not to mention the radiation." I offered her my iPhone. "No! Too complicated!" she snapped. "Just dial this number and say that we're ready now."

I dialled the number on the serviette. A man's voice answered, "Hello. I am listening."

"Who's that?" I asked. There was no answer. Just breathing.

"Do what I say for once, Nastya. Tell him that we're ready."

"All right, Mama." With a catch in my voice I said, "We're ready." Immediately the phone cut off. "Now what?" I asked.

"Just wait, Nastya."

This was when I could have asked my mother the obvious questions. *What is my sister's name? When was she born? Where is she? Who is her father?* And, most importantly: *why have you never told me and why have I never seen her?* But what would have been the point? With my mother I only learned what I was meant to know when I was meant to know it. This wasn't San Francisco.

"Let's sit down," my mother said. "We might be some time." The pancake kiosk had a blue awning. Beneath it were green metal chairs around circular white metal tables. My mother rubbed a chair with the back of her hand to check that it was dry, and we sat down. I read the menu in the kiosk window: sweet pancakes with jam, condensed milk, Nutella, bananas, Nutella and bananas; savoury pancakes with butter, ham, cheese, ham and cheese. My childhood, basically. The rain dripped from the awning, which was advertising Baltika beer. I checked the prices.

Visitors to the New Tretyakov were still arriving from the Krymsky Val gates: pairs of Europeans in hiking jackets and practical shoes, a Chinese guided tour, Russian pensioners and the occasional skinny student. An arty type was walking towards the cafe. He was a pale specimen, walking with a springy, prancing gait that made him look as though he was about to start skipping. His gelled, swept-back hair and his short beard looked as though they had just left the salon. He had a leather satchel. Probably an art student. Probably gay. (I can say that. Stereotypes are my profession. If I didn't have stereotypes, I'd be like a painter with twenty tubes of white paint.) The man was peering shortsightedly at his phone through glasses. They had chunky, pale blue plastic frames. Pale blue = голубой = gay. He sat at another table and hid himself behind a newspaper. Novaya Gazeta, obvs. A libtard.

Funny how sweet pancakes are always cheaper than savoury ones. It seems against the laws of nature.

I watched my mother. She had drifted off into waiting mode i.e. that Soviet/Russian meditation practice where your eyes glaze over, your thoughts turn inwards, you stare into nothing, time stops, and you float in an alternate plane of existence. Not being of that generation, I just fidgeted and yearned to get out my phone. So, I had a sister.

My phone rang.

"Hello?"

"Good afternoon, Nastya," said a smooth voice. "Let's get acquainted."

"Who is this?"

"May I join you and your mother?"

The art student lowered his newspaper and came towards us, tucking his phone into the pocket of his tight jeans.

"Sit down and join us, Anton," my mother said with a rather flirty smile. "Anton, this, as you know, is my daughter, Nastya. Nastya, this is Anton. You know Anton, but you don't know that you know Anton. Anton works for the FSB like you. In fact, I he's a bit of a high-flier, aren't you, Anton. Marked out for higher things. Head of station, maybe in one of your groovier western capitals. See how he blushes when I praise him, the sweet boy. And it's rude of you to look so surprised, Nastya darling. Spies don't all have to look like nightclub bouncers. You of all people should know that. Anton, what would you like? Coffee? A pancake? Nastya, Anton's got a terrible sweet tooth, don't you Anton?"

Mum ordered Anton a condensed milk pancake and cappuccino. She put two spoons of sugar in his coffee, stirred it for him, and made sure his napkin was perpendicular to the edge of the table. Anton smiled with patient indulgence.

"Anton is my handler," Mum said. "Or rather, Anton is my fifth handler. I've had a lot of young men from the FSB handling me." She giggled. Yuck. "I asked Anton to explain himself to you. Maybe you thought you knew all about your family. But listen to Anton. You might learn something." She turned to Anton and looked up into his eyes.

This was going too quickly.

"Theoretically, everything that I am now about to tell you about your family is top secret," Anton began. "So, before I start, Nastya, you must tell me: are you in or are you not in? I mean that we have a mission for you. It is vital for Russia. It is a big job, and it is also an assignment which will play to your abilities and your interests, personal and professional. If you tell me now that you are in, then your status will change. You are currently a freelance contractor for the FSB. If you take on this assignment, you shall become an employee, with the implied benefits. It is not a short-term commitment. Mmm. Condensed milk in a pancake. Sometimes the simplest recipe is also the best."

"And what if I say no?"

"If you say no ...". Anton dabbed the serviette to his lips. "Then I will finish my pancake and walk away, and you will never see me again - except maybe at your mother's graveside, at the back of the crowd." He pulled out of his satchel a pink A4 envelope and slid it across the table to me. "But then you will never learn about your family. You will go through life wondering about the photograph in this envelope. When you are a mother, telling your children about their grandmother, you will know that part of her story is missing. When you are a lonely old woman, you still won't really know where you came from." Anton scraped his spoon around his coffee cup, turned the spoon upside-down and sucked off the syrup. "And in a few weeks your mother will die, knowing in her heart that she couldn't tell the truth about herself to her own daughter." Anton slid the envelope back towards himself, flicked back his fringe and looked me in the eyes. "I will walk away, and leave you to bury your mother," he said.

The three of us sat in silence. A Chinese tour group went from left to right and another went from right to left.

Mum tapped Anton's plate with her spoon. "So, what is your decision, daughter?"

"I'm in," I said. Mum's shoulders sank with relief. She smiled, a different kind of smile from before.

Anton and Mum both laid their hands on the envelope. As it slid back towards me, Mum said, "Take your first look at your big sister, Nastya. It's not a great photo, unfortunately. Her name is Mikhaila. I called her Misha. Now Anton can tell you everything."

"I am not exclusively Anton. Nastya, you also know me as Gleb. I am your supervisor. Under my guidance, Nastya, you have been planting online Ragebombs for Russia. So far, your clever little Ragebombs have been the information war equivalent of a precision-targeted drone attack. But now, Nastya, you and I shall together destroy Russia's enemies with the most powerful online Ragebomb of all time. The thermonuclear Ragebomb."

Chapter 11 - Piraeus, 7th of Boedromion, 378 BC

So I'm lounging with Chorismos the dog and Arete the woman in the shade of a fig tree. I am savouring the most sublime ecstasy gifted to humankind by the Olympian Gods: that of watching other people working.

Aristotle's slaves are looping the ropes around the statue of Alcibiades: one around his neck, one under his armpits, and one three times round his nob and belayed up his bum-crack. Aristotle's tourists are in a gaggle by the dockside. They are starting to look bored, so Aristotle is starting to look worried. Behind them, another team of slaves is loading a kerkouros galley with amphorae. The ship's name is painted on its side: the *Jolly Flogger*. The figurehead is a girl in bed etc. etc.. The ship's Nubian captain is whipping the slaves but it's obvious that his heart isn't truly in his work. From time to time, he calls them 'filthy, white-skinned, bastard, honky, gobshite, bumwipe, cracker Thracian scum' and absent-mindedly slices their backs with his oxhide whip, but his mind is clearly elsewhere. This son of the Blue Nile is preoccupied. He is frowning. Maybe he's impatient to finish the loading and set sail before the wind changes.

Now Plato is talking with the Nubian. What's all that about? The Philosopher King, who considers himself too noble for the smell of his own farts, chatting with a salty sea-captain. Something doesn't add up. I can't hear what they're saying, but from the way they're nodding and shaking hands it's like they've just done a deal. Weird, and slightly unsettling.

Now Plato shakes the sea-captain's hand, pats him on the back, and rocks up to my fig tree. "Oh look," he drawls, "It's a dog, a woman and Diogenes. I suppose that's what you call a love triangle." He giggles at his own joke. "But back to business, Diogenes. I'm not paying you three drachmas to savour your body odour. Aristotle's tourists haven't come all the way from the four corners of the rectangular earth to see you lolling around with your two lovers. They've paid good drachmas to be shocked."

"I told you. No masturbation."

"A dump then."

"Already have. This morning. I don't do piecework."

"Some sacrilege, then. Anything to shock the tourists."

"I can think of no greater offence to the Gods than your existence upon this earth, O Plato of Athens."

"Well, you'd better think of something quickly, Diogenes of Sinope."

And over it goes. The statue of Alcibiades topples gently onto the quayside. With almost no noise, Alcibiades's glory sublimates into a puff of grey dust, which swirls in the bright air for the duration of a laugh and then is gone. The sea laps gently against the jetty. Chorismus pants. Distant seagulls squeal across the sparkling waves. So much for Alcibiades, history's darling.

I shout across the dock at the tourists. Harken! Ye Thebans, Boetians and Macedonians, examine your lives. Behold! Here was Alcibiades. Cheering crowds lined his path whenever he went for a pee. He led Greece's second-mightiest army. He watched Aeschylus's mind-numbing tragedies from the front benches. He knocked the willies off Athens's finest statues, and still the *demos* loved him. Alcibiades's fame extended from the pizzerias of Sicilia in the west to the doner kebab shops of Asia Minor in the east. And now even Alcibiades is nothing, not even a memory.

"So, ye grockles of the Hellenic peninsula and beyond, think of your own petty glories. Shame on you all. Ponder your pursuit of money, titties and cocks, your jewellery and horses, your nubile, elastic slave-girls. Your ambitions are so much tinier and squalider than the ambitions of Alcibiades, and even he is toppled. So, ye rubberneckers of Corinth and Miletus, abandon all your trifles. They are a handful of dust. You are a handful of dust. Throw away your finery. Tame your erections. Slurp lentil soup from a wooden spoon and live a virtuous life."

And now the tourists are crowding around me, elbowing each other to get close. Plato is looking smug. Was that a bit too strong? Are they going to beat me up?

The biggest of the tourists is leaning over me. A hulking, hairy Macedonian. I see the muscles throbbing in his forearm. I am regretting my recumbent position. The advantage of verticality, when lecturing Greeks on the pathetic shallowness of their lifestyle, is that it affords a rapid retreat.

"That made me feel virtuous all over," purrs the Macedonian. "How much is the usual tip?"

We agree on a drachma per tourist. They file past, pressing the coins into my palm, smiling and grateful because I have told them how worthless they are. It's a fair deal.

A man has taken a mallet and chisel out of a wooden toolbox and is now making quick work of the inscription on Alcibiades's statue. Sic transit etc etc.

But now it's the Nubian from the kerkouros galley who wants to talk with me. He's with Plato again. Yes, I know. Watch out for Plato! There's nothing he'd like more than to get shot of me. To have me booted out of Athens so that he can strut and prance without any commercial or intellectual competition. You can understand his position, of course. He's onto a nice little number, with the soft-skinned youth of the Athenian aristocracy lining up at the doors of his Academy. At nine every morning they start talking about virtue, at lunchtime they start drinking, at three in the afternoon they're glancing under each other's tunics and - bingo - by five in the evening they're virtuous. So, the last thing Plato wants is me totally owning him in word-battles on the Agora. The last thing he wants is me telling the gilded youth that virtue means living the simple life and demonstrating - by example - that slapping the monkey can serve as the foundation and cornerstone of a righteous existence. Oh, yes, when I'm wandering around the Stoa with my lantern looking for an honest man, Plato knows I'm lowering his share price. So, whatever he's cooking with the ship captain, he's not thinking of my welfare.

Plato hails the tourists. "Noble kosmopolitans," he cries. "Gather round and hear the great Diogenes of Sinope. Come close, and don't miss a word. Diogenes once said, "When I look upon mariners, man is the wisest of all creatures." Well, now you have the opportunity to hear him in disputation with a sea captain. May I introduce to you, the one and only Captain Sukkot of Nubia, master of the Jolly Flogger."

The tourists draw up in a circle around us, wide-eyed and silent.

'I am indeed Captain Sukkot," says the Nubian. Now, I'm afraid we must jettison our stereotypes at this point. When someone says 'Nubian sea-captain' you probably think, like me, of some tall, broad-shouldered gentleman with a six-pack and a voice like bronze thunder. Sukkot, however, is medium-sized in the vertical dimension and rather weedy in the horizontal one. His voice is squeaky, and his twisted teeth make him speak with a lisp. He is dressed like a Greek, but he's got a blingy amulet of Amon-Ra hanging from a gold necklace.

Straight up, I get that feeling. It always happens when I meet a Nubian. I can't resist it. I go wobbly at the knees, my head bows down and my face twists into a cringing smile. Yes, put us Greeks in front of a dark-skinned Nubian and we come over all subservient. Trapped by history, that's us. While we Europeans were living in caves bollock-dangling naked, the Nubians were building pyramids and expounding the universal philosophy of Hermes Trismegistus. That's why we can't resist the urge to grovel whenever a dusky Nubian's around.

"Diogenes of Sinope, I have a question for you. It's about my slaves, the filthy bumwipe white cracker Thracian scum. Look at the lazy honky gringo bastards." Sukkot gestures to the *Jolly Flogger*, where a tiny, barefooted old man is staggering under the weight of an amphora, his eyes and veins bulging like earthworms out of his shiny, bald head.

Captain Sukkot tucks his whip into his belt and pulls back his scrawny shoulders. "So, you're a philosopher, O Diogenes of Sinope, innit? You discern the parameters of a virtuous and fulfilled life, right?"

"Guilty as charged," say I. Plato is leaning forward. He doesn't want to miss a word.

"Behold yonder white trash crackerjack honky slave" the good seaman continues. "Is he not the happiest person alive?" (Plato is smirking now.) "I mean it's like this, innit. Yonder honky slave lives the simple and virtuous life, just as you prescribe, O Diogenes of Sinope. He breakfasts on dry bread, he lunches on lentil soup and he dines on lentil soup and dry bread. A modest but nutritionally adequate diet, exactly as you prescribe, and moreover rich in fibre and micronutrients when you take into account the weevils and other invertebrates. Yonder honky slave, just as you prescribe, is neither troubled by material comforts, nor by the vain pursuit of reputation, nor by the futile chase for wealth. He wears rags, precisely as you recommend. His life consists of virtuous labour by day and the dreamless snoring of the innocent moron by night. Is yonder honky slave therefore not the happiest and most virtuous person alive, according to your precepts?"

Plato nods approvingly at Sukkot and turns to me, eyebrows raised.

Obviously, I could have responded more than adequately to the Nubian. Unfortunately, however, No-Tits Arete of Cyrene chose this moment to barge through the ranks of tourists and insert herself into our conversation, thus preventing me from whipping out my dialectic prowess. "Step aside, O Diogenes of Sinope," she purrs, shoving me out of her way with an elbow to my cavea thoracis. "Come hither, slave."

The pop-eyed slave freezes half-way across the gangplank. The sinews of his knees are quivering under the weight of the amphora. His once-pale north-Thracian skin, bereft of the blessing of melanin, is erupting in sunburnt blisters across his back and shoulders. He glances briefly at Sukkot's whip and lowers his eyes fearfully in expectation of his next thrashing. Sukkot nods approval without even looking at the slave. The slave totters towards the three of us.

"What is your name, slave?" says Arete.

"He's called Omphalos," Sukkot replies. "The bellybutton. He had a Thracian name, natch, but buggered if I could pronounce it. So I call him Omphalos, innit." (The slave's navel is indeed a wondrous protrusion.)

Arete glares at Sukkot. "Tell Omphalos that he can put the amphora down," says Arete.

"Go on then," Sukkot mutters.

Omphalos lowers the amphora gently, and then watches it fearfully as though it might shatter on contact with the scalding dust.

"Behold, Diogenes of Sinope, and behold, Plato of Athens," Arete begins. "I am going to demonstrate that, in the absence of an abstract moral framework, the purpose of Mankind is to achieve tranquility, absence of fear, absence of pain, and physical pleasure in all its forms. I am going to prove that the airy-fairy virtues of Plato are just words, and that the lentil-based lifestyle recommended by Diogenes is just a pose for poseurs. I am going to prove that the sole purpose of existence is to cultivate the pleasures of the body. Tell me, O slave Omphalos," Arete continues. "What is the ultimate purpose of your life?"

"Purpose, ma'am?"

"Let me put it in plain language for this simple fellow. What is your preferred lifestyle choice, O Omphalos?"

"Choice, ma'am?"

And here's Plato butting in and placing his geometrically imperfect body between Omphalos and Arete. "Look, I'm sorry to be a bore," he whines, looking rather like a chap whose plan is about to be derailed, "but this is supposed to be a dialogue between Diogenes the cynic of Sinope and Sukkot the sea-captain of Nubia. No Epicureans invited, I'm afraid. So you can jolly well take your lifestyle choices, your pomegranate hummus wraps and your non-binary sexuality away and stick them where the golden chariot of Apollo doesn't shine."

Arete ignores him and turns back to Omphalos. "O thrice frog-like Thracian," she continues, "do you live in fear?"

Omphalos sneaks a glance at the tip of Sukkot's whip, to which the captain has attached a sprig of rusty fishhooks. "No, ma'am," he says. "Ah does not live in fear. Ah has achieve de state of ataraxia, which is to say that Ah ain't a-scared of nuddin'."

"Hmm. But tell me, O Omphalos of the creaky bones, do you live in a state of pain?"

Omphalos grimaces as he slowly straightens his back. When, eyeballs popping, streamers of sunburnt skin exploding off his shoulders, he finally reaches twenty degrees from vertical, he forces a gap-toothed grin and says, "No, ma'am. No, sirree. Ah do not live in pain. Ah has achieved de state of aponia, which is to say that Ah has de privilege of inhabiting a material body as lithe and flawless as de inner thighs of Hestia's sacred virgins. Oh, yes. Ah is truly living de good life. Mah best life. Oh, yes indeedy-doody, ma'am."

118

"In fact, you're happy, aren't you, Omphalos?" Sukkot says sweetly.

"Sho' ting, massa! I's so happy I's jus' about jivin' wi' joy." Omphalos shot a watermelon smile to the assembled company.

But Arete isn't discouraged. "False consciousness!" she cries in triumph. "The slave Omphalos has proved my point!" Plato looks puzzled and, frankly, I'm puzzled too.

"Yes, false consciousness!" Arete warbles. "You two philosophers claim to base your teachings upon reason. But it's not reason. It's oppression. It's the patriarchy. Plato, you teach that the only things that matter are Wisdom, Courage, Moderation and Justice. And thanks to your airy-fairy virtues, this pale-skinned Thracian doesn't realise that he's ground down by society and that what he really needs is solid food and a mattress. Diogenes, you teach that poverty is noble. And thanks to you, this trailer trash Omphalos doesn't realise that he's living in misery. False consciousness. Virtue is the invention of the oppressor."

"Hang on a moment," says Plato. "If Omphalos had answered 'yes' to all your questions, saying that he wanted a comfier life, wouldn't you have taken that as proof of your Epicurean philosophy."

"I certainly would, O Plato of Athens," replies Arete.

"But on the other hand, when Omphalos answered 'no' to all your questions, saying that he is perfectly happy as he is, you also took that as proof of your Epicurean philosophy."

"I certainly did, O Plato of Athens," replies Arete.

"So, whatever the evidence shows, you're always going to conclude that you're right?"

"Exactly. Which proves I'm right. If I'm right whatever the evidence shows, then I must be really, truly right."

"But what if I don't agree with you?" Plato asks.

Arete of Cyrene shrugs. "If you don't agree with me, Plato of Athens, that proves you're a part of the patriarchal oppressive construct."

"That doesn't make sense."

"You're in denial."

"I was in de Nile once," says Omphalos. "Dat crocodile nearly done swaller me."

"Whatever," says Arete.

And we all stop talking. There's no point. Our words lie where we have dropped them. A faint sigh of wind briefly stirs the sails of Sukkot's galley. The sun glares with contempt on the litter of broken syllogisms in the hot sand around our feet. The indifferent cicadas sing at us. Chorismos's hind leg thumps slowly against the dust as he scratches his neck. The tourists whisper. Omphalos looks at each of us through his watery, pale blue eyes: the Platonist, the Cynic, the Epicurean, and the whip. "Oh me, oh my! Is dat de time?" he exclaims, looking at the sun. "I'd best get me back to mah honest toil. Tote dat barge, lift dat bale." With a toothless whistle and a dry rattling of lumbar vertebrae, Omphalos stoops down to lift his amphora.

Plato nudges Sukkot.

"Ah, yes!" says Sukkot. "Tell me, O Diogenes, do you still insist that hard work, rags and lentils are the accoutrements of a virtuous life?"

"I do. It is the privilege of the Gods to want nothing and of godlike men to want little."

"Tell me, therefore, O Diogenes: would you be willing to join my crew aboard the Jolly Flogger as a slave?"

Ah.

Ah.

Now I understand. Plato has paid Sukkot to make me look stupid in front of the tourists. Plato wants me to contradict myself so the tourists will tell everyone back home that Diogenes of Sinope is rubbish. The truth about my philosophical incompetence will spread to the four corners of the rectangular world. Then who's going to pay to see me have an argument or a crap? But I'm not going to fall for Plato's little stratagem.

"Well," he sneers. "Aren't you going to answer the captain? Would you be willing to become a slave?"

I turn to the tourists. "I am a man of principle," I cry, and I leap from the quay into the Jolly Flogger. I slap an astonished Omphalos on the sunburnt geological extrusions that pass for his vertebrae. "Pass me that amphora, good fellow," I roar. The tourists applaud as I shoulder the amphora and parade in circles around the deck. (Bloody hell, it's heavy though. No wonder little Omphalos is vertically compressed. Obviously, I'm only going to keep this up until the tourists have buggered off to wherever. Then it's back to my barrel for me and, if the goddesses Hubris and Nemesis and the three Fates aren't too bloody-minded, a learning-by-doing dialectic with Arete on the physis and nomos of physical desire.)

"Look at me, look at me!" I shout, somewhat breathlessly. "I am modelling the good life. Honest toil and no concern for wealth or fame." Omphalos's sky-blue eyes, which have somehow stayed fresh and bright while the rest of him turned into dried poop, spin around and around as they track my gyrations.

Now it's Arete skipping towards the quayside with a determined frown. She hitches up her tunic, revealing a splendidly hairy pair of legs, and springs like a gazelle into the kerkouros galley. "Most noble Omphalos," she declaims, extending both arms to the astonished Thracian. "Now you are free to enjoy the pleasures of life. The cynic Diogenes has offered to take your place. This is your chance. Liberate your mind, come ashore, eat, drink and be merry, for tomorrow we die."

Then things started happening rather too quickly.

Omphalos glances up at Sukkot. "Massa," he croaked, "does Ah do what de madam says? Is Ah really free?"

And Sukkot glances sideways at Plato. Plato nods, pulls a jingling purse out of his toga and throws it to Sukkot. With his left hand, Sukkot catches the purse and with his right he uncoils the Jolly Flogger's mooring rope from its bollard. He leaps into the galley.

"Wait, wait," I cry. "When I said, 'modelling the good life', I only meant for a few minutes." I drop the amphora and suddenly there's olive oil and broken pottery all over the deck. I try to jump onto the quayside, but I slip up on the oil and land on my bum in the bottom of the boat.

"Hoist the mainsail," Sukkot calls. A rag resembling a larger version of my oft-fouled tunic quickly climbs the mast and catches the feeble breeze. The galley creaks in resignation and slides lazily away from the quay.

"Think of the bint as a bonus," Plato shouts across to Sukkot.

"I already do," Sukkot shouts back. "For resale only, obviously. As my papa said – don't get high on your own supply."

Omphalos is smiling and drops onto all fours. He is joined by his crewmates. They begin eagerly licking up the olive oil.

"All breakages come out of your salary," Sukkot hisses to me.

"I get a salary?"

"No."

Puh-thump! Puh-thump! Puh-thump! Suddenly there's this noise in my head, and I don't know what it is. Could it be a ship's carpenter at work? Does Sukkot keep a set of bongos on board? Or is it the outraged throbbing of rebellious arteries in my temples?

Chapter 12. Streatham, at exactly the same moment

Puh-thump! Puh-thump! Puh-thump! There's a noise in Mikhail's head, and he doesn't know what it is. He tears off the headphones and the virtual reality goggles. Humpty the parrot is dancing on his perch from one claw to the other. His neck's jutting out. He's eyeballing the door in alarm and screeching, "Plato talks bollocks! Plato talks bollocks!"

Puh-thump! Puh-thump! Puh-thump! Someone is hammering on the door of Mikhail's flat.

Mikhail doesn't yet know that the next twenty minutes will change the course of American history.

"We know you're in there," called a woman with a west African accent. "You might 's well open up, 'cause we're not going anywhere in a hurry."

Mikhail peered through the spy hole to see three grimacing faces: Dumitru, Ruby and old grey-haired Dr. Bannerji. Mikhail opened the door.

"And about time too," said Ruby, hands on hips.

"We don't have any quarrel with you," began Dr. Bannerji, "but..."

"Yes, we do," interrupted Dumitru. "A big problem. A stinking big problem."

Mikhail was still adjusting to the flat reality of Streatham after taking off his Virtual Reality gear. His mind was whirling. He had that vacuum feeling in his bladder that reminded him of being told off at school.

"Plato talks bollocks!" screamed Humpty. Ruby and the parrot glared at each other.

"The thing is ...", began Ruby.

"You just crossed the red line, my friend" Dumitru said. "Tell him, Dr Bannerji."

"Well, my wife ..." Dr Bannerji wrung his hands and looked at the floor. "No, I can't say this. I just can't. It goes against my nature."

"Come on. You're a medical man, innit," said Ruby. "I mean, you must have seen it all, right. Plenty of bottoms and stuff."

"No, no, no!" stammered Dr. Bannerji. "I'm not that kind of doctor at all. I have a Ph.D. in English literature from Calcutta University. I wrote my thesis on the works of Margaret Oliphant, an underrated Scottish lady novelist of the Victorian era. So, in fact, I have hardly seen any bottoms at all, apart from ...". His voice tailed away.

Ruby edged closer to Mikhail. Her eyes narrowed. She inhaled slowly and deeply, her blouse rippling like a curtain in a summer breeze. "Dr. Bannerji's wife - right now - is lying semi-conscious on her sofa," said Ruby. "Wheezing and gasping. Mrs. Bannerji - you know she's an elderly lady?"

"I know, I know," stammered Mikhail. "Old."

"Mrs. Bannerji struck her head on the floor when she fainted. And you know why she fainted?"

"I don't know why she fainted."

"She fainted because when she stepped into the lift to go down, BOOM! She was whammed in the face by the fart that you left behind you at three twenty-three p.m.. You know, when you took the lift upstairs. After the police gave you that telling off." Mikhail's mind clicked back into focus. He was in Streatham in 2019 and there had been a misspelt notice about foreigners taped to the wall downstairs. Mikhail didn't know what to say, so he just waited.

"Hey? Hey? You listening to us, sunshine?" Dumitru said, waving his hands in front of Mikhail's eyes. "You just crossed the red line, mate. You farted in the lift."

Mikhail still didn't know what to say.

"You just gonna stand there? You mental or something?" Dumitru was rolling his shoulders like a boxer.

"I think I'd better go now," said Dr. Bannerji. "See to my wife."

"You're not going anywhere 'til I've got you an apology for your missus," said Dumitru. "I said - I said, are you mental? Or are you just taking my piss? Cause, if you're taking my piss, I know what to do with people who take my piss, you nawa mean?"

"I wasn't taking the piss," Mikhail explained. "I was just thinking."

Dumitru was jiggling his shoulders again. "Oh yeah? And what were you thinking, my son?"

"I'm wondering why the lift was going down."

"Uh?"

Mikhail smiled in relief. He had found the door into the conversation. "I was thinking about the fart," Mikhail explained. "I was wondering how long after I farted it was that Mrs. Bannerji entered the lift and fainted. Because lifts are designed to permit the entry and exit of gases, so as to eliminate the risk of suffocation in the event of an accident or a mechanical failure. Moreover, each time the lift doors open and shut, there is a substantial exchange of air between the inside and the outside. Many lifts also have electric air extractors to facilitate the evacuation of noxious gases, and yes, I can hear it whirring right now.

"Now, if Mrs. Bannerji was stepping into the left to *go down*, as Ruby said, then that means she was *already up*. So, before she even stepped into the lift to descend, the doors had already opened and shut three times since I used it: once when I stepped out, once when the lift came down to the ground floor to pick up

Dr. and Mrs. Bannerji, and once when Mrs. Bannerji stepped in.

"So, in addition to the continuous seepage of gas and the extractor fan, there must have been at least three complete exchanges of gas. It is therefore highly improbable that the fart which caused Mrs. Bannerji's unfortunate injury was mine.

"Dr. Bannerji, please pay close attention to this question. The reputation of more than one person may depend upon it." Mikhail reflexively twirled an imaginary moustache. "When you and Mrs. Bannerji called the lift to go downstairs, did the lift come up to you or did it come down?"

Dr. Bannerji shook a forefinger. "It definitely came down. Without a doubt it came down."

"So," said Mikhail carefully, "You live on the penultimate floor. We can therefore be certain that the person who dealt the fart entered the lift on the top floor. It must therefore be Ruby or Dumitru. It is logical."

Ruby, Dumitru and Dr. Bannerji stared at each other. "Plato talks bollocks!" squawked Humpty.

"You think you're so fucking clever," said Dumitru.

"I don't think I'm clever at all," said Mikhail. "I've got Archilochus-Hesburger Syndrome. It is not intelligence. It's not a disability either. It's a condition."

"Please allow me to go downstairs now in order to attend to Mrs. Bannerji's condition," pleaded the doctor. "I should be at her side." Nobody took notice of him.

"Wait a minute," said Ruby, waving a plump finger under Mikhail's nose. "You stop right there. Just because you didn't supply the actual fart which injured Mrs. Bannerji, that don't mean you're not guilty as sin. You know what I'm talking about?"

Mikhail tried to understand whether he was supposed to answer. Was that what they called a rhetorical question?

"I'm talking about the doctrine of parasitic accessory liability," proclaimed Ruby. "Step aside, gents. I'm a lawyer, so listen up. You heard the accused. He said, and I quote, "It is highly unlikely that the fart which caused Mrs. Bannerji's injury was in fact mine." His exact words. "Highly unlikely." Not "impossible". So, in essence, the accused is admitting that he did indeed fart in the lift. I'll just let that fact hang in the air for a moment, gentlemen. The doctrine of parasitic accessory liability states that if two persons had the intention to fart and the knowledge that their farts could cause distress, then they are both equally responsible in law for the consequences of their farts, regardless of which fart actually caused the injury in question."

Mikhail bit his lip. "Ruby, I think you are right. I did not cause Mrs. Bannerji's distress, but I am just as guilty of causing her distress as Dumitru because I knew the potential consequences of my fart. The fact that Mrs. Bannerji entered the lift when she did is a purely random event, and it is not logical to base guilt or innocence upon a random event. Dumitru and Ruby cannot be more guilty than I. They did not know that Mrs. Bannerji would enter the lift within seconds of their misdemeanour. Calling Dumitru or Ruby the guilty party would be like sending a lollipop lady to jail because a child was struck by lightning while crossing her road. And if Dumitru or Ruby cannot be more guilty than me, then I cannot be less guilty than Dumitru or Ruby. Dr. Bannerji, please tell your wife that I am very sorry."

Dr. Bannerji forced a smile. "I think I'd better go now," he muttered, and scurried down the stairs.

"Bwaar! Plato talks bollocks."

Mikhail shrugged, and then he smiled. "I did have the right to break wind in the lift," he said, 'but that does not mean that it was right. "Right" and "right". It is the same word meaning two different things, which is probably the reason for thirty-five to forty percent of disagreements."

And thus was released the fart, that, like the first musket shot at the Battle of Concord, was heard around the world and was to set western civilization ablaze.

Chapter 13. Still at the pancake kiosk of the New Tretyakov Gallery

"Your mother has many talents," began Anton/Gleb, "but it was her skill at chess which mattered in the end. In January 1983 she was on the Soviet junior team. They were competing in Oxford, England. She was only in England for six days, but that was long enough for her to fall pregnant."

"Don't pull faces, Nastya," said my mother. "Your eyerolls and winces wouldn't suit an unkissed schoolgirl, let alone a twenty-seven-year-old troll. Anyway, sex was different in the USSR."

Anton/Gleb didn't seem to mind the interruption. "Fortunately, the team's chaperone caught your mother as she returned to her lodging in the early morning. Your mother immediately revealed the name of the man who had taken her virginity a few hours earlier. It was Brent Lundscum Junior. When the chaperone reported back to Moscow through our embassy in London, the KGB couldn't believe its luck. Yes, Brent Lundscum Jnr, Yale alumnus, Rhodes Scholar, heir to the Lundscum processed pork empire, son of Brent Lundscum Senior, Republican Governor of Missouri, about to follow his father into a sordid and successful political career and, though the world didn't know it then, future Governor of Missouri himself.

Your mother couldn't have done better for the Motherland, even if she had been following written orders from the Lubyanka. This was platinum-grade blackmail material - kompromat. Not only had Lundscum had casual sex with a Soviet citizen, but moreover statutory rape of an under-age girl, who moreover (and this was the jackpot) happened to be black-skinned - well, half-black, which is enough to count as a negro for Americans. With such kompromat on Lundscum Jnr, surely we could blackmail Lundscum Snr. And if, as his parenthood and his wealth predicted, Lundscum Jnr entered the top level of American politics, what would he not do for us to keep this liaison secret?

"The only problem was that we had no proof. Nowadays the chaperone would collect a semen sample without being told. But this was 1983, long before we stole DNA testing technology from the Americans. Moscow did what it could. It arranged for your mother to stay in England another ten weeks. The embassy in London put her up in the Third Secretary's apartment. And we waited for Lundscum Jnr. to make contact with your mother. Even a little love-letter would have sufficed. But there was no sign of him.

"It was already March when we realised that Lundscum wasn't even in Oxford. The day after he impregnated your mother, he flew home to Mom and

Pop in Jefferson City. We thought maybe he had left Oxford because of moral guilt, but Lundscum's subsequent career ruled out the possibility of Lundscum having a conscience. It was just an unfortunate coincidence.

"We had your mother phone Lundscum at the Governor's residence in Jefferson City, but she couldn't get past the switchboard. We wrote letters for your mother to copy out and send. We smudged the ink with teardrops made of tap water and salt. But she only got one letter back. It was even on Oxford University notepaper."

"They gave me the original," Mama said. "I left it in England."

"But of course, we kept a copy," said Gleb/Anton. "It's in the envelope."

I read it:

Dear Anna,

In response to your long epistle, as I said, it all comes down to the Continuum Fallacy - color and age. There is a point at which small differences become impossibly big. I will not take responsibility for a child, which, for all I know, is not mine. I have nothing more to say to you.

"What does it mean?" I asked. "The continuum fallacy?"

Mama shrugged. "It means that many trivial complications together added up to an insurmountable objection. It meant that he would not acknowledge me or our unborn child."

"It also meant that it amused a Rhodes Scholar from Yale to show off his learning to a Soviet teenager," said Anton/Gleb.

"Anyway, it wasn't all bad luck," Anton/Gleb said. "At least your mother was pregnant."

"Nastya!" my mother snapped. "Don't look so shocked, you hypocrite."

"Mama, I mean..."

"I know, I know, Nastya. You thought I was just a drab old Soviet remnant. How typical of the young to assume that nothing of interest happened before they came into the world. Now you're astonished to discover that I have a past. Well, just keep listening to Anton, my dear. And you'll learn that my past is a lot more interesting than your present, and certainly far more interesting than your future will ever be."

Anton had been pretending not to take notice of our conversation. Now he said, "With any luck, it would be a boy with a facial resemblance to Lundscum, and that would be proof enough of his statutory rape. Twelve weeks after conception, as soon as an ultrasound could show the foetus's sex, the London station had the embassy doctor give your mother the once-over. The outcome was a severe disappointment; it was going to be a girl. Add to that the inevitable dilution of your mother's African genes, and there was really no hope of a family resemblance.

"So in April 1983 the order came from Moscow to give up. Your mother's pregnancy was becoming visible. There wasn't any point keeping her in London. We booked her onto a flight to Moscow.

Nastya's mother continued, "And they were so kind to me. The day before I was due to leave, just before I closed my little pasteboard suitcase, the Third Secretary's wife gave me ten pounds to buy a pair of jeans from Woolworths. But I didn't go to Woolworths. I went to Queen Anne's gate. I marched into the Home Office. I told the receptionist that I was a Soviet citizen and that I wanted to defect."

"But why?"

"Why, Nastya? You still don't get it, do you? With the arrogance of your generation, you think that nobody was young before you. I was seventeen, darling. I'd just spent two months sitting on the couch all day watching Boy George and David Bowie on the TV. In the evenings I was lying in bed, listening to the sounds of Holland Park, smelling the diesel and the fried potatoes. Don't you think I wasn't dreaming of freedom?"

"I'm sorry, Mama." I was surprised. I'd never heard my mother say what she wanted. I'd only known her saying what other people shouldn't want. Just for a moment, I was wondering whether I had underestimated her. Tacogirl513 once wrote that you become an adolescent the moment you see your parents' failings, and an adult the moment you see their qualities again. Maybe Mama had once been more than a sovok.

"Yes, Nastya, and maybe you'd also better remember that I was pregnant with your sister. I wasn't just thinking of my own future.

"So the British took me to their Special Branch Headquarters. For two days I was indeed special. There was a policewoman, Detective Sergeant Jane Briscoe. She was always asking me if everything was all right, giving me Fanta and Kit-Kats whenever I asked. She was so kind when I threw up in the morning.

"I'd left all my clothes in Holland Park, so Jane took me shopping - to Marks and Spencers, not to Woolworths. She bought me two full outfits, plus an extra two sets of underwear.

"Apart from Jane, I didn't know the names of the people who questioned me. They asked me why I wanted to defect. I told them that I liked London. They asked me if I had been told to defect by anyone back home or in the Embassy. I said no. One of them kept looking at his watch.

"On the second day, Jane told me that the Embassy had demanded my return. The Embassy said that I was a minor so I could not legally defect, and anyone who prevented the Embassy from taking me to Moscow was kidnapping me. So Special Branch took me to see a judge. Jane sat next to me in the back seat of the police car, which smelt of sick. The judge said that I was a ward of the court. That meant that the Soviet Embassy had no claim on me. I belonged to Britain.

"They gave me a bank account, a few hundred pounds, a council bedsit in Stoke-on-Trent and a form to apply for social benefits.

"I needed a job, but it was 1983. The contradictions in British capitalism were manifest. A tenth of the workforce was unemployed. Margaret Thatcher had provoked a war against Argentina to placate the proletariat. And now she was closing coal mines to provoke a class war. The streets were filthy - full of hamburger wrappers.

"And by now my belly was beginning to show. I asked for jobs in shops, cafes, everywhere. There was no work in Stoke-on-Trent for an unmarried pregnant Soviet teenager.

"To begin with I worried that I was doing nothing, just sitting in my bedsit on my second-hand sofa. I joined the Stoke-on-Trent chess club, but the games were too easy.

"But they had this new programme on the TV called 'Countdown'. The players had thirty seconds to make a long word out of nine letters. I watched it every afternoon. When I started going to prenatal classes at the Royal Stoke Hospital, I found that all the other women were also idle and I stopped worrying about my idleness. So I started the day with Good Morning Britain, except on Saturdays when it was Roland Rat. There was also Sons and Daughters from Australia. I watched the news, which had its own logic. Irish freedom fighters escaped from jail -twice -, the United States invaded a little Caribbean island, Falklands veterans had mental disorders, the British re-elected Margaret Thatcher and there were still no jobs. But there was also always Countdown, wonderful Countdown. Everything made sense on Countdown, and the contestants spoke a language that I could understand. I was watching Countdown when I went into labour with Mikhaila in September.

"And the next six years passed. I thought briefly about educating myself, but I couldn't go to college because of Mikhaila. There was a woman who came from the benefits office occasionally. We sat at the kitchen table and she played with Mikhaila and showed me what to write in the forms so they kept paying my benefits. I told her once that I'd been invited for a job interview at a supermarket and she told me not to turn up. I got books from the library. Sometimes I took Misha to the park. There was a place called Rhyl by the sea. If I got restless we could take the train to Rhyl and feel the wind on the beach. In winter the wind reminded me of back home. Also the people in Rhyl don't say much.

"I didn't know anybody. Not even my neighbours. There was just me, Misha and the TV.

"So you regretted being in Stoke when you could have been in Moscow, huh?"

"No, Nastya. How could I regret anything? I was seventeen. Regret is the sign that you have reached the stupidity of adulthood. Before adulthood, you know that everything that happens must happen, so there cannot be anything to regret. Regret is the definition of growing up. When you are a child - and I was a child- you are therefore happy simply to let time pass. You know that every day is taking you closer to the future when, you sincerely believe, all things will become clear. Anyway, Nastya, I was a Soviet, remember? And in the Soviet Union we were all children waiting for the future, weren't we? So I was happy to let time pass, watching Sons and Daughters and Countdown.

"When Mikhaila was four, I started taking her to school. The mothers I met at the gates of the infant school confirmed that I was normal. Their lives were also devoted to the passing of time, by means of young children and television. I found that I was assimilated.

"I think that Channel Four chose me to compete in Countdown because of my accent. Naturally the mathematics was not a problem, but I didn't do so badly with the nine letters, dear Nastya, especially when you consider that English was my second language. I beat the champion on my first try and I won the pale blue teapot in the shape of a stopwatch, but it was not my destiny to become an Octachampion. I was interrupted after my sixth victory.

"While I was still pregnant, I worried that they'd find me and take me back on that plane to Moscow. But after Mikhaila's birth, I gradually forgot where I came from. When they said, 'Let's bomb Russia' at Margaret Thatcher's election rally, I heard it as though they were talking about somewhere I didn't know.

"So it was actually a surprise when they kidnapped Mikhaila and me in Leeds Station. They must have observed our Countdown routine: stop recording at six o'clock, taxi to Leeds Station and train to Stoke. We stepped out of the Channel 4 studio into the wind and rain at five past six. A taxi pulled up. We got in. Mikhaila asked for her teddy bear and I told her

I'd give it to her on the train. Then she asked for her sandwich. The taxi turned a corner and stopped at red traffic lights. A man got into the taxi and chloroformed me. When I woke up, I was in Moscow. They told me later that the Third Secretary's wife, who had been sanctioned for sending me to Woolworth's to buy clothes, reported my location. It turned out that she was a Countdown fan.

"Yes, Nastya, everything I told you about Chernobyl was a lie. I was in Stoke-on-Trent all that time. I watched Chernobyl on the BBC. I probably knew more about it than most people in Kiev."

Anton/Gleb laughed. "And here's the funny thing. We brought back your mother for interrogation because we were sure that British intelligence had turned her. But you knew nothing at all, did you?"

"Nothing at all, Anton."

"Oh my God!" I explained. "My sister! You left Mikhaila in the taxi."

"But at least we had her adopted," Anton/Gleb interjected. "Chervyakov and Alekhina, alias the Litvaks, a refusenik couple from Kiev. Or at least that's what they looked like. We established Chervyakov and Alekhina as Sleeper Agents in Bury St. Edmunds in 1987. They slept and they slept. (Suffolk, and especially Bury St. Edmunds, is a good place for sleeping.) However, we decided that a pair of bored Sleeper

Agents was an unacceptable risk, so we gave Mikhaila to the Litvaks to keep them occupied."

Sometimes - not very often, thank God, but sometimes - I get this strange sensation in my nervous system. It's hot and sharp, and a bit like those few seconds when the first gulp of a Bloody Mary flushes through my capillaries. I had a friend who described the prickles in her nerves during the onset phase of Multiple Sclerosis, but when I get them it's a symptom that I'm starting to take an interest in somebody else. And I was getting them now. "My sister, when she was with the Litvaks, was she, I mean was it ...?"

"You want to know whether she had a happy childhood," Anton/Gleb interrupted. "Her childhood was *normalno*."

Normalno. Our Russian word meaning, "as usual". Allie from California cannot conceive of *normalno*. For Allie, everything is either awesome or a total bummer. Allie's from the West. She doesn't know how to let things be.

Anton/Gleb continued, "Mikhaila went to Imperial College in London. A nice name, don't you think? She studied Computer Science, specialising in artificial intelligence and advanced computer graphics. She was, of course, brilliant. For her final year project, she designed and coded a virtual reality model of the Agora in Athens. Your own sister Mikhaila won the prize for the best undergraduate dissertation of the year. She had PhD offers from Imperial, Oxford and Cambridge to continue her virtual reality work. The head of faculty at MIT personally offered her a full scholarship.

"But the Litvaks also told us that Mikhaila was being investigated for some kind of neurological disorder. We never found out exactly what it was. She had a 'Beautiful Mind', people said."

"That beautiful mind, she got it straight from me," says Mama.

"In fact, the Litvaks were driving from Bury St. Edmunds to Mikhaila's graduation when they were both killed in the road accident."

"Because you killed them," I said. It was a reflex.

"This time no," Anton/Gleb laughed. "Not the FSB. A small stone. It cracked their windscreen, resulting in an unfortunate head-on collision."

"I don't believe you. The FSB killed the Litvaks"

Anton/Gleb shrugged. "And then Mikhaila Krutova disappeared from our radar. One day a rising star, the next nowhere to be found. Of course, we didn't look for her too hard. Mikhaila was nobody to us.

"But now things are different, Nastya. We would really like to locate your sister. To reassure you that she's all right."

"Oh, Gleb, darling, please," I laughed, teasing the skinny little spy. "It's the American election, isn't it? My sister is a walking, talking piece of kompromat. A positive DNA match between my sister and Lundscum, and you have the perfect blackmail for Governor Lundscum."

Anton/Gleb smiled. "...Governor Lundscum, who is running in the Republican primaries for President. A perfect target, but we'd lost your bloody sister. No Mikhaila, no evidence and therefore no blackmail.

"But then our luck changed. A sallow-skinned woman walks into the consular department of the Russian Embassy in London with an application form for a birth certificate; she wants her first passport. First name Mikhaila. Family name Krutova. But no father's name and therefore no patronymic.

"The consular official says that he can't issue a birth certificate without a patronymic. Krutova says she doesn't know her father's name. 'Happens all the time,' says the official. 'Just write down your best guess.'

"And what does the woman write? *Brentovna.* The daughter of Brent."

"The consular officer enters the name into the database, the FSB systems spot a match and flag it for priority attention. After three decades, we'd found your half-sister.

"FSB Moscow immediately orders our London station to tail Mikhaila. To follow her every movement 24/7. Not to let Mikhaila out of their sight.

"But what do those London station fuckwits do? They mix up Streatham in south London with Stratford in East London and stake out the wrong flat."

("The Soviet KGB used brains," interjected my mother. "They recruited chess players – like myself. And now they're all nightclub bouncers and pugilists.")

"So, when these thugs realise their screw-up, they find a way to make it worse. Instead of obtaining Mikhaila's travel plans, our FSB bullyboys treat her as a standard intimidation case. What do they do? They pin up some racist rant on a wall and call in the police to arrest Mikhaila of hate speech. And Mikhaila simply strolls out of the front door, suitcase in hand, unobserved, and flies to America!"

"To think we were once a great nation," my mother mutters.

"The best kompromat of my career, a mulatto rapechild carrying Lundscum's genetic material in every chromosome, and I can't fucking find her!" Anton/Gleb's shoulders sagged momentarily. He coughed and sat up straight again.

"And me?" I say. "You're asking me to find Mikhaila and turn her in to the FSB? Because I speak

147

English? Because I already work for you? Because, as her blood relation, I can win her trust. Is that it?"

"Well, Nastya, I can either ask you pretty please - or I can order you as your ranking officer. All we need is for you to collect two samples of DNA: Mikhaila's and Lundscum's. A coffee cup. A napkin. A hair. Anything we can give to the Washington Post to prove that Mikhaila is Lundscum's daughter by statutory rape. After that you can do what you want. Tearful family reunion? That's your business. Be my guest."

"And if I refuse? Haven't you got a hundred other agents who could do this?"

My mother, who had been fingering her paper napkin, said very gently without looking up, "You have heard that I am going to die soon, Nastya. I want to die in Tiraspol, where I came from all those years ago. Beside the river Dniester. Where the grapes still grow. I am asking you, Nastya, to tell your sister that I didn't abandon her. Tell Mikhaila why I hid for the last thirty years, and then tell her that I hope very much to see her before I die. Tell her to visit me in Tiraspol and hold my hand before it is too late. Only you can do that. Nobody else." She looked at me, eyebrows raised.

"But the DNA first," Gleb said. "First the DNA."

Chapter 14a. Horringer, 3 miles by the A143 from Bury St Edmunds, Suffolk, 1992

The monthly farewells began when Mikhaila was nine and finished when she was eleven. Every second Sunday of the month, Magda Hesburger (Auntie Magda) said goodbye to Mikhaila with the same fifteen words and little Mikhaila would reply with the same four words.

This was when Mikhaila was living with her adoptive parents the Litvaks, in their pink thatched cottage in the village of Horringer, about three miles from Bury St. Edmunds in Suffolk. Between eleven-fifteen and eleven-thirty on a Sunday morning, a weary woman in brown corduroy trousers, supermarket trainers, a dark blue backpack and a light blue kagoule would ring the Litvaks' doorbell. This woman had short grey hair with a 360-degree fringe that ran horizontally around her head like the rings of Saturn. She always walked from Bury St. Edmunds station, and often, when the door opened, she would be peering shortsightedly through rain-spattered glasses. She never seemed happy to see the Litvaks and would brush past them into the living room, clutching her backpack to her thin chest, with wrinkles on her blouse or cardigan where breasts would have been. She took her shoes off at the door in the Russian way. Magda Hesburger spoke Russian with the Litvaks, even though the Litvaks only spoke English with each other, at least when Mikhaila was around. If Mikhaila's foster-father or foster-mother asked how her journey was, Auntie Magda would growl back, "Normalno". Sometimes Mikhaila would hear the word, 'Cheltenham', and, after Mikhaila had looked up Cheltenham in Mrs. Litvak's atlas, she wondered why Auntie Magda came all the way from Gloucestershire every month (via Paddington and Liverpool Street stations) to meet a couple that made her so uncomfortable and anxious. But when Auntie Magda came into the living room and Mikhaila looked up at her from her jigsaw, book, paint-by-numbers or Lego on the floor, Auntie would dart Mikhaila a pained smile, as though to say, "You're the only thing I like in this house."

After the visit to the toilet and the silent glass of lemon tea, Magda Hesburger would pick up her dark blue backpack (with brown shoulder straps) and follow the Litvaks into their study at the back of the house. (Mikhaila had never seen inside the study; the Litvaks kept it locked.) Then Auntie would return to the living room, now without her backpack. The Litvaks would remain about an hour in the study, and Mikhaila would hear Mr. Litvak's photocopier whirring and clicking.

The photocopying hour - that was when Auntie Magda would talk to Mikhaila. The first month she only spoke one sentence: a question. She was watching Mikhaila play with her Lego, following Mikhaila's hands with her eyes as though she were guessing where the orphan would place the next plastic block. "What will appear, Mikhaila?" she asked. Not "What are you making?" or "What will it be?", but "What will appear?" as though the idea of the object was already somewhere else and waiting to take material form.

"Two things," Mikhaila whispered.

"What are they?"

"A spoon. And Lego." Auntie Magda nodded in agreement.

The second month, Auntie said nothing at all to Mikhaila but watched her paint by numbers. Or rather, her eyes scanned the canvas and then closed, as though she could already see the pirate ship, the *Jolly Roger*, in all its future angles and colours.

The third month, Auntie Magda began helping Mikhaila with her jigsaws. She would sit on the edge of the sofa and peer down at the scattered pieces like a bird, her eyes darting from side to side behind their thick glasses. She didn't have to reach down. She would just point at a piece and then point at the place where it belonged, and she was almost always right, even when it was a case of blue sky on blue sky. Once, Auntie Magda arrived just after Mikhaila had opened the jigsaw box, tipped out the pieces and stirred them up with both hands. All the pieces were scattered on the floor, some upside down.

"It's ancient Athens in the evening," Auntie Magda said. "There. That's the Akropolis."

"How can you tell? You can't even see the box." Auntie Magda shrugged and giggled like a little girl.

Mikhaila thought for a moment. "Do you have a job?" she asked.

"Yes, I do."

"Is it in Cheltenham?"

"Well, you are a clever little girl. Yes, it is."

"What's your job?"

"I do puzzles."

"Jigsaws?"

"Different puzzles."

"Do you work at GCHQ?"

"How did you…?"

"It's on my map. What does GCHQ stand for?"

"Government Communications Headquarters. Now, Mikhail, that's enough questions."

"Why did you call me Mikhail and not Mikhaila?"

"I ... I... I...," Auntie Magda stammered. "I confused you with somebody else."

The fourth Sunday, during the photocopying hour, Auntie Magda suddenly broke the silence with a question. "Do you know about the Fox and the Hedgehog?"

"No."

"The was a poet in ancient Greece called Archilochus of Paros."

"What's Paros?"

"It's an island. There is Paros. And opposite Paros there is Anti-Paros, which means *Opposite Paros*. And there is a tiny islet in-between them. I suppose they ran out of names, so they called it *Reumatonese*. It means *Flow Island*."

"Can we go to Flow Island when I'm a grown-up? I never went on holiday since Mama... What did Archilochus say?"

"Archilochus was the High-Priest of Paros in ancient Greece, nearly three thousand years ago. He was a very special poet."

"What made him special?"

"Archilochus was the first person ever to write from somebody else's point of view."

"Like invisible quotation marks?"

"Exactly. My, you're so sharp, Mikhaila!"

"So, when Archilochus's poems said bad things, people didn't know whether to blame him or his words?"

"You understand, Mikhaila. Well, the people of Paros hated Archilochus because they hated his poems. But the god of truth – Apollo - got angry at them. Apollo was in a rage because the people of Paros had confused Archilochus's words with Archilochus. So, Apollo told the people of Paros that they would not be able to have children unless they built a temple in the honour of Archilochus."

"Did they build the temple?"

"Indeed they did, Mikhaila. On that tiny island between Paros and Antiparos. And for eight hundred years people came from all over Greece to worship at the Temple of Archilochus on Reumatonese."

"But what did Archilochus say?"

"He said, *The Fox knows many small things, but the Hedgehog knows one big thing.* I've been watching you, Mikhaila. You know what I think? I think that you're a hedgehog. Am I right, Mikhaila?" Mikhaila froze. "I can see from your eyes that I am right," Auntie Magda said, blinking down at her through her glasses. "You and I are the same, Mikhaila. We see all the pieces at once.

"What were your biggest thoughts?" Auntie Magda asked. Mikhaila could not speak. How was this possible? Here was somebody who saw inside her the same way that she saw paint-by-numbers and jigsaws. It was like Auntie had X-ray vision.

"Come on, Mikhaila. I don't bite, love. What were your biggest thoughts?"

Mikhaila looked up into the grey, blinking eyes. He saw how Auntie's glasses magnified the grey creases beneath them into metallic furrows. She did not see any sign of malice through those glasses, so she answered the question. "I have had three big thoughts," she said. "The first one was over there." She pointed out of the living room door and across the hallway. "Sometimes I sit under that dining room table. The carpet has patterns and a special smell. I was sitting there, and I thought, "How does a deer think, if a deer doesn't have any words to think with? And then I tried thinking without any words, and I couldn't do it. Words kept popping into my head. I asked my teacher the next day, and she said, "What questions you come up with, Misha!" so I didn't bother anybody with my other two big thoughts.

"The second big thought was at school in Morning Assembly. Mrs. Anderson (she's our headmistress) said, 'Some children, and I won't name any names, have taken up bullying. Let me make myself clear as crystal, girls and boys. Bullying is not acceptable in my school.' Even though she didn't name

155

any names, everybody knew that the names were *Kevin Sweetman* and *Christian Pike,* and everybody knew that the name of the person they were bullying was *Mikhaila Krutova*. They used to shout, 'Hey boy-girl! You a girl or a boy, Mikhailurrrr?'

"So suddenly you could hear chairs creaking, and everybody was turning around to stare at me. I looked out of the window, because I didn't want to see faces. Our Assembly Hall is in the new annex, so it has big windows. And while I was looking out, I started to think, 'Maybe bullying is not right and not wrong, and maybe bullying is just something that happens like when a dog barks at a bike going past. Nobody says that the dog is right or wrong. Everybody knows that barking at bikes is just what dogs do.

'So right there I had my second big thought. My eyes stopped looking through the window into the playground and they started looking at the window glass. I saw dust. And I saw my own reflection. As soon as I saw my face in the window, I knew that being good to other people is right. It's like this: s'pose it was a reflection of me on the other side of the glass. S'pose nobody could tell which was Mikhaila and which was the reflection of Mikhaila. Then everybody would have to treat me and my copy as well as each other. There wouldn't be any reason to treat us differently because they can't see any difference between us.

"Then, s'pose Kevin Sweetman and me were both looking through the window, and there was a person on the other side but that person was so far off, or the window was so fogged up, that we couldn't see whether it was a copy of me or a copy of Kevin Sweetman. Then there wouldn't be any reason for Kevin to treat the other person differently from the way he would treat himself, which means that there wouldn't be any reason for Kevin to treat *me* differently from the way he would treat *him*self. So being nice to another person makes sense unless I can actually see a difference between me and the other person – a difference that makes them deserve niceness less than me.

"I had my third big thought underneath the table, the same table where I had the first one. You know how sometimes suddenly a word just turns into a sound and letters, and the word stops meaning anything? Not always, but often?"

"I know," Magda said.

"And then the letters and the sound and the meaning come together again?"

"I know exactly."

"Well, suddenly I realised that everything in the whole world and everything that happens in the whole world is like that. You can see anything two ways. Either you can see a house or you can see bricks. Either you can see a pirate ship or you can see planks of wood. Either you can see the Akropolis or you can see the jigsaw pieces. Either you can see a story or you can see lots of different stuff happening. Either you have a plan or you just do things as they happen. Either the dog is trying to scare you on purpose, or the dog is just barking because that's what dogs do to cyclists. Either Kevin Sweetman is bullying Mikhaila Krutova or noises are coming out of Kevin Sweetman in the playground. *And both ways of seeing everything are always right at the same time.* Always always always. And if people understood that, I wouldn't be so upset all the time."

"You get upset because you have X-ray vision, you dear girl," said Auntie Magda. "Look about you as much as you can, with your X-ray vision, and we can talk about what you see."

That visit, the third visit, was the first occasion that Auntie Magda spoke the ten-word farewell and Mikhaila gave Auntie the four-word reply. The photocopier stopped whirring, the study door clicked shut and the Litvaks returned to the living room. Without a word, Mrs. Litvak placed the documents in the backpack and returned them to Auntie Magda. A floorboard creaked.

Auntie Magda went to the toilet again and, after she had tied her laces in the hallway, she straightened up stiffly and peered at Mikhaila, saying, "Never forget that it is *you* who sees things clearly,"

And Mikhaila replied, "Never shall I ever."

Ten months and ten Sunday visits later, Mikhaila spoke first. "Auntie," she said, "I think I have worked it out now. It took me a long time. I watched television for months. All the way through the summer holidays. Non-stop.

"Your … parents let you watch non-stop television?"

"They're not my parents. They're Mr. and Mrs. Litvak."

"But you should be out playing with your friends, Misha."

"I don't have friends. The other children at school just call me the following names: Robot. Spakbrain. Mikahilurrrrr. Unisex."

"Oh, my gracious. You and I are different from them, that's all. (It's a blessing and a curse.) Come and have a hug, my darling." Auntie stretched out her arms.

Mikhaila didn't move. "But now I've worked out from TV that I don't have to be different. I watched all the programmes with stories in, to see the rules of what you're supposed to do. The Clangers. The Double Deckers. Rupert Bear. Bagpuss. Jim'll Fix It. Hickory House. Rolf Harris. I worked out all the rules for how you're supposed to behave. If I follow the rules, I'll be like everyone else, so nobody will bully me. There are ten rules. I will read them." Auntie frowned and nodded.

"Rule Number One is to look after yourself and stop trying to make other people happy. Rule Number Two is to make other people happy and stop looking after yourself.

"Rule Number Three is to do what you think is right, like a superhero, and don't listen to other people. Rule Number Four is to do what other people want you to do, so you're not a selfish shellfish.

"Rule Number Five is that girls and boys are the same. Rule Number Six is that girls are better than boys because they are nicer and less selfish shellfish.

"Rule Number Seven is that you have to have fun now and stop worrying about the future. Rule Number Eight is that if you have to think about the future or you'll get into big trouble.

"Rule Number Nine is you've got to be brave and say what you think. Rule Number Ten is you've got to be patient and keep quiet. What do you think about the ten rules? Did I get them right?

"You did."

The last Sunday that Auntie Magda visited, she left without saying goodbye and she forgot to take her blue backpack. Mikhaila saw the backpack on the dining room table and asked Mr. Litvak, "Will Auntie come back to get it?"

"No, she won't, Misha."

"Why not?"

Mr. Litvak looked up from his newspaper. "Well, it's like this. Do you remember how it was before you knew Auntie Magda?"

"Yes."

"Good, Misha. Well, now it's like that again," and he pulled up his newspaper like a drawbridge.

The story must have been important, because it appeared twice that evening: first on the national news at six o'clock and then again on the regional news from Look East. The Litvaks had gone together to the phone box in front of the village hall, as they always did after Auntie left. So, Mikhaila was watching TV alone:

"A woman identified as Magda Hesburger was killed in a hit-and-run accident on the A143 between Bury St Edmunds and Horringer." A photo of Auntie Magda appeared on the screen, with her 360-degree fringe and all. She was smiling. "Police are not ruling out foul play. According to rail tickets on her person, she was on a daytrip to Bury St. Edmunds from Cheltenham in Gloucestershire, where she worked for Government Communications Headquarters. She was captured by CCTV at Paddington Station carrying a blue backpack, and police are seeking information from

161

any member of the public who may know the whereabouts of the backpack, as it may be important for the investigation." Mikhaila wondered how Mr. Litvak had known that Magda was not coming any more before seeing the six o'clock news.

Auntie Magda's visits had only been once a month, i.e. there had already been twenty-nine or thirty days a month when Auntie did not visit. Now there was just one more day per month like that, which was not a big difference. So, Mikhaila did not miss Auntie Magda's visits. But she didn't forget them either.

Chapter 14b. Imperial Magazine/45, Winter 2019

In this edition of Imperial Magazine, we step into the brave new world of alternative realities. Imperial College alum and Queen guitarist Brian May tells us why for him music is more real than astrophysics. Labour leader Jeremy Corbyn paints for us his alternative vision for Britain. And PostDoc researcher Mikhail Krutoy takes us on a journey to Ancient Athens to show us what reality means for people with Archilochus-Hesburger Syndrome, a rare and little-understood neurological condition.

But first, we join Dr. Ileana Stigliani, Associate Professor of Design and Innovation at Imperial College Business School, who asks, "Do we need a #Metoo for machines?"

***

yada yada yada

***

Greece is the word! Mikhail Krutoy takes us back to classical Athens

Hello. My name is Mikhail. I told the editor of Imperial College Magazine that I would only write this article on condition that she did not change it <u>in</u>

any way. I mean: she must not even correct my speling or my punctuation!. This is because there are two possibilities: either her edit does not change the meaning of my text, in which case it is pointless, or it does change the meaning of my text, in which case the edited version is not what I meant. Either way, therefore, she should not change my text. (That includes the number of words.) She agreed.

The reason that I asked for no changes is that I have Archilochus-Hesburger Syndrome, which is a condition and not a disease and certainly not a disability.

Archilochus-Hesburger Syndrome sounds like Asperger's Syndrome because they both contain the letter sequence -rge-r, but, like their two names, the two conditions are partly the same and partly different.

My doctor says that I am unhappy when something doesn't make sense because I have Archilochus-Hesburger Syndrome. But when I ask him, "Doctor Wadhwani, what is Archilochus-Hesburger Syndrome?" he reads from a red book, "Archilochus-Hesburger Syndrome is characterised by a subjective affect of anxiety and distress when the patient is exposed to a situation or a statement which is experienced as illogical." This in fact does

164

not make sense itself! If the phrase "Archilochus-Hesburger Syndrome" *means* me getting distressed, then Archilochus-Hesburger Syndrome cannot be the thing that *makes* me distressed. A description of a thing cannot make that thing happen.

It's as nonsensical as saying that bad weather is making it a day rainy. It's as nonsensical as saying that inflation is making prices go up. It's as nonsensical as saying that gender inequality makes women worse off than men.

Never mind. Close the eyes. Seven deep breaths. Inhale, count slowly to 10 and exhale. Lion breaths, so-called. That's what my doctor recommends for the distress.

I remember myself sitting under the kitchen table on the grass matting. It was a bright morning, and the legs of the table and chairs were throwing angular shadows onto the floor. Maybe I was six - small enough to sit under a kitchen table, anyway. I was thinking; I had two thoughts, one after the other. My first thought was a question: if a deer doesn't know any words, what are *its* thoughts? My second thought was like a vision: sometimes you can make all the words in the universe just evaporate. A table stops being a table, and now it is pieces of wood. A face stops being a face and now it is a pattern of curves and shades, and then the pattern of curves disappears as well, and you are just left with lines and shades. You watch the shapes and noises around you, and they do nothing to you, because they are just shapes and noises. You can make this fragmentation take place across the whole universe at once, without any mental effort. Just by deciding that it will be so, you can dissolve the cosmos into atoms. And the dissolving doesn't only work for objects. It works for actions too. One moment it's a game of football, and the next it's people running around after a ball. One moment it's a waterfall, the next it's zillions of individual splashes finding themselves suddenly unsupported. And, under the kitchen table, I perceived how the universe is either dissolving or coalescing, non-stop, depending on how you look at it. After that, I could never feel words the same way again. Words would suddenly go transparent, so I could see right through them. When I told this to my child psychologist, he turned to my Mum and said, "Easiest diagnosis I've ever made. Classic Hesburger-Archilochus".

Archilochus-Hesburger Syndrome is a spectrum condition, which means that nonsense makes everybody anxious a bit. Some people, many of whom make a career in politics, religion, the arts or journalism, are able to tolerate elevated quotients of nonsense without distress. Others, like me, experience high levels of distress. That means I have Archilochus-Hesburger Syndrome. Or conversely, Archilochus-Hesburger Syndrome causes me to experience high levels of distress (vide supra).

There is also the secondary distress, which I shall now explain. Sometimes, when I explain that somebody has talked nonsense, people get annoyed. Their annoyance creates secondary anxiety and distress in addition to the anxiety and distress caused by the initial nonsense. I want to alleviate the primary distress by talking logically but I know that the more I talk logically the more people will get annoyed. It's a feedback loop. My doctor's red book says that such a spinning feeling is labelled "the Hesburger's Vortex".

When I am in the Hesburger's Vortex I put my fingers in my ears and run to somewhere quiet where there are no other people to get annoyed. This breaks the feedback loop.

That is why I created the Diogenes Project.

For my undergraduate thesis at Imperial College I created a virtual reality version of the Agora of Athens in 378 B.C..

While I was testing the programme, I made a discovery. "Eureka!" I cried. I found that when I was in the electronic Agora, all my Hesburger distress vanished. It was like penicillin for the mind. Suddenly I was a normal person, without any medical condition. I was cured.

You say to me, "You weren't cured, Mikhail Krutoy. The virtual Agora only relieved your symptoms, the same way that a paracetamol only relieves the symptoms of the flu without eradicating the virus."

You would say that, and you would be wrong.

When I was in the virtual Agora, I was not only cured, but I was hyper-cured. Hyper-cured means that the disease itself had ceased to exist. There was no Archilochus-Hesburger Syndrome. Archilochus-Hesburger Syndrome could not be a real thing in a reality where everything was logical, and in the virtual Agora everything is logical. The pillars of the Stoa stood at the only possible distance apart. The sun shone at the only possible angle and made the shadows form the only possible patterns on the dust. In the virtual Agora, everything was the only way that it could possibly be, given my programming (using the proprietary Unity 3D platform) and the laws of geometry and electronic physics. And if everything in Diogenes Project Athens is logical, then in Diogenes Project Athens Archilochus-Hesburger Syndrome cannot exist. Hyper-cured. Eureka!

When I told Imperial College that I was hyper-cured, the Medical Research Council offered me a research grant. They asked me what I wanted to do next with my virtual Agora.

I said to Imperial College, "Colleagues, I have e-populated my Agora with objects which follow the universal laws of geometry regarding their shape and location and the universal laws of Isaac Newton regarding their motion. Now I want to populate the virtual Agora with ideas that follow the universal laws of logic."

"How can you populate a virtual reality simulation with ideas?" asked my colleagues from Imperial College. "What explanation shall we give in your grant application to the Medical Research Council?"

"I am going to fill the Agora with fools and charlatans," I replied. "For the fools, there will be crowds of idiots. For the charlatans, there will be philosophers. And then I shall join them in the Agora. I will be Diogenes of Sinope. The fools will talk crap because they are fools, and the philosophers will talk crap because they are frauds. But in my virtual Agora

I will now, finally, be able to reply to them in a way that I cannot in the real world where my talking makes everybody angry."

I said, "IN THE VIRTUAL AGORA I WILL BE ABLE TO EXPRESS MYSELF. IN THE VIRTUAL AGORA I WILL BE MYSELF." [Please do not edit the upper-case letters. That was how I said it.]

DO YOU HAVE ARCHILOCHUS-HESBURGER SYNDROME?

Archilochus-Hesburger Syndrome is the latest neurodiversity that's got everyone buzzing. So don't miss out; take this fun quiz to find out whether you have Hesburger's.

It's simple. Give yourself one point for every 'yes' answer to an even-numbered question and one point for every 'no' answer to an odd-numbered question. (If that's not clear to you, then you probably don't have Archilochus-Hesburger's. And if you don't fancy doing this quiz, then you certainly don't have it.) For your convenience, we've shaded in the response boxes that will give you a point.

NB The *Do You Have Archilochus-Hesburger Syndrome Quiz* is not a substitute for medical advice. If you think that you or someone you know may have Archilochus-Hesburger Syndrome, ask your doctor whether she has heard of it yet. And remember, Archilochus-Hesburger Syndrome isn't a disease. Archilochus-Hesburger Syndrome isn't a disability. Archilochus-Hesburger Syndrome is a condition.

1. Be honest - does it make any difference whether this quiz says that you have Archilochus-Hesburger Syndrome or not?	Yes ☐ No ☑
2. Do you always try to treat other people fairly?	Yes ☑ No ☐
3. Are you sure that you know whether abortion is OK?	Yes ☐ No ☑
4. Do you often make problems for yourself by questioning the opinions of your boss or your teachers ?	Yes ☑ No ☐
5. When two politicians are arguing on the television or the radio, is it obvious to you that one is right and the other is wrong?	Yes ☐ No ☑
6. You're in a meeting at work and somebody says something that doesn't make sense to you. Do you feel uncomfortable?	Yes ☑ No ☐

7. Do you like any slogans?	Yes ☐ No ☒
8. Are you sometimes jealous of people who have religious faith?	Yes ☒ No ☐
9. Do you post uplifting sentiments on social media (e.g. tomorrow is the first day of the rest of your life) ?	Yes ☐ No ☒
10. Do words sometimes lose their meaning for you?	Yes ☒ No ☐
11. Do you like brands?	Yes ☐ No ☒
12. When you see somebody else having bad luck (e.g. getting poor, sick, or injured through no fault of their own), do you feel bad that you're luckier than them?	Yes ☒ No ☐
13. Do you ever describe your views with a word that ends with -ist ?	Yes ☐ No ☒

14. Do you sometimes think it's unfair that people eat animals (and generally not vice-versa)?	Yes ☒ No ☐
15. Can you be sure whether somebody's a woman without asking them?	Yes ☐ No ☒
16. Do you keep quiet in discussions about racism because you're not 100 percent sure you know what the word 'racism' means?	Yes ☒ No ☐
17. Do you believe in the wisdom of crowds?	Yes ☐ No ☒
18. When you see somebody's face, does it sometimes stop looking like a person ?	Yes ☒ No ☐
19. Would you rather listen to Gustav Mahler than the Beach Boys?	Yes ☐ No ☒
20. Would you rather listen to J.S. Bach than Ed Sheeran?	Yes ☒ No ☐

Count up how many shaded boxes you have ticked.

Score: 1-5   You probably don't have Archilochus-Hesburger Syndrome. But if you have concerns, ask your GP about Hesburger's.

6-10   Get with the programme

11-15 Welcome to the club

16-20 Yay, babe! You're officially Hesburger's

Chapter 15. The United Club™ Lounge, Dulles Airport, Washington DC

In one corner of the dark, rectangular space sit a bulky man and a slender woman. They have put their trolley bags on the neighbouring chairs to stop others from sitting too close. The woman sits alertly on the edge of her seat, leaning forward over her laptop, knees and ankles clamped efficiently together beneath a pencil skirt, her gaze fixed tightly upon the man's face.

"Shaun, the flight's actually showing delayed. Since we've got this downtime, maybe we could run over your RRP."

"Huh?" Shaun Shaughnessy was the Democratic Senator for Maryland. He was the frontrunner for the Democratic nomination for the 2020 presidential election. But mostly, this evening, he was weary.

"Your Reputational Risk Profile," continued Emily. "The sin list haha. We think it would be good to have it finalised before Sunday's debate with Lundscum."

"Debate with Lundscum?" Shaun mused. "How ironic!" Forty years ago in Oxford, Shaun Shaughnessy and Brent Lundscum had been pals. Both Rhodes Scholars - the two Yanks of St. John's College. Drinking buddies. God, once he'd even told a girl he *was* Brent Lundscum. That Russki schoolgirl with the wrinkled tights and the babushka hat that they'd picked up in the Lamb and Flag. But some things were best forgotten.

"Shaun? Shaun? The Reputational Risk Profile."

"You forget, Emily. I am a Catholic. God forgives my sins when I confess them."

But there was one sin to which Shaun had never confessed. For decades he had kept that one sin under lock and key. But in recent weeks the repressed memory had escaped from its cage and was now gnawing at his conscience day and night. Maybe what was why he was tired.

"Well, Shaun, maybe Lundscum and Tox News are less accommodating than God when it comes to past sins. For example, how do you respond if they raise the black-eyed peas gaffe?"

"A gaffe, dear Emily, is when I mixed up Theresa May and Angela Merkel. The Black-Eyed Pea Incident was not a gaffe but the death of Truth in the West. You know, I checked on the Library of Congress website, and I was right. (Oh, yes, Emily - you're not the only one with a laptop.) Black-eyed peas <u>are</u> beans. Peas are from the genus pisus. Black-eyed peas are from the genus vigna. Vigna unguiculata. Ergo, black-eyed peas are not peas. They are beans. So I have nothing to apologize for. Gaffe my ass (pardon my French)!"

Emily quickly checked over her shoulder that nobody was hearing her boss disgrace himself. If a significant percentage of the Democrat demographic called a bean a pea, then it was a pea. She had a major in Brown University in political science, for God's sake. She sighed inwardly. Did she really have to go over this again? "Shaun, this is important. We have to be on message. You went to the First Missionary Baptist Church, a historically African-American place of worship, in…"

"Scruggsboro Arkansas. I haven't forgotten, Emily. You dragged me out there for the black vote. It was New Year's Day."

"Which made it even worse," Emily cried. "The worst possible day to confuse ethnically-charged side dishes. After the service the pastor served up black-eyed peas and collard greens. And you were right there up on the stage, paper plate in one hand and microphone in the other, and said…"

"Ma'am, you sure do make a great plate of beans," Shaughnessy had chortled into his microphone. The congregation had fallen silent as the word 'beans' reverberated around the church hall.

Well, how was he to know a bean was now a pea? He hated beans. He hated peas. He hated pulses of any kind. At his age it didn't do to be hobnobbing around with legumes. Mangetout - that was another thing, in moderation, of course. And haricots verts fried in olive oil with finely chopped garlic and a soupcon of lemon juice, it went *sans le dire*. But a Mississippi-mud-coloured mess of neolithic pottage like this, please. How could anyone seriously blame him for calling them 'beans'?

A rose by any other name would smell as sweet.

The 'B' word had rung out across the church hall. Men in bulging waistcoats and matrons in ample dresses gawped up at Shaun. Their eyeballs protruded through the expansive frames of their imitation tortoiseshell glasses. How could someone make such a ...

No. Not a gaffe. The biological truth. Black-eyed peas were of the genus vigna. They had previously been of the genus phaseolus. You couldn't be more of a bean than a phaseolus. Phaseoli were the thoroughbreds of the bean world. The Inner Circle. The royalty. You could trace their lineage back to Ancient Rome. Didn't the gladiators eat phaseoli? Didn't Marcus Aurelius? And what about taxonomy? Had Linnaeus and Darwin lived in vain? Did nobody care about the real names of things? Was Truth dead?

Emily (God bless bright young Emily, and God bless her Brown degree) had quickly flipped open her iMac and hammered out a hundred words of humble pie. Shaun had dutifully read it aloud. He said how deeply it had touched his heart to share black-eyed *peas* with the African-American community of Scruggsboro on New Year's Day. (Shaun curled his lips and popped the P of 'peas' explosively into the microphone, so that nobody could mistake it for a 'B'.) He said that he understood and respected the historical significance of black-eyed peas on New Year's Day, as a symbol of a proud African heritage, of a shared legacy of unspeakable collective suffering, and of the community's hope for a prosperous future.

But the damage was done. He could tell, just by looking down into the array of sullen faces. He concluded his speech to a brief and desultory patter of pro forma applause, looked at his watch and made a dash for the safety of his entourage at the back of the hall. He could feel the congregation's collective glare boring into his scurrying back. One thing was for sure, he thought, as his bodyguard slammed shut the door of his Lincoln: the honest worshippers of the First Missionary Baptist Church of Scruggsboro would be staying at home on polling day.

And now Emily felt a stab of anxiety. What was all this about Darwin and calling things by their correct names? And Truth? *That* was the problem with boomers. They got so anal about Truth. What bit of

'Truth' would Shaun's semi-senile white male mind wander off to next? *True* women? *True* marriage? She shuddered and clutched her iPad for reassurance.

"Shaun... ? Shaun ...? The Reputational Risk Profile?"

But the senator's slouched back and grey face spoke of exhaustion and defeat. His shirt was creased, his collar open and his St. John's College tie skewed to one side. He was remembering the Russian schoolgirl again and the regret was sapping his strength.

He still had a good head of hair, this Shaughnessy – 'leonine', the New Yorker used to say - sweeping back from his forehead in bushy waves of white and auburn. From time to time, Senator Shaun Shaughnessy would run his fingers through these opulent locks, as though to reassure himself that at least one vestige of his golden youth had not deserted him. He also had the remnants of a firm, square chin, now embedded between those moist, flabby jowls, a chin which was currently sagging despondently into his chest.

"I'm ready to throw the whole thing in," Shaun Shaughnessy muttered. He tapped the small, white bowl in his lap. "Look. Peanuts! I'm a fudging Senator, for heaven's sake, a fudging congressman in a fudging first class lounge in the fudging capital city of the fudging free world and all I get is fudging salted peanuts."

Emily's glance flicked anxiously around the lounge, checking that nobody's phone was filming her boss's off-message moment.

"Come on, Emily. Sorry I shouted. You're OK. Nothing wrong with you, Emily. The innocent ambition, vanity and egotism of youth, not yet sapped by four decades of compromise and disappointment. Look, Emily - you're my aide. So give me some aid. Explain to me, please, Emily, why I shouldn't throw in all this horse manure.

"When I was at Oxford, I played the jazz piano in pubs, for Christ's sake – Tuesdays and Thursdays at the Turf, Fridays and Saturdays at the Eagle and Child." Suddenly his mind's eye was back in the smoke-and-beer fug of the Eagle and Child, with Lundscum and the nervous Russian schoolgirl. Quickly, he pushed the memory out of his mind.

"Professors of Anglo-Saxon literature used to drop coins into my beer mug. I was happier then than I am now, Emily. I played the American Songbook: Fats Waller, Gershwin, Irving Berlin. I was good. I had blue notes. I had rhythm. I had pizzazz. And when I played those American classics, I was the most patriotic yank in the world. The dominant sevenths in the right hand, the walking bass in the left. Oh, I was happy. You'd better fudging believe it."

Emily stared with horror into the congressman's eyes. The careers counsellor at Brown had warned her about the steep learning curve. He'd got that wrong. It had been a steep *disillusionment* curve. One by one, all Emily's beliefs had been shattered: her belief in power, her belief in deal-making, her belief in cunning, her belief in expediency, and, most of all, her belief in her own unstoppable career, had all turned to dust before her eyes. Working as Shaughnessy's aide had been like being told every morning for eighteen months that Machiavelli was as honest as Santa Claus.

And now this? Just as she'd resigned herself to the fact that her boomer boss was neurotically obsessed with this '*Truth*' thing, here he was reminiscing into a plate of peanuts about crooning *My Funny Valentine* in limey bars. WTF!

"That was a serious question, Emily. Tell me. Help me. What's politics for? Why shouldn't I just throw it all in?" The senator stared pleadingly into his assistant's eyes. She stared back into his and realized in terror that she was gazing deep into the soul of a truthful human being.

"Er... you're cruising awesome in the polls," Emily ventured. "Winnepac's got you five points ahead of the field in the Democratic primary, and Gallup gives you the edge in the head-to-heads over any Republican candidate, including Brent Lundscum."

"I wouldn't have beaten Trump."

"Well, thanks to erectile dysfunction medication, you don't have to beat Trump, sir."

"Yeah. Who knew that those little blue hard-on pills could make the human brain explode - like an egg in a microwave, the poor sonofagun. Splat. All over Mike Pence." Shaun and Emily paused a moment to contemplate the alternative history of the world if Trump had survived to win a second term in office.

"Shaun, I can show you the polling numbers. I've made a spreadsheet ..."

"Sorry, Emily, but fudge the fudging spreadsheet, you know what I mean? Like, what's the point? There's no point being at the front of the race if you don't even want the prize, right? Emily, my head hurts, my back hurts, my doc's giving me pills for my blood pressure, pills for my cholesterol, pills for my insomnia. It's not like I need the money. Boxers, they're not dumb, not like us politicians. The only reason boxers fight is so that they can stop fighting. Smart guys, eh? And you know what? When I look at other people's families, I'm realising that Shirlee and the kids are getting cute again. So, guess what - I could spend some time with them. Play the piano. Call beans beans. Grandkids if I'm lucky. It doesn't sound like a fudging hardship, does it? I mean, we're supposed to be the fudging liberals, aren't we, you and me? It's the Republicans who need the McMansions, right? We're supposed to be content with jazz, clean air, social justice and true love. Isn't that the idea? So, come on, Emily. I have a lot of respect for your intelligence and your ambition. Just give me one good reason to carry on."

"Er... the New New Deal?"

And there it was again: that vision of the Russian schoolgirl in the Eagle and Child. Her face was so pale, her lips so thin. Was this feeling what they called 'guilt'?

"It doesn't work any longer, Emily. Idealism won't cut it. Sorry. Sure, I want a better deal for poor people and black people and gay people and black-eyed peas and whatever. I mean, who doesn't? But I'm not so fudging conceited to think that if I dropped out there isn't someone else who could fight the good fight just as effectively as me. I mean, that would be like the ultimate arrogance, wouldn't it, imagining that I was the best guy on planet earth able to fix this mess." It was the memory of the Russian schoolgirl again, undermining his confidence. Was this what people called 'shame'?

"Power pose!" Emily said to herself. "Feet apart. Hands on hips. Stop hyper-ventilating. You can do this, girl. Focus." Out of her laptop case she pulled an A4 document stapled at one corner and fumbled it onto the carpet.

Shaughnessy smiled, picked it up and passed it back to her. "Everything's gonna be OK, Emily," he said. "Anyway, what've you got for me this time? The Harvard Political Review, eh? Well, I'm more Oxford, England than Cambridge, Massachusetts, but I'm always ready for another tidbit of political education from my brightest aide. Shoot."

"It's this really amazing paper. Like it's a total gamechanger. Wait 'til you hear this. Like it's going to totally re-inspire you."

"I'm listening, Emily." The aide checked her boss's face for any sign of sarcasm or impatience, but all she saw was the smile of a kind and tolerant old man. That sincerity again. It was freaking her out.

"OK, then. So basically, what she's saying is that we're now in a new political epoch. That's what the article's called: *Hail to the Fourth Epoch*. It's like: in the Middle Ages you had the feudal system, and everyone was fighting over land, right? Then you had the epoch of the big sailing ships, and everyone was fighting over sea trade. Then you had the Industrial Revolution and all the factories and everything, and it was the fighting for coal and steel and working-class revolutions and all that. And now you've got the *Fourth*

Epoch, which is basically the media and the internet and everything, so all people care about is ..."

"Labels," said the congressman. "All the voter cares about is labels."

"You've read it."

"No. But I don't need to. I saw the movie, you know what I mean? Labels. Yeah, I got it; beans are peas and I'm past my sell-by date. Look, Emily, I'm a Shaughnessy. As in 'The Roosevelts, Kennedys and the Shaughnessys.' And being a Shaughnessy means you go into politics to help the ordinary guy, the Average Joe. When I started out, the whole point of being a Democrat was to help the poor guy who's having a rough time because the rich guys are having a fine time. Kinda straightforward, huh? Like, if you're a Democrat you tax the rich sonofaguns and spend the cash on Medicare and food stamps, and if you're a Republican you borrow money from the Chinese and spend it reducing taxes for the rich sonafaguns. It was simple enough in the old days, right?

"But now, Emily, who gives a damn about the poor? All people care about is the label. The African-Americans say I've got to say they're special, and then it's the Latinos who've got to be special, and then it's the Asians, and then it's the gays, I mean the LGBTQ-plus, whatever the plus stands for. Everyone's got their label, right? So I tell everybody that they've got the special label. You know, like Blue Label Johnny Walker's the special label. And the rich sonofaguns can screw 'em over, and they just don't care, so long as I get their label right. Oh, yeah, and they all want to be told that they're suffering. All they want from me is to pay my respects to the label. Don't say 'beans'. Say 'peas are suffering', and you'll be President of the USA.

"You know what, Emily? If I went out tomorrow, and I said, 'Hey, folks, you elect me, and I'll raise the minimum wage to fifteen bucks an hour', nobody would even fudging care. It wouldn't get five minutes on CMM. But if I said, hey, folks, beans are beans and Latinos are OK, suddenly the whole world's on fire. You've got That Tacogirl513 saying, 'Dontcha mean *LatinXes*? And any reference to beans is dog-whistle racism.' CMM says 'Wuddabout the African-Americans'? Tox says, 'Wuddabout the poor whites?' Oprah says 'Sean Shaughnessy's got White Saviour Syndrome'. Labels, labels, labels. Americans prefer to be poor, so long as I use the right labels to describe their victimhood. And so it goes, on and on and on. Yada-yada-yada.

"Emily, dear, I'm getting too old for this. How am I supposed to remember all those labels? I can't even remember any more which month it is: Black History or Hispanic History or Pride. I want a rest.

"You know what finally did it for me? That - oh, Lord, I don't even know if I'm supposed to say 'boy' or 'girl' - from London. You know, the one who had surgery to their eyelids to make them look ... more Asian because they said they identified as Korean. 'Identified as Korean?' I just thought, 'Shaun, when nothing makes any sense, pack it all in.' Let someone else build the New Jerusalem. Someone fresher. Maybe someone with breasts. Or at least a smaller prostate."

Emily's stared into the congressman's bloodshot eyes and bewilderment turned to alarm. Shaughnessy's outburst wasn't that famous Irish-American blarney which made him the go-to Democrat for every late-night host from Colbert to Conan. Shaun Shaughnessy really was thinking of giving up politics and only she, the rookie aide, stood between the congressman and the door marked Exit.

"Aw, don't blush, Emily. Ok, I shouldn't have said 'breasts'. Inappropriate."

But Emily was blushing because she had realised how totally important she now was. Her leadership coach had told her the name of such moments. 'Praxis.' This was a moment of praxis, when you had to balance your in-breath with your out-breath, and with your out-breath your inner potential, your atman, expanded beyond you into the instant, empowering you to manifest your agency. Fate had placed upon her padded shoulders the responsibility for the future of the United States of America, the Home of the Brave and the Land of the Free. If she, Emily, didn't find the right words right now, this moment, Shaun Shaughnessy would abandon his presidential bid, someone competent in a pantsuit would win the Democratic nomination, the Republicans would retake the White House (largely because of the pantsuit), and America would descend even further into an apocalypse of race riots, road rage, poisoned air, forest fires, school shootings and crystal meth. And then Emily switched to a vision of herself standing beside (and only slightly behind) President-elect Shaughnessy at the National Nominating Convention. In front of her were arrayed infinite ranks of political activists waving their red, white and blue merchandise items. Cellphone flashlights flickered like stars as far as the horizon. Shaun was, yes, he was turning towards her and saying, "And I dedicate this nomination to someone who believed in me when I didn't believe in myself." The crowd rose to its feet and roared. "I dedicate this nomination to a woman who, despite her youth, had the wisdom and the courage to save the Democratic Party. I dedicate this nomination to..."

"Emily, are you OK?"

"Sure, sure."

"You looked like you were wandering off there, Emily. Well, then, please, tell me. See my cell phone here? I've got Shirlee on speed dial. I can just press this button and ask Shirlee, my wife and soulmate of thirty years, to pick me up from the airport. And you know what? As soon as I press call, the story changes. I'm out of politics. Suddenly I'm not Senator Shaughnessy. I'm Grandpa-to-be Shaughnessy. Sounds good, huh?"

"Jesus!" Emily thought. "He's entering his password." We're seconds away from the apocalypse.

"Just give me one good reason, Emily."

"The Shaunsters?" Emily ventured. The Shaunsters were a syndicate of minor billionaires, officially known as the "Pan-American Political Action Committee for the Election of Shaun Shaughnessy."

"What the fudge about the Shaunsters?" Shaughnessy growled. "Pond-dwelling reptiles! One moment it's 'We're totally committed to gay rights and the New New Deal', and the next it's 'Congratulations, Mr. President. And how about a federally-funded strategic bacon stockpile?' Give me a goddam break. Wet-skinned carrion-feeders!"

"You can't say 'wet-skinned'," Emily whispered. "It sounds like wetback. A slur for LatinXes."

"My point exactly, Emily."

"But Sean", Emily said, and now there was a shade of firmness in her voice, "you know, don't you - if you don't run for President, the Shaunsters will ask for their donations back."

There was a pause. Suddenly Emily and Shaun became aware of the lounge muzak: "It's Christmas time in Texas, And the feeling is infectious."

Shaun swallowed a peanut. "They can't do that, can they? I mean, it's my money now, right?"

Emily shrugged. "We advised you not to sign that contract. Lawsuits for misrepresentation? Breach of contract? Class action? Massive legal fees? I mean, who knows?"

"Hmmm." Shaun sank even further back into the armchair. "Hmmm." His chin receded into the folds between his grey cheeks. "Legal fees, eh?"

Emily felt a surge of relief. The moment of danger was over. Shaun Shaughnessy the Gaelic charmer was back in the game again. "Hey, Emily, that Reputational Risk Profile of yours - it's like a kinda list of all the really bad stuff I've done, right? In case it comes up during the campaign."

"Yup, that's it, Shaun."

"Like, er, photos of me in blackface at a frat party? Amazonian hookers at the Global Environment Forum? Calling Liberace a faggot over a hot mic? That kinda stuff, right?"

"Uh-huh."

"Or, for the sake of argument, unprotected sex with an under-age, mixed-race Soviet schoolgirl?"

"Yes, or that."

Shaun grinned broadly. "Well, Emily, you can tell your PR clowns that I have no reputational risks. I'm as pure as the lily-white snow. The debate with Lundscum's on Sunday, right? Now, if you don't mind, I'll get myself another bowl of these excellent salted peanuts."

Chapter 16 - In the other corner

The chairs in the United™ Club Lounge were arranged symmetrically around the central bar; so, in the opposite corner to Shaun and Emily there was an identical cluster of armchairs, where another man and another woman had barricaded themselves behind their hand baggage. His carry-on was Rimowa aluminium; hers was Samsonite pink. The man was sitting legs splayed wide apart and was tapping on his iPhone. His white shirt was smooth, his Oxfords glistened, and his silk mauve necktie glowed modestly in the dimmed lighting of the lounge. His hair was glossy and neatly parted, with the necessary minimum of grey at the temples, just where it belonged, and his skin was a mellow bronze, almost too luminous to be natural.

"Hail to the Fourth Epoch!" sneered the man, waving a photocopied document at the woman. "What kinda elitist north-eastern campus socialist BS are you making me read now, Mackenzie? I pay you to be my aide so I don't have to read things, I believe. Which bit of the word *downtime* don't you understand?"

Mackenzie was wearing a pinstripe pantsuit above high heels. Her blonde-dyed hair was pulled back into a ponytail so tight that it smoothed her forehead and lifted her painted eyebrows into an arch. She pulled on her smile, the spokesperson smile that she used for shutting down reporters from the mainstream media (*I believe that Governor Lundscum has made his views very clear on that point, Dave. Do we have another question?*), the orthodontic masterpiece of a smile for which her parents had taken a nine thousand dollar equity release. "Sincerely, Brent..."

"Legs an eight, tits a seven," Lundscum thought. "She wasn't a complete waste of my time, this Mackenzie. Would I do it again? Probably not, but what the hell."

Mackenzie registered reflexively that his eyes were on her chest. The top three buttons of her white blouse were open, and the Governor's red-eyed gaze had drifted downwards to the third from the top. "Sincerely, Brent, I think that this paper is really worth your attention." Mackenzie tried peering into her boss's eyes to regain his attention.

"Why are you waving your head around, Mackenzie? Makes you look like a retard. OK. Sure, sure, sure. Hail to the Fourth Epoch. I'm listening."

"So, basically, it's this paradigm-shifting paper in the Harvard Political Review..."

"Written no doubt by a bunch of Hispanic lesbians."

Mackenzie did a quick assessment and decided that her boss did not expect a reply. "Basically, they're saying that we've had the feudal age, the age of sea trade and the age of industry, and now we're in the ..."

"Just hold it right there a minute. Are you quoting Karl Marx to a Republican Governor? Are you giving me the three stages of historical materialism?"

Mackenzie blanched. Shit. Had she just done a CLM - a Career-Limiting Move?

"Just kidding, Mackenzie. God, you should see your face. I'm totally cool with Karl, right. I mean, these old Jewish guys, somehow they always hit it right on the nail, don't they? Had to read some Karl Marx in Oxford. Well, obviously I read the study guide, not the actual book, right? I was like, 'Are they seriously making us study this shit?' And, then, after I'd read a bit, I was like, "Hey, the old Hebrew dude's got it completely worked out. I mean it all just boils down to one thing: us rich guys gotta keep those poor suckers down, right? That's what business needs. That's the American way. And if those work-for-a-paycheck mugs get a bit uppity, you know what I mean, then it's..." - the Senator put on his best Mahalia Jackson and began to sing, "Gimme dat ole time race and religion. Gimme dat ...". He fell silent and looked around, just in case.

"And now we're in the Fourth Epoch," Mackenzie continued, holding the same brightly orthodontic smile. "Basically, now that we're in the age of media, all that people care about is labels. Basically, it's like, you get the words right, and nothing else matters."

"Jeez, honey!" Lundscum snorted. "Tell me something I don't know! No, don't look so disappointed, Mackenzie, my dear. It doesn't suit your pretty little face. Yes, I get the words right and nothing else matters. And that's why people like you and me, real Americans, rich people, are gonna keep running this country for the next thousand years. Trump got it, God rest his rotten soul. That Boris Johnson guy got it. But those Democratic libtards won't ever get it. They'll keep handing the country to us every two years. They're telling Americans which words to use and which words not to use, and us Americans we goddam hate that. LatinX not Latino. LGBTQ-plus not queer. Woman not man. Negro not black. African-American not negro. Minorities not foreigners. Minoritised people (what-the-fuck does that mean?) not minorities. Enslaved people not slaves. Gender not sex. We can take away someone's health care. We can send their kids to Afghanistan to get their balls blown off by an IED. We can put import tariffs on their pantyhose. We can borrow money in their name from China, spend it on our pals' yachts and leave the grandkids of the bare-assed poor to pay the tab. But I'll tell you what: we're not dumb enough to mess with their words. 'Cause putting your own labels on stuff is something we Americans hold dear. Only a Democrat would be dumb enough to mess around with people's language. You can put an American on the breadline, but you can't put him in quote marks. Every time you tell people that your labels are better than their labels, you piss them off. You tell white people that they're racist if they say, 'All lives matter' instead of 'black lives matter.' You tell women they're misogynists if they don't vote for Hillary. You tell black people they aren't black if they don't vote for Shaughnessy. You tell proud people the word 'pride' doesn't belong to them anymore. Pretty soon you're gonna piss people off. 'Cause ordinary Joe and ordinary Josie don't want any politician messing with their labels. June gets labelled for the homosexuals. September gets labelled for the Latinos and October's for the blacks. And if some white soccer mom says, 'What about me?' well then, you tell her that she should kindly shut the fuck up because you've got another label for her: 'Karen'. Oh, my Lord, how dumb can those Democrats be? You've just gotta watch Oprah for five minutes - which is about as much as any sane person can take - to know that every American thinks they're a victim, but these Dems go around calling people 'privileged'. Well, that's just not smart politics because, last time I checked, white heterosexuals made up two thirds of America. Yup, thank the Lord that the Democrats are morons, and that's why I'm gonna be Governor of the great state of Missouri until I'm President of the USA." Lundscum chuckled softly. "Hey, Mackenzie, since you're standing up, how about another scotch?"

Mackenzie put the *Fourth Epoch* back into her laptop case. She checked over her shoulder. Nobody was close enough to hear. There was just some cheesy, dandruff-speckled old white guy in the opposite corner of the lounge, holding forth to what looked like his assistant. "And about that other thing," she said.

Lundscum raised his right eyebrow. He'd taught himself to raise his left eyebrow when he was starting out in politics. For years - decades, even - his ascending left eyebrow had carried him through press conferences, debates and congressional enquiries, conveying stern, patrician scepticism, telling the American public, 'I'm too much of a statesman to use the word bullshit, but here's my eyebrow calling it out. Lately, however, he'd noticed in the mirror that he'd raised his left eyebrow so often over the years that his face had become permanently asymmetrical, just as his British nanny had warned him. "If the wind changes, your face will stay like that." Now, instead of saying 'patrician', his perennially-elevated eyebrow was saying, 'cerebrovascular incident'. So he had to train his face muscles all over again and recruit his right eyebrow to duty.

Lundscum raised his right eyebrow. "What other thing, Mackenzie?"

Behind that smile the aide's teeth were clenched. "You know quite well what other thing. What were we talking about just an hour ago? You know: you and me."

"Oh, *that*. Come on, my dear," he murmured coolly, his blue eyes still on his phone. "Sit down, Mackenzie. Is this how you want to be seen? The angry woman? The shrill female? Really?"

"No, I won't sit down!" Mackenzie snapped. "Do you actually hear what I'm saying?"

"Just name the amount," the Governor murmured, "and we'll take the discussion from there."

"You fucking don't get it do you, Brent? It's not always about the fucking money."

"In fact, Mackenzie," Brent Lundscum drawled gently, "from where I'm sitting, it looks like the fucking money is exactly what it's about. OK, I get it. It's blackmail. So just sit down, Mackenzie, darling, and we'll go over some numbers."

"It's not blackmail and it's not about the fucking numbers, Brent. It's about you and me and trust."

Brent stifled a wry laugh, sighed and put down his phone. "Well, Mackenzie, that's certainly not how it sounded a moment ago when you mentioned your living expenses. You're my aide. I pay you a decent salary - probably more than you're worth, but let's not get sidetracked. We had a truly splendid time at the Marriott in Houston. We had a so-so time at the Intercontinental in San Diego. We had a quite excellent time at the Hilton in Philly. You enjoyed yourself, or at least that's the way things looked from a vantage point six inches above your chest. You're not pregnant, darling; we've already established that scientifically. And even if you were, there's ways and means. So, what's the big deal? If this is your way of asking for a raise, you know I can't give you more than the other girls. We can't have jealousy in the hen coop."

Mackenzie was at a loss for words. Or rather, she had the words, but she couldn't use them. She wanted to howl, "You used me!" but she couldn't, because women are free to make their own mistakes and live with the consequences. She wanted to say, "You're my boss and I didn't have a choice," but she couldn't, because everything is a choice in a free country. So, there was only one thing left to say.

"Governor Brent Lundscum, you're a shit, and I'm going to bring you down. I'll go to the press. Yeah, yeah. I mean it."

Lundscum sighed. "Oh, Mackenzie! Dear, dear Mackenzie, you're supposed to have your finger on the pulse of the Republican voter. And you still don't get it. You're white. You're blonde. You wear crimson lipstick. You've got a tight ass from behind and you're moderately attractive from in front. You think our voters are going to hate me for screwing you? Give me a break. They're gonna love me. Jesus! When Donald Trump, God rest his soul, bragged that he was grabbing girls by the pussy, they adored him even more. And I was watching, and I thought, "Shit, Brent Lundscum, you're one dumb sonofabitch. All these years you've been going to church and paying off the chicks to keep quiet. I mean, never mind the money. It's just the stress and the goddam hassle of having to perform day after day like some presbyterian prick with the Book of Leviticus stuck up his ass. And then the Donald comes along and shows us all what dumb fucks we've been. The more he screwed around, the more Joe average and Josie average loved him. They said, 'Hey, this guy's an asshole just like me.' I mean, obviously, nobody wants to snuff it like Donald, his head exploding like napalm all over pious Mike, so let's all go easy on the hard-on meds, right? But Donald Trump taught us a priceless lesson: if you fuck up the way other people would like to fuck up if they only had the cash and the balls, then you're not fucking up. You're a role model. You're aspirational."

Brent chuckled. "I mean, obviously, there are limits. Like you don't want to do a black girl, even if that's your thing. Half-black? Stone cold suicide. Or with a tranny. Or with a Russian agent, I guess. But with a whitebread all-American babe with two ovaries, two X chromosomes and one uterus like you? No problemo. So, yes, you can go to the press, Mackenzie. Actually, I beg you to go to the press. I'm on my knees."

Brent's phone pinged. "Hey, here it is, Mackenzie. The Gallup poll's out. Why the long face? Yep, Brent Lundscum. You're still looking good! Pulling ahead of your old Oxford buddy and wingman, Shaun Shaughnessy."

Ah, yes. Those happy days with Shaun in Oxford, the city of dreaming spires. And one happy night in particular, when he and Shaun welcomed a half-caste virgin Russian schoolgirl into a crowded pub. Mackenzie was just a transaction. But that night in Oxford was history and sometimes history had to stay in the past.

For a couple of minutes Mackenzie stood and watched her boss scrolling on his phone. Then she asked, "So, Brent, shall I reach out to Blair?"

Without lifting his face from his phone, Lundscum waved the question away. "Sure, sure, Mackenzie. Just tell him how much you want. Blair'll take it from there. About time that sonofabitch lawyer started earning his salary."

Lundscum kept scrolling. Same old same old. There were the texts that Mackenzie had sent to donors in his name and there were the texts from donors reminding him that it had been 'an honor to contribute financially to your campaign' and asking him if they could 'drop by to touch base on an important matter'. Thank God for texts and instant messaging. Only a moron or a Democrat, or, in Hillary Clinton's case, both, would use emails and leave a trail of incriminating evidence. Scroll. Bla bla bla. Delete. Scroll. Bla bla bla. Delete.

Lundscum's thumb froze above the screen. Wow! Jesus! From her profile photo, she couldn't be older than twenty-five. And those tits. What was her name? Kaboomshka69 from Irkutsk. Siberian journalist requesting an interview, eh? Well, Kaboomshka69, yes, if you've got something you want to discuss one-on-one, then so does Brent Lundscum.

Monday, 8 March, 2020

Wcrbym265: hi Nastya - yr sis applied for passport @ Russemb London Dec/19. Stated travel date 12/3/2020. Stated destination - John Hancock Hotel Washington DC.
tacogirl513: hi Gleb I'm @ Sheremetyevo airpt now
wcrbym265: we will blacklist hr passport so she cannot leave USA
tacogirl513: cool
wcrbym265: in America U'll be who? Tacogirl?
tacogirl513: Kaboomshka69 blonder sexier bigger boobs Republican bait
wcrbym265: ☺

Chapter 17 - Passport control, Newark Airport, March 12, 2020

The woman behind Mikhail addressed him in a language that he did not understand.

Mikhail turned around. The woman was younger than him. She had long hair and blue eyes. Slavic? "I don't speak, er ..."

"Russian," said the woman in good English. "Your passport. The eagle with two heads."

"I don't speak Russian," Mikhail said. "My passport is not my language."

"This line. Jeez. How long do you think it'll take?" the woman said. "I've got a connection to DC in an hour and twenty minutes." She stared into Mikhail's eyes, like someone who was waiting for an offer. "Hi. My name's Nastya. But everyone calls me Allie. Or Kaboomshka. I'm an influencer."

Mikhail thought that he should answer her question about the expected duration of the wait, even though she had changed the subject after asking it. "There are one hundred and fifty-one people in front of me, clearing immigration on average at the rate of one every 21 seconds. That means that I have approximately another fifty-two minutes to stand in the queue. For you it is slightly more, because you are behind me. Of course, if an immigration officer arrived or left, that would change the average clearance rate, and I would revise the calculation. But as of now, I think we might or might not make it. I am also flying to Washington." They shuffled forward, nudging their hand baggage forwards with their toes.

"Jeez! I just hope to God I don't miss my plane. I'm going to Washington to look for my sister. It's been so long. She's called Mikhaila. Like I'm totally pumped! Like wow! Meeting your own sister for the first time in your life! Like how crazy is that!"

"You don't talk like a Russian," Mikhail said. "Russians speak with fewer exclamation marks. Are you American, despite speaking Russian?"

"Yup, you got me. I'm a west coast girl... I'm just so worried I'm going to miss my plane."

Mikhail wondered why this woman was repeating that she might miss her plane. It had been clear the first time, and now this was the third. And after each time that she said that she was worried, she then looked at him as though she were expecting a specific reply. Mikhail said, "I don't know why you have told me three times that you are worried about missing your plane. I have got Archilochus-Hesburger Syndrome. It is not a disease. It is a condition. It means that I am distressed when I do not understand the reason for things, and right now…"

"… I get it. I totally get it. OK, Hesburger's guy, the reason you didn't understand me is that I was speaking the language of Blonde. When I say, 'I'm really worried about missing my plane,' what that means in Blonde is, 'Please may I go in front of you in the line?'"

"Thank you, Allie. That is a lot clearer."

"Sure. I guess it's just translation. From the Blonde language to the Hesburger language. Two ways of saying the same thing."

"I can relax now. That's better. Allie, please come in front of me."

"Well, thank you, kind sir."

"You're welcome, Allie."

As they were swapping places, "I'll tell you how you can fucking help," came a high-pitched voice from behind. "You can start off by telling me what the fucking cunting shit is this." Mikhail turned to face a shrivelled old man with a tuberous nose, a crest of crazy white hair and a liver spot on his right cheek. He wore baggy jeans, shapeless red sneakers and a tartan jacket with patches on the elbows. The old man was haranguing an African American woman in a black uniform and a badge which said *How Can I Help?* "I'm ninety-two fucking years old and they couldn't give me

208

a fucking scooter ride through immigration, the cocksucking motherfuckers."

"Please mind your language, sir," said the ground staffer. "I'm just trying to do my job. The courtesy people-movers are fully occupied. We will try to have one available momentarily."

"You don't tell me to mind my fucking language, bitch," said the old man. "Do you know who you're talking to? I'm Noam fucking Chomsky. Yeah, you heard that right, bitch, Noam fucking cunting Chomsky, the father of modern linguistics, the most cited word-wanker of the whole fucking Anthropocene epoch. So don't tell me to mind my fucking language. 'Coz I fucking invented language. And momentarily means 'in a moment', not 'for a moment'. Look it up, you skanky ho."

"Sheesh. That's one crazy old linguist." The ground staffer shrugged and walked away.

"Hey bitch!" Chomsky shouted after her. "If we don't believe in freedom of expression for people we despise, we don't believe in it at all." He turned to Mikhail. "See what this country's coming to. 'How can I help?' used to mean 'How can I help', not 'Keep your opinions to yourself, old man'. People should just say what they mean, and the world would be a much better place." Chomsky looked at his watch. "Jesus H. Crap, my connection's in an hour and fifteen. Hey, how long do you think this is gonna take? Yeah, kid, I'm talking to you."

Mikhail smiled. He understood. "Please take my place in the line, Mr. Chomsky."

"Don't you fucking patronise me!" shouted Chomsky. "I don't need your charity, lard-butt. I just need one of these beaner bitches to get Chomsky's Hebrew ass on a courtesy people-mover pronto. And, hey, dude, are you doin' ok in the hormones department? I mean, I'm looking at that chest of yours, hombre, and I'm just thinking 'man-boobs' You need to see an endocrinologist, know what I mean? Anyway, maybe my question wasn't clear. I asked you: how long do you think this is gonna take? Or don't you understand American?"

Mikhail looked around the immigration hall. "Approximately ten minutes, unless the number of officers is increased or reduced, in which case I will have to adjust my calculation."

"Hey, the hell it's ten minutes, fat boy," growled Chomsky. "You were just telling that broad it's fifty minutes. How come it's ten now?"

"Because you're in the wrong queue. The queue for US passport-holders is over there."

"Cocksucker!" Chomsky shuffled away.

That had been Mikhail's first flight ever and his first jet lag. He was alarmed by the unfamiliar combination of exhaustion, lightheadedness and alertness.

Wherever he looked there were screens hanging from the ceiling playing the same hallucinatory video on an infinite loop. Smiling faces. Black, white, brown, Native American, freckled, young, fresh, old, wrinkled faces saying 'Hi! Hello! Hola!" Mikhail's oxygen-starved brain was spinning.

The video brought Mikhail's mind back once again to the old question of telephone directories. What a pity that you didn't have telephone directories anymore! BBC Radio London was always saying that the point of books (or statues, or reality TV, or sitcoms, or sports, or theatre, or murals), was to represent the diversity of the population. Represent? *"Diversity* is easy to say," Mikhail thought, "but what does *represent* mean? If only three percent of the UK population is Afro-Caribbean like Mikhail, did that mean that we had to reduce the share of black people like Mikhail on the radio and in football matches to three percent? Did we have to increase the number of Eastern Europeans correspondingly to three percent, Polish now being the UK's second language? And how about the idiots and bores and nobodies? How were they to be represented in a correct percentage? Only the telephone directory had done the job perfectly: every social group was represented, more or less proportionately to their share of the population. The telephone directory was the perfect book, the immaculate book, the book to end all books. In fact, if you had a telephone directory, you didn't need any other books at all, because it represents the population so entirely. So why did they get rid of it? Were telephone directories too expensive and pointless, now that everybody owned a cellphone? OK, fair enough. We must be practical. So, here's another more efficient approach. We could take a random sample of the population of the UK, say, one in a hundred thousand. But it would have to be a rigorous and robust scientific sample. You could pay Gallup, or Ipsos or YouGov for some randomly selected names from their database. They probably wouldn't charge you much for a statistically significant sample of seven hundred individuals. Then you'd print them out. If you arranged the names in three columns on A4 paper, it would come to no more than ten pages. And, allowing for inevitable statistical variation (which cannot be helped), the list would contain exactly the right proportion of idiots, bores, people with two X chromosomes, geniuses, left-handers, Poles, people with and without penises and/or bunions and/or wheels, black people, Man U. supporters, lefties, righties and redheads to reflect and represent the UK population. Then you could send a pdf of the list to everybody, and you would have the whole of the UK reading the only perfect book in existence, the only book which would satisfy the perfected objective of art: to represent undistorted reality."

"Then," Mikhail mused, as the queue inched towards the immigration counters, "You could go a step further, and improve upon perfection. You would ask the seven hundred people to say in one sentence what they were thinking at a very specific moment in time. Gallup, Ipsos or YouGov would ask the question if you paid them enough. They'd phone the numbers on their sample list, and, after asking 'For which candidate would you vote in the next general election?' they would say, "Please tell me what you were thinking just before the telephone rang." And people would reply things like:

a) 'I was wondering whether I should pee now or wait until this programme is finished', or

b) 'Of course he's a nob; got to be with a name like Martin', or

c) 'My shoulders hurt', or

d) 'Is three toothbrushes for the price of two worth it, or will I lose the second and third ones before I use them?', or

e) 'If I just keep quiet and say nothing, will she annoy me less or more?' or

f) 'If deer don't have words, how do their thoughts go?' or

g) 'Is the world made of little things which have been put together into big things, or big things which can be taken apart into little things?' etc etc

"Then you could put these seven hundred sentences into a book, and it would no longer just be the only perfect book in the world, it would be the ultimate book in the UK, the only necessary book in the UK, because it would represent accurately and proportionately the thoughts of the UK population. It would be the most diverse book in the world. We could call it the *Diversouniversopedia* and we would distribute it free of charge (online and through newsagents). Anywhere, in fact, where you can buy a lottery ticket or a cellphone top-up voucher, you would be able to pick up a hard copy of the *Diversouniversopedia*. For environmental reasons, we would promote the online (or e-reader) version, obviously. Or the app. However, even if people took the paper version, it would soon be net emission-reducing because anybody, having once bought the *Diversouniversopedia*, would never need to acquire another book, magazine or newspaper, being already in possession of a representative sample of total thought.

"Jorge Luis Borges recommended a library consisting of all the 410-page books which could be written by rearranging the letters of the alphabet.

However, this would not be very practical or even useful, not compared with the *Diversouniversopedia.*

"Anyway, as well as reducing greenhouse gas emissions, the *Diversouniversopedia* will save time and promote peace. No sitcom writer, tennis-player or sculptor would ever have to appear on BBC Radio London again, to say that their jokes, book, victory or statue were striking a blow for the representation of any type of human being, because the *Diversouniversopedia* had already struck a blow for everyone in proportion to their characteristics along every conceivable dimension: internal anatomy, melanin production, place of birth, chromosome Xq 28, for example. There would be no woke people, because there would be nothing left to criticise, so there would be no anti-woke people either, or no angry conversations over dinner among flatmates. It would be a kind of nirvana.

"We could still have musicians, though, I suppose, to tickle our neuro-aural synapses. Abstract sounds are OK - so long as there are no lyrics.

"Yes, of course, the neuroconvergent majority will complain that the *Diversouniversopedia* is boring. Well, if they're bored, after an hour of practice you can play four chords on the guitar, which covers 25 percent of hit songs.

"Oh, God! My eyes! My eyes! I've got to jump the queue. This is a medical emergency." Mikhail turned around. A young woman with long hair and a swollen face had taken Chomsky's place in line. The skin around her eyes was mauve, wet with tears, and so inflamed that she was squinting at Mikhail through a pair of narrow slits. Mikhail then realised that she was talking, not to him, but to the phone on the end of her pink selfie-stick. "I'm in a state of crisis," she wailed. "They won't let me move to the front of the line. Oh, my God, my eyes are literally burning. Well, if you're watching this, Delta Airlines, you should have put me in Business. Refuse to upgrade me, me with my four hundred and fifty-nine thousand followers?"

Mikhail stepped aside. The woman weaved to the front of the line preceded by her upraised selfie-stick, and calling, "Medical emergency! Psych trauma!"

Mikhail could feel a Hesburger crisis coming on. He tried to calm himself by constructing logical statements about the *Diversouniversopedia*, but his train of thought was broken. His kicked his suitcase forward and resumed watching the video. "Hi! Hello! Hola! Namaste!"

"Hi, sir! So what brings you to America today?" the immigration officer asked Mikhail.

"I have come to meet my father."

"Uh-huh. And what is your father's residence status in the U.S.?"

"He is a United States citizen, for sure. Born in the U.S.A.."

"Father's name?"

"I don't know."

"Uh...huh... I geddit. You don't know your father's name, but you're coming to America to meet him. This is the bit where I get a little suspicious, you know what I mean?"

Mikhail turned up the sides of his mouth, to make it look like he was smiling. (He had read that this was helpful.) "Don't worry, officer. I have done the necessary research on my father's identity. In fact, I have narrowed it down to two names."

"And those names are?"

If the officer was asking for the names, he clearly believed Mikhail's story and there would be no difficulty from here on. "The first name is Shaun Shaughnessy."

"Uh... huh... the guy who's gonna be the Democrat running for prez, right? He's your Pop, yeah?"

"No, no, no! Not necessarily him. My father could be the other name."

"Which is?"

"Brent Lundscum."

"Oh, yeah! I should've guessed. The Republican guy who's running for prez too. Well, that makes sense, I guess. Either you're a nut job or you're pulling my chain, and you make too much sense to be a nut-job, so I guess you're pulling my chain. Suit yourself." The officer looked a second time at the cover or Mikhail's passport. "And you're coming in on a Russian passport, huh?"

"Yes."

"Do you have a U.S. passport?"

"No."

"Even though you have an American parent? You never thought of applying for a U.S. passport? Most people would in your situation."

"Why?"

"I dunno. To visit America, I guess." Mikhail curled up his lips again.

The officer looked at his watch and sighed. "Uh-huh. I get it. O....K..., so that's how it's gonna be, huh? Let's have a look at this Russian passport, then." With an unrushed left thumb, he opened the passport and flicked through the pages until he reached the laminated page. His right hand hovered over his keyboard. He looked down at the passport photo. He looked up at Mikhail. He looked back down at the passport and back up at Mikhail. "So, what is your family name actually, er, sir?"

"Krutoy."

"Spelling, please."

"K-R-U-T-O-Y."

The officer scratched his bald patch. "It says here, 'Krutova'." It rhymed with 'shoot over'.

Mikhail smiled again. "Krutova is the feminine form. Krutoy is the masculine form."

The officer exhaled slowly. "O..K.., O...K..., I get it. And your first name is..."

"Mikhail."

"It says here, 'Mikhaila'."

"Mikhaila is the feminine form, Mikhail is the..."

"Yeah, I get it."

"But you can call me 'Misha' in any case," Mikhail added. "In Russia, they call Mikhails 'Misha' and they call Mikhailas 'Misha'. Misha can be both masculine and feminine, so maybe this will make our conversation simpler."

The immigration officer rubbed his eyes. "So, what are you, male or female?"

Mikhail smiled. "I am male."

"O.K. You could make this easy for us both, you know. Or very difficult. I'm going to ask that question again. Think very carefully before you answer - just decide if you want to make it easy or difficult. Unnerstand, pal?"

"I unnerstand, sir. I have Archilochus-Hesburger Syndrome. It is not an illness. It is a condition. Archilochus-Hesburger Syndrome means that I can only say logical things. Otherwise, I get anxiety."

Officer Romero raised his eyebrows. "O.K., then, ma'am. Here we go. See this here on your passport." He slid the passport through the hole in the perspex screen and pointed at the laminated page. "It says 'sex', right? And underneath there's an F, meaning 'Female', right? All clear? So, let's try again. Are you male or female?"

Mikhail smiled again. "I am male." He looked down. "Probably you have observed these protrusions on my chest and you are thinking that they signify that I am female. Is that the problem? But they are man-boobs, gynecomastia. They are not a woman's breasts, in case that was your misapprehension. I have gender dysphoria, sir. It is not an illness; it is a condition. And now it is a proven fact, accepted by all, that I decide what sex I am. So, I am a man and it logically follows that these," (Mikhail poked his nipples), "are logical man-boobs."

Border control officer Romero sighed and shook his head. "I'm afraid I must ask you to step aside, ma'am," he recited. "You appear to be entering or attempting to enter the territory of the United States of America with false representation, which is an offence under the Immigration and Nationality Act."

"But it is not false representation, sir. I received this passport from the Embassy of the Russian Republic through the established procedure. My passport has all the features and devices of modern Russian security printing, including the engraving, the watermark and the holographic image of the double-headed eagle."

"Yeah, yeah, yeah. Have it your way, ma'am. But if this passport is genuine, then you gotta be a genuine female 'cause that's what it says in your genuine passport, and if you're female and you keep telling me you're a guy, then you're making false statements to an immigration officer, which is also an offence under the Immigration and Nationality Act. Either your papers are bogus or you're lying. Take your pick."

Mikhail smiled.

"Are you smirking, madam? You think this is funny?"

"No, officer."

"So, what's with the happy face?"

"I thought that a smile would make you happy too."

Romero rubbed his eyes. But when he opened them again, Mikhail was still there, smiling gently. "Gender dysphoria, eh? I might wear a uniform, but I know the world's changing and I'm cool with that. My dog, Rolf, used to go around trying to hump the cat.

Each to his own. So, O.K., look, I'm feeling generous today, ma'am. It was my daughter's birthday yesterday and she had a great party, ten candles and no arguing with my ex, and I'm in a good mood, you know what I mean? So, I'm gonna give you a last chance. Three strikes and you're out, right? It's all the same to me. I'm an open-minded guy. I'm just trying to do my job, right. So, one last time. Are you male or female?"

"My doctor told me that my sex is just a word. He said that whatever I choose it to mean, that's what it means. So, logically, there is only one answer which is not a lie: I am male."

"OK, have it your way."

A security officer escorted Mikhail to collect his suitcase from the baggage carousel. As she waddled across the baggage hall, Mikhail took note of her geometry. The fat on her legs meant that she couldn't put her thighs together, which meant that her knees had to be even further apart than her thighs and her feet even further apart than their knees, because the thighs, the knees and the feet were all governed by the same angle where her legs met at the apex of her crotch. As the three of them walked to the holding room, Mikhail remembered with relief the proper term: her triangles were similar but not congruent. Similar and isosceles, indeed. Euclidean geometry, courtesy of Euclid of Mikhailia, the man who made shapes follow the rules of shapes. Maybe Diogenes would bump into Euclid someday soon. They would have a lot to talk about.

Jet lag aggravated the symptoms of Hesburger's.

The security officer led Mikhail to a door marked, "No Entry to Unauthorised Persons". (Whenever Mikhail saw that very common sign, it upset him because it did not convey any meaning. If somebody already knew that they were unauthorised to go through that door, then they did not need a sign to tell them so. If, on the other hand, they did not already know that they were unauthorised, they would think that the sign did not apply to them, and would go through the door anyway.) The security officer entered a four-digit code into the keypad next to the door, thus proving that she was authorised, and that the sign was not only redundant, but doubly redundant. Mikhail tried not to memorize the code.

The corridor down which Mikhail followed the security officer was lit by humming fluorescent tubes in wire cages. The floor was grey linoleum tiles. To right and left was white plasterboard. They passed a sheet of paper taped to the wall with the words, "Don't forget to sine back in your TASER" printed in Arial 48. An empty snack vending machine had blue tape over the coin slot. At the end of the corridor was a pale green melamine door. Mikhail could hear a man shouting on the other side. The sign on the door said, "Holding Room - Identity Verification." The security officer entered the same code into the keypad.

"Wait in here, ma'am," said the security officer. "The Examiner will be with you momentarily. The Examiner will retain your passport until an appropriate determination has been made."

"What's going on?" asked Mikhail. "I need to catch my flight."

"Please do as I say, ma'am. It's nothing personal. Just procedure." She showed Mikhail through the door and it slammed behind him.

The Holding Room for Identity Verification was about five metres by four metres. It had no windows and was lit only by a buzzing fluorescent light in a wire cage on the ceiling. A dozen stackable beige plastic chairs sat against the four walls facing the middle of the room, where, on the stained grey industrial carpet, lay the woman with the red, swollen eyes. She was on her back and sobbing to the phone held at the end of the glittery pink selfie-stick above her face. "Aaarh, aargh, the pain! It's doing me in!"

"Are you all right?" asked Mikhail.

"Fuck you!" the woman yelled, turning to Mikhail. "Now I've got to do this whole TikTok all over again, you wanker."

"I'm sorry," said Mikhail. "I didn't understand. I thought your eyes were hurting."

The woman turned towards him. Maybe it was a glare, but it was impossible for Mikhail to tell through the swelling. "Are you saying there's something wrong with my eyes?"

"Be careful," came a voice from the corner of the room. It was Noam Chomsky. "You're about to enter the labyrinth of ethnic semiotics. And she's a fucking fruit loop."

"I asked you a question," repeated the woman. "Are you saying there's something wrong with my eyes?"

"Well, they're all puffed up," Mikhail said.

"Now you're fucked, lardass," muttered Chomsky. "Fools leap in where angels fear to tread. Abandon hope, all ye who enter here."

"OK, since I don't want to give offence, I will just repeat my original question," Mikhail said. "Are you all right? You seem to have a lot of pain in and around your eyes."

"They're not just my eyes. They're ethnic signifiers." The woman lay her selfie stick beside her. "And I don't like the way you're leaning over me," she said. "It's making me feel oppressed."

Mikhail pulled up a grey chair and sat down. "Is that better?" he asked. The woman just stared at him,

225

possibly glowering. Her forehead was the colour of strawberry ice-cream and botox-smooth. Her hair was cut into a mop-top and dyed salmon, with black roots, and her wide, comma-shaped black eyebrows somehow didn't seem to be where they belonged.

"Yes," the woman sniffed. "I am more relaxed now. Not a hundred percent, though." Her forehead attempted to frown. "You really don't know who I am, do you? I'm Livvi Birmingham.

"Don't tell her you've never heard of Livvi Birmingham, lardass," sniggered Noam Chomsky.

"I won't," Mikhail assured her. "But are you all right?"

"Does it fucking look like I'm all right?" Livvi shouted. "A hundred and seventy-five thousand pounds of esthetic surgery exploding in my face. I asked for an upgrade. I told them, "My name is Livvi Birmingham. I'm an influencer. I've got four hundred and fifty-nine thousand followers on Vevo. I've been on This Morning with Holly Willoughby and Matthew Schofield. I'm supposed to be on a flight to LA to meet with my agent and make a media strategy. You upgrade my ass to business, and I upgrade the image of Delta Airlines to Dope. But no. I end up flying in coach next to some guy in dad jeans, I fall asleep and when I wake up the silicone pouches under my fucking eyes have ruptured."

Probably right now I'm leaking toxic fluid all over underneath my skin.

"And then, and then, when I get to passport control, guess what. This total dorkhead immigration officer, he looks at my passport and he says, just like that, the nationality on your passport doesn't match your nationality on your I-94 form. Well, yeah, duh. Why would it? The nationality assigned to me at birth was British."

"Middle class and within fifty miles of London, by her accent," Chomsky interjected.

"But, like, for the last eleven years, I've identified as Korean. Society has Britishised me, but I'm actually Korean. When I found out the truth, it was like suddenly everything was clear. I knew what I had to do. First, I had my eyelid creases, that's my supratarsal folds, lowered by about two millimetres. Then I've my jawbone shaved down eight times. And now I'm just living my best life.

"I cannot judge you for that," Mikhail commented. "I read in a magazine in the barber's that everyone is on a search for their Best Life."

"Kiss my ass!" sneered Chomsky.

"I've done five nosejobs. I've had my chinbone cut off and reattached, so I've got titanium screws in my mandible. I've had my cheek bones reduced. I've recently had my browlift. I've had fat reduction on my

227

chest. I've had liposuction. Nipple correction. I've had whitening injections in my skin. I've also had filler in my lips and under-eye area, and you know, it just makes me happy. It's just like me being what I was meant to be, returning to my fabulous amazing me-ness. People understand that it's a new concept but at the same time not a new concept. At the end of the day, this is my truth."

"And the filler under your eyes, that's what exploded?" Mikhail enquired.

"Yeah, duh! Anyway, so the waeguk-saram immigration guy, he just says, 'Look, lady, why don't you just apply for Korean citizenship, OK?' and I say, 'I did, but I was rejected,' and he says, 'Tell you what. You come back to me with a Korean passport, and then you can write on this form that you're Korean.'"

"Some swog bufty guy, this cop," said Chomsky.

"So, then he said, 'Are you smirking, lady?' and I said, 'Smirk? You kidding me? With this botox? It's just the way Dr Kapoor left my mouth turned up at the corners,' and he said, 'Look lady, you don't screw with me,' and then they put me here. And I'm gonna miss my flight to LA. And my agent said he can get me on Oprah.'"

"Fucking typical," snarled Chomsky. "Get a beaner off his fucking lawnmower, put him in a cop uniform and he thinks he's Juan fucking Peron."

"Well, I think you urgently need medical assistance," Mikhail said. He went to the door, but the handle was locked from the outside. He entered the security code which he had memorized, opened the door and shouted, "Hey, someone come here quickly. There's an influencer here leaking silicone. Help! Help!"

"Chill, bro!" said Livvi. "I still gotta finish this vid, OK?" she picked up the selfie-stick and checked her face in the font-view camera. "I won't be a tick. Then you can call the medics, all right?" Mikhail let the door slam shut.

"What you in here for, nigga?" asked Chomsky.

"The officer and I could not agree whether I am male or female," Mikhail explained.

"That figures, with those honkers."

"Man boobs."

"Please yourself. Jeez. What happened to free speech? This Holding Room for Identity Verification. What a fucking joke! I know who I am. I'm fucking Noam Chomsky, the father of modern linguistics, so they can stick that up their spic ass." He took out a dirty handkerchief and blew his nose like a trombone. "Jesus, that fucking limey blow is shit. Thank God I'm back in the U. S. of A.. Hey, wanna know why these fascist fuckwits put me in this so-called Holding Room for Identity Verification? Because I used a word the right way. Can you fucking credit it? You actually use a word to signify the only, the single, sole, fucking unique meaning that it's got, and still they take it the wrong way. Wanna know what word I'm talking about? Yeah, I bet you do, you voyeuristic pricks. I asked for mobility assistance. You know, one of them spaz carts with the Puerto Rican at the front and the siren and the flashing light, and the bench on the back for the geriatric curry-muncher. And you know what I get? A fucking wheelchair. So, there I am, cruising through the airport on my wheely droid, this skinny little Somali dude back in the engine room, and I see some lard-butt dyke in a uniform, and I tell her that I.M.H.O. the airport is 'excessively frugal', know what I mean, and next thing I know I'm here in the slammer. Identity verification my ass." Chomsky blasted his nose again, stuffed the handkerchief back into his trouser pocket, leaving the corner hanging out, and wiped his fingers on the lapel of his sports coat.

"I've finished my video now," said Livvi from the floor. "You can call for help."

Soon after Livvi had been wheeled away, strapped to a grey steel gurney, another officer returned. Her badge said 'Rawlins'. She was carrying a clipboard and handcuffed to a tall, slender African American man who walked with a gentle, easy, loping gait.

The tall man's grey hair was neatly trimmed. He wore olive corduroy trousers, a tweed jacket, a pressed white shirt, a club tie and half-moon glasses and was carrying a battered leather briefcase. Officer Rawlins removed the detainee's handcuffs and shoved him into a chair.

"That's *Professor* Charles Granville to you, officer."

"Well, you jus' sit there, *Professor* Charles Granville," Officer Rawlins growled. I guess the more lies you tell, *Professor* Charles Granville, the longer you gonna be sitting on yo' skinny ass here. You just wait while I do your paperwork. Gonna book you in for false statements, oh yes!"

"Nice suit, bro," said Chomsky.

"Thank you," said the Professor.

"What they got you in for, nigga?" Chomsky asked.

"The good people of the US Immigration and Citizenship Services have surmised that I misrepresented my profession."

"You're a prof, right?"

"I retired from the groves of academe in the fall of twenty seventeen. I'm now a sensitivity reader."

Chomsky raised his eyebrows. "And what the fuck's that?"

Professor Granville sighed. "Well, suppose an Englishman called Nigel is writing a novel, and one of his characters is Indian. Then Jocasta, his editor, will say, 'Oh my Gawd, Nigel, darling! Damn and blast. Did you really have to put that ruddy Indian person in your book? Now I'll jolly well have to hire a sensitivity reader. Otherwise, we'll get absolutely bloody hammered in the Guardian." And then the sensitivity reader revises Nigel's novel. He takes out all the inaccurate racist cliches, and thus ensures that the Indian character is authentic."

Mikhail nodded. "Your sensitivity reader job is useful," he said. "You make African American characters realistic."

Professor Granville winced. "Well, actually, that's the problematic error. One assumes that African Americanisms are my field, whereas my specialty is actually upper-class Caucasians – posh Brits to be precise, preferably Old Etonians. You see, I've spent the last thirty years teaching Jane Austen, Evelyn Waugh and Virginia Woolf at Durham University in England. I possess the melanin, I grant you, and I trust that I still retain some vestige of my dulcet Barbadian twang, but no...". Professor Granville chuckled. "... me, make a realistic black American? The very idea is perfectly risible. But when I told immigration that I was coming to America to advise Ta-Nehisi Coates on late eighteenth century white slave owners for his forthcoming moving picture, they wrongly surmised that I was making false statements."

"Well," Mikhail commented. "All the same, if somebody ever writes a novel about me, I would expect it to be reviewed by a quarter black Russian with Archilochus-Hesburger Syndrome who was brought up by Lithuanian Jews in Suffolk."

"Fat frickin chance anyone wanna write about yo man-boobs!" muttered Chomsky.

Officer Rawlins held out her ballpoint. "Just sign here, Mr. Granville. Sensitivity reader? Authentic my ass! I'll tell you what ain't authentic, and that's you.

"Right! Chomsky!" she shouted. "We got a Noam Chomsky in here?"

"Sheesh," Chomsky whispered loudly, "now ain't that the ethnicity I was a-hopin' to avoid."

Rawlins looked at the photo on Chomsky's passport and then at her clipboard. "I guess you're, Noam Chomsky, huh? Says here you used a racist slur on an employee of the Transportation Security Administration. The N-word. Well, my friend, turns out you just committed an offence against the 2001 Aviation and Transportation Security Act. Uh-huh. Verbal assault. Can you give me one good reason why I shouldn't just haul your ass off to the NYPD?"

"Verbal assault?" Chomsky sneered. "Sticks and stones may break my bones, but words will never hurt me. Goddam. I spend all my fucking life telling people that a word is just a fucking signifier, a frigging sound in the mind, and then they pop me for 'verbal assault'. 'Niggardly', darling, is from the Anglo-frigging-Saxon. Meaning 'excessively frugal'. Sorry to tell you this, sweetheart, but you've got no right to be offended. I think you'd better let me catch my plane."

"Well, my friend, you ain't got no right in hell telling me to be offended or not to be offended. It's not up to some old Jew-boy to tell me my feelings ain't valid."

"Excuse me," Mikhail said. Rawlins and Chomsky turned to him and glared. "Officer Rawlins, could a person of colour decide whether to be offended?"

"I guess," Rawlins replied.

"Oh, good!" Mikhail said. "I think I can help sort this out, then. I'm a person of colour, and I'm telling you, as one person of colour to another person of colour, not to be offended. I am so glad to be useful. I become happy when I stop an argument. Oh, I think that I see incredulity on your face, officer. Please do not imagine that I am an impostor. My mother's mother was African, so my mother was as black as Barack

Obama, Booker T. Washington, or Frederick Douglass, notwithstanding the fact that my father is a honky."

The officer looked Mikhail up and down. "Sir, you sure ain't black," she said.

Mikhail smiled as his therapist had taught him to smile when the Hesburger's compulsion came upon him. "Nonetheless, regardless of my skin colour, it's like farting in a lift."

"Please stay out of this, sir. I ain't got no quarrel with you, sir. This is between me and Grandpa Moses here."

"No, I have to speak," Mikhail said. "I have Archilochus-Hesburger Syndrome. It's not a disability. It's a condition. It means I sometimes am compelled to say things."

"Well, I ain't heard of no Cheeseburger's Syndrome."

"Guess it's a new fashion," Chomsky said.

Officer Rawlins clucked and took out a pen and notebook. "Well, I guess I'm gonna have to get the medical examiner. Don't want you suing my ass. Sir, please could you oblige me by writing down the name of your disease."

"It's not a disease. It's a condition."

"Whatever."

Mikhail surmised that he could continue talking because nobody else was. "No, it's really like - like

235

farting in a lift. I mean elevator. We are all born with the inalienable right to fart in an elevator. And yet, how often do any of us take advantage of that right? Never. We clench our collective sphincter and wait until we reach our desired floor. So, there are two things I don't understand: one is why you, Madam Officer Rawlins, take offence at a mere word, and the other is why you, Mr. Chomsky, insist on using a word which offends Officer Rawlins, when you would never fart in a crowded elevator, at least not deliberately."

"Yup. I've got the goddam right," said Chomsky. "Niggardly, niggardly, niggardly." Then Chomsky let rip a colossal, eyebrow-searing fart that had Mikhail and the officer leaping back for cover.

"OK, you're coming with me, asshole." Rawlins grabbed her taser.

As Chomsky's curses faded into the distance down the corridor, Mikhail felt a surge of anxiety. After so much nonsense in the Holding Room for Identity Verification, the Hesburger's was hitting him hard. Hands trembling, he pulled his laptop out of his backpack. Thank God. There was a good signal from the airport wi-fi. He fumbled in his backpack for his earphones and VR goggles, and put them on his head.

Chapter 18 - The Myrtoan Sea, 10th of Boedromion 378 B.C.

It was only my second morning as a slave and the outlook was already negative for your humble narrator and travelling companion, Diogenes of Sinope. My owner, Captain Sukkot, was staring at the horizon. His skin had turned from black to ashy grey overnight. I think he was regretting an executive crisis management response decision that he'd taken during the storm: he had thrown our helmsman Palinurus overboard. It was one of those things that had seemed a good idea at the time: sacrificing a colleague to appease the mighty sea god Poseidon and thus calm the raging tempest. In the rosy-fingered light of dawn, however, the downside was becoming apparent.

"Anybody here know how to steer a ship?" Sukkot called to the crew, galley slaves and cargo slaves. Nobody answered. The galley slaves didn't seem to care that we were lost on the wine-dark sea. And why should they?

"Or know how to navigate?" Sukkot's voice tailed off. "Anyone?" He grinned and looked to the left and right, as though a spare helmsman might jump out from under an oar-bench.

The blind dude Aesop pipes up from the front end. "There's no such thing as mistakes - only lessons. Two frogs had to leave their pond because it dried up, but then they saw a well, and..."

"Fuck off, Aesop!" shouts everyone in the boat, myself included.

This Aesop is a short man with a long white cane and a nose like a mangold. He is crouched in the bow of the Jolly Flogger, smiling inanely as his milky eyes scan the featureless grey sky. Aesop of Mesembria and I had made acquaintance as fellow-pukers during the previous night's and I must say that, despite his visual handicap, his aim was faultless. When you puke with a chap, you very quickly get to know him on the inside.

"The frogs came upon a well. One of the frogs says, 'It'll be wet in there. Let's jump in.' But the other frog replies, 'Yeah, but how will we get out?' And the moral of the story is..."

"FUCK OFF, AESOP!"

Despite the absence of wind, courtesy of the great Poseidon and the selflessness of our late helmsman Palinurus, the Jolly Flogger was bobbing on the grey billows like a gassy turd in a washtub. The riff-raff galley slave oarsmen were sprawled over their benches, grabbing a cheeky kip after their night of futile exertion. Occasionally one of these rough-handed rower oiks would lift his head a moment for a quick

238

upchuck. I, for my part, was ready for my breakfast, having comprehensively voided both ends during the storm. Chorismos, bless the little chappie, was already slurping down his third portion of oarsman barf.

"You realise, Sukkot, you dickhead, what a dickhead you are?" says I. "We needed Palinurus the helmsman."

"Well, it worked, didn't it? We're alive."

"Couldn't you have waited for another ship to throw a crewmate overboard? Then we'd have got a freebie, you moron."

"Yeah, well I'm a businessman, not a philosopher, aren't I?"

"Obviously."

Sukkot reflexively lifts his whip-hand and then drops it with a sigh. "Tut Tut, Sukkot", say I. "Let's not forget the first rule of retail: never flog the merchandise. Don't get high on your own supply."

The stock, in this case, in addition to the sundry groceries in the amphorae, consisted of (i) your humble author (ii) my newly-acquired disciple/stalker/sex-object, Arete of Cyrene, she of the moustache and the titless chest (iii) Aesop, the blind dude with the zoo stories, (iv) Chorismos my dog, and (v) a pair of Lesbians.

Sukkot wasn't a bad chap when you got to know him and, had we met in other circumstances (i.e. me

239

not being his working capital), I could have seen myself sharing a jar and a plate of salted beans with him down the Agora. After tight-arse Plato and his crew of sphincter-burglars, Sukkot's mercantile pragmatism was a welcome breath of fresh air. Indeed, if my experience of coinage, poultry, and life in a barrel had taught me anything, it was that a man who lives without principles deserves society's utmost respect.

And Sukkot was a true liberal to boot. Notwithstanding the way he called Omphalos and me 'cracker white-trash, honky ass-wipes', he said that some of his best friends were white. "I don't see the colour of a person's skin," he said. "I just see their price. I'm very open-minded. Going through life, I've learned that there are just two kinds of people: slaves and potential slaves. Travel broadens the mind. It makes you realise that people of all races have the same value - somewhere between two hundred and four hundred drachmas." What a wokester!

We'd chatted a bit, Sukkot and I, and he'd explained his business model. "I'm targeting a niche market. I stay away from the lower end of the slave trade, the manual labour market segment, you know: galley slaves, aphedron-cleaners, olive-pickers and so on. What with all the prisoners from the effing wars, pardon my language, the market's for beefcake's totally flooded. The prices are at a twenty-year low and the margins are practically zero. Back when I was starting out as a slaver, no self-respecting warrior would ever let himself be taken prisoner. It was 'either return with your shield or on it', right? But now, ex-hoplites are two a drachma. No, no, no. If I've got that kind of slave, it's better for my bottom line to work them to death rather than sell them. Like this old git." He gave Omphalos a playful flick of the whip. "Total waste of space but he just won't croak. Will you ever kick the bucket and get off my hands, Omphalos?".

"Doing my best to, massa."

"Hmmm." Sukkot rubs his chin. "Maybe I should have thrown Omphalos overboard instead of Palinurus. Do you think Poseidon would have known the difference? Would the Earthshaker have been pissed off by me sacrificing this negative-net-worth scrotum? I mean, do the Gods know our intentions? And if they do, do they care? I mean, I had a girl once in Luxor. She was that pissed off with me when I gifted her a fake amulet. I mean, it was real lapis lazuli, but I hadn't paid for an enchantment, so it didn't cure her itch. She wouldn't speak to me for two menstrual cycles. Do you think it's the same for deities - they want our worship to be sincere?" The Nubian shrugged. "Anyway, what's done is done. Pity about Palinurus but here's the bottom line: always look forward with hope, not backward with regret. Man cannot discover new oceans unless he loses sight of the shore. You've got to push past the negativity."

Well, I wasn't going to argue with Sukkot, he being the one with the whip.

Omphalos had a concave chest, not unlike an inverted turtle shell, and during the night I had observed how he had acquired this deformity. Omphalos was so weak and scrawny that he often failed to lift the blade of his oar out of the sea when he was reaching for his next stroke. The forward motion of the ship would then whack the oar handle back into his chest. The frying pan shape of his thorax was the legacy of those cracked ribs.

"And still I keep Omphalos alive," Sukkot sighed. "I think of him as my corporate social responsibility programme. Anyway, basically, I'm targeting the high-margin, premium market segment with a differentiated product: philosophers and sex objects. Unless the merchandise can give you either a syllogism or a blowjob (or, in very rare cases, both), sorry guvnor, but I'm just not interested. I don't like to boast, but I was way ahead of the peloton on this one. In the ownable personal services market, it's a case of *you snooze, you lose*, my friend. I call it Sukkot's Hierarchy of Needs. Once a punter's got food, water and a roof over his head, what's the next two things he wants? A shag and a reason for living. Honestly, I've often thought I could jack in this capitalism racket and become a motivational speaker like Plato. 'Sukkot of Nubia shows you how to triple your sales with the *Sukkot Five-Step Approach* © that will have your competitors gagging. Step One: find your client - anyone with anomie, weltschmerz and/or a hard-on.' You for instance, Diogenes of Sinope, I see you going for top dollar to some parvenu nouveau riche pseud if we get to Corinth. (*When* we get to Corinth, I mean. No negativity.) I visualize your future owner, Diogenes: some high-roller wannabe who's done well in trade, married above himself, just bought himself a few hectares on the cheap side of the valley, and wants a house slave to tutor his brats and make him look like a gent when the in-laws pop round. Aesop, on the other hand, he's a different market niche. I mean, Aesop's got a bit more class than you. No offence meant..."

"None taken."

".. but Aesop lives on a higher plane. You see, Diogenes of Sinope, I monitor the market trends, and apparently there's this new thing called 'Classical Fart'.

"Art?"

"That's the one. So, basically, you buy up a story, or a tune, or some porno, and, if you're lucky, some aristokratos starts calling it 'Art' and basically you're golden. So, Aesop, I'm calling him a Novelist.

"The woman, though, Arete, whatever her name is, frankly, I don't know how to market her. Sex object? Obviously, Corinth would normally be the place, Corinth being the acknowledged knocking shop of the plate-shaped world. One thousand working girls at the Temple of Aphrodite, they say. Thing is, I'm not so sure that Arete's bankable in that regard, nawa mean? But a woman philosopher...? Anyway, she just fell into my hands, jumped into my ship of her own free will, like. If she didn't cost me anything, then it's easy come easy go, right? Maybe a novelty item."

"I resent the way you treat me as an object for your profit and pleasure." Again Arete! Inserting herself into the conversation as though she had a willy – with that loud, grating and unfeminine voice. I notice that her moustache is quivering with rage. It seems to have sprouted a little since Piraeus.

But Sukkot, being a broad-minded liberal, was prepared to reply to a woman: "If you're not an object, then what are you?"

"I'm a human being."

Sukkot scratched his head with his whip-handle. "Oi, Diogenes, you're gonna have to help me on this one. Can't she be an object and a human being at the same time?"

Well, as a rule, I don't get involved in other people's arguments, but, as I mentioned earlier, it seemed to me that it wouldn't do any harm getting into Sukkot's good books, seeing as I belonged to him and his whip. (Plus of course us Hellenes got all our culture from Africa, apparently, which makes respect dark skin. I suppose we'll have to liberate our minds at some point, but for now grovelling and awe do the trick where black people are concerned.)

"O Arete of Cyrene," I say, "Behold yonder noble ebony-hued Nubian, Sukkot the mariner. What is he to you?"

"He is the captain of the Jolly Flogger, the ship whereon I travel, O Diogenes of Sinope."

"And yonder cringing parody of humanity, Omphalos: what is he to you?"

"He is a galley slave of the Jolly Flogger, the locomotive force of the ship whereupon I travel."

"And I, O Arete of Sinope, what am I to you?"

"You are Diogenes of Sinope, the great philosopher, upon whose lips I travelled the wine-dark sea to hang."

I continue. Although you've probably worked out where this dialectic is going, dear reader, one must see these syllogisms through to their end. "So, Arete, in fact all these people are objects to you. Sukkot is a captaining object because he is a captain to you. Omphalos is a rowing object to you, and I, inexplicably, am an object of attraction to you. Is that not so?"

"It is so, O Diogenes of Sinope," she hisses. She's obviously pissed off with me, but she started it. Then I come in with the killer question.

"So, the moment somebody has any kind of significance for you or effect upon you, does not that significance or effect immediately make them an object to you?"

"It does indeed, O Diogenes of Sinope."

"So, in fact, the only people who are not objects for us, are those who mean nothing to us?"

"It is indeed true."

Sukkot grinned at me. And why shouldn't he be impressed? It was the first time he'd seen me perform as a stunt philosopher. "Can you pull a routine like that for the punters in the slave market?" he asked.

So here we were, supposedly on a short-haul from Athens to Corinth, two days max, where I was to be sold as a tutor-slave-cum-conversation-piece. Except now we were fuck knows where heading and fuck knows whither while the corpse of Palinurus our helmsman was feeding the cephalopods. Now, I'll tell you, dear reader, I wasn't exactly pining for my barrel on the Agora. Sure, the barrel was home, and there's no place etc. etc. but what with the lack of privacy, the sanitary arrangements and Chorismos's stentorian farting I was ready to let go of the past, open up the next chapter in my life and explore the magic of beginnings. In fact, I rather fancied myself as an intellectual ornament in the home of some crass parvenu in the leafy suburbs of Corinth. And who knows, maybe some clap-raddled retiree from the Temple of Aphrodite might allow me to confer respectability upon her. All this is to say that right now I was more than usually reluctant to drown.

"OK, OK, you lot," Sukkot calls to the crew and cargo. "This is your captain speaking. What do you want first, the good news or the bad news?"

"Da good news, if it please you, massa," wheezes Omphalos.

"Okey Dokey. The good news is that, thanks to the selflessness of our dear late colleague, Palinurus the helmsman, may he sink in peace, we are all afloat and alive. The one life is given for the many. Greater love hath no man than this; that a man lay down his life for his friends.

"The other good news is that the storm has had minimal financial impact, thanks to my foresight in investing our retained profits in upgrades to the hull, the mast and sail, which are now not only operational but fully depreciated. And the bad news is that we are lost.

"But let's reject negativity. You can't start the next chapter of your life if you keep re-reading the previous one. So, I want everyone in the ship to have a forward-leaning growth mindset and focus on the potential of the future. Never forget that in the slave trade our greatest asset is our people, and...."

Just as Sukkot is revving up, a boy's treble voice pipes from the rigging. "Ship ahoy!"

"Yay! We're saved!" Sukkot trilled.

"It's a Macedonian trireme," cried the lookout.

"Oh, shit." Sukkot's face turned greyer. I immediately understood. With the arrival of a Macedonian vessel, my dream of domestic bliss in suburban Corinth was blown to buggery. Instead of gently coasting westwards towards the one thousand plucked, perfumed and powdered hetairae of the Temple of Aphrodite, we had sailed north and entered the territorial waters of Macedonia. And you know what's the problem with Macedonians? Well, obviously one wants to avoid ethnic stereotypes. But on the other hand, it is important to be sensitive to cultural differences. The cultural difference between Macedonians and everybody else is that Macedonians are all fascist, moronic, shitfaced wankers.

Chapter 19 - Back in the Holding Room for Identity Verification, Newark Airport

Officer Rawlins tore the headphones from Mikhail's ears. "I said - sir, ma'am - I said I checked with the Medical Officer and he's saying there ain't no such disease as Archilochus-Hesburger Syndrome."

"It's not a disease, it's a ..."

"...Condition. Yeah, whatever. Well, personally it don't matter to me whether it's a disease, a condition or a pain in the ass. The medic says it plain don't exist."

"I have it. Therefore it exists," Mikhail explained.

"Let me at him," drawled an obese Caucasian man with a red sweaty face, a comb-over and ketchup splashes on his white coat. "I'm the Medical Officer. That's me." He pointed to his badge. "Doctor Chester Appleby. Customs and Border Protection. Onetime cosmetic surgeon to the beau monde of Akron, Ohio, and now an emblem of failed white masculinity. If you don't want to end up like Dr Chester Appleby, just stay away from medical malpractice lawyers and Colonel Sanders, my Russian friend."

"OK. I will."

"Yeah. Anyway, this conversation will be at zero cost to you, but you are hereby informed that nothing that I say should be construed as medical advice. Do you understand?"

"But what if you give me medical advice?" Mikhail asked. "Is that medical advice not medical advice?"

"Smart guy. If I give you some medical advice, it ain't medical advice. You got that?"

"OK, doctor." Good. Here was a person who understood the difference between a word and a thing. This physician would understand Archilochus-Hesburger syndrome, even if he had not heard of it yet.

With a grunt, Dr Appleby shifted his weight from his left buttock to the right and peered through thick glasses at his notes. "Well, I've consulted Dr. Google and Dr. Yahoo, and both these renowned physicians, you know what, they told me that there's no such thing as Archilochus-Hesburger Syndrome."

"There is, doctor, because I've had it all my life. The symptoms are obvious: I am very polite; I try to be nice to people; I am anxious when things do not make sense; and I have X-ray vision."

Officer Rawlins chortled. "Come on, sir. Ain't nobody in the world got X-ray vision."

"Doctors say that a Hesburger's person sees through the word to the thing behind," Mikhail explained.

Officer Rawlins sighed. "Mr Krutoy, Ms Krutova, whatever you are. This is America; in this great country you can have whatever superpower you choose. My problem is that you been telling a badged employee of the United States Customs and Border Protection Service you got a 'condition' which stone cold don't exist. And that means you're lying. And lying means I gotta deport you and you will never, ever get admission into the US. Do you understand me, sir?"

"But I do have Archilochus-Hesburger Syndrome."

"Well, how come Dr Chester's saying there ain't no such thing?"

"Finally you ask the right question, officer. The reason Dr Chester doesn't know about Archilochus-Hesburger Syndrome is that I named it myself."

"OK, I see. So you invented Archilochus-Hesburger Syndrome."

"No. I named it."

"You made it up."

"No. I gave it a name."

"OK, so you created it."

"No, but I decided what to call it."

"If I could just come in here," interjected Dr Chester. "There's this little thing called the DSM - the Diagnostic and Statistical Manual of Mental Disorders. If you're think you're nuts, first thing you do, you look yourself up in the DSM. If you're in the DSM, congratulations: you're mentally ill and you get my sympathy. Hey, maybe insurance will cover it. But Archilochus-Hesburger Syndrome is not on the DSM list. That means you're just a weirdo. As our psychology professor said at med school, *"If it ain't on the list, it doesn't exist."*

Officer Rawlins exhaled. "OK, sir, madam. Let's go. Your ass is on the next plane to Russia."

"It makes no sense," Mikhail wailed. "I thought we were allowed to choose our own labels."

Officer Rawlins unclipped her handcuffs from her belt.

Chapter 20 - North by north-east of the Sporades, 13th of Boedromion, 378 B.C.

The Macedonian patrol ship has spent the grey morning gradually closing in on us; I can see its hull now. For a moment I feel tempted to row myself. After all, I do not wish to be captured by Macedonians. I am sensitive to the culture of our Macedonian neighbours: they are humourless, fascistic brutes.

I say, I say, I say - why do you bury a Macedonian twenty metres underground? Because, deep down, Macedonians are nice people.

In the Elysian Fields, the Corinthians are in charge of the sex, the Athenians are in charge of the jokes, and the Macedonians are in charge of the police. In Hades, the Athenians are in charge of the sex, the Corinthians are in charge of the police and the Macedonians are in charge of the jokes. Boom Boom!

I say, I say, I say - how many Macedonians does it take to change a lamp wick? One.

I say, I say, say - why is there no crime in Macedonia? Because it's illegal.

If the Macedonian trireme catches the Jolly Flogger, I can forget about the handmaidens of the Temple of Aphrodite in Corinth. No way will those neckless Macedonian sausage-noshers appreciate my value as a philosopher. I will face premature death as a clapped-out galley slave.

Obviously, with Omphalos and a bint in the engine room, there's no way we can outrun a Macedonian warship. But if we can at least keep rowing until nightfall, it will be a cloudy moonless night and then we'll give them the slip in the dark. So, I watch our shipmates *literally slaving* away, and again I ask myself whether I shouldn't take an oar myself.

But then I think, "Nah - what's the point?" There's thirty-eight of them, not counting the woman, and only one of me. I'm hardly likely to tip the balance, am I? It would be like giving money to the poor. Ethical, but futile. Moreover, with Palinurus the helmsman departed, Sukkot obviously can't steer the ship and operate the whip at the same time. So, it's left to me to supply motivational incentives to the rowers.

"Look lively, there, you lazy lubberly lumps of lard!" I cry, applying the lash generously in the collective interest. Mostly I am flogging Omphalos, because he is nearest on my left, and I've always had a strong backhand. "Teamwork makes the dream work!" I call. "Our organisation's greatest assets are its people and its passion. If you want to lift yourself up, lift up someone else. Alone we can do so little, together we can do so much." I chant my motivational quotes in time with the oars, occasionally applying an artistic flick on the syncopated up-beat to the beefy shoulders of Arete, not because I'm a misogynist but because it would be sexist to treat her differently.

Aesop, his well-flogged shoulders beaded with blood and sweat, cries out, "Shipmates! Comrades! We may live or die by our efforts in the coming hours. So let me tell you a fable about the importance of hard work. The grasshopper sang all summer while the ants worked hard and ..."

"Fuck off, Aesop!" we all shout.

However, notwithstanding my leadership qualities, in the dreary twilight the Macedonian galley pulls alongside the Jolly Flogger. Our galley slaves are slumped over their oars, panting, puking and crying for water, their bloodied hands dangling beside their sweat-greased flanks. Omphalos throws up on Arete, and Aesop throws up on Omphalos, but I (being in a supervisory role) skip up to Sukkot in the stern. "I did what I could, boss," I say. He gives me a pat of appreciation. A true manager.

"Damn," says Sukkot, slapping his forehead. "I could have thrown Omphalos overboard as a sacrifice to Helios the Sun God. Then the sun would have set earlier, and we'd have given those Macedonians the slip. Still, the only real mistake is the one from which we learn nothing."

"There's no such thing as mistakes, only lessons..." Aesop starts off.

"Shut the fuck up, Aesop!" we all cry.

"...a fir tree and a bramble were growing side by side. The fir tree sneered, 'You know, Mr. Bramble, you're a titchy, tangled up waste of space. I, on the other hand, am tall and strong, so people use me for building houses.' The bramble replied, 'Oh, yeah? Just wait until the men come with their axes to chop you down.' And the moral of the story is that I'd rather be a slave right now than standing in your shoes, Sukkot." The other galley slaves give Aesop a patter of applause. Proletarian solidarity. The blind poet takes a bow in the wrong direction. He's about to fall overboard but Arete catches him by the ankle.

The Jolly Flogger drifts to a halt alongside the Macedonian ship. All we can hear is the slapping of water against our keel and the hollow knocking of the two hulls. Despite his shield, helmet, and full suit of hoplite armour, and despite the pitching of both ships, the Macedonian captain leaps like a gazelle across the gunwale of the Jolly Flogger. Ye Gods, this soldier boy sure is in love with himself. The crimson crest on his helmet waggles around like a rooster's arse. He is followed by half a dozen hoplites in battle gear.

Straight off, the captain addresses Sukkot. Typical. They see one Nubian and they assume he's in charge (even though he usually is). Like I said, us brothers have got two thousand years of history against us.

The captain flicks back a blonde fringe. "I am Captain Ektaktos of ze Macedonian maritime militia. Now zen, you are avair, I presume, zat you are trespassing in Macedonian territorial votters." Sukkot doesn't speak. "Come on zen. Papers!"

With shaking hands, Sukkot pulls his documents out of the gauntlet compartment. "The Macedonian peruses them, pursing his lips and rocking on his heels. "'Allo, 'allo, 'allo," he says. "Ve've caught ourselves a nice fish today, lads. Ze notorious pirate Sukkot of Nubia. Macedonia's most vanted." Poor Sukkot. He's gone a whiter shade of pale.

"Don't you be vorrying about ze merchandise, pirate," says the Macedonian captain. "Zat's all ze property of our beloved King Amyntas ze Zird now."

"Hang on a moment, officer," say I. "What exactly are the charges?"

"And who is zis?" the Macedonian asks Sukkot, jabbing the exquisite point of his *kopis* sword rather too close to my sternum.

"This is Diogenes of Sinope, our Director of Strategy and Operations," says Sukkot, with the agile thinking of the cutting-edge entrepreneur. "Diogenes translates our broad corporate objectives into measurable key performance indicators and ensures that they are owned and actioned by the front-facing cost-centres."

The Macedonian now seemed ready to give me a bit of respect. He turned to me. "Ze charge," he grunted, "is piracy. Sukkot ze Nubian is ze most notorious pirate betveen Egypt and Thracia."

"I think there must be a misunderstanding. Officer," I say. "Sukkot is an entrepreneur, not a pirate."

"Vat's in zem?" barks the Macedonian, pointing his *kopis* at the amphorae.

"Low-margin consumer goods," I reply. "You know, wine, olive oil, wheat, that sort of thing."

"Did Sukkot grow the grapes, the olives and the wheat?"

"Well, obviously not. He ..."

The Macedonian shrugged. "So - if he didn't grow zem, zen he must have stolen zem. Some poor bastard vas out zere sweating in the fields, aching in his back, hands all blistered, sunburned probably, but zis rich bastard ends up with ze profit. Sounds like theft to me. Sukkot's a pirate. And zerefore you're a pirate too, you manager of strategy and operations."

"No, no, no. it doesn't work like that," I say, with my agora smile. "Sukkot <u>bought</u> the wine, the oil and the wheat. Bought. With money. Not stole."

Ektaktos scratched his head. "So vere did he ze money get?" Like I told you, these Macedonians are not big-picture thinkers.

"All right," I say. "Let's do a deep dive. He got the money by selling other wine, olives oil and wheat."

"Did he grow those other grapes, olive oil and wheat himself?"

"No, obviously."

"Zen he is a pirate."

Now you see what I mean about Macedonians. They lack vision. You need vision to understand how one person's sweat becomes another person's property. It's almost spiritual.

I tried another tack. "O Ektaktos of Macedonia," I begin, "What is your favourite dinner?"

"A chicken doner kebab in the style of Asia Minor, O Diogenes of Sinope."

"Do you have a slave who makes chicken doners in your kitchen?"

"Of course, O Diogenes of Sinope," snaps Ektaktos.

"And what is your kitchen slave called?"

"Something to do with beans."

"Never mind. We don't need the name. But when the doner is cooked and in your hands, is it your doner, O Ektaktos of Macedonia?"

"Naturlich."

259

"So, if the doner made by the effort of a slave becomes your doner, why cannot the wine, olive oil and wheat produced by the effort of another slave become the wine, olive and wheat of Sukkot?"

"Hmmm," says Ektaktos. "Vould you mind awfully if I had a time out mit my colleagues?"

The Macedonians go into a huddle. Eventually Ektaktos turns back to Sukkot and me. "Fine," he says. "I grant you that the wine, the olive oil, the slaves and the wheat are the 'property' of Sukkot of Nubia. (He makes big air quotes around the word 'property'.) He hooks his thumbs into his belt and pushes out his chest. "But theft of miscellaneous dry goods and beverages was only the secondary charge, so you're not off the hook yet. The main charge, the vone which is going to get you both a premium-grade crucifixion, is the theft of zis wessel."

Damn. I should have admitted that I was a slave. Now I'd told Ektaktos that I was a key player in Sukkot's senior management team, I'd have to take executive responsibility: i.e. an agonising death on a wooden cross.

Ektaktos cracks his knuckles. "Regarding ze second charge, did you, Sukkot ze Nubian, three days after ze vernal equinox, three hundred and eighty years before Christ, knowingly capture the Macedonian vessel formerly known as ze 'Feelin' Nauti', enslave its captain, thrice-noble Kalamindar the Thracian, sell its crew and change ze ship's name to 'The Jolly Flogger'? Do you deny any of this?"

Sukkot looks at his horny toenails. "I deny everything," he mumbles.

"I'm Sukkot's attorney," I say. "And you have no evidence against him."

There is a pause. We hear the waves slopping against the sides of the two ships.

"But I am the evidence!" shrieks a familiar voice from the rowing benches. "It is I who speak to you thus, I thrice-noble Kalamindar the Thracian, prince of the seas and former captain of the Feelin' Nauti. I, Kalamindar, mariner of the northern kingdoms, whose valour and virility were renowned from the snow-capped peaks of Thracia to the croc-infested swamps of the Nile. I, Kalamindar of Thrace, bear witness that Sukkot the Nubian committed all these vile crimes, and many, many more infamous acts of such base foulness that the Olympian Gods themselves barf to hear them recounted." We all turned our heads towards the voice. Who on the Jolly Flogger could have spoken in such with such aristocratic assurance?

Then we saw.

Crikey O'Reilly! So Omphalos was Kalamindar. Even I had heard of Prince Kalamindar, the glorious Thracian mercenary who had risen to become Lord

261

Admiral of the Macedonian fleet. Kalamindar was none other than our larval shipmate, Omphalos. With a clanking of armour, the Macedonians turn to face him. Ektaktos's soldiers kneel and press their hands to their foreheads.

"Omphalos?" says Sukkot.

"Well, only because that was the name you gave me, you cheap bastard. Calling me after a belly-button. The effing cheek."

"Well, well, well," harrumphs Ektaktos. "I zink you'd better be coming with us, Sukkot the Nubian, and, er... vat's your name?"

"Plato," I say. "Plato of Athens."

"Ja, the name rings a bell. You're ze famous pervert, aren't you?"

"Define 'pervert'."

Ektaktos shrugs. "Anyway, it's getting dark. Ve'd best be on our way. Ve should have you up on your crucifixes by Thursday - Friday tops. Come on lads. Noble king Amyntas will surely shower us in silver for returning his High Admiral, Kalamindar of Thrace."

I feel a sharp, stabbing pain in the small of my back. "Let's be having you," says the spear's owner, "and no funny business."

This is probably a good time to say a few words about my crucifixion, an topic upon which I have firm views. This is how crucifixion works: first my legs will

262

lose their ability to support my body, then my shoulders will dislocate, and my arms will stretch about 20 centimetres, and then finally the strain on my chest and the internal bleeding in my lungs will suffocate me, all of which will take, say, a day and a night.

I don't want to be crucified. I really don't. But this raises an interesting question, if you think about it. Here I am, Diogenes of Sinope, the bloke who lives in a barrel and goes around lecturing everybody that physical pleasure is a sad illusion. I eat beans and dry wholewheat pita. I dress in rags, and I sleep with a flatulent mongrel. So, if I'm not interested in physical pleasure, why do I have a such a problem with physical pain? Or, to put it the other way around, if I'd prefer a lifetime of bean soup to twenty-four hours on a Macedonian crucifix, why wouldn't I prefer a nice lamb doner to a bowl of bean soup? If I tramp around Athens preaching that physical pleasure corrupts the soul, why do I put so much effort into staying alive? I mean, what's the point of living, if you're not going to enjoy yourself?

Another stab in my back pierces my skin. "Come on, Plato of Athens. You're nicked."

Chapter 21 - Virginia State Route 267

"I shall draw a line in the sand," resolved Shaun Shaughnessy, Democrat, senior senator for the state of Maryland, as his black limo sailed away from the kerb. "I just don't know which side of the line I shall find myself." The senator checked his Rolex. Seven forty-two. OK, he had forty minutes. At eight twenty-two, he would reach his five-million-dollar townhouse in Kalorama, and by then he would have made the big decision. The whopper. The big kahuna.

By eight twenty-two he would have chosen either (a) to declare his candidacy for the presidency, or (b) to drop out of politics altogether.

In forty minutes, therefore, his chauffeur would be holding the limo's rear door open, and he would step out. His face would glow with determination. His eyes would be steely. His bags would be on the kerb. The chauffeur would pocket his tip. Shirlee would open the door of their home and, from behind her silhouette, the sound of sweet jazz and the aroma of coq au vin would pour down the steps into the street and transport him back to Europe and his youth. Then Shaun would say ...

Either (a): "Shirlee, darling, I've got something to tell you. I've been thinking about this for a long time."

Or just (b): "That smells delicious, darling."

One the decision was taken, that was it. No looking back. No regrets.

The senior senator from Maryland slumped a little further on the black leather seat of the airport limo. He was almost horizontal. Seven fifty-one already. No problem. That still left thirty-one minutes. Thirty-one minutes was more than half an hour. Plenty of time for a capable politician to take a decision.

But God, the drive from Dulles Airport to downtown Washington D.C. was such a downer these days! He used to get a kick out of the Dulles Expressway, cruising eastward in the dark with the office lights of American private enterprise flashing past at 60 miles per hour. He would ask the limo driver where he came from. When he got the answer (Ethiopia, Nigeria, Pakistan, wherever) he'd ask, "And how's America treating you?" and he'd always hear the words that he needed to hear: "Doing fine in the US of A, thank you, sir. It's a great country. Anybody can make himself a somebody." Sean would reward these reassuring words with a 15 percent tip rather than the regulatory 10 percent and feel like a philanthropist as he passed the receipt on to Emily for the expenses claim. Back then, the ten-lane Dulles Expressway at night was like one of those inter-galactic wormholes on *Star Trek*. You would shoot through the flashing lights of breakneck capitalism and burst out into a parallel universe of grandiose constitutional vistas and floodlit obelisks. There was that rush of optimism when your limo glided onto the Memorial Bridge, the majestic Potomac River twinkling below, Abraham Lincoln hunched and brooding in his shrine to your North American honesty, the squat and stalwart Kennedy Centre hunkered down on the riverbank, guarding your national culture like a dragon on its gold, and the Washington Monument rising proudly ahead of you like a splendid golden Johnson, announcing to the solar system that your U.S. of A. was still the big swinging dick. Ignoring the angry, toadlike, impenetrable, corroded bronze of the Museum of African-American History (because it spoilt the view), you would sail along Constitution Avenue, your manly heart swelling, as the United States Capitol, your place of employment, loomed broader and taller in the windscreen and seemed to call your name in the plump womanly tone of an operatic contralto: "Come hither to me, Shaun Shaughnessy, Senior Senator of Maryland. I am the Mother of Democracy. Come to my bosom. Rest thy weary head within my ample, bountiful cleavage and draw strength from me!"

But that was then. Right now, Shaun Shaughnessy was feeling a weird unfamiliar emotion. It had begun the day that President Trump O.D.ed on erection pills, and his head exploded all over Vice-President Pence's coiffure in the White House briefing room. Normally, the spontaneous detonation of a Republic president in an odd-numbered year would have elated Senator Shaughnessy; it left enough time for the sympathy vote to evaporate before the 2020 Presidential Election.

But the eruption of Donald Trump's cerebellum did not leave Senator Shaughnessy energized. It left him with this new, alien feeling. What was it? Regret? With a tincture of emptiness and a soupcon of melancholy? He kept remembering that whiney proverb: 'Be careful what you wish for; you might get it.' Was that one of Aesop's?

At two o'clock one morning, Shirlee Shaughnessy had crept downstairs into the living room to find her husband hunched over his laptop, Googling search terms like 'alienation', 'void', 'angst' and 'anomie'. But all these abstract nouns were too grey. They sounded too much like a dull ache and not at all like the sharp mental pain that would suddenly stab him from behind at any time of the day or night.

Then, one oppressively humid evening, he left Shirlee watching the Kardashians, slipped on a pair of jogging pants, and slipped out into the street through the kitchen. He wanted to clear his mind. It was the Interns' Hour, when hundreds of young idealists poured out of the office suites of congresspeople, lobbyists and corporate lawyers, and into the bars of Dupont Circle and Kalorama. The boys had loosened their tie knots, and the girls had switched their pumps for trainers. The interns sat around sidewalk tables, and, with bright eyes and flushed faces, they twittered and roared at each other across savory fries and microbrew in plastic cups, swapping anecdotes about their glimpses of powerful people, before creeping to studio apartments in singles and pairs.

Shaun turned right after the World Bank Treasury, for no other reason than that he liked the name of that little alleyway - St. Matthew's Court. It sounded quaint and un-American. The senator walked between the concrete geometry of an office building and the windowless red-brick side wall of the Catholic cathedral. Then he turned left onto Rhode Island Avenue.

Suddenly, up on his left, Shaun saw the Big Guy himself. St. Matthew, stern faced, square-jawed, and as butch and Caucasian as a 1930s quarterback, was admonishing him, the senior senator, from the portico of his cathedral. The saint's left hand was thrusting out

268

an open gospel and his right hand was giving Shaun the finger.

Right away, Shaun remembered the name of the new emotion.

Guilt.

Yes, Shaun Shaughnessy, the senior senator from Maryland, was guilty. He was guilty of being a lousy father and a crap husband, leaving Shirlee to handle their teenage son's increasingly obvious mental illness while he spent his evenings in Annapolis hotels brown-nosing his donors. He was guilty of hypocrisy, sucking up to that pant-suited egomaniac Hillary Clinton, who despised the ignorant, obese proletariat whom Shaun claimed to represent. (Oh, yes, anybody who'd listened to Hillary after a couple of martinis knew that 'Basket of deplorables' was just the start of it.) Shaun was guilty of cowardice, keeping his mouth shut when he should have been telling Sanders or Ocasio-Cortez that they were scaring off ordinary folks, flying in first class when he should have been screaming that the planet was on fire, wrapping himself in the Stars and Stripes when he should have been calling the Iraq invasion a bonehead cowboy show. He was guilty of betrayal. He had betrayed a child (a long time ago, in another country, and only once, but it was bad), he had shafted the decent, hardworking people who campaigned and voted for him like dumb sheep year after year and got nothing in return. But, most shameful of all, he had screwed *himself* over. Yup. Shaun the politician had screwed over Shaun the guy. The only things that Shaun the guy really cared about were beer, the kids, fairness, firm boobies, good manners and the blues scale, but Shaun the politician had spent the last thirty years totally stiffing Shaun the guy out of all that good stuff, and had left him with nothing except a career, a large wooden desk, a disappointed assistant called Emily, a bloated gut, cholesterol meds and insomnia.

Oh, Emily! She was now his most recent betrayal. She was sitting at the other end of the leather seat, scrunched up against the limo's door as though about to fling herself onto the Dulles Expressway. No, Shaun didn't *literally* screw his assistants. That was more Lundscum's style. Shaun was betraying Emily the liberal way. Day by day, Shaun was gradually dismantling Emily's ambition. Guilt, guilt, guilt!

Twenty-five minutes to go. No, there was no joy on Virginia State Route 267 anymore. The Dulles Expressway was no longer the portal to a wondrous parallel universe. It was a monstrous conveyor belt of oversized cars, spewing out greenhouse gases into a sprawl of grey-beige buildings commissioned by golf-loving Chief Financial Officers, a sprawl of ugliness, greed and mediocrity that had already oozed from

Washington across the meadows of Loudon County like a bacterial colony in a petri dish, and which would just keep on devouring the fields and forests of America because there was nobody left in America who cared enough for beauty to stop it.

Twenty-one minutes to go. So, what was it to be: the presidency or cool jazz? Maybe he should just toss a coin.

"You OK, Emily?" Shaughnessy asked. He hadn't got the tone right. He'd been aiming for a compromise between 'caring' and 'professional', but it came out as 'creepy uncle'.

"I'm fine," Emily said to the car door. He heard her sigh. Her red face turned and looked him straight in the eyes. "Tell me you aren't really going to quit," she stammered. "Tell me you aren't going to hand the presidency, on a silver plate, to that shit Lundscum."

***

And suddenly Shaughnessy is back in the Eagle and Child in Oxford, England. It is January 1983. Sean Shaughnessy, Rhodes Scholar of St. John's College, is knocking out *'Ain't Misbehavin'* on the piano. His buddy Brent Lundscum, the other Rhodes Scholar at St. John's, downs his fourth Jack Daniels and looks at his Rolex.

"Those chicks aren't coming," Lundscum said. "Let us face the hard truth, comrade mine. You and I have been stood up. The young ladies of St. Catherine's have somehow proved impervious to our stateside wealth and charm. Or - in your case – just wealth. Maybe it's true what they say: all Catz girls are lesbians. Let's split. I'm as horny as hell, comrade mine, and I have it on good authority that there is proletarian pussy to be had at Shades nightclub."

Shaughnessy cascaded Fats Waller's final diminished C minor across the keyboard and took a mouthful of IPA. "You bugger off if you want, Lundscum, you skank. I humbly suggest that try your luck on Christ Church Meadows. I saw some rather cute sheep there." He fluttered his hands in arpeggios up and down the keyboard - the opening augmented G chord of *Blue Moon*.

"Don't be an asshole, comrade Shaughnessy. We yanks must stick together."

"OK, OK." Shaun gulped down the dregs of his Theakstons Old Peculier. The two Rhodes Scholars pulled on their identical green Barbour jackets and their St John's College scarves, and pushed their way past the crowded bar towards the door.

Just as Shaun was reaching for the handle, a girl burst in and landed in his arms.

"Watch where you're going, honey!" said Lundscum. "First let's introduce ourselves, and then you'll want to throw yourself at me, not at him."

"I'm very sorry." It sounded like a Russian accent. Shaun stepped back and looked the girl up and down. She was mixed race – like the girl in that movie – *Flashdance* – that was it, and, yes, she was pretty, especially with her hair wet and tangled, but she looked like she was only sixteen, for heaven's sake. She was wearing a knee-length quilted coat with purple fake fur trim and an old-lady purple felt hat, trimmed with a mauve feather.

"Come on out of the rain, darling," said Lundscum, grabbing her hand and dragging her into the crowd at the bar. "What are you having?"

"I do not drink, please," said the girl. "I am coming from chess tournament. I am losing oneself. Tell me, please, what is the way to St. Johns College?"

"Well, you're in luck, honey!" Lundscum roared, tugging her arm. "We're both gentlemen of St. John's College, as you can tell from these scarves. You're safe with us. Much safer than out alone after dark on the mean streets of Oxford."

The girl looked bewildered. She was blinking in the smoke. "But our chaperone Tatiana Mikhailovna is waiting," she said. "And my coat will smell of cigarettes. Tatiana Mikhailovna will notice."

"Aw, come on. Tatiana Mikhailovna won't mind waiting and she won't smell a thing. Tatiana Mikhailovna is a martyr to chronic nasal congestion of

273

the worst kind. I happen to know that for a fact. Now, have you ever heard of Babycham? Did you know - they make Babycham from pears? It's practically lemonade. That'll make you feel better. Then we'll take you to Tatiana Mikhailovna. I'll confess that was all the fault of the American imperialist devils. When Tatiana Mikhailovna sees me on my knees pleading your cause, her Soviet heart will thaw like springtime in Irkutsk. You have my word as a gentleman. I am known to charm disappointed and lonely women of a certain age."

"You are American, yes? It is not convenient to be with you."

"Well, I think that it is extremely convenient for both of us. Serendipitous even. But, seeing as you're in a hurry, I shall instruct my dear Comrade Shaun Shaughnessy to buy us a round of drinks while we get to know each other. Off you go, Shaun. Babycham for the lady. My name is Brent, Brent Lundscum."

"My name is Anna Krutova."

Lundscum cocked his head towards Shaun. "I would like to apologise regarding Comrade Shaughnessy. To be quite honest with you, Anna, he is not my friend, but we're the only two yanks in St John's so I have to stick with him, you know what I mean. Between you and me, Anna, I'm sure he's gay."

The girl looked confused. "Gay?"

"Yeah. But don't tell him I said so. Still in the closet."

"Closet?"

"You got it. He's a Democrat, you see. A liberal. They're always talking about sex, but none of them actually enjoy it, you know what I mean?" He tapped the side of his nose. "I, on the other hand, am a Republican. I believe in God, freedom, t-bone steaks and the heterosexual life. Oh, Shaughnessy - are you still here? I've got one word for you. *Babycham*." He pointed to the bar. "Off you go."

"Come off it, Brent," Sean whispered. "Let's get her back to her chaperone in St. John's. She can't understand half of what you're saying." Indeed, the girl was frowning in bewilderment and her head was turning from one American face to the other and back again. "She's just a schoolgirl, Lundscum, for heaven's sake. Let's go. Then, I swear, I'll find you the cutest sheep in the county of Oxfordshire, OK?" He pulled Lundscum's arm, but Lundscum's hand was clamped onto the girl's wrist.

Lundscum raised one eyebrow. The hardworking left eyebrow. "Get the goddamn Babycham, Shaughnessy. Can't you see that Anna's in a hurry?"

"Brent, old pal, old buddy. She's under-age. She probably hasn't eaten. Alcohol will go straight to her head." Shaun cringed at the sound of his own whiney voice.

"Russkies drink, don't they?" Lundscum guffawed. "They're famous for it. You know what? Make it two Babychams, Comrade Shaughnessy, because she's a Russky. Three. We don't want to have you toddling backwards and forwards to the bar to satisfy her Russian needs." Then, almost in a whisper, "And don't make me ask again." Shaun drew breath and was about to speak, but he shrugged and disappeared into the noisy crowd of students.

When Shaun returned with a tray (three Babychams, Lundscum's Jack Daniels and a half of IPA for himself), Lundscum and the girl were seated at a corner table. Shaun had to pull up a chair from another table.

"Well, you took your time, Comrade Shaughnessy. That, Anna, is why you must always date a Republican and never a Democrat," Lundscum roared. "A Republican man is right there up at the bar thumping the mahogany. A Republican's like, 'Here's the money. Let's have the good stuff.' But a Democrat just stands around waving his arms and whining that everyone is getting served before him. Isn't that right, Shaughnessy? Anyway, it's a good thing you came back. Anna and I were kinda starting to run out of conversation, weren't we honey?" He pushed the first of the three Babychams in the girl's direction. "Anna, it transpires, is rather better at chess than she is at speaking American. But I did glean one rather fascinating piece of intelligence. Anna's mother is from, where was it, Anna? You mother - where from?"

"Mozambique."

"You see, Shaughnessy, half Soviet, half African. She's a goddam special issue of National Geographic. To think I've only had pureblood Caucasian girls! It's high time for me to expand my horizons, don't you think? Now, Anna - drink up. Cheers. No frowning now. Look, Shaughnessy. She's practically downing it in one. Amazing stuff, Babycham. Tastes like apple juice and does the job like Uncle Jack."

Shaun watched the Brent pour Anna's second Babycham out of the slender bottle with the cutesy deer on the label. Shaun saw the shiny, grey smudges of pencil lead on her little finger as her pale, bony, blue-veined hand clenched her glass. Then he watched the first flush of crimson come to her cheeks and the bridge of her nose.

When she was half-way through her third drink, the girl said she needed to go to the toilet. Lundscum's eyes followed her as she swayed tipsily into the crowd and the cigarette fug. Then he turned quickly to Shaun.

"All right, Shaughnessy. Quickly. I'm gonna be fair, not that you deserve it, old boy. Heads or tails?"

"What the hell ...?"

"Who takes the Russky home of course, Shaughnessy, you faggot. She's in no fit state to choose between us, so ... we have to choose for her."

Shaun sighed. "I don't ... I don't ... You know what they call it here in England? Statutory rape."

"She's skinny, Shaughnessy. She's from the frigging Soviet Union so she doesn't eat right. Skinny girls don't have boobies. They don't get their period til they're, like, twenty or something, right? Right? What was she called, that gymnast? Olga ... Olga.."

"Olga Korbut?"

Lundscum slapped Shaun's shoulder. "You see? Twenty years old and flat as the Siberian tundra. I rest my case. Come on - heads or tails?"

"You know we're friends, Lundscum ..."

"Aw, come off it. Don't give me that 'friends' shit. Sure, we're hanging out here in Oxford. But we both know, don't we? We both know we'll hate each other's guts when we're back home. I'm a God-fearing Republican, old boy, and you're a Democrat pussy faggot. And don't tell me you haven't got a hard-on for her. So, heads or tails?"

"For God's sake, Brent. Didn't you see her pinky? Pencil dust, for Christ's sake!"

"Jesus, Shaughnessy. Now she's coming back from the john. Why must you always make matters so frickin' complicated? Well, I guess I'll just have to take her myself." He waved the fifty-pence piece in Shaun's face. "And the coin goes back in my pocket. Going once … going twice …".

"OK, OK," Sean cried. "Heads. I call heads."

"And even the Democrat finally sees reason," Lundscum chuckled. He lay the seven-sided coin on the back of his thumb and flicked it spinning into the air.

And before the coin even fell back into Lundscum's sweaty hand, Shaun Shaughnessy felt ashamed.

***

Yes, guilt! Guilt was the knife stabbing Shaun, as his limo cruised through the premier real estate of Kalorama. Shaun the coward-politician had betrayed Shaun the decent guy too many times. Now it was time for Shaun the decent guy to stick it to Shaun the coward-politician in return. Time to fix the guilt. Something brave. Something right.

And something to royally shaft that sonofabitch Lundscum. No way was Shaun going to give him a free run to the White House.

"Don't worry, Emily," Shaughnessy said. "We're gonna do the right thing. And by the right thing, I mean we're gonna grind that bastard Lundscum's nose into the dust."

The limo slid to a halt. All the windows of Shaughnessy's house were lit up. The door opened and Shirlee's silhouette appeared in a wreath of brightness on the front porch. His driver counted his tip and looked up in some surprise as the Senator bounded up towards his wife three steps at a time.

Chapter 22 - In transit, Newark Airport

Mikhail was happy. As www.sleepinginairports.net recommended, he had made his Gate B16 his home. There was a bench without armrests and the wi-fi was free, so long as you reconnected every hour. There was a power socket where Mikhail could recharge his virtual reality goggles. A cleaner called Jesus had given him a United Airlines polyester blanket and pillow. "Jesus cares," Mikhail inferred. The shuttered refreshment kiosks (donuts, pretzels, smoothies, sandwiches plain and toasted, burgers) promised a filling breakfast. "Airport food prices are substantially higher than prices in the city," Mikhail thought. "However, this would only be a problem if I could get to the city."

After stamping his passport "ENTRY REFUSED WITH PREJUDICE", Officer Rawlins had dropped Mikhail's suitcase at his feet. Mikhail was therefore able to change into his pajamas, bathrobe and slippers, brush his teeth, wash his hands and face, and fold his clothes ready for tomorrow. Having rolled up his coat as a pillow, he lay flat on the perforated metal bench, pulled up Jesus's blanket to his chin and slipped on the free eyeshades from the plane. All was good.

Being refused entry into the United States, that was not the surprise. Having wrongly decided that Mikhail was lying, it was only logical to deport him. Mikhail saw it from Officer Rawlins's point of view. It was her function to deport liars.

Also, when United refused to let him check in back to London, that was not a surprise either. He had a Russian passport without the right of abode in the United Kingdom (despite being born there). So why ever would he be allowed to fly home?

What surprised him, though, was when the Aeroflot check-in machine said, "Check-in denied. Please see customer service agent." At the Aeroflot counter Ekaterina Orlova was polite, helpful and not at all impatient. She said there was a 'block on his passport' in the *system*. No, she didn't know who put it there; that information was not available in the *system*. Here was Aeroflot's customer service email address. Now, if Mikhail didn't mind, there were other passengers in the line.

There was a machine that said, "How was our service today?" Mikhail punched the green smiley button because Ekaterina Orlova had done her job.

Mikhail sent Aeroflot Customer Service an email and received an immediate reply that they would respond within ten working days. No problem! Imperial College would let him work from anywhere, and there was wi-fi in the airport. What was more, hotels.com gave free cancellation, so the savings on accommodation would pay for pretzels and smoothies. It was true what the neurotypicals without Hesburger's said about silver linings.

There were only two annoyances. The first was minor. The second was big.

The minor annoyance was the noise from Jesus's motorised mopping-machine. "I suppose Jesus must do his job," Mikhail kept repeating to himself, "because if he didn't have to do it, it wouldn't be a job."

The big annoyance was the televisions mounted way up high on the walls. Each screen was as big as a door. When Mikhail lay down and shut his eyes, he could hear CMM in his left ear and Tox News in his right. Tox was always praising the recently exploded Leader of the Free World and Mikhail's potential father, Brent Lundscum. CMM, on the other hand, was saying bad things about the ex-President and praising Mikhail's other potential father, Shaun Shaughnessy. Jesus said that nobody could switch them off.

After two hours, Mikhail had worked out that the televisions followed a direct recursive loop algorithm: (1) you describe a real event e.g. a congressman sent a jpeg of his penis to a teenager (2) you play a fanfare and project the logo of your channel (CMM or Tox) onto a blue background (3) words slide along the bottom of the screen reporting the denial or denying the report (4) a mouth with red lipstick and shiny teeth quotes Twitter (5) quick detour for a story about a famine in Mozambique (6) a man in a suit (white face and slick hair on Tox, black face and shiny hair on CMM) reports in outraged tones what people are saying on Twitter about what people were saying on Twitter about the jpeg (7) GOTO (2).

The loop gyrates faster, the outrage gets more righteous, the eyebrows rise higher, the flashes of Mozambique get briefer, the teeth shine brighter, the chyron spins like a washer-drier approaching its orgasm, and, just when Mikhail thinks that the two bickering screens will shatter into a million shrieks and shards of blue glass, the newsreaders abruptly pull their crazy-kid eyeballs back into a grown-up face, draw a deep breath, tap their earpieces, turn solemnly to the camera and say in measured, mahogany tones, "Just coming in, we have some breaking news. Megan the Duchess of Cambridge ..." and (8) GOTO (1).

Jesus didn't mind. "I turn on my machine and I hear nothing," he told Mikhail. "My machine, she make noise, but she better than that TV news trash. You got one guy talking trash, that's like back home in Guatemala. You got two guys talking trash, that's democracy. You got guys talking trash about the other guys' trash talk, that's America. I love this country."

But the TV news was too much for Mikhail. The worst was the stereo effect: CMM in the left ear and Tox in the right. "Each of them alone pumps out enough contradictions for a Hesburger's seizure," Mikhail thought, "but when Tox and CMM collide in the middle of my head, the harmonic vibrations in my neural synapses cause exquisite Hesburgerian pain." He tried lying on his stomach, so that CMM was to the right and Tox news to the left, but the relief was only temporary. He searched the airport for a quieter sleeping-spot, but the screens were everywhere.

After forty-eight hours of this torture, Mikhail decided to write to comments@CMM.com and foxfeedback@foxnews.com. He explained to them about Archilochus-Hesburger Syndrome, about the harmonic vibrations, about the border agency's misunderstanding regarding his maleness, and about his floating life in the extraterritorial limbo of Newark Airport. Then he shut his laptop and waited to see what would happen. He was encouraged to receive an immediate reply from each news channel assuring him that his opinion mattered to them. CMM and Tox were both sorry not to have met his expectations. Both promised to respond within three working days. Mikhail was therefore reassured.

But meanwhile the torrent of contradictions and *non sequiturs* emitted by the televisions was driving

Mikhail nuts. Time to seek the consolation of reason.

He put on his VR goggles.

Chapter 23 - In Macedonian waters; dusk

"Come along quietly, then, Plato of Athens," says the Macedonian rozzer, tickling the small of my back with a razor-sharp spear-tip. "We'll have you up there on your crucifix in no time."

Some of you might say that it serves me right. You might say that I, Diogenes, made bad life choices: debasing Sinope's currency - check; flooding Athens with contaminated poultry - check; pooping in the Agora for personal gain - check; masturbating - idem; taking the piss of eminent philosophers - check; impersonating a lawyer - check. But these were all victimless crimes. I may have offended the Olympian Gods, but I did it with no malice in my heart.

In short, I really don't deserve to be crucified for piracy just because Sukkot helped himself to Admiral Kalamindar's ship.

And there is Sukkot, wailing and gnashing his teeth: "Dedun, Mandulis and all the ebony-skinned Gods of my beloved Nubia, guardians of the desert and the cataracts, may I never forsake you if you spare my life! And why, oh why, O my African spirits, did you let me spend all my working capital on ship repairs if you the Macedonians would confiscate the *Jolly Flogger*?"

Ah, the repairs! Suddenly, like a streak of lightning across the night sky, the solution comes to me.

"Stay yonder spears, ye cheesebrained flatfoots of Macedon," I cry. "Be grateful for the divine genius of Diog - I mean, Plato of Athens. For I am about to save you from committing such a miscarriage of justice, such a violation of natural law, as would earn you the wrath of Olympian Apollo himself."

Sukkot just groans, "Just give it a rest, bro. It's all up for us." But the Macedonians are listening. They know the score: if we skinny-arsed mortals commit an injustice, those Olympians don't mess around. Take Oedipus. He didn't *know* he was murdering his Dad and shagging his Mum, but the Gods punished him anyway. The Gods didn't give a toss that Oedipus's Dad picked the fight or that his Mum was clearly gagging for it. Here in classical Greece, you break the rules, you do the tragedy. That's why the Macedonians are pricking up their ears when I warn them about the Gods' wrath if they so much as tap a carpet-tack through my lily-white hands.

I turn to the Macedonian captain. "Please remind us, officer, what is the charge?"

"Ze charge is zat Sukkot ze Nubian, aided and abetted by Plato of Athens, did, knowingly and mit malice aforethought, steal ze Feelin' Nauti, ze flagship of ze Macedonian fleet in ze Aegean, and zen did proceed to massacre or enslave her crew, zuss committing an egvegious act of piracy, for vich ze penalty ordained by ze laws of Macedonia is death by crucifixion."

"And where is this vessel, which you allege to have been stolen?"

"You and I are standing on it."

I raise my eyebrows. "You mean the Jolly Flogger?"

"I mean ze Feelin' Nauti, which is vot zis ship really is."

He's stepped right into my trap, this guileless Macedonian numpty. I puff up my chest and assume the declamatory posture. "Will you tell us, O Sukkot of Nubia: have you made any repairs to this vessel recently?"

"Uh? What? Oh, yes. Of course. We are an ISO 23326 employer and our first priority is the safety of our employees. Having paid a dividend to our shareholders, that is to myself, we still retained excess cash reserves, so we envisioned and co-designed a bottom-up zero-base systems renewal called Slaving 2.0."

"You and who else?" asks the Macedonian.

"Just me," says Sukkot, rather too smugly.

"So if it's just you, vy do you keep saying 've'?"

"Sukkot is an inclusive manager," I explain. "Anyway, Sukkot of Nubia, I presume that Slaving 2.0 was implemented stepwise in discrete phases."

"Naturally," Sukkot beams. "We followed a multi-stage process, with a lesson-learning post-innovation huddle after each implementation sprint."

"And could you describe Phase One?"

"We replaced the hull," Sukkot says.

"Indeed, a bottom-up approach! Ha ha!" say I. The captain's face doesn't even twitch. "Anyway, after you had changed the hull, was it still the same ship? Still the Jolly Flogger?"

"Yes, it was still the Jolly Flogger," Sukkot replies.

"The Feelin' Nauti - which he stole." (This Macedonian keeps digging himself deeper and deeper.)

"Sukkot of Nubia, would you please tell us, what was Phase 2 of the implementation of the Slaving 2.0 programme?"

"We replaced the mast."

"Of the Jolly Flogger?"

"Of course."

"Very good, Sukkot of Nubia. And Phase 3?"

"The sail and the keel."

290

"I see. You have replaced the hull, the mast, the sail and the keel of the Jolly Flogger. So, Sukkot of Nubia. Is there any part of the Jolly Flogger which was not replaced as part of Slaving 2.0?"

"Everything is new. Our management team implemented a blue-sky zero-base vision of greenfield reengineering."

"Aha!" I cry. "Then this ship is not the Jolly Flogger. It is a completely new ship." Those square-jawed Macedumpkins are gawping in amazement at my brilliance. They rarely see a performance like mine where they come from. "We can therefore conclude, quod erat demonstrandum, that the ship on which we are standing is not *and never has been* the Feelin' Nauti. This is merely a random assemblage of timber, hemp, slaves and tar bobbing around the northern Aegean. Why, it's hardly a ship at all! Flotsam, more like. A clump of maritime spare parts. I therefore put it to you, O Ektaktos of Macedonia and your retinue of dutiful but sadly rectangularly-minded rozzers, that all charges of piracy related to the alleged capture of the Feelin' Nauti should be dropped forthwith."

Ektaktos flicks back his blonde fringe and shakes his head so that the red feathers in his helmet flop and jiggle. "Can't argue with that," he says ruefully. I think I see a spark of gratitude in his eyes - gratitude that I have saved him from angering the Olympian Gods with a false conviction. That's a Macedonian for you. Always relieved when someone tells them what to do.

"Sorry," says Ektaktos. "I vos only obeying orders."

"So you'll be off then, lads?" say I. "Your galley slaves have had a little break, which is nice for them, isn't it, lads? Lovely meeting you all. Best regards to King Amyntas. How about a push off?"

But Ektaktos winces and pouts. "I'm zo sorry, sir, but if you could just give us one more moment," he says. "Ve're not altogether finished. Ja, I indeed ze charge of slave-trading drop vill. Also, ve ze charge of piracy drop vill. But zere is von more problem, unfortunately. It is zer kfestion of *vacism*."

"Racism?" Sukkot and I exclaim in unison.

"Ya, vacism. I mean, look at zem - all your galley slaves are European. Zey are vite, not zo? Zis is discriminatory slave hiring practices, ya?"

I was getting that sinking feeling. You know what I mean? You've gone the extra mile. You've put in a hundred and ten percent. You've overdelivered. And then, just as you're ready to head off home to your barrel, somebody shoots a new task into your inbox.

"I'm not racist," Sukkot says. "I'm the least racist person in this ship. I'm the least racist person anywhere in the world. I'm the least racist person you have ever met." He points at me. "And you can speak to Plato of

Athens. He knows me very well. He's European. You can speak to any of my galley slaves. They'll tell you there's nobody less racist than me. I don't have any friends, but if I did, I would ensure that they were ethnically diverse."

"Keep your vords inside your mouth," Captain Ektaktos snaps. "Ve haff a zero-tolerance approach to vacism in Macedonia. Non-discvimination is central to our core values. Your Royal Highness, Prince Kalamindar – pray tell us. Has Captain Sukkot been vont to use racial slurs or epithets in the vorkplace?"

"Yessiree," says Omphalos.

"Could you repeat them?"

"Please excuse me, massa Ektaktos. I don't like to repeat dese bad words. Dey trigger me. Yessirree."

"I know it's hard for you to relive this," says Ektaktos, "but we're all here for you, Prince Kalamindar." The Macedonian militiamen nod in agreement.

"Well, massa Ektaktos," Omphalos squeaks. "Captain Sukkot does sometimes call me a 'cracker white-trash, honky ass-wipe'. But, you know, it's just friendly banter. Locker-room talk."

"I was being ironic," says Captain Sukkot. "Can't nobody take a joke these days?"

"And, and … I don't know if I should say this," Kalamindar stammers.

"Take your time," Ektaktos says gently.

"Well, once ... the massa, I mean Captain Sukkot ... it was about two years ago ... once ... we were returning from the slave auction at Syracuse and the massa was in a good mood ... and ... and ... he put this white paint all over his face."

"Whiteface!" gasped the Macedonian.

"And then, with his face all whited up, he started singing ... singing ... in Attic Greek .... the final chorus from Euripides's *Hippolytus*."

"It was ironic!" the Nubian wails.

"He's in denial," says the Macedonian master at arms.

"Of course I'm in de Nile. I was born in de Nile. I grew up in de Nile."

Captain Ektaktos and the Macedonian militiamen catch their breath and take a step back. They look at each other for a moment. "I think I'm being triggered," gasps a big hairy bloke with a ginger beard and no neck. "I'm going into hyperventilation. Someone hold my shield. I'm reliving a trauma. Like, all the progress I've been making on my mental health is..." He cannot finish his sentence. One of the other Macedonians hugs him and helps him to sit on a rowing bench, where his voluminous red facial hair dangles between his legs.

Ektaktos shakes his head. "Well, obviously this isn't a crucifixion offence. However, I am unfortunately going to have to suspend your mariner's licence. Think of it as an opportunity for personal growth, Sukkot of Nubia. You'll be able to take some time out to educate yourself, to learn about the historical inequities in the eastern Mediterranean and to reflect on your role in sustaining systemic, institutional racism."

"But what about my slaves?" Sukkot whines. "Do I have to free them?"

"It's racism we've got a problem with," says the good captain. "Not slavery. Nothing wrong with hard work, so long as it's non-discriminatory. We'll confiscate the slaves, of course. Prepare the shackles, master-at-arms."

What a day! For the third time my hopes of a cushy life as a house-slave in Corinth are evaporating like the dawn mist on Mount Ida. I say to myself, "I blame the system! The system makes me hope to be a house-slave, just as a way of keeping me quiet and stopping me from questioning its norms. How I envy those oiks on the rowing benches. He that is down shall fear no fall, he that is low no pride. Just my luck to have been born to higher things, only to have my good fortunes torn from my grasp."

Sukkot has turned grey again. The poor sap has just learned that refuting a charge of rac/sex/narciss -

ism is logically impossible. As any smooth-cheeked sophomore from Plato's Academy knows, you can't deny that you're in denial by denying it. So, our master mariner tries another tack, so to speak. "I want to begin by speaking directly to racialized northerners like Omphalos, I mean Prince Kalamindar, who face discrimination every single day in their lives. What I did - it hurt them, hurt people, who shouldn't have to face intolerance and discrimination because of their identity. Wearing whiteface is something I deeply, deeply regret," he says, with an expression - eyes upwards and to the left - like that of an actor remembering his lines. "But I am not the man I was all those years ago. Whitening your face, regardless of the context or the circumstances, is always unacceptable because of its historical connotations. I didn't see that from the layers of privilege that I have and for that I am deeply sorry, and I apologize. I am certainly conscious that in my career as a slave-trader who's taken many concrete actions to fight against racism, to fight against intolerance, to fight against anti-northern racism, specifically, to recognize unconscious bias and systemic discrimination that exists in Nubia and elsewhere in the human trafficking sector, to work to overcome and recognize intersectionality so people live within it in a way that so many of us dealers in human cargo simply cannot understand or appreciate the micro-aggressions and the challenges being faced. So even though we've moved forward in significant ways in the slave industry, what I did, the choices I made, hurt people[1]."

"Ya, ya, ya," sighs Ektaktos with a dismissive flick of his bronze bangles. "Ze apology is necessary. And now, you vant to show zat the apology genuine is by *stepping back*, not true? You put ze career on pause and take time to reflect, ya? Master-at-arms! Load ze slaves and ve sail for Macedon."

"Oi!" says Sukkot, whacking my septum with his whip-handle. "Stop your daydreaming, you pasty-skinned, Eurotrash honky cracker. Go do your philosophy stuff - and prove to the Macedonians that I'm not racist. Otherwise, both of us are up shit creek, you lily-arsed waste of space." He takes me aside and whispers into my ear, "Hey, honky, and don't think I won't tell them who you really are: Diogenes of Sinope, the notorious forger. Oh, yeah. You know what's the punishment for counterfeiting in Macedonia? Yeah, that's right. Crucifixion. Those Macedonians are really into monetary stability."

The gist was clear: both Sukkot and I were wedged far up our respective creeks, but my creek was distinctly the shittier of the two.

---

[1] Justin Trudeau, Prime Minister of Canada, plagiarized Sukkot's speech and got away with it.

Sukkot and I rejoin the Macedonians. I take a deep prefatory breath. This will have to be the dialectic of a lifetime.

Now, my verbal duels in the Agora, my willingness to take on all comers in the no-holds-barred combat of ideas, may have created the impression that I am a proud, brave individualist, willing to endure any peril in pursuit of Truth. Well, just so that there's no misunderstanding: I am a *scaredy-cat*. Taking the piss out of Plato and his posse of diaper-wearing toffs was more of an amusement than a challenge - a diversion for a superior mind, an *amuse-gueule*: Plato's ego takes a hammering, I earn a few minutes' relief from Chorismos's farts, and the tourists get to shower me with drachmas - everyone's a winner. But arguing for my life, splitting syllogisms as I watch the sun set on what may be my penultimate day on this flat earth, that, Dear Reader, is another bowl of bouillabaisse entirely. So, with Sukkot threatening to turn me in for crucifixion as Diogenes the forger of Sinope - should he be convicted of racism - I should by rights be crapping myself into my perizoma.

But I know that I have two things going for me. One, natch, is my superlative intelligence. The other is the literal-mindedness of the Macedonian race. I am cautiously optimistic that, about twenty minutes from now, Captain Ektaktos and his trireme will be heading back home to Thessaloniki to tell the state of Macedon that they no longer understand what racism is.

Let's see how I fare.

Chapter 24 - Mikhail's nook, Newark airport: the LED screen on the left as you face the window

Don Citrus: Well, if you thought the Republicans' immigration policy couldn't get any weirder, get a load of this story from Newark International Airport. A passenger on an incoming flight from London was denied admission to the United States on the grounds, yeah, get this, that his declared gender was different from the gender in his passport. Brianna Collins is in Newark Airport with the full story. Hi, Brianna! I heard you had to make some unusual travel arrangements.

Brianna Collins: That's right, Don. I'm speaking to you now from the transit zone. I guess you could say I'm in no-man's land. Or should that be no-woman's land? According to airport procedures, the transit area is exclusively for passengers in possession of a valid boarding card for an international flight. So, to get here, Vince my awesome camera guy and I actually have flights to Acapulco booked for two hours from now.

Don Citrus: Wow! That's crazy! Still, any excuse for a trip to the sun, right?

Brianna Collins: You got it, Don. Anyway, this amazing story is about Mikhail Krutoy, a Russian citizen who flew into Newark on a scheduled flight from London.

["Hey, look!" Jesus shouted. "They got your photo on CMM. Wow, man. You something! You only in America two days and you already on CMM. I'm telling you: what a country!"]

Brianna Collins: According to a statement provided to CMM by the United States Customs and Border Protection Agency [reads from clipboard], 'Ms Mikhaila Krutova was denied entry to the United States on three counts of misrepresentation. First, Ms. Krutova represented herself to the immigration officer as female, in contradiction to the information on her Russian passport that she is of the male gender. Secondly, Ms. Mikhaila Krutova declared her name to be Mikhail Krutoy, contrary to the name on her passport. Thirdly, Ms. Krutova claimed to be suffering from a neurological condition which was found, upon investigation by a senior medical expert affiliated, to be an invention. Ms. Krutova's visa was therefore cancelled with prejudice. Well, Mikhail Krutoy is with me here in transit. Mikhail - or should I call you Mikhaila?

Mikhail: It doesn't make any difference. It's just a sound in the air. Misha works best. It stands for

301

Mikhail and Mikhaila. Call me whatever makes you happiest.

Brianna Collins: Er... OK. So, Mikhail, let's start with the basics. Would you describe yourself as a man?

Mikhail: *I* would, but that's just me.

Brianna Collins: A transgender man?

Mikhail: What does transgender mean to you?

Brianna Collins: It means ... Why do you want to come to America?

Mikhail: I am looking for my father. If I find my father, I will be American and allowed to live in America.

Brianna Collins: So, how do you feel when the US Government, the very moment that you step into your future homeland, refuses to let you enter?

Mikhail: I am disappointed, but they are doing their jobs.

Brianna Collins: But what about having your gender identity denied?

Mikhail: Oh, that was not a problem.

Brianna Collins: Er ... let me put it another way. Many people would say that the US Customs and Border Protection Agency is being transphobic when it says that you are a woman. Many people would say that it amounts to gender violence. What would you say to those people who feel that you have been a victim of transphobia?

Mikhail: I'd say that I don't own the English language. I'm not in charge of what words mean to other people. Words are sounds. If you look at words closely for a long time, they dissolve into noises and letters on a page. If a British person thinks that football is the game with a spherical ball and an American thinks that football is the game with a peanut-shaped ball, nobody calls that a problem. If a British person thinks a rubber is for erasing pencil-marks and an American thinks that a rubber is for preventing unwanted pregnancies and sexually transmitted diseases, nobody calls that a problem. And if the word 'man' means one thing to me and another thing to Officer Rawlins, I can't say that I'm right and Officer Rawlins is wrong. I don't call that a problem. So, I am not angry.

Brianna Collins: But we're talking about your identity as a human being.

Mikhail: Logically that makes no difference. Just because a word is being used to describe me, that doesn't mean I own it. What if I had an identical twin, exactly the same as me, mixed race just like me, and I described myself as white and my identical twin sister described herself as not white? You can't follow the example of both of us, and say that exactly the same shade is white and not-white at the same time. That would be claptrap. Wouldn't it? Wouldn't it? What about Pringles?

<u>Brianna Collins</u>: Er ... yeah, what about Pringles?

<u>Mikhail:</u> It is an obvious question. Are Pringles potato crisps or potato chips?

<u>Brianna Collins:</u> Ha ha! Well, I suppose it depends on where you come from. We Americans call them potato chips. You Brits call them chips, I guess.

<u>Mikhail:</u> But it doesn't depend on who is eating them, I think, right? If John Wayne is eating Pringles, and then he passes them to Prince Charles, they don't suddenly change from chips to crisps, do they? Of course not. That would be claptrap. The person holding the Pringles doesn't own the words that describe them. And so I don't own the words that describe me.

<u>Brianna Collins:</u> Er ... Erm .... Mikhail, this is your chance to share your truth. What do you want to say to the United States Customs and Border Agency? Do you want to tell them, 'Hey, you stopped me from finding my father, and I'm not OK with that?'

<u>Mikhail:</u> Well, it was OK that Officer Rawlins called me a woman because nobody owns the word 'woman'. But it was not OK when Officer Rawlins punished me for calling myself a man, because nobody owns the word 'man' either. That upset me because I have Archilochus-Hesburger Syndrome, which is a

304

neurological condition, not a disability or a disease. Have you finished? Taco Bell is about to close, and I haven't had dinner yet.

Brianna Collins: Just one more question, Mikhail. As someone living with Archilochus-Hesburger Syndrome, do you think that society, and I mean particularly the medical profession, should be taking Archilochus-Hesburger Syndrome more seriously?

Mikhail: I don't know. What difference would it make? Did you know that there is a breed of dog called a Basenji?

Brianna Collins: Er, no.

Mikhail: Well, they come from Central Africa.

Brianna Collins: Is that a fact?

Mikhail: It is a fact. When Barenjis are defending their territory, they go 'Barooooo, Baroooo.' Sometimes people buy Barenjis because they have read on the internet that Barenjis don't bark. Then they find out that the 'Barooo Barooo' is worse. 'Barooo. Barooo.' Like CMM and Tox News. It drives the Barenjis' owners out of their mind. So, does it make any difference to a Barenji bitch whether we describe her call as a bark or a yodel? No. The bitch doesn't care. Does it make any difference to the Barenji bitch's owner? No. The bitch's sound is the same whatever you and I call it, Brianna. So, it doesn't make any difference to me whether doctors recognise Archilochus-Hesburger Syndrome or not. The important thing is that I have it.

Brianna Collins: And back to Don in the studio.

Don Citrus: Thanks, Brianna. Well, we know that immigration is a real hot-button issue in the Presidential primaries. And transgender identity is another. And here we've got them both - a perfect media storm.

Brianna Collins: Yes, Don. And let's not forget that Mikhail is biracial. And of Russian descent.

Don Citrus: Wow. A perfect storm indeed. We'll be giving you the latest news on Mikhail Krutoy in real time, so stay tuned to CMM. And, hey, Brianna. Have an awesome trip to Acapulco.

Brianna Collins: Yeah, right, Don.

Don Citrus: And, after the break, what did Meghan the Duchess of Sussex really say to Prince Philip?

Chapter 25 - 2500 Penn, operated by Whyhotel

Nastya here.

I'll be honest; I didn't think America would be this easy. Look, I'm a child of the 90s, OK? I grew up in a broken nation. Born in the Soviet Union. Raised in - no, not in Sodom. Sodom would have had more parties and sunshine. And a beach, I guess.

Raised in Yeltsin's Moscow. We ate potatoes three times a day. We fitted steel front doors with triple deadbolts. We rushed home before dark. The stairwells were twilight zones, perfumed with urine and vodka-laced puke, where our hearts pounded, and we strained our ears for the sound of footsteps. Sometimes we tripped over your neighbours doing it *crab-style* on the sweating concrete steps.

I had a girlfriend, Varvara. Her mother was a cleaner in the Hotel Ukraina. She had Varvara turning tricks with foreigners in the Ukraina to pay for groceries. Then, thank goodness, Varvara got her lucky break. One of her customers was an ambitious young Third Secretary from the Italian Embassy and by 1999 Varvara was on commission, procuring her schoolmates for his ambassador. #Metoo? Well, nothing is ever completely black and white, is it?

I had another girlfriend, Sonya. Her twin brother Vanya was a nice kid. He never said much, but he did smile, unlike the rest of us. He had a floppy fringe, which he was always blowing off his forehead. I let him feel my tits twice. He never asked for more. Just enjoyed what was available, like a good Soviet kid. Then they sent Vanya to fight in Afghanistan. And when the army spat Vanya out, Vanya was a psycho. He sat in the kitchen in the dark.

I had another girlfriend, Veranika, with a kid brother called Pashka. A skinhead in a black fake leather jacket came round to Veranika's apartment and said he had a driving job for Pashka. That was the last time we saw Pashka.

That's enough, you! I told you before, didn't I? We never talk about the 90s. If you're looking for a book or a movie about the 90s, it was never made. We don't need reminders.

So, of course, we all thought America had got it together. We Russkies were the losers, right, shagging in stairwells and burning chairs to stay warm? So, if we were the losers, then the Yanks must be the winners. As Karl Marx wrote, *If you're wallowing in shite then logically somebody else has their bum in the butter. Their happiness is why your life is crap.*

308

And that's why we Russkis need to hate the West. If America is eating t-bones while we're eating cabbage, it follows that they are shafting us in a way which we haven't yet discovered.

My modest mission, coming from Russia to America, was to bring on the downfall of the West and the collapse of liberal democracy. It's always nice to have a reason to go to work in the morning.

Thanks to Gleb, I was an accredited journalist from *Russia Today*. I was in the USA to cover the presidential primaries, to portray American democracy as a mud-wrestling freak show managed by wannabe mobsters and financed by psychotic billionaires.

As well as my quality reportage for RT, I was gonna, in the words of the song, keep on trolling, trolling, trolling. And this time I had a whole troll farm working for me.

texasranger327 is mad as hell. No fucking way did Donald Trump have a freaking anoorysm, writes texasranger327. *My daughter's a lab tech in Bethesda. When Trump's blood samples came in, the director of the hospital he comes into her lab. He puts all Trump's bloods into a disposal bag and tells Cindy she's canned if she says a word. So what kinda stuff was in Trump's blood that the deep state doesn't want even his medics to see, huh? That's all I'm asking. Repost if you care about freedom, justice, God, the truth and America.*

Nine million shares.

tacogirl513 is mad as hell too. Why? Because the transphobic state of Missouri won't allow people to use the bathroom of their gender preference. tacogirl513 is triggered. It's so Jim Crow. So tacogirl513 is calling on you to make February 1 into Bathroom Freedom Day. There shall be a mass Poop-In.

Two million shares.

Destroying civilisation was hard work in the old days, Gleb said. Now all you need is a billionaire with an algorithm. I have it easy.

But I digress. I get carried away. I love my job too much.

As well as RT and my baby trolls, my third mission, of course, the most entertaining, is to obtain a sample of Brent Lundscum's DNA. Gleb's buddies at the FSB will match Lundscum's DNA to Misha's. Brent Lundscum, the father of my half-brother, will soon be President. Then, kompromat and blackmail! And bingo, he's taking care of Mother Russia from the Oval Office.

When Lundscum's press officer refused me an interview, all I had to do was to email Lundscum my CV and I got the appointment. OK, my CV had a photo with the top three buttons of my white silk blouse undone, and my email specified the location as his room in the Mayflower Hotel.

Goebbels said that people will believe any lie if you repeat it often enough. Well, these Yanks are so just gagging to be made angry, they'll believe anything the first time. Repeat a lie? Why bother, when you've got 350 million morons with smartphones? God, this is too easy!

You know why the West is screwed? Two words: happy endings. "Your dream can come true, so long as you want it enough." Every movie, every comic book, every Netflix special, every politician and every schoolteacher promises a happy ending. It's the magic of Disney.

Well, Amerika, your lives ain't getting better and there ain't no happy endings. Your median household income was the same in 2015 as in 1990. Your streets are dirtier. Your hospitals charge you six hundred bucks for a pair of crutches. *You can be whatever you want to be?* Those guys who sleep in oily jeans and hoodies, who wait for work at 5am at the gas station outside my hotel, are you saying it's their fault for not dreaming hard enough?

We Russians, on the other hand ... Well, can you think of one famous Russian movie, opera, ballet, novel or love song with a happy ending? I rest my case. Мы любим страдать. We love to suffer.

The West is a clinically obese toddler watching his happy ending melt away like an ice cream dropped onto the sidewalk. The West is throwing a century-long tantrum. Which is why we Russians will be left standing when America has masturbated itself to shreds.

And your Western God! A simpering, whimpering babe in a manger! All things bright and beautiful, all creatures great and small. Give me a break! We Russians have got a God with balls and a beard. Our Russian God scattered His beloved children across eleven time zones of tundra. He left us in thirty degrees of frost, with His snow drifting to the roofs of our huts, smoke from the hearth stinging our lungs and our eyes, and His wolves howling at us out of His dark woods. He commanded us to break our backs pushing ploughs and grubbing potatoes from His knee-deep mud. He blighted our crops so that we would be grateful for His berries and mushrooms, blessed be His name. Like all my Russian brothers and sisters, I have heard God's message to humankind: "Life's a bitch and then you die!"

So, dear Europe and dear America, we will bury you.

I know what nouveau riche bad taste is; I'm from St Petersburg, for God's sake. Lundscum's room in the Mayflower Hotel could have been the boudoir of any oil oligarch's trophy wife: gold-framed mirrors, gold brocade curtains, gold carpet so thick that the heels of my Jimmy Choos left dents, gold scatter cushions inviting you to the bed, and in the corridor, the ultimate in ostentatious North American elitist luxury: a Caucasian housekeeper.

Lundscum let me into his room. "Hey, Alisa. How ya doing?" he purred, perusing my slender legs and long, lithe body up and down. While we shake hands, he stares into my lovely, limpid Slavonic-blue eyes. He waves me onto the sofa.

I size Lundscum up in return: pressed white shirt with the top two buttons undone and a few grey curls peeping out; a Republican head of hair - thick, greying at the temples and chemically lustrous; shirt sleeves crisply folded to his elbows as proof that he was prepared to labour alongside the hard-working middle class; luxurious, leather-soled, biscuit-brown handmade brogues as reassurance that he wouldn't have to. Everything about him radiated superficiality, ego, arrogance, hunger for power, artifice and cunning. Totally my type.

In the far corner of the room, above the holographic log fire, there is a large TV screen flashing red and blue. It's Tox News. The volume is turned down, so I can hear noise but no words. In the Siberian taiga you have the whistle of the wind in the pines. On the Black Sea shore, you have the rattle of the surf on shingle and the screech of the gulls. On Nevsky

Prospekt you have the midnight hum of the taxis. But the soundtrack of America is the crazed muttering from a million television screens of an angry man with bouffant hair and a shiny face the colour of raspberry milkshake.

"Hey, Mackenzie! Happy snappy time, right? A photo of Alisa and me and then off you go, OK?"

A sulky girl with bad skin emerges from the corner of the hotel room, a thousand-buck Nikon SLR in her porky hands. Lundscum sits beside me on the couch, grasps my hand a little too tightly and flashes his shiny Republican teeth while his bag-carrier Mackenzie snaps away angrily. I guessed what was up with Mackenzie.

"Whoa, girl! That's enough, Mack!" Lundscum keeps his eyes on me, more specifically on my chest, while he waves this petulant Friesian away. This Mackenzie, she's already starting a double chin. Her calves are lumpen, and her doughy ankles are swelling out of the tops of her shoes. "Sorry, honey," thinks I. "If you wanna sulk like a Russian babe, you gotta look like a Russian babe. While I was fuelling my adolescence with black rye, beetroot soup and vodka, you were putting away those milk shakes and fries. What goes around, honey, comes around."

"Now then, Alisa? Whaddya say? Shall we get to know each other?" Lundscum pulls a chair up too close, spins it around and sits with the chair-back clasped between his thighs. I bend my deep red lips into a slow smile, run my hand through my lustrous blonde hair, recross my legs and bite the end of my Cross brushed steel pen. Let the games begin.

I'll spare you the interview and what followed. They were both tediously predictable. But don't worry. You're soon going to see my genius.

When it's over, I tell Lundscum I need to freshen up in the bathroom. Once I've locked the door, I spit a generous portion of Lundscum's DNA into the standard issue FSB specimen jar. I drop the jar into my bag, run the faucets for a few seconds and flush the toilet.

When I return to Lundscum, he doesn't even turn to face me. But no problem. He's a guy. He's pointing the remote at the television and turning up the volume.

Tox News is running a split screen. On the left, the man with the flabby throat is having apoplexy. On the right there is a still photograph of an oval face. I think it's a man's face, even though there are no corners at the jaw or cheekbones. A Humpty-Dumptyish face. Like a hard-boiled egg with a mat of hair resting flatly on top. I vaguely remember this face from the immigration queue at Newark Airport.

In a few seconds my genius will kick in. Be patient.

The flabby-throated gentleman is ranting. "I mean, what did she expect? Did she think she was entitled to enter America on false pretences? She's a woman. She was born a woman. It says on her birth certificate that she's a woman. And more to the point, it says in her uterus and her double-X chromosomes that she's a woman. And her passport says she's a female called Mikhaila Krutova."

Mikhaila Krutova! The egg face is my half-sister! I've found her. It was so simple. But of course. This is America, where craziness floats to the top. So why not?

The TV keeps haranguing us. "But this woman Mikhaila Krutoy has the audacity to declare to a federal officer that she is a man, and that her name is not Mikhaila Krutova but Mikhail Krutoy. So, suddenly the whole liberal world loses its shit. CMM and all the mainstream liberal media are crying out that her human rights are being violated. The liberals believe that anybody can lie to the United States Customs and Border Agency. The liberals believe it's a human rights violation if we don't just wave every perjurer right into America. Well, I've got something to say to you, Mikhaila Krutova and the Democratic Party and the mainstream liberal media. Facts are facts and lies are lies. Science is science and truth is truth. A man is a man, and a woman is a woman. And if you think your liberal views entitle you to say that two and two make six, maybe - like Mikhaila Krutova - America just ain't where you belong."

And now came my moment of genius. Suddenly I knew how to set America on fire.

"Wow! That sure is one hell of a story, Brent. You know what? You should make a campaign statement on Krutova. Rallying the base."

Lundscum rubs his chin. "Hey, that's not such a bad idea."

"Make Krutova into a wedge issue, Brent. Use Krutova to split the Democrats. Force Shaughnessy to comment on Krutova. If Shaughnessy takes Krutova's side, he loses the blacks and the white working class. Believe me. Joe and Bill from Philly, they don't like politicians telling them what their words mean. But if Shaughnessy takes Border Protection's side, he loses the gays and the libtards. Either way, Shaughnessy is screwed four fingers up his liberal ass."

Lundscum is already on his phone. "Hey, Mackenzie, honey! Get back in here! You've got work to do."

"But you have to be quick, Brent. If you don't, someone else will."

Always remember, dear Reader: Vladimir Putin doesn't play chess. He plays judo. In judo you don't have a plan. You have an opponent. In judo, you let your opponent's own momentum trip him up. And when your opponent is the obese, angry, top-heavy, off-balance West, well, frankly, bringing it down is a piece of piss.

"Yeah, yeah, you're right. Jesus, you're right. I bet that cocksucker Ted Cruz is watching Tox right now." Lundscum's frantic. "Hey, Mackenzie!" he yells. "I said I need your ass in here right now." Mackenzie bursts in through the door. "Tell Tox I've got a statement on this Krutova dyke. And tell them I've got to be first or not at all. You got that? First..."

"...or not at all," Mackenzie mutters. Ungrateful cow. Instead of sulking, she should be thankful that I'm doing her job for her.

And that, dear reader, is how I, Nastya, did my bit, a good Russian who doesn't believe in happy endings, to help Americans shred their once-great country into ever-smaller fragments, whilst also providing the Motherland with the Mother of All Kompromats. I take a little curtsey to your applause. Oh, really, you're too kind!

Chapter 26 - Capitol Hill

Shaun Shaughnessy gazes through the frost-glazed window of his cabin. It is early afternoon, but the wind-torn Appalachian winter sky is graphite grey like dusk. The distant silhouette of the Grandfather Mountain fades into the monochrome horizon. The trees are whining. One of the cabin's log joints squeals as though in pain or ecstasy. Shaughnessy presses his fingertips to the window and feels its trembling. "It will snow," Shaughnessy says - and now it is indeed snowing.

"The snow will settle," Shaughnessy says. "We will have a real winter again." And great sloppy clods of wet snow are now fastening themselves to the windowpane, layering the hood of his faithful all-electric truck in the driveway and tugging down the boughs of the pine trees. As Shaughnessy watches the snow first plaster the ground and then climb towards the cabin window, he feels a glow of satisfaction. This winter, the first winter of the New Age, is his creation, his life's work.

President Shaun Shaughnessy has beaten Global Warming.

Behind Shaun they gather, tiered in rows like a choir in Madison Square Gardens, the congressmen and congresswomen, the Republicans and Democrats, the bishops, rabbis and imams, the community leaders, the blacks, the Asians (south and east), the LatinXs. Their murmur rises to a chatter, then swells to a roar and finally explodes into a chant of praise, a hymn in gospel harmony to a LatinX beat, whose swaying chords ring out so loud that the cabin itself quakes: "Shaun brings winter! Halleluiah! Our diverse souls rejoice!" Global warming is history. Swoosh: the sea is falling. Crunch: the glaciers are stacking up. Ker-ching: the ski resorts are re-opening. All races, creeds, caucuses and socio-economic profiles are arrayed in a rainbow phalanx behind Shaun Shaughnessy to welcome America into its Golden Age. It's the late 50s again!

"Senator Shaughnessy! Senator! Senator!" a woman's voice was calling, clear and melodious. It silenced the wind and the hymn of praise.

Shaun opened one eye and then the other.

"Senator Shaughnessy! Senator! Senator!" He looked around. This wasn't the New Age. This was his Capitol Hill office and Emily was waving an iPad in front of his nose.

"Sooo sorry for waking you up, Shaun," Emily said with a tone that said, "No, I'm not sorry. I, for one, am doing my job. I am sad and embarrassed, but mostly humiliated. I am from Brown University and my life has taken a wrong turn; I staked my youthful promise on a loser."

Shaughnessy pushed his feet against the side of his desk in to achieve a respectably upright position. His bum made a farting noise as it slid across the dark green Italian full-grain leather. "What's the matter, Emily?"

"We've ... you've got a crisis, Shaun. It's all over social media. There are memes already."

"Memes, huh? Already? Jeepers!" Shaughnessy tried to look worried. What was a meme? "Going ... er ... viral, eh, is it? Tell me more."

"There's a woman ... I mean, there's a man. Definitely a man. Mikhail Krutoy..."

At the end of Emily's breathless exposition, Shaun was still perplexed. "And what has this to do with me?"

"It's a wedge issue. Lundscum's team has been looking for a chance like this for weeks. It'll cut our demographic right down the middle. If you call him Krutoy, you're going to lose the working class. If you call her Krutova, you're going to lose the college-educated liberals and the LGBT pluses.

LGBT pluses? Was that a kind of sandwich?

"Listen," Emily raced on. "It's all here on Twitter. You've got Tacogirl513."

"Taco...who?"

"We're not exactly sure who she is, but she's got over a million followers. LatinaXes. LGBTQ plus pluses. Practically all of them in the top quartile by social media reach and engagement."

"And this means?"

Emily clenched her iPad in frustration. "Shaun, it's simple. You lose Tacogirl513 and her social media cluster, you lose eight percent. And Tacogirl's calling on you to make a statement. Listen: 'Yo, Shaun Shaughnessy! Time to call out institutional transphobia on Krutoy. What U waiting 4? Prove you ain't SWM-slash-WMP.'

"SW...?"

"Single white male slash white male privilege, Shaun."

"OK, Emily, so I'll make a statement on institutional transmacallit. It doesn't cost me anything."

"But it's not so simple, Shaun" Emily groaned. "Here's another tweet from orneryjoe18."

"Who in the name of...?"

"No, we don't know who he is either. Linguistic meta-analysis of his tweets indicates that he's either from Pennsylvania or Georgia. Anyway, the point is that he's very popular among white working-class independents. Over a million followers. You lose orneryjoe and you lose another eight percent."

"And what does Joe say?"

Emily read from her iPad. "Hashtag Shaughnessys Washington libtards going nuts 4 Krutova WOMAN. Totally out of touch again with hardworking middle class hardworking Americans. #krutovanotkrutoy. #peoplewhomenstruate".

"So basically, I'm damned if I do and I'm damned if I don't."

Emily was talking faster and faster. "I've got a mole in Tox News. Lundscum's just arrived in their DC studio and he's in make-up right now." She looked at her Fitbit health tracker watch. "He's going on air in twenty."

"Oh, that little shit!" Shaughnessy was sitting up now.

"We're a hundred percent certain that Lundscum's going to talk about Krutoy. He won't miss a break like this. He's going to say that Krutoy is Krutova. He's going to say that US Border did the right thing refusing him entry, and then he's going to challenge you to agree or disagree. And whatever you do," Emily wailed, "you lose eight percent!"

"Emily, Emily! Calm down. I'll just say what I think. Americans are reasonable. Americans are always ready to hear sincerity and common sense. A politician who speaks from the heart. A politician who cuts through the spin and the, er, memes and gives a straight answer to a straight question."

"But, er, Shaun - what <u>do</u> you think? Krutoy or Krutova?"

"Erm ... what <u>do</u> I think? What do <u>I</u> think? What - do - I - think?" Shaughnessy frowned. "Erm, Emily ... what do you think I think? Or, to put it more precisely, what should I think?"

Emily pursed her lips. "There's nothing else for it, Shaun. We need to pivot."

"Pivot?"

Emily sighed. "Block and bridge, Shaun."

Pivot? Block and bridge? Was this a game of Twister?

"When they ask you about Krutoy-Krutova, you just change the subject."

"But people hate politicians when we dodge the question. I don't want to be that kind of asshole. I'm Shaun Shaughnessy, the ordinary Joe from the MD burbs. I'm the guy with five o'clock shadow who looks straight at the camera and tells it how it is."

Emily was shaking her head.

"OK, OK," Sean murmured. "Let's block and twist. Or whatever. He who fights and runs away, lives to fight another day. That's Tacitus, Emily."

Emily wasn't listening. She was already muttering to herself. "Pivot to religion? No. No God after 9pm. The border wall? No, it's too soon since Trump's head exploded. There's still residual sympathy. Oh, well – there's always the default pivot."

"What?"

"The race card, Shaun, obviously."

Shaughnessy frowned. "But, Emily ... but ... but what has Krutoy got to do with race?"

"For God's sake, Shaun. This is America. Everything, everywhere is always about race. Or can be. If you want it enough. It's just a question of finding the angle. And that's what I'm for." Emily did a little shimmy. "Look!" Beaming with pride, Emily thrust her ipad under the senator's nose. "What do you see, Shaun?"

The senator saw a screenshot of a CMM news report. The strapline said, 'Customs and Border Agency accused of transphobia.' The picture was of a smooth ovoid face, with dark brown hair that looked as though it had been pasted on top. It was captioned 'Mikhail Krutoy - stranded in Newark Limbo'. The pink elliptical head. The worried frown. For some reason they made Shaughnessy think of Humpty Dumpty.

"I don't get it, Emily. What am I supposed to be looking at?"

"Can't you see? His nose."

"It looks like ... a nose. Am I missing something?"

"Oh, God. Do I have to spell it out? He's one quarter African!" Emily said in an exasperated whisper, even though there were only the two of them in the room.

"You saw that he's African yourself?" Shaughnessy asked in puzzlement. He held the iPad close to his eyes and then at arms' length. "I'm not seeing it. Does that mean I'm race blind?"

"Shhh. We don't say those words, remember."

"But if she doesn't look black, how do you...?"

"Well, actually, I read it in RT International."

"Russia Today? Russia? The Russians? Do we really get our intel from the ...?

"Shhh. Here it is." Emily cut him short. She swiped onto another browser tab and passed the tablet to her boss. "Here. It's the article by RT's special correspondent in Washington. Alisa something."

Shaughnessy read aloud. "In what appears to be the beginnings of a major scandal that will shake the US Presidential election campaign, Russian citizen Mikhaila Krutova was denied entry to the United States Bla bla bla. Currently stranded in Newark Airport... Forced to survive on American fast food... Bla bla bla. Transgender activists have called upon Democratic frontrunner ....egregious act of transphobia. Bla bla bla. Here we are: according to RT analysts, Krutova's story follows the familiar pattern of the targeted exclusion of racial minorities. Krutova's mother was half African, and highly placed sources believe this may have been why the Customs and Border Agency refused her entry. The United States...hypocrisy on human rights...Rodney King... Third World conditions... Legacy of slavery ... Jim Crow... Race riots."

"But Emily!" the senator whined. "He doesn't even look ..."

"His appearance doesn't matter," Emily snapped. "For God's sake, Shaun. Krutoy's race isn't what he looks like. Race is the historical legacy. Have you forgotten about Jemima Kroger already?"

Shaughnessy sagged back into his chair. "I think I may have forgotten."

"Jemima Kroger. AKA Jemmie la Bombalera. AKA, 'an unrepentant and unreformed child of the 'hood.' Jemima's own words, Shaun. Puerto Rican. Associate Professor of History at George Washington University. *Que viva Puerto Rico libre!* says Jemima Kroger. *I'm fully committed to dismantling US imperialism. I'm out of the Bronx. Organizing against the police since I was born.*" Emily drew a long breath. "But Jemmie was a fake, Shaun. She was a middle-class Jew from Kansas City. She looked black, if you wanted it enough. People thought she was black. But she wasn't black because she didn't have the historical legacy, you see. Mikhail, on the other hand, he doesn't look black but he's got the legacy. So, he is black, You see now?"

"Well..."

"For God's sake, Shaun. Do I have to spell it out? Aren't you Irish every time you go to Boston, and Catholic every time you go to New Mexico, and old every time you're at an AARP conference, and doesn't that make you a victim everywhere you go?"

"Hmm. I guess so. So - this Jemima Kroger can't choose to be black because she was born Jewish?"

"Damn right she can't. It's cultural appropriation. It's whitesplaining."

"But Mikhail Krutoy can choose to be a man even if he was born a girl? It's OK."

"Exactly."

"And everybody's fine with this. I mean, on our side?"

"Yes."

Shaughnessy looked up from the tablet screen and slapped his thighs. Thank God for Emily. One day somebody would write down all these new rules and he'd get the audiobook and listen to it on long journeys. Why not? He'd done the catechism when he was a kid, and these millennial inquisitors couldn't be tougher than their role models back in sixteenth century Spain.

Love your neighbour as yourself. That was a principle. Turn the other cheek. That was a principle.

328

All suffering comes from attachment. That was a principle. (These Buddhists, they sure know a thing or two, hey?) There is only one God, and Mohamed is his prophet. That was a principle. Well, you might not agree with the Muslims, but at least they didn't mince words.

But with this new catechism - if you wanted to save your skin you had to be like Alice in Wonderland and believe a dozen impossible things before breakfast.

You were fiercely convinced that harming children was bad, and you also howled in righteous fury at anyone who felt queasy about killing an unborn child.

You told the feminists, in an upward cadence of virtuous passion, that gender was made by society, not innate, and then you turned around and told the LGBT pluses, in a downward cadence of melancholic sympathy, that gender was innate and society had nothing to say about it. But don't overdo the sympathy, for God's sake, or you're appropriating the LGBT+ experience.

The right to free speech was inviolable and the very essence of what it means to be an American. But only up to a point, obviously.

Discrimination based on race was an abomination, the abomination of abominations, the sin against the Holy Ghost. People should be judged by their ability, obviously. For God's sake, did we still have to say that in 2019? But, having said that, the next judge on the Supreme Court bench must be a Latina.

Women and men are the same (we hold this truth to be self-evident) and the other eternal truth, in the next sentence, is that women make better managers, investors, parents, friends and politicians.

You respect the holistic values of the Shawnee, the family values of the Mexican and the work ethic of the Chicago striver, and then you pout virtuously at the vile racist who makes a generalisation, a *stereotype*, about the culture of any ethnic group.

Hmmm. Sigh. There wouldn't be an audiobook, would there? Nobody could write down the rules because, the moment you tried to put the rules all in one place, people would notice that the rules were all contradicting each other. Damn. Being a Good Person these days was like getting near the end of a Sudoku and discovering that you can't make the numbers add up.

He sighed. "OK, Emily. I know the drill - what I have to say to the media. Back to work, I guess. But just tell me one thing, Emily? When you study political science these days, is there a module on what to do when you're sick and tired of the whole shebang?" All those political theorists whom his port-addled brains had devoured in the wood panelled libraries of Oxford.

Your man Plato. Your man Montesquieu. Your man Karl. Every one of them had skipped over the big kahuna: "I mean, isn't that the main question in politics, Emily - why the hell bother?"

But Emily didn't hear him. She was on the phone to CMM.

Chapter 27 – WhatsApp (with end-to-end encryption)

"Hey, hey, hey! Mikhail, my friend. You in trouble."

Mikhail woke up from a dream about Sudoku. There were too many equations and not enough variables. He couldn't make the numbers add up.

He lifted his eye shade and winced at the fluorescent lighting. Jesus was waving Mikhail's smartphone in his face. The screen said, "Metropolitan Police Streatham."

Mikhail took the phone and Jesus returned to his big yellow cleaning machine. It was two in the morning. Outside on the airport apron, a United Airlines plane, bejewelled with flashing lights, was pulling regally into its berth.

"Hello. Is that Mikhail Krutoy?"

Mikhail thought for a moment. "Er...Yes, yes, it is. It definitely is."

"This is PC Cook. As you may remember, I attended a call to your address regarding an incident of alleged hate speech."

The ensuing conversation confirmed Mikhail's understanding of disagreements: when people stopped arguing, it was not because they had changed their opinions; it was because they had loosened the meaning of words.

"Yes, I remember you," Mikhail said. "Your shoes looked comfortable."

"Er, yes. I am asking you to help us with certain enquiries regarding the display of written material at your abode with intent to cause racial hatred. At the moment you are not being charged. I should warn you, however, that, on the basis of the evidence, we would like to question you with regard to a possible offence in terms of Section 4a of the 1994 Criminal Justice and Public Order Act."

"Good. I like laws. Also, I will tell you the truth," Mikhail said. "I am bad at lying because I have Archilochus-Hesburger Syndrome. It is not a disease. It is a condition."

"OK. So, sir, did you write a note beginning with the words, "BREXIT IS COMING"?"

"No."

"Well, sir, the author was obviously targeting immigrants, and you were the only British native with access to the property."

"Are you racially profiling me, officer?"

"Oh, very clever, sir."

"In fact, I'm not very clever, officer. My IQ is approximately 110. I may appear smart, but it is an illusion caused by honesty. It is a neurological condition.

"Why do you say that I am a British native? Is it because my country of origin, the USSR, is no longer a foreign country because it no longer exists? Or is it because I am white, which, to some, I am not?"

"Let's make this easy for both of us, shall we sir? Do you know who posted that message on the door?"

Mikhail beamed, happy at last to be able to help. "Oh, yes! That was me! You see, I was on my way to the Russian Embassy, where I was about to apply for a passport because a lady in the Home Office had threatened me with expulsion from the United Kingdom. I needed the Russian passport to visit America - to look for a father so that could have a nationality."

"So you're Russian then, sir?"

"No. As I explained, I am from a country that does not exist. I have no father yet, but my mother was born in the city of Tiraspol, which is either part of Moldova, Transnistria, or the Pridnestrovian Moldavian Republic, depending on your outlook. If you look at Tiraspol from the west, then the city is in Transnistria, because you are looking across the Nistru River. If, however, you look at Tiraspol from the east, then the city is in Pridnestrovie, because it is on the near side of the Dniester River.

"Anyway, officer, when I opened the door onto our courtyard, there was a big thump and there was a man lying there on the ground. He had been bent over, trying to push a sheet of paper under the door, and the door had hit him on the nose. The door is of reinforced construction, due to the high level of criminality in Streatham, and the man appeared to be in considerable discomfort, judging by the way he was swearing in Russian."

"In Russian, sir?"

"Definitely. Then he said to me in a Russian accent, 'Could you please help me? I don't have the code for the *domofon*. Please affix this letter in a visible location inside your *korpus*.'"

"Er, I see." The officer sighed. "And I suppose you didn't read the message before you posted it?"

"Oh, yes, officer. Of course I read it. It was meant for all of us to read."

"So you knew it was material intended to cause racial hatred, then?"

"Oh, yes, officer! I knew that. But I said to myself that nobody would consider me the world's greatest poet for posting a Shakespearean sonnet. So nobody would consider me a racist for posting a hate letter."

"I see... I see... And this man with the bleeding nose, sir. Could you describe him?"

"With great ease, officer. He was either a Russian immigrant who dislikes immigrants or a Russian FSB agent spreading social discord."

PC Cook sighed again. "I'll elevate the case to my superior officer. There may be charges."

"Rules must take their course."

Chapter 28 - The departure lounge of Newark Liberty Airport (EWT), with a boarding pass for Montreal in my Gucci bag

Zdrastvui, dear reader. (I greet you in the second person informal now, since you and I have become *besties* over the last 200 pages.) Yes, it's your Nastya here again - the only bona fide troll in your modest circle of acquaintances. As you would expect, I am where the action is: in the departure lounge of Newark Airport. A *Russia Today* press pass adorns my left boob. I'm crushed up against the crowd barrier by the obese citizenry of the West.

Except you Americans don't call it obesity these days, do you? You call it 'realistic body shape'. 'Body Positivity.' So what are the slender Russian babes like me, then, if we're not realistic? Imaginary? Body Negative? Fantastic? Fantasmic? I'll take fantasmic.

Misha is standing at a lectern. We, the press, the Fifth Estate, the guardians of truth, are gathered around her. On Misha's lectern is an open laptop. Behind her is CMM's greenscreen.

My online creations, tacogirl513, texasranger327 and many like them, have tossed Misha into that tumble-dryer of hysteria called 'the news cycle'. Thanks to the non-stop online jabbering of my cyber-spawn, my half-sister half-brother Misha has been on every TV news bulletin for the last week:

1. First it was the liberals, God bless them, hammering wild digital shrieks into their iPhones at the injustice of Misha being denied entry to the Land of the Free for claiming that she was a man.

2. Then it was the conservatives, reliable as ever, screaming outrage that a specimen of homo sapiens with boobs and a uterus should deny her own womanhood.

3. So, of course Brent Lundscum practically ejaculates his righteous anger all over Tox News. He's moaning orgasmically about the men and women of Customs and Border Protection who put their lives on the line to keep America safe.

4. Next in line, tired old, cheesy old, flakey old Shaun Shaughnessy whines on CMM about the institutional transphobia of the United States Customs and Border Protection Agency. You can tell from his wandering eyes that his heart isn't in it. But what the hell? A liberal whine is a liberal whine.

5. So far, so predictable. But Phase 5 took even me by surprise.

Misha, my half-sister, is dressed as a man. Her egg-like head wears her lank black hair in a greasy parting. She is perspiring under the studio lights because someone has put her in a navy blue polyester suit.

You wouldn't notice Misha's breasts unless you already knew they were there. Most American men have man-boobs anyway, so the gender of Misha's chest is in the eye of the beholder. They are not the Platonic ideal form of woman-boobs. They are Aristotelean man-boobs.

Anyway, I digress.

In front of Misha are the two cameras labelled CMM and Tox News. That's what you call 'balance' in the west: naivety on one side and lies on the other.

CMM and Tox have converted a Hudsons News Store into their control room. Cable-strewn consoles face the concourse.

Peering into CMM's laptop and twiddling Tox News's joystick, Misha is scanning the Kennedy Center auditorium 300 kilometers away in Washington. In telephoto mode, she only sees humans. But when she presses the '-' key to zoom out, the humans disappear and society appears. By the time the camera hits full wide-angle, the ethno-generational-spatial contours are distinct: the human beings in the Kennedy Center are arranged in strata. As Misha's camera descends from the upper tiers to the orchestra or traverses from the sides to the centre, the black faces thin out while the grey hair, boiled ham faces and sportscoats densify. Misha surmises that the tickets cost more the closer they are to the stage.

There is a discontinuity in the gradation, however, like a fault line on a geological map. In the central segment of the two front rows, the percentage of black and brown faces is markedly higher than that in the overall US population, sports coats and ties were scarcely to be seen, and the numbers of men and women were conspicuously equal. Diversity seating?

My half-sister Misha checks out her avatar on the laptop screen. CMM's lavalier microphone is clipped to her tie. Tox's earpiece is wired down the back of her shirt to the transmitter on her belt.

Misha holds the 'w' key down. Her view swivels anti-clockwise, away from her avatar and onto the stage of the Kennedy Center. She sees the digitized backdrop of stars and stripes and, downstage, two empty lecterns.

Tacogirl513 started it, my Tacogirl of the unshaved armpits and shoulder blade tattoos. As you recall, I was planning to reveal that Tacogirl513 was not in fact a Latina called Roxana but a Jewish princess from Long Island called Rachel Eidelmann. Rachel Eidelmann's father was to own 12 dental practices in

New York and New Jersey. Rachel Eidelmann was to have majored in Eng. Lit. at a colonnaded liberal arts college for women. But Tacogirl's engagement stats are still rising, so she will remain Roxana until the presidential campaign hits peak hysteria. Good things come to those who wait.

To be honest, I wasn't expecting even Americans to fall for Tacogirl513. It was what you yanks call a 'Hail Mary pass' - stupidity retrospectively redefined as heroism. I am intimately familiar with the ruminant Anglo-Saxon, the paranoid Ashkenazi, the godless Scandinavian and the boorish German. The grass-eating liberal and the ear-twitching conservative paid for my apartment in New Holland, St. Petersburg. But even I was amazed by how quickly they amplified Tacogirl513:

"Shaughnessy vs. Lundscum now!!!!! We The People demand a debate on live TV

"Misha Krutoy in the chair.

"Hesburger Kid vs. Spawn of Trump.

"#Hesburgeristruth #bringiton"

Once Gleb had injected a few hundred thousand bucks up the algorithmic ass of the social media, Tacogirl's demand for a debate tore through the internet like a wildfire. First it burned across the hinterland of Twitter and Facebook. Then it swept into the GenX frontierlands of Insta and TikTok.

341

I got a message from Gleb. "For God's sake, Nastya, you're climaxing too soon. Chill, girl!" But I couldn't slow down my wondrous digi-wave. My creation was out of control. Moscow pulled the paid promotion, but the cyber-tsunami was already surging under its own momentum. The whole liberal tribe was shrieking online for a debate between Shaughnessy and Lundscum - to be moderated by Misha.

"OMG!!!!", thought I. "The conservatives have to jump now. If the debate is just a Democrat thing, then Lundscum won't bite."

So I mobilised my army of bigots. Not just my frontliners like texasranger327 and orneryjoe18, but my reservists, my cadets, my rejects and my retirees. I was General Kutuzov at Austerlitz.

I called up my righteous Baptists, my semen-leaking incels, my proud-2b-karens, my Floridian pensioners, my Annapolis midshipmen, my Proud Boys, my soccer moms and my closet gay catholics. I called for back-up from Moscow and my colleagues delivered. Yuri lent me his Friends of Israel. Natasha lent me her cryptocurrency tipsters. Pasha lent me his Farmers' Wives For Trump. My virtual battalions marched and counter-marched, posting, cross-posting, commenting, up-voting, liking and sharing across the golden plains of North America. Within a week the conservative metaverse was aflame with calls for Misha to chair a debate between Shaughnessy and Lundscum. Oh, yes! I am good.

And then Brent Lundscum tweeted those five magic words:

"Hey, Shaun - BRING. IT. ON."

And then I knew. I'd brought off the most epic trollery since the Protocols of the Elders of Zion. Bigger than Hillary's Benghazi emails. Way bigger than Donald's pee pee party. I had rammed a stick of semtex up the ass of the goddam Statue of Liberty!

At my bidding, a cross-dresser with a neurological condition, boobs and a blue suit was going to dismantle western liberalism and western conservatism on prime-time live TV. Mikhaila Krutova, thanks to me, was going to demolish the Jenga towers of chop-logic, tantrums and posturing that you Americans call politics. And afterwards there would be nothing left but the shrieking, grunting and howling, as you westerners tear each other apart with the animal hatred of toddlers in a ball-pit: blacks and whites, rich and poor, men and women, north and south...

And then ... and then... and then ... when all the eyes of America are on my quadroon half-sister, I am going to whisper her father's name into her ear. And then Misha, because she's got Archilochus-Hesburger Syndrome, will announce on live TV that either

Shaughnessy or Lundscum knocked up an under-age, mixed-race Soviet girl – our mother.

America will pull itself apart.

And I will be the Troll Queen.

BOW DOWN TO THE TROLL QUEEN!

Now, if I may crave your indulgence for a brief detour through the byways of your western culture...

***

I realise, dear Westerner, that you have certain expectations of a story; you expect the good to end happily and the bad unhappily. But this is a Russian story, so the good will end unhappily. (Maybe the bad will too, but that's by-the-by.)

So, this story is not what you like.

But you do like burritos. When you order a burrito, first you choose a carb (white rice for Republicans, brown for Democrats). Then you choose a protein (chicken, pork, beef or, God help us, tofu). Then you decide whether to pay an extra $2.70 plus tax for guacamole. It's the western way.

So I'm going to let you choose your own story, burrito-style, as follows:

First, dear reader, please select one of your two basic plots: (A) the liberal plot and (B) the conservative plot.

The liberal plot is where your protagonist has a hard time because she is (Ai) female, or (Aii) not of western European origin, (Aiii) poor, (Aiv) sexually different, (Av) new to the place (Avi), raised by a psychotic mother, or (Avii) extra-terrestrial. For the first two-thirds of the liberal story, the protagonist gets roughed about. Then s/he has the epiphany: Fairy Godmother, gay kiss, sunset by seashore, lottery win, affirming friend, white saviour - you get to choose. After the epiphany, for the final third of the story, s/he gets her shit together. Roll the credits. That's your option A, the liberal plot. Simple, huh?

And the conservative plot, Option B, is even simpler. First you choose your villain from the following categories: (Bi) females / shemales (Bii) Russians / Muslims (Biii) poor people (Biv) sexual deviants (Bv) new arrivals (Bvi) psychos (Bvii) extraterrestrials. Or you could have a twofer villain, for example a sexually deviant Russian; that's intersectionality. For the first nine-tenths of the story, the sexually deviant Russian knocks the shit out of the American. Then the American knocks the shit out of the Russian. That's the conservative plot.

There you have them: your two western stories. Now we can return to our Slavic story, the Tale of Mikhaila Krutova from Pridnestrovie.

***

Look now! They're counting Misha in. *You're live in 5-4-3-2-1.* There's a breathless hush in Newark

345

Liberty International Airport. There's a breathless hush in the Kennedy Center.

***

CMM	And now, coming to you live from our nation's capital ...
Tox	... and from Terminal C at Newark International Airport, Tox News ...
CMM	... and CMM ...
Tox	... bring you the pre-presidential debate between Governor Brent Lundscum ...
CMM	... and Senator Shaun Shaughnessy. To be moderated by Mikhaila Krutova.
Tox	To be moderated by Mikhail Krutoy.

(Long pause)

Tox	*Miss* Krutova. Over to you.
Misha	Oh, right. [Taps microphone] Three, two, one, testing. Can you hear me?
CMM	We hear you loud and clear, *Mister* Krutoy.
Misha	Hello. Do you want the rules? There must be rules. Here are the rules. I will ask one of you a question, and then I will keep asking questions until I understand what you mean. I have got Archilochus-Hesburger Syndrome. It is not an illness; it is a condition. It means that I want to

346

keep asking questions until things make sense. Is that OK?

Shaughnessy OK by me, Mikhail.

Lundscum Aye aye, cap'n! [Gives a knowing smile to the live camera]

Misha That's good, then. Question number one is for Governor Lundscum. Here comes question number one: is it ok for me to say that I am a man?

Lundscum Ha ha. How did I know that question was coming my way? Ha ha. Well, where I come from, if a person is born with two X chromosomes and a uterus, we simple folk call that person a woman. I have profound respect for transex ... transgen ... respect for people who want to change their, yeah, but that doesn't make a man into a woman and it doesn't make a woman into a man. That's how I see it. And you know what? I'll bet that's how the ordinary, hardworking, middle-class people on Main Street America see it too.

Misha Thank you. That was a good answer.

Lundscum Well, *ma'am*, you're most welcome.

Misha I mean it was a good answer to another question. But not a good answer to the actual question which I asked.

Lundscum	I beg your pardon, but I ...
Misha	[waves hand exasperated] No, no, no! It's a bad start. I knew it would be like this. That's why I said I didn't want to be a moderator. Already they're confusing things and making me upset. Somebody with Archilochus-Hesburger Syndrome should not have to listen to politicians.
Lundscum	I beg your pardon, but I ...
Misha	And don't keep saying, "I beg your pardon." You do not want my pardon. It is therefore passive aggression. Listen carefully, please. I didn't ask, "Am I a man?" I didn't ask, "Do you say that I am a man?" I asked, and I was very specific, and these were my exact words: "Is it OK *for me to say* that I am a man?" For me to say. For me to say.
Lundscum	[his smile freezes and his eyes turn skywards for guidance from the Lord, but God and his spin doctor are not to be found.] No, with the greatest respect, it's not OK for someone to say they're a man if they're not a man. I mean, we have teens in high-school locker-rooms, teens who just want to strip off their athletic

348

clothing, innocent naked teens in showers, who …

Misha   It's OK. I see. So basically, you're saying that you have ownership and control over a word. You get to decide what the word 'man' means.

Lundscum No, I'm just saying that a man doesn't have a uterus and a woman does.

Misha   Says who?

Lundscum Says pretty much everybody.

Misha   Thank you. At last. Finally, we're getting somewhere. So, what you're saying is that if pretty much everyone thinks that the word spelt M-A-N means a person born without a uterus, then that's what the word spelt M-A-N means.

Lundscum [smirks] Yup, that's pretty much it.

Misha   So a word is defined by the majority opinion?

Lundscum That's what we Americans call democracy! [Scans the audience for a round of applause, and receives it.]

Misha   So if you had a location, let's say Islington, which is in north London, where most people said that a man can have a uterus, then they get to define the word M-A-N for Islington, right? After all, they are the majority in Islington. Or, if I'm here in the departures lounge of Terminal C in Newark Airport on my own at night, do I get to define every word in the English language all by myself because I'm the majority in this corner of the departures lounge of Terminal C? But if my very good friend Hay-zus comes around with his floor cleaner and we disagree on the definition of a word, then there's a 50:50 split. It's a dead tie. Then who's the majority? Does a man lose its meaning at an intersection of time and place when and where people do not agree on its meaning?

Lundscum [smiles conspiratorially at the audience] I'm sure the hard-working people of America don't want to watch us, may I say *childishly*, bickering over the meaning of words.

Misha I hurt when words change their meanings. I've got Archilochus-Hesburger Syndrome. It's a condition, not a disease. Anyway, you started the bickering.

Lundscum [chortles anxiously] I don't think I did.

Misha You said that it's not OK for somcone to say that they're a M-A-N if they're not a

M-A-N. So you were bickering over the meaning of a word.

[An uncomfortable pause. The audience shuffles. Chairs squeak. Lundscum looks around.]

Misha   [jerks to attention] There are rules in this debate. There must be rules. I oversee the rules. According to the rules, I am now going to ask Senator Shaughnessy the same question. Senator, is it OK for me to say that I am a man?

Shaughnessy [smiles at camera 1] You know what, Misha. It's OK with me. You know why? We've got a word for it in America: and that word is Diversity. It's the inalienable right of every human being to define themselves how the heck they want.

Misha   That is very kind of you. Thank you. So, if I, or any Mexican for that matter, want to call myself an American citizen, then that's our inalienable right? Is that a good example of diversity?

Shaughnessy [alarmed] Yes. No. But let's get one thing straight. If I am elected President, I will make sure that our laws on citizenship are enforced to the letter and without prejudice.

Misha	You just said it's everyone's inalienable right to define themselves how they want. You said it. You said it. My buddy Haysus and I can define the word 'American' just like we can define the word M-A-N.
Shaughnessy	Well, we gotta be reasonable. Most people in the world wouldn't say that the word American applies to you. Sorry, but no way.
Misha	Ah! Thank you thank you. Most people in the world! So, you're agreeing with Governor Lundscum, then? A word is defined by what the majority thinks it means. That is good. We have a consensus. I feel better. You and Governor Lundscum both believe that someone with a uterus is not a M-A-N because most people do not define the word M-A-N to include people with uteruses. Now I can relax.
Shaughnessy	[extremely alarmed] No, no, no. I don't mean that at all. Trans men are men. Trans women are women. It's pure transphobia to deny it. There's no room in the 21st century for transphobia.
Misha	[crestfallen] What is transphobia?

Shaughnessy I'm glad you asked that. Now we're hitting the heart of the matter. Transphobia is prejudice against transexual or transgender people. And I'm against it. And if I am elected President . . .

Misha Thank you for being against transphobia. I am against transphobia too. You said that it is pure transphobia to deny that trans men are men, yes?

Shaughnessy I certainly do.

Misha Very good. Now we can achieve clarity. This is how we shall achieve clarity: we shall refer to the natural world. A tomato is a fruit, not a vegetable. So, if I say that a tomato is a vegetable instead of a fruit, does that mean that I have prejudice against tomatoes? If I say that a whale is a fish instead of a mammal, does that mean that I have prejudice against whales? If I say that a spider is an insect instead of an arachnid, does that mean that I have prejudice against spiders?

Shaughnessy Obviously not. That is ridiculous. They're not the same cases at all.

Misha Why?

Shaughnessy Well, for one thing, like I said, I guess it's about human rights. A human being has

	the right to define the words that apply to them.
Misha	So Hay-sus and I are Americans? And whatever Vladimir Putin says is true if he says it is true? And President Donald Trump was the victim of a witch hunt because he said so? I am trying to make sense of this.
Lundscum	Hey, you know what, Misha? You've been asking all the questions [rolls eyes at the camera] making us both look like a pair of stooges. How about you tell us what you think? Do you think it's OK for you to say that you are a man?
Misha	Yes. And, Governor Lundscum, it's also OK for you to say that I am not a man. Any opinion on the meaning of a word is always OK, because a word is just a momentary vibration of the air or a few black lines on a white background. But now we are breaking the rules. I am supposed to be asking questions, not answering questions. Breaking the rules is bad. By the way, Senator Shaughnessy, do you think that transgender people have a harder time than other people?

Shaughnessy Without a doubt. Transgender people often encounter stigmatisation, discriminatization and oppression.

Misha So then you believe that it is OK to encourage transgender people not to want to be transgender people? Because if they decide not to be transgender people, then they will not encounter stigmatisation, discrimination and oppression.

Shaughnessy I vehemently disagree with that proposition. Conversion therapy is abhorrent. Period. And conversion therapy is based upon a fundamental misunderstanding. People don't choose to be transgender. People don't choose their gender identity. Trying to repress or change a person's gender identity is unequivocally wrong. It is damaging to emotional and mental health and a violation of human rights.

Misha Are you just saying that to make me happy?

Shaughnessy Not at all. I am saying it from deep conviction.

Misha [looks at his notes] Deep conviction ... OK. I'm just thinking...Hmmm... I have decided to ask you another question,

Senator Shaughnessy. The rules allow me to ask a follow-up question, meaning a question which is logically consequent from your answer to the previous question. Also, it is me who decides the questions. Not you. That is the rule. Here is the question: Senator Shaughnessy, do you think that different preferences and behaviours are part of the difference between men and women?

Shaughnessy [Scans the audience and juts out his chest] I am deeply convinced that every American has the right to chase their dream, irregardless of their gender, faith, sexual orientation or colour. That's what the word 'America' means.

Misha   Oh, dear! 'Irregardless' is not a word. Are you inventing a new word, Senator? If you are inventing a new word then we will have to agree on its meaning, and that will take time.

Shaughnessy [Presses his earpiece] I meant 'regardless'. Or 'irrespective'.

Misha   Thank you.

Shaughnessy You're welcome.

Misha   But you did not answer my question. Again, you answered a question which I did not ask. That is against the rules. My question was, "Do you think that different preferences and behaviours are part of the difference between men and women?"

Shaughnessy I am deeply convinced that men and women are both born with infinite potential.

Misha That was not my question. I asked: do you think that different preferences and behaviours are part of the difference between men and women? You know: girls hug dolls, boys drive hydraulic diggers, men fart freely, women collect cushions. That kind of thing?

Shaughnessy It's very simple. I want an America where any little girl can look at an astronaut, a surgeon or the President of the United States, and say, "Mom - one day that's gonna be me!" I'm not ashamed to say this: I'm a feminist and a true-blooded American, and, heck, I'm damn proud of it.

[applause from around 50% of the audience]

Misha All right. You are refusing to answer the question. But you do not have to answer the question because I already know what

357

you believe. I can work it out by logic. You just said that people do not choose their gender identity; they discover it. As soon as you use the phrase 'gender identity', you are saying that men and women are born with different preferences and behaviours. That's what 'gender identity' means, isn't it: that a person identifies with the preferences and behaviours of a man or a woman. Or do you have a different meaning of the phrase 'gender identity'?

Shaughnessy [reaches out very slowly and takes a long drink of water] Let's move on.

Misha My next question is also for you, Senator Shaughnessy. You were second in the first round so you shall be first in the second round. My next question is extremely difficult. I am sorry for that, especially as you were unable to answer the previous question. It is about Amber Bowling of Clay County, Kentucky. Have you heard of Amber Bowling?

Shaughnessy [laughs for the camera] I guess I'm about to.

Misha In December 2018 Kentucky State Police arrested Amber Bowling because she murdered her baby when it was two hours old. She put the baby boy in a plastic bag and threw him off a balcony to kill him. Was it OK for her to kill him? This is obviously a very hard question, so you can take time to think.

Shaughnessy [looks perplexed, then sniggers] Well, I don't need to reflect, Mikhail. There is no doubt or equivocation in my mind. What you have just described to me is a heinous crime that deserves to be punished to the full extent of the law. And I think that everyone watching this debate at home will agree with me. [applause]

Misha Thank you, senator. So what is the general principle here? Are you saying that is not OK to kill innocent babies? Take your time.

Shaughnessy Of course, it is definitely not OK to kill innocent babies.

Misha Thank you. That is a clear answer. So you are saying that abortion is not OK?

Shaughnessy [turns to camera] It has always been my firm position, and my voting record confirms it: women have the right to choose. In 2023, we will commemorate the fiftieth anniversary of Roe versus

	Wade, which confirmed that every woman, rich or poor, white or black, has the right to control her own body.
Misha	It did not ask you about the right to choose, but we can continue. So, you are certain that it is wrong to kill people who have not done anything wrong, and at the same time you are certain that it is OK to kill a foetus. So, then you must also be certain that a foetus is not a person. Is that correct?
Shaughnessy	If I could make a point here about the American woman - the American woman deserves ...
Misha	No. You are only allowed to answer my questions. That is a rule. It is important to have rules. In news interviews you are allowed to change the meanings of words and to answer questions that were not asked. But this is not a news interview. It is a Hesburger's debate. So I will repeat my question. You must be certain that a foetus is not a person. Is that correct?
Shaughnessy	OK, OK. Yes, that is correct. A foetus is not a person.
Misha	Thank you. So, if a foetus is not a person, when does it become a person? Does it

change instantaneously from a non-person into a person when its head passes through the birth canal. In other words, does it become human at the precise moment when the cranium moves through the vulva? Or is it the final toe that marks the acquisition of personhood? Or, in the case of a caesarean section, does it become a person when the surgeon lifts the head out of the pelvis? [murmur of disgust from the audience] I am just asking so that I understand. That is the rule of the debate.

Shaughnessy Er... one of those, I guess.

Misha So it was Amber Bowling's constitutionally-protected right to kill her male foetus two hours before its head (or toe) passed through the vulva, but it was a heinous crime for her to kill her baby boy two hours afterwards. Is that correct?

Shaughnessy Er...I guess so. Could I have a glass of water?

Misha Next question. How are you so certain of when a foetus becomes a person?

Shaughnessy [looks straight to camera] Well, you know why I went into politics, Mikhail? My mother. To me, my mother was the greatest goldarn hero in the world. Like millions of hard-working women across America, Margaret Shaughnessy would have done anything for us children. She held down two jobs just to put food on the table for my sisters and me. Every morning, while it was still dark, she would leave our little clapboard house to catch the bus to ...

Misha	Please stop. I did not ask any questions about your mother. If this debate was about whose mother is the best mother, I would tell you about my mother. The same question is for Governor Lundscum. Was it OK for Amber Bowling to kill her baby boy?
Lundscum	Absolutely not.
Misha	Is it wrong to kill people who have done nothing wrong?
Lundscum	Absolutely.
Misha	So are you saying that abortion is not OK?
Lundscum	Abortion is absolutely not OK.
Misha	Why?
Lundscum	Like you said, because a foetus is an innocent human being.

Misha	I did not say that a foetus is a human being. I only asked questions. That is the rule. I have got Archilochus-Hesburger Syndrome. It is a condition, not a disease. Is a sperm cell a person?
Lundscum	Huh - do I have to answer that question? OK. It's a rule. I get it. Hesburgers. Whatever. No, obviously a sperm cell is not a human being. And neither is a human egg, which I assume is going to be your next question.
Misha	But when you put them together, they become a person. Is that correct?
Lundscum	Absolutely.
Misha	Instantly?
Lundscum	Absolutely.
Misha	My next question is like my last question to Senator Shaughnessy: how are you so certain of when a sperm cell and an ovum become a person?
Lundscum	I guess you'd just have to put it down to my deep Christian faith.
Misha	"Deep Christian faith." I cannot disagree with that answer. Because I don't know what it means.
Lundscum	I believe that many decent, hardworking Americans agree with me, Mikhaila.

Misha	I did not say that I agree with you. I said that I cannot disagree with you.
Announcer	We-e-e-e-ell, how about that? We're going to take a short break now to catch our breath. Part 2 of the Hesburger's Debate will continue in 30 minutes on CMM and Tox after the news bulletin. Next up - racism. Don't miss it.

Misha's face is pale and sweaty. She rips the Lavalier microphone from her lapel and runs to her friend Jesus. Jesus takes one look into Misha's panicked eyes, and he knows exactly what Misha wants: he passes Misha her backpack. Misha clutches the backpack to her chest and dashes into the men's bathroom. I don't know what's in that backpack, but Misha is clearly desperate for it.

Anyway, dear reader, I have work to do. It's time for me to let off the shot, to quote Emerson, which will be heard around the world. The envelope is in my hand. Assuming my famously cute smile, I saunter towards Hudson News. Through the plexiglass wall, I see a broadcast director leaning back in his chair, hands clasped behind his head. He won't be relaxed much longer.

I knock on the door. He jumps up to attention when he sees me. I have that effect on men, especially men with tee shirts, acne and technical skills. He opens the door.

"Hey, wow, how can I help you?"

"What's your name?"

"Eric."

"OK, Eric. I suppose your parents gave you a Viking name out of a misplaced pride in their Caucasian heritage. You don't reply? I'm cool with that. So, tell me, Eric - who pays your salary: CMM or Tox News?"

"Tox."

"I know, Eric. And your producer is Danny Caputo. So, you shall now do three things in the following order. First, you shall read the contents of this envelope." I hand it to him. Eric pulls out my paper. The letterhead says, "DNA Paternity Testing USA - only $99." The logo is a double helix against a background of the Stars and Stripes. I can tell from his eye movements that Eric is a slow reader.

"Second, Eric, you shall be astonished."

"Holy crap! I mean - Hectic! Shook! Holy crap!"

"Well done, Eric! And third, my young Aryan, you will now phone your producer and say, 'Holy shit, dude! You've gotta see what I just seen.'" But Eric is already dialling. Like I said: this shot's gonna be heard around the world. God bless America."

Chapter 29 - Back in Macedonian territorial waters, 10th of Boedromion, 378 BC

You know what the water in the pot looks like when you've boiled black beans in it? Yes, that's how the sea was, the grey, sudsy sea upon which the motley crew of the Jolly Flogger were now engaged in dialectic with the Macedonian maritime police. The topic under discussion was whether the aforesaid Macedonian fuzz would (a) let us resume our passage to Corinth and its fragrant temple virgins, or (b) convict us of racism, take us to Macedonia, and crucify me for counterfeiting. The waves were making a sloppy-slappy noise against our hull and the Macedonian captain was tapping his fingers against the exquisitely sharp and curved blade of his kopis. Tense.

I need to prove that we're not racists. And the only thing in my favour is that all Macedonians are dumbass squareheads. And I mean all.

"Sukkot," I say, taking my owner aside. "May I give you some constructive feedback in a safe space? Although I've only been your chattel for a few weeks, and I'm still in my guarantee period, I totally respect you as a slave driver, particularly the way that you empower your junior slaves. With you it's a 'what you see is what you get' leadership style. Every flogging comes with an objective performance appraisal based upon clearly defined key performance metrics. Awesome. Indeed, I see you less as my owner and more as my mentor, and ..."

"Fuck me, Diogenes," says Sukkot. "Why are you sucking up?"

I throw myself onto my belly and kiss his big black flaky toes. "Please don't tell the Macedonians I was a counterfeiter," I whine. "Pleeeeease! I don't deserve to be crucified."

Sukkot jabs a crusty toenail up my left nostril. "It's simple," he growls. "You get me off the racism charge and I won't tell the Macedonians you're a forger. Quid pro quo, as your white-ass Roman cousins might say."

"But that's not logical," I sob. "What good does it do you if I'm crucified for counterfeiting?"

Then Sukkot utters three words that pierce my heart like an ice dagger. "Management by results." I let out a wail of despair. Sukkot squashes the sole of his odorous sandal into my snivelling nose. "Consider yourself incentivised," he hisses. "There's your Key Performance Indicator: prove to these arsewipe, whitebread Macedonian crackers that I'm not a racist, or else you die."

I stagger to my feet and wipe the toe-crud off my nose. Arete of Cyrene runs up and grabs my wrists with a grip worthy of Milo, the legendary wrestler from Croton. She stares straight into my eyes, her moustache twitching with emotion. Her Adam's apple bobs up and down as though she is holding back a sob. "Oh, Diogenes of Sinope," she sighs in her mellifluous baritone. "If the weak and trembling heart of a female can lend you strength in your moment of need, take it. Take it now, for it is yours."

I push her away. "Step back from me, woman!" I cry. "Step back, lest my resolve be weakened by the vapours of your oestrogens." I push back my shoulders, cough, spit a green gob of manly phlegm onto the deck, draw myself up and stride into Ektaktos's personal space.

"O Ektaktos of Macedon!" I cry. Sukkot skips back in astonishment at my booming, virile tones. All the galley slaves lean towards me across their oars, so as not to miss a word of my exposition. Even Aesop falls silent. Arete quivers femininely. The only sound is the slop-slip-slap of waves on the hull. "O, Ektaktos of Macedon, thrice-officious police officer of the wine-dark sea! How do you define 'racism'?"

"That is an easy one, O Diogenes of Sinope," declaims the Macedonian captain. "Racism is any attitude or behaviour that assumes that someone is inferior because of their colour or race."

"OK, Ektaktos of Macedon, let's just park that for a moment. Ektaktos, you are a member of the Macedonian constabulary, are you not? In other words, a rozzer, a bluebottle, the fuzz, a smokey, the po-po, a cop, a bobby?"

"I am indeed a police officer, O Diogenes of Sinope."

"And would it be correct to say, indeed, that you are a rather senior police officer? A captain?"

"I am."

"Hmmmm. And as part of your career development, have you at any time been on cultural awareness training."

"I have. I don't see where this is going."

"You soon will, O Ektaktos of Macedon. And what did you learn from your cultural awareness training?"

"I gained cultural competence, O Diogenes of Sinope."

"And what is cultural competence, O Ektaktos of Macedon?"

"Being 'culturally competent', O Diogenes of Sinope, means having the knowledge and skills to be aware of one's own cultural values and the implications of these for making respectful, reflective and reasoned choices."

Suddenly a voice cries out from the bow of the Jolly Flogger. "Don't go there, Ektaktos!" It's Omphalos the grub-like galley slave, Omphalos, previously known as His Excellency Prince Kalamindar, Admiral of the Macedonian fleet. "Whatever you do, don't say, 'one's own cultural values', Ektaktos. You're throwing the game away."

Ektaktos would have done well to listen to Omphalos. But the captain just shot the galley-slave a dismissive stare. "Commitment to diversity, O Prince Kalamindar, means we understand and accept that everyone is different, that we respect those differences, and that we're open to listen to different points of views and leverage them to learn from each other."

"So, O Ektaktos of Macedon," I cry, "do you maintain that people from different societies have different cultural values?"

"I do, O Diogenes of Sinope. That is the wondrous beauty of diversity."

"Let me run that past you again: are you insisting that a person's beliefs and values are correlated with the social group whence they come?"

"Don't say it!" yells Omphalos.

"I do insist," Ektaktos affirms, "zat a person's beliefs and values are correlated with ethnicity and

370

race. Zat is vy cultural awareness training and cultural competence are essential tools for modern community policing in the fifth century BC." Omphalos groans and facepalms.

This is just too easy. "Tell me, thrice-noble Ektaktos," I cry, "are all beliefs and values equally good?"

"Be not a numpty, O Diogenes of Sinope. How can all beliefs and values be equally good?" Ektaktos puffs out his chest. "Obviously, discipline is <u>better</u> than creativity. Blind obedience is <u>better</u> than freedom. Hard labour is <u>better</u> for the soul than education. Fear is <u>better</u> than love. Men are <u>better</u> leaders than vomen."

I give him one last chance. "Are you absolutely sure that some beliefs and values are better than others?"

"We Macedonians hold these truths to be self-evident," Ektaktos harumphs. Omphalos has slouched onto his oar in despair.

"Well, we Athenians beg to differ," say I. "We Athenians believe that creativity is better than discipline, that freedom is better than blind obedience, that education is better for the soul than hard labour and that love is better than fear."

"And we Cyrenians believe that women can lead as well as men," growls Arete.

"And what do you think of my Athenian values?" I ask Ektaktos.

"I think they're bloody immoral."

"So, O well-born Ektaktos," I say, "if, per your creed of diversity, a person's beliefs and values are correlated with their ethnic origin, and if some beliefs and values are better than others, then does it not follow that the values of people from one ethnic group might be better than the values of people from another ethnic group?"

Ektaktos's face falls. His chest sags. Even the plume on his helmet droops. "Vell, it's a fair cop, and you got me bang to rights," he sighs. "You have conclusively proved, O Diogenes of Sinope, zat disdain for people from other colours or races is not a punishable offence but is in fact a logical corollary of cultural competence and a sense of morality."

"So now what do you say?" I ask.

"You're free to go," Ektaktos mutters. Then he calls to his crew: "Cast off the hawsers! Crew members to your benches. Hoist the mainsail. The Macedonian boarding party shall disembark immediately! We shall make straight for the port of Torone. I shall go to the Commissioner of the Maritime Police and request early retirement on the grounds of a shattered value framework."

"And what else do you say?" asks Arete.

"Sorry," says Ektaktos.

"Oy! What about me?" calls Omphalos. "I'm Prince Kalamindar. I command you to take me home with you to Torone."

"Don't be a vazzock," says Ektaktos. "You're Omphalos the galley slave." Ektaktos leaps across into his own ship. He turns, clicks his heels and salutes. "Sorry to have troubled you, sir," he says, and, with a lusty 'von-two von-two von-two," the Macedonian oarsmen row off into the inky night.

I raise my eyebrows at Sukkot. "You owe me one," I say.

"Don't be a wazzock," Sukkot growls. "You're my slave." He cracks his whip across the back of my head. "I hope you realise that I took a loan out to buy you. Every hour you waste with your philosophical wankery, all this verbal self-gratification with every random honky we meet, is costing me in interest. By the great black Gods Tefnut and Hathor, the sooner I sell you to some poncey Corinthian the better."

And so, with the natural social order restored, the Jolly Flogger and her crew of wazzocks settle down for the night. Tomorrow we set sail for the slave market of Corinth. But we still don't have a helmsman, Sukkot, having sacrificed Palinurus to Poseidon.

The night, though calm, is dark and starless. Aesop chatters away to himself in the gunwales -

something about a crow and a stone. Arete's mellow baritone voice wafts mournful Cyrenian sea shanties through the blackness, which I find highly arousing. I sidle next to her. "You're an epicurean," I say, "so why don't you and I get kinetic together?" Sometimes the classic lines are the best.

"If we did get kinetic, you might have a nasty surprise," she replies. "You betta sublimate yourself, Diogenes."

"What kind of nasty surprise, Arete?"

"If I told you, it wouldn't be a surprise," says Arete. "Enjoy the tautology. Good night, Diogenes." I hear her clambering across the benches to the far end of the ship.

Before long a strong wind rose up. It was a sleepless night for Diogenes of Sinope. When the rosy-fingered dawn finally broke, it was as though all the colours had been washed out of the world. The sea was grey and the sky was greyer.

"Look lively, my hearties," cries Sukkot. "Hoist the mainsail. Westward we shall plough our furrow through the waves! Before the sun sets once more into the wine-dark sea, we shall be in Corinth."

"Look, Sukkot," I protest. "None of us know which way is west, do we? There's no sun."

Sukkot points to port. "Well, the Macedonians headed off that way, so obviously that must be north.

We just do a U-turn. Easy." No sooner said than done, and with the wind swelling at our backs, the Jolly Flogger speeds across the waves to Corinth and my destiny.

Chapter 30 - The Vacation Cottage Express, Newark Liberty Airport

Zdrastvui! Hold on. I'm in my rancid hotel room, and I'm thinking up a simile.

Have you seen those declassified videos of underground nuclear tests? Sometimes I watch them for relaxation, with a glass of chablis. Not those early *atmospheric* nuclear tests. No, not the over-ground bangs. God, they're so mundane. Just one big poof and it's all over. Story of my life.

But an *underground* nuclear test is poetry. It begins with a disappointment - a literal let-down. The ground sags. It slumps. But then suddenly the earth heaves upwards and an expanding, radial earthquake, a ring of leaping rocks, races away from the epicentre. All is shattered. Exquisite.

A neutron bomb? Oh, purleeease, darling! A neutron bomb is hardly a show at all, just a coy little whiff silently wiping out the population. Like a plug-in mosquito killer. How middle-class! And a vacuum bomb, sucking the air out of people's lungs? Kitschy!

No, I am spectacular and subtle at the same time: subtle in my ways, spectacular in my effects. I am an underground nuclear test.

Well, that evening in the transit zone of Newark Liberty Airport, Mother Russia (me) set off two nuclear bombs beneath America. In the three days since then, the expanding shockwave has shaken the foundations of the United States. America will now crumble and fall like the walls of Jericho. Partly thanks to me. (But mostly because the USA was already rotten.)

Three minutes after the commercial break, my half-sister Misha posed her nuclear question: "Governor Brent Lundscum, so if a person's beliefs and values are correlated with their ethnic origin, and if some beliefs and values are better than others, then is it not likely that the values of people from one ethnic group might be better than the values of people from another ethnic group?"

The governor paused for a second, two seconds, three seconds. We journalists in the transit area looked at each other. Would Lunsdcum walk off? Would CMM and Tox News cut to a second commercial break? I watched Eric the producer. His hand hovered over the console, ready to switch the video feed. But the senator looked straight into the camera, and said, "Well, I guess it's logical."

My half-sister Misha turned to Shaun Shaughnessy. "Senator, what about you? Is it not likely that the values of people from one ethnic group might be..."

"I know the question," Shaughnessy snapped. "Let me think." His shoulders sagged. He sweated. We could hear his laboured breaths. "Just give me a moment." He dabbed his forehead with a white handkerchief. He bit his lip. He looked briefly to the sky. "Yes," Senator Shaughnessy mumbled. "It's logical."

And the shockwave hurtled outwards! Through the networks, through the cable channels, the late-night satirists, the mainstream media websites, yea, to the outer reaches, even unto the scream-filled asylum corridors of Twitter and Insta, where Reason flakes off the walls like old paint. Not only the Republican Governor, but even the Democratic Senator had, of their own free will, declared themselves on live network television to be racists.

Youtube crashed. Facebook crashed. Twitter crashed. AT&T and Verizon issued service outage advisories. Twitter's server farm caught fire. Palo Alto had a power cut. The nuclear shockwave hurled up shards of triumph, hate and anxiety as it raced outwards across the western hemisphere.

What is it with you westerners, you and your approval ratings? 36 percent of Americans think that Brent Lundscum's a good ole boy who says it like it is, just like their uncle Walter. Another 36 percent of Americans, on the other hand, rate Brent Lundscum slightly lower than a raccoon turd. So Lundscum has a net approval rating of zero. Meaning neutral, right?

No. A cocktail of sycophancy and loathing. Not neutrality. Frenzy.

Neutral would be the way that we Russians see our leaders. Apart from a few nutters in showbiz or west London, we don't like or dislike our President. We simply acknowledge his existence. He just IS: commanding our lives. He is like the wind in November, the taste of salami or the price of a return ticket to Antalya. He is our context. To approve or disapprove would be silly. It would mean as much as agreeing or disagreeing with the number of legs on a spider. If it didn't have eight legs, it wouldn't be a spider. If our President wasn't our boss, we wouldn't be us.

That's why we shall bury you, dear Americans and Europeans. Our Russian indifference makes us solid. Our fatalism is our strength. Russians shall always stand firm, exactly where we are. For the simple reason that we love to suffer. And if our don't-give-a-fuckness leaves us poor, cold, spotty-faced, greasy-haired, and dressed in 1990s polyester blouses, then ... we are True Russians.

CMM and Tox News wound up the broadcast in haste. After Shaughnessy's mumbled "It's logical", whatever followed would be anticlimax. The reporters scattered; they had their headlines. The LatinX and

African-American *untermenschen* rolled up the cables, dismantled the lighting rigs and crated the consoles under the supervision of Eric the Viking.

My phone was buzzing like a Soviet fridge: three thousand plus Twitter notifications: atoms of enhanced uranium in a pressurised water reactor. Neutrons of anger. I scrolled through them. The chain reaction was underway. Each tweet triggered three more. The USA was freaking out.

I didn't feel any excitement. It was too predictable. Boring.

And one notification from Viber. A message from the Rayon militia in Moscow. They had found my mother dead in her apartment. (I got the details much later; they had discovered her sitting at the kitchen table beside her radio. The neighbour had called the militia to complain that the state news channel had been playing at top volume for two days. Pancreatic cancer. Well, I guess she had the last laugh on me.)

The departure lounge was emptying. I could have left, but I wanted to watch my half-sister Misha for a few minutes. Curiosity, maybe. She somehow seemed shrunken. She was tired, I suppose. As soon as the debate finished, she ripped off her necktie and jacket and slumped into a chair. She ignored the commotion. She was oblivious to the airline passengers who thrust their cellphones into her face for selfies.

"Hey, you leave my friend in peace," called Jesus, the cleaner, but the passengers ignored Jesus and pressed closer around Misha. So Jesus went into his storeroom and came back with some of those retractable tape barriers and yellow 'Wet floor' signs. He fenced off Misha's corner of the departure lounge and the remaining passengers drifted off to their flights.

I watched as Misha pulled the earphones and goggles out of his backpack. The moment she put them over her ears and eyes, her face and body relaxed, like when a baby starts feeding.

There were two TVs on the wall of the departure lounge. I'm not interested in CMM. I'm watching the Tox News screen, and I don't have to wait long. "And now, in breaking news - you remember Misha Krutova, the transgender activist who just got Senator Shaun Shaughnessy, the Democrats' likely presidential candidate, to confess to racism. Well, hold onto your hats, because we're got an even bigger shocker for you. 'What could be bigger than a lib admitting he's a racist on live TV?' you ask. Well, just when you think it can't get any crazier in lib land, it turns out Senator Shaun Shaughnessy is Misha Krutova's father. Yes, you heard that right. Senator Shaun Shaughnessy, who is, I repeat, the front-runner for the Democratic presidential nomination, had sexual relations with an under-age, mixed race, Soviet girl." They show a crappy photo of a teenage girl. She's kinda cute. She ought to be. It's my mother, receiving her chess trophy in Oxford in 1983.

That was my second underground nuclear bomb. There was nothing more for me to see or do. Before leaving the airport, I take one last look at my half-sister. She's lost to the world.

Chapter 31 – An uninhabited islet supposedly west of our previous location, 14th of Boedromion, 378 BC

"You are exhibiting symptoms of hysteria, darling," I reassured Arete the woman. "It is on account of your anatomy."

"I despise you and your stinking heart, Diogenes of Sinope!"

"Calm down, dear. If you stop flapping about and just listen for a moment, you might learn something. Hysteria, Arete, arises in your womb, as is shown by its etymology; the word 'hysteria' is derived from 'ὕςτερα', which is to say your uterus. Your vessel of conception. The peoples of the far East use the word 'ystri' for an unmarried virgin, while the peoples of the far north have a fertility goddess called Yostre. All these uterine words are proof positive that your reproductive apparatus has consigned you to this irrational and excitable state. It's scientifically proven that your womb moves around of its own accord, like an octopus, between your hips, as well as up to your ribs, rightwards to your liver, leftwards to your spleen and downwards into your fanny."

"What gives you the right, a man, in the fourth century BC, to talk about my womb?"

I sighed. "It's all in the writings of the great physician Hippocrates, who learned it from Aesculapius, the god of healing, who got it from Apollo. You can't argue with scrolls and gods, dear."

Sukkot laughed. "Huh! Hark at the white man talking like the big expert!" he sneered. "Hippocrates Schippocrates! Our Nilotic scientists discovered the Wandering Womb while your white-arsed ancestors were still living in trees."

You see, the Jolly Flogger had weighed anchor for the night in the lee of an uninhabited island. I had been fast asleep on my bench, dreaming of the hundred-limbed sacred whores of the Temple of Aphrodite in Corinth, when suddenly, a baritone scream woke me from my innocent slumbers. I sprang up, to see Arete the woman in the blue-black moonlight. She was scrambling over the oar-benches towards Sukkot, Aesop and myself and she looked as though she'd seen a ghost; her eyes were gaping like a Spartan's arse and the bushy, black hair on her arms was standing up like Hercules's pubes. I was strangely aroused.

"A specter!" the woman stammered. "He – I mean she – I mean it - was stark naked. With droopy old-woman tits, and a saggy old-man willy and balls. It was turquoise and translucent like a jellyfish. It shimmered in the darkness and wisps of grey vapour were leaking from its hair and fingers and floating in the air like gossamer."

"Uh-huh," said blind Aesop, nodding like he knew what the hell was going on. "Your visuals mean nothing to me, but I suppose there was an utterance, right?"

"Of course there was an utterance, blind man!" retorted Arete. "The ghost clutched my wrist in its icy fingers and recited a riddle:

"'I came to you from Hades' halls.

'But I was born with a cock and balls.

'Now I have boobs, so riddle-me-ree!

'Will you call me 'he' or 'she'?

'Answer wrong to this my verse,

'And you shall have my mortal curse.'"

"And you got the answer wrong, I suppose," said Aesop.

"How do you know?"

"Everybody gets it wrong. Same old story ever since the Temple of Hera," Aesop laughed. "You have met the ghost of Tiresias, the ΤΕΡΦ of Thebes. There's no right answer, because the answer is whatever the ghost wants it to be. You call the ghost 'he', and the ghost says that it's a sad reflection upon Hellenic so-called civilisation that any psychologically fragile young woman should feel that she needs to justify her gender identity. You call the ghost 'she', and the ghost says

385

you're a misogynist for denying the exclusive right to femininity of biological females. And I suppose you tried arguing with the ghost?" Aesop laughed again. "And then – let me guess – the ghost said that it wasn't transphobic..."

"Yes..."

"And, Arete, then it told you that Lesbians shouldn't be called bigots for not being sexually attracted to hermaphrodites, right? That it's deeply concerned about how a socio-political concept of womanhood is influencing politics and medical practice. It said it's worried about the dangers to young people and the erosion of women's and girl's rights. Am I right?"

"How did you know?"

"You're done for, Arete. You just got cursed by the ΤΕΡΦ of Thebes. You have my sympathy. Very soon you will come to a nasty end."

"TERPH?" Sukkot asked.

Aesop chuckled. "Tiresias of Thebes, the Trans-Exclusionary Revolting Phantom. Let me give you the back-story." He cleared his throat.

"Tiresias of Thebes's mum was the nymph Chariklo and his dad was some shepherd. Never mind his dad; focus on his mum. One day Tiresias accidentally stumbled across Chariklo in the woods. The catch was that Chariklo was bathing in a limpid

386

mountain stream along with Athena, the goddess of olives. Well, back in those days you weren't supposed to see a goddess naked without an invitation. That was before philosophers, when the essence of the Gods' divinity was forbidden knowledge to mortals. Athena therefore quite naturally struck Tiresias blind. So far so inevitable, right?

"But Chariklo, Tiresias's mum, protests to Athena that this punishment is a bit over the top. Athena sees Chariklo's point, so she gives Tiresias a white stick as compensation."

"Just a white stick?" says Sukkot.

"Yeah, but it's a magic white stick. It steers him around, the lucky bastard. Also, Athena gives Tiresias the ability (a) to see the future (b) to live for seven generations and (c) to hang around as a ghost when he's dead. What you lose on the swings, you win on the roundabouts.

"So, Tiresias put his new powers to good use. He set himself up in Thebes as the municipal seer. In this capacity, he advised pretty much all the kings of Thebes. For example, Tiresias warned King Pentheus not to go to Mount Cithaeron, or else a frenzied mob of crazy women would tear him limb from limb. But Pentheus didn't listen, so he got shredded. Then Tiresias warned King Oedipus that he was going to kill his dad and shag his mum. But Oedipus took no notice either, and wham bang he goes."

"Why didn't anyone follow Tiresias's advice?" Arete asked. "I mean, they knew he was the seer, right?"

"Because if they had heeded Tiresias's prophecies, then his prophecies wouldn't have come true - obviously. And that's the thing about Tiresias, as you just discovered: we're always wrong and he's always right. In fact, our being wrong is what makes Tiresias right. Same for Pentheus, Oedipus and you."

"OK. But why is Tiresias a Trans-Exclusionary Revolting Phantom?"

"I was just getting to that. One day, Tiresias accidentally stepped into the Temple of the Goddess Hera, the wife of Almighty Zeus."

"How can it have been 'accidentally'?" Arete said. "Didn't he have his magic white stick?"

"Accidentally on purpose, more like," Sukkot said.

"Maybe his stick wasn't working," said Aesop.

"How could it not be working? It was from an immortal Olympian goddess."

"All right, all right, maybe Tiresias left his magic white stick at home." Aesop sighed. "Anyhoo, when Tiresias was in Hera's temple, he inadvertently saw ..."

"How could he see anything?" Arete interrupted. "He was already blind."

"Who's telling this story?" Aesop snapped. "I dunno. Maybe it was in his mind's eye. The fact is that Tiresias <u>saw</u> two of Hera's sacred snakes shagging on her holy altar. Tiresias whacked the female snake with his stick ..."

"But how, if he ...?"

"... so now Tiresias had to be punished again. Well, Hera couldn't blind him this time, because he was already blind. So she gave him the worst punishment there is: she reassigned him into a woman."

"Whoa!" murmured Sukkot. "Cold."

"Only for seven years."

"But still extreme," Sukkot said. "Hot damn!"

"For seven years, Tiresias served as a priestess for the goddess Hera, she married, she had children, she worked as a sacred prostitute – all the usual girl stuff. Then, on the exact seventh anniversary of her sex reassignment, she whacked the male snake with her stick and Hera reassigned her back into a man."

"Phew!" exclaimed Sukkot. "Lucky for him!"

"Not lucky at all," corrected Aesop. "Tiresias's troubles were far from over, and it was Hera again. This time the Queen of the Immortals was having a row with her husband, Almighty Olympian Zeus, the King of the Gods. Hera was claiming that men enjoyed sex more

389

than women and Zeus said it was the other way around. Obviously, there was only one person on earth who could resolve the argument; they called in Tiresias to adjudicate.

"'So, who enjoys sex more, O Seer of Thebes, men or women?'

"'That's a no-brainer, O Olympian Zeus. Sex is nine times better for women than for men. Not eight. Not ten. Nine.'"

"'That's not the truth,' Hera yelled.

"'It's <u>my</u> truth,' Tiresias replied coolly. 'And on matters of gender my personal truth is always right.'

"And right there, dear friends, Hera struck Tiresias blind."

"But, Tiresias was already..."

"Shut up, woman!" Sukkot, Omphalos and I said. "Let the dude finish his story."

"So that's it," Aesop sighed. "Tiresias of Thebes was shot dead with an arrow by Apollo at the exact age of 175, and now his restless spirit wanders back and forth between earth and Hades, asking mortals riddles about his identity and cursing them if they answer him wrongly."

"When will he stop?" I asked.

"When he gets the right answer."

"And when will that be?"

"Never, because all answers are equally wrong." Aesop gazed sightlessly at Arete. "You, woman – now the curse is upon you."

"What will become of me, O Aesop of Mesembria?"

"How in the name of Hades should I know? Bloody stereotyping. You see a blind guy, and you immediately assume he can foresee the future."

Chapter 32 - Some Aegean shoreline, 15th of Boedromion, 378 BC

Things got worse for Dionysus of Sinope just now. Far worse. Twice.

Sukkot! I'm not gonna lie; he really chose the wrong time to find religion.

After we had bidden farewell to the goose-stepping brassnecks of Macedon and escaped the ectoplasmic clutches of the Trans-Exclusionary Revolting Fantom, a stiff wind rose behind our arses and puffed us briskly across the wine-dark sea. Sukkot was gleeful and so was I. Even with a rabble like Aesop, Omphalos, Arete and me behind the oars, the trip from Piraeus to Corinth should have taken the Jolly Flogger a day or less. But, thanks to Sukkot chucking our helmsman Palinurus overboard in an attempt to placate Poseidon, instead of rowing one day to the west, we had rowed four days to the north, wandered into Macedonian territorial waters and got ourselves charged with piracy, forgery and racism. Anyway, we did a U-turn four days ago, so any time now Cape Sounion should have been rising into view. And then Corinth.

But a fifth day passed. And a sixth. "Sukkot," I said, on the morning of the seventh day, "I think you've got us lost again."

"Silence, slave!" yelled Sukkot. "We're on course. We'd be in Corinth already if you slobs rowed a bit faster." He cracked his whip across my blistered thorax. I decided to shut up.

On the morning of the eighth day the sky finally cleared. And we saw the sun. Ahead of us. Which meant that we were rowing east. Away from Corinth. "You see, Sukkot," I said. "We're adrift."

"Well," Sukkot whined. "It's obvious what happened. I knew it all along. One of you slaves on the port side was slacking off, quietly quitting, and we've therefore deviated from the totally correct course which I established. Hmmm. Someone isn't a team player. And I think I knew who it was. Diogenes of Sinope, you are the free rider."

"It could have been a slave on the starboard side rowing too fast," suggested Omphalos. "Bloody suck-up overachievers!"

"There are no mistakes, only lessons," came a voice from the stern.

"Fuck off, Aesop!" we all roared.

"Well, I know what to do," said Sukkot. "Sometimes the boss just has to follow his gut and take an executive decision." He inhaled deeply. "I hereby promise to Poseidon the Thunderer, the almighty god of the wind and the waves: when we arrive safely in Corinth, I shall sacrifice the philosopher Diogenes, as a thank-offering to Poseidon for bringing the Jolly Flogger safely to its destination."

"Hang on," said Arete, her moustache twitching with anxious care. "If you allow the tender heart of a woman to be heard, let's keep our eyes on the bottom line here. Diogenes is high-value cargo."

"Exactly!" said Sukkot, waving a finger in the air. "This is why I'm the manager, and you numpties are slaves. Diogenes is a premium asset, and that's exactly why Poseidon will steer us safely to Corinth. Suppose I offered him Omphalos? Poseidon would be so insulted with that stick of turd salami, he'd probably blow us around the Med for a month and then get bored and shipwreck us off the Pillars of Hercules." Sukkot tapped the side of his head. "Always think long-term, boys."

"Well, thinking long-term," I said, "none of us have eaten or drunk anything for days. We're not gonna be worth much in Corinth as corpses. And I don't think Poseidon will be impressed by a dead philosopher either."

"Damn!" muttered Sukkot.

But right at that moment Aesop cried out, "Thyme! Oregano! I smell land!" And, sure enough, straight ahead, the limestone crags of some unknown shore were rising above the horizon. "Didn't I tell you we were on course?" shouted Sukkot, slashing his whip to left and to right with gay abandon. "Full speed ahead, me hearties!"

Take it from me: when you've seen one Hellenic coastline, you've seen them all. The mournful call of the gulls. The merciless blaze of the sun. The herb-cupboard fragrances. The sharp underwater rocks waiting to slice your keel to shreds. You get the idea. It's the standard set-up from Ithaca to the Hellespont.

But there was something disturbingly familiar about this particular shoreline. It recalled faraway memories - and not good ones. I just couldn't place them.

Soon a stone breakwater and a bustling port were coming into view. Fishwives, married females of the proletarian orders, kitchen slaves and other riff-raff were haggling over the red snappers and octopuses flapping in baskets on the quayside. A gang of slaves was lining up amphorae in front of a clapboard warehouse, supervised by a white-haired merchant who was scrabbling busily on his abacus. A sharp-eyed pimp was lining up his wares too, no doubt having spotted the first rays of dawn strike the mast of the Jolly Flogger. (Well, wasn't he just in for a disappointment!) The members of a rather laid-back squad of elderly militiamen were variously snoozing, scratching, stretching and yawning in the shade of the warehouse. Yes, this could be any port in the ancient Greek cosmopolis, but somehow the scene was worryingly familiar.

"Right-ho," said Sukkot, as the Jolly Flogger rounded the breakwater and the calls of the πορναί declaiming their price list wafted across the harbour. "We're only here for food and water and then it's off to Corinth. And remember that you're representing your ship, so I want you all on your best behaviour. Most importantly, anywhere beyond the harbour is strictly out of bounds. Diogenes and the wossname – woman - you're with me to carry the shopping. Omphalos, you load the barrels of fresh water."

"Yes, massa."

Well, I must admit it was nice to be back on terra firma, as Arete and I followed Sukkot along the harbour mole with our recyclable hemp shopping bags. We were getting plenty of attention, though. The merchant had forgotten his abacus and was gawping at us. The πορναί suddenly fell silent and their pimp was staring in our direction. "Bloody provincials!" I said to myself. "I suppose they've never seen a black man, a barrel-dwelling philosopher or a woman with a fully-grown beard." I felt a surge of pride that I was from cosmopolitan Athens, the navel of Hellenic civilisation, the fount of western liberal ideals, the ground zero of diversity.

The merchant dropped his abacus and came running towards us. "Friggin' Ada! It's him. I'd recognise that wanker Diogenes a mile off." The pimp likewise rushed up, his arms outstretched to the blue sky. "O great goddess Aphrodite, the lover of smiles, the delayer of old age, the deceiver, the friend of flowers, O great goddess, you have heard my prayers! He has returned!" His πορναί bustled behind him in a gaggle. They were calling and beckoning to the geriatric militiamen, who picked up their rusty spears and cracked shields and ambled in our direction. The fishwives and their customers gathered round, and pretty soon we four were trapped on the mole by a yelling crowd of perfumed πορναί and unwashed citizenry.

"Militia! It's that tosser Diogenes!" cried the merchant, red-faced, clutching his fists and practically spitting with rage.

And then it came to me. Of all the fish markets in all the towns in the world, we'd walked into mine. We were in Sinope. Yeah, Sinope. As in 'Diogenes of Sinope'. My hometown.

"Sinope!" explained Sukkot. He looked embarrassed - and well he might. Sinope is in Asia Minor. Yeah, Asia Minor, as in Asia. The opposite side of the Aegean Sea from Corinth. As far in exactly the wrong direction as we could have possibly sailed.

397

Anyway, let me explain. With the benefit of hindsight, I now realise that I may have rushed over some key details earlier when I was introducing myself. The thing is...

I used to run the Sinope mint, having inherited the position from my dear father. The mint's job was to turn sheets of pure silver into Sinopean currency. Under the sharp-eyed gaze of the city magistrate (aka the Archon), we used to cut the precious metal into portions of exactly one ounce. Then we used to stamp them with a goddess, an eagle or a dolphin or something and, then, tadaa, they were suddenly drachmas. At least, that was how my father did it, the old sucker. He obeyed the laws of Gods and men and he therefore lived off bean stew his whole life.

The goddess Apate made me do it. I had a mate called Linus. He owned Sinope's armoury. He used to buy sheets of tin from Britannia, mix it with copper to make bronze and sell it to me for my economy range of coinage. Well, Apate, the goddess of tricksters, came to me in a dream one night. I couldn't see her directly - only her reflection in a mirror, which was floating and turning in the air like a feather or a wisp of smoke. Apate was stark naked, totally hairless and as pale as milk. Her slender body was curving, stretching and swaying.

Suddenly, Apate metamorphosed into a strip of white metal. It flexed and gyrated in the cold moonlight, and I could hear the wind whistling around its edges. And in my dream her voice called to me sweet and soft: "Diogenes, O Diogenes! What am I? Am I silver? Or am I tin?"

I woke up in a sweat. I knew exactly what this meant. I had just received a direct instruction from the goddess Apate. She was ordering me to replace some of the silver in my drachmas with tin. Yes, Apate is the goddess of deceivers and liars. But Apate is also the assistant of Prometheus, and Prometheus, well, he's the god of molten metal, I thought, so Apate is practically the patron goddess of minters of money. I knew what I had to do. I went against my professional ethics, but who was I to disobey the orders of a divine being, even a down-market D-list goddess like Apate?

You guessed the rest. Business was booming (record profits, customer satisfaction metrics through the roof). The only problem was that I couldn't receive the glory and praise that were due. If the secret of Apate's instructions had got out, confidence in the Sinopean drachma would have collapsed and Sinope's prosperity would have vanished like morning mist. But what could I do? I'd received my orders from a divinity. I was under the orders of a celestial power. It was my sacred duty to replace silver with tin. The personal profit was just an accidental side-effect. Collateral impact.

Until that prick Linus had to spoil everything. He came to the mint one morning and leaned on the counter. "My dear friend, Diogenes," he said, "I was visited in my dreams last night by Nemesis, the goddess of fair distribution."

"I thought it was retribution."

"Redistribution."

"Hmmm," I say. "And how are you so sure it was Nemesis?"

"Because she was measuring my cock with a ruler."

"Fair enough," I said. "And?"

"Nemesis was worried. Stressed out, I'd say. The thrice-feared goddess whispered to me (in my dream) that you'd just installed a marble floor on your house and had two new Circassian horses in your stable. In sublime tones, the deity said that it's very strange that a microenterprise which used to scarcely keep your father in bean soup had now become a veritable profit centre. Nemesis – I quiver at her name - moreover added that your consumption of my tin had mysteriously outstripped your production of bronze coinage. So, to cut a long story short, the goddess strongly believes that you should pay me a thousand drachmas a month plus ten percent of your dividends,

400

with an option to go to 50 percent equity. Sorry, Diogenes. It's not me. It's Nemesis. These goddesses. You can't argue with them."

"Go screw yourself up the bum with an artichoke, Linus."

"Don't you want some time to think about it?"

"I just did. Fuck off." Well, I assumed that Linus would understand that we were in the initial phase of a multi-stage nested negotiation and that 'fuck off' was simply my opening position. I certainly didn't expect that Linus would run off telling tales to Menandros, the city magistrate. I didn't expect that in eight hours I'd be Sinope's Most Wanted, bundling my silver and my dad onto a midnight galley. I didn't expect to be disembarking in Piraeus two weeks later as a stateless refugee, deprived of my basic human rights. But here I am now, back in Sinope. And, as it happened, yes, they still remembered me.

The militia had pushed to the front of the crowd. I had nowhere to run. "It's that tosser Diogenes!" yelled the merchant. "Thanks to him I ended up with a shedload of dodgy drachmas on my balance sheet."

"And my poor girls!" cried the pimp. "Working their asses off 24/7, and paid in tin! In the name of gender equity, I demand justice for my sexually exploited women!"

Then this greybeard with a six-foot staff steps forward. The crowd murmurs, 'Oooh-errr', shuffles back and falls silent. The greybeard strikes the foot of his staff three times on the jetty. "Do you recognise me, O Diogenes the coin-stamper?" he booms.

"Menandros?" I try. "Wow, yes, Menandros. How long has it been, mate? Oh God, I can't believe it." I slap him on the back. "Honestly, you're looking really ... Are you working out? By Aphrodite, buddy, you just get younger and younger. How are Daphne and the kids? I can hardly ..."

"That's Menandros the Wise, Archon of Sinope to you, Diogenes."

"Yes, I remember."

"Well, then you'll also remember that you were condemned to cancellation for debasing the currency."

"Oh, shit. Yeah. Right. OK."

"Guards! To the Place of Cancellation! Take the counterfeiter Diogenes to the *orygma*." In seconds I'm face-down on the jetty with two bloody eyes, and my hands tied behind my back.

Now, in case you didn't know, an *orygma* is an ugly gaping pit, strewn with spiky rocks and surrounded by vertiginous precipices. And before you can say 'joyous homecoming', I'm standing on the brink of Sinope's municipal *orygma*, peering down at the mangled and putrefying corpses cancelled at the bottom, my bowels churning in terror.

"Any last words before we push you off?" calls Menandros.

"If you don't mind, maybe I could just come in here for a moment," says Sukkot. "I don't want to minimise what Diogenes has done. Obviously, I'm absolutely appalled. In my book, counterfeiting is never OK. Totally unacceptable. But, strictly speaking, Diogenes is my property, so I was wondering whether, perhaps..."

"The law is the law!" cried Menandros, waving his staff. "Diogenes the Counterfeiter must be cancelled."

Sukkot steps back. "OK. Like I said, totally unacceptable."

"Guards! On the count of three. One... two..."

"O Menandros the Wise, Archon of Sinope, I prithee hold!" Everyone turns to see the owner of this booming baritone voice.

"Who speaks to us so boldly and so loud?" asks Menandros.

"'Tis I, Arete of Cyrene, seeker of wisdom and devotee of pleasure. Pray tell me, O Menandros of Sinope, of what act is Diogenes accused?"

"He is accused of debasing the silver coinage of Sinope with tin, O Arete of Cyrene."

"And do you insist, O Menandros, that tin is less valuable than silver?"

"I do," says the Archon.

"Aha! I bid the πορναί approach." Arete beckons the whores to come to the front of the crowd. The sluts giggle and look at the ground, as they should, the dirty skanks. "What is your name?" Arete asks the most brazen and shameless slapper.

"Sir, my name is Chlamydia," she replies to Arete, "on account of my pink cloak, sir."

"But she's a woman!" splutters Menandros. "She only exists to give pleasure and ease to men. She has no right to speak in a public space. She cannot testify. She is only partially human."

"That's not what you said last night, love."

"Hrmph." Menandros clutches his staff for reassurance and thumps it thrice on the ground to show who's the patriarch.

"Well, Chlamydia," says Arete, "don't be scared. Just tell us all exactly what happened when the tin drachmas went into circulation."

"Yes, Arete, sir." Chlamydia coughed. "Well, Arete, sir, when the tin drachmas appeared, Sinope entered its Golden Age. Suddenly, the whole city had extra money in its pockets. It was spend, spend, spend. We sex-workers called it trickle-down economics. The taverns were selling fried fish as fast as the fishermen

404

could catch them, and Samian wine as fast as the slaves in the harbour could unload the amphorae. The price of octopus quadrupled; you could only get two tentacles for the price of eight. Fishermen were buying shiny new boats. So the boatbuilders were making a fortune too. All over Sinope you could hear sawing and hammering - the sound of nouveau riche tradesmen building faux-Athenian mansions. The price of a cubic meter of wood went through the roof. The slave sector could hardly cope with the demand from the boatbuilders, tavern-keepers, merchants, builders and fishermen. Slave dealers were doubling their investment from capital gains and stock revaluation alone, never mind their operating margins. It was boom time, and all thanks to Diogenes's tin drachmas. We girls scarcely had time to make our beds and Master Epididymis, our pimp, was never so generous. We nominated him for the Procurer of the Year award from the Asia Minor Chamber of Commerce – and he won!" The whore nods demurely and steps backwards into the crowd.

"Thank you, Chlamydia, my dear," says Arete. "Now, O Menandros the Archon, if the tin coinage led to such prosperity, is not tin therefore more valuable than silver?"

"It appears that tin is indeed more valuable than silver, O Arete of Cyrene."

"And, rather than counterfeiting, has not Diogenes been performing a service to the state - yea, a veritable *quantitative easing*?"

"To coin a phrase," I interjected.

"This hairy alpha male from Cyrene has got a point," says the merchant, nodding so fast that his double chins wobble.

"Those were good times," agreed Epididymis the pimp.

Menandros rubbed his grey beard. "Diogenes has indeed blessed the politeia of Sinope with quantitative easing, O Arete of Cyrene, and Sinope is grateful. As Archon of Sinope, I decree that the cancelling is hereby cancelled."

And no sooner than you could say, 'theory of value', we were back at sea and sailing westward for Corinth. The decks of the Jolly Flogger were laden with amphorae of fine Tyrrhenian wine and Cappadocian corn, a gift from the grateful merchants of Sinope. Chlamydia the slut was with us too, a thankyou present from the pimp to Sukkot. (It was nice to see the two women getting on so well together, Chlamydia playfully tugging Arete's beard or massaging the stiffness out of her thighs.)

And we had some new passengers: six emaciated young men with shaved heads, orange robes and orange umbrellas. They had paid the merchant for a passage from Asia Minor to Athens, which the merchant had subcontracted to Sukkot for a 60 percent commission. Fortunately, one of the travellers, called Siddhartha, could speak a little Greek. Siddhartha explained that they were monks from a country far to the east, even beyond Persia, named Bharata. They were disciples of a holy man called Gautama Buddha. They had heard that in the city of Athens one could find an academy of philosophers (Plato's mob, obvs.) who believed that the world was real, that words had fixed meanings, and that people only lived once. In the land of Bharata everybody knew that the world was an illusion, that words were words, and that people lived many times, so the monks were keen to meet these exotic Europeans with their mysterious occidental spirituality.

Sukkot was more than happy to transport these 'Buddhist' monks to Athens. They would not eat meat or fish, or anything at all after midday, so the cost of catering was minimal. They were polite to the crew and slaves. They would even bow to my little doggie, Chorismos. Siddhartha explained that Chorismos's serenity and optimism when we kicked him were evidence of his noble soul, and that the dog was in all probability the reincarnation of a great holy man. Siddhartha also explained that the monks had to avoid contact with women. But, although they kept as far away from Chlamydia as possible, they seemed to have no problem arm-wrestling with Arete. They always lost.

"Westward ho, me hearties! Hoist the mainsail" roared Sukkot. "O, Prometheus, great God of the seas, mighty Thunderer! Bear us safely to Corinth, and Diogenes of Sinope shall be your burnt offering!"

But one thing we *still* didn't have: a helmsman.

Chapter 33 - Off the Lycian coast, 19th of Boedromion, 378 BC

"Those are definitely Lesbians," I said. "I can spot them a mile off. That means we're lost again, Sukkot. Instead of west, you've taken us due north to Lesbos. And that port you're heading to is therefore Mytilene."

"There's no such thing as mistakes," called a voice from the bow, "only lessons. There were once a tortoise and a hare who decided to run a race, and ..."

"Fuck off, Aesop!" we all shouted.

"Well, it's not OK to say they're Lesbians just by looking at them," Sukkot whined. "Not in 378 BC. That's stereotyping. Moreover, you need to watch your attitude, Diogenes. You ought to remember who's slave and who's master. Or I'll, I'll..."

"You'll what? Sacrifice me to Poseidon?" I asked. Omphalos sniggered. "Oh, for God's sake, see those butch militia types in uniform? Yeah? Just look at what's painted on their shields," I said, waving at the squad of hoplites waiting for us on the quayside. "That pointy letter - it's a lambda. Letter 'L' for Lesbos."

"Ah," sighs Aesop. "Then we're in deep doo-doo. Let me explain.

Aesop coughed and scanned his audience with his sightless eyes. "Not so long ago, the Lesbians revolted against Athens. Then they invited Sparta, Athens's mortal enemy, to send a fleet to protect Lesbos from the inevitable Athenian counterattack. But the Spartan fleet arrived too late, found that the Athenian task force had recaptured Lesbos and sailed straight back to Sparta.

"Back in Athens, the assembly debated how to punish the Lesbians. Not only had they rebelled against Mother Athens, which was a heinous crime in itself. They had also invited the fleet of Athens's greatest enemy into Athenian waters. The assembly voted by a large majority that every adult male Lesbian should be put to death. That's democracy, folks. As soon as the votes were counted, an express galley set sail for Lesbos with the death sentence.

"The next day, Diodotus and some other members of the Athenian assembly realised that they had made a tactical error. What if another Athenian colony rebelled? They would remember what happened to the Lesbians, and fight Athens to the last man, expecting that surrender would only lead to their mass execution. Far better therefore, Diodotus argued, just to execute the ringleaders of the Lesbian revolt. Creon, on the other hand, insisted that the original verdict was correct. 'Laws are laws', said Creon. 'You rebel, you get cancelled.' Well, they debated the whole day and into the evening; and all the while they were speechifying, the express galley was carrying the sentence of execution closer and closer to Lesbos.

"Finally, the Athenian assembly held a revote. Diodotus won by a whisker; instead of sentencing all adult men to death, the assembly condemned only one thousand Lesbians to lose their lives. The Assembly immediately dispatched a second galley, promising its crew a substantial cash bonus if they overtook the first galley and countermanded the original sentence. The rowers laboured around the clock until their hands bled, sleeping in shifts and eating at their oars, and ...

"...well", Aesop continued, this is where the liberal mainstream media start spreading fake news. According to Thucydides, the second galley arrived just as the head of the Athenian task force was reading out the order to annihilate the men of Lesbos. But actually, there was an HR issue. Typical unionised public sector workers. The night shift on the second galley was pissed off because the rowers on the day shift were going to get the same bonus for rowing during normal working hours. Result? They had to park the galley off Cape Sounion while the captain asked the oracle of the Temple of Poseidon to clarify overtime policy. By the time the second ship reached Mykonos, it was too late;

every Lesbian man had been put to death. Lesbos was a female-only island. And it still is."

"Oh, shit!" Sukkot gasps. "So..."

"Exactly," says Aesop. "It's an island of angry women. Galleys make them angry. Athenians make them angry. Men make them angry. And men in Athenian galleys make them triple angry. Here come the arrows."

"Turn around! Turn around!" cries Sukkot. But it was too late. The Jolly Flogger was already within range of the angry Lesbian archers. A hail of arrows whooshed from the harbour towards us. We all ducked and cowered over our oars. But there was nowhere to hide.

Aesop was the first casualty - a direct hit in the little toe. Chorismos was running up and down the boat in terror. Only the six monks seemed completely unperturbed; they observed the proceedings calmly. But Big Lysandros, my rowing partner, took an arrow in the heart. He fell back off our bench and slumped lifeless on the deck in a pool of blood.

Something pink cried, "I want to be a Lesbian!" and leapt out of the Jolly Flogger into the sea. It was Chlamydia, still wearing the cloak that had given her name. She doggy-paddled towards the shore.

Then I saw a chilling sight, a sight that I shall never forget, a sight that still comes to me in my nightmares. Arete of Cyrene was standing at full height upon her bench, presenting a full-frontal target to the angry Lesbians. She had ripped open her tunic, presenting her hairy flat chest head-on to the archers. Her beard fluttered in the wind, as did her willy. She had no boobs at all. Just the outline of a woman's breasts tattooed onto her muscled torso. And saggy ones at that. "Don't kill me, O sister archers of Lesbos," she cried. "I am a woman, just like yourselves! I am under the dire curse of Tiresias, the spectral blind seer of Thebes, whose personal truth puts all others in the wrong for eternity. Let me join you. Let me be break free of the curse of Tiresias, the Trans-Exclusionary Revolting Phantom. Release me from my fate."

The arrows stopped. The angry Lesbians were peering at Arete and talking excitedly to each other. Then they shook their heads, raised their bows and launched a ferocious volley of nine arrows directly at Arete. Three arrows dropped short and fizzed into the sea. Three whistled overhead. And three tore right into Arete's chest.

Arete looked astonished. "Sisters?" she gasped. "I am a woman like you. Pleasure is the sole purpose of life." Then her knees folded. Arete of Cyrene tumbled from the bench into the wine-dark sea and was no more.

Aesop shook his head. "Didn't I tell you? The Curse of Tiresias strikes again. So long as we've got prophets banging on about their 'personal truths', the rest of us are done for."

We rowed hell for leather. Soon we were out of range of the angry Lesbian archers. We stopped to catch our breath. You know, I was dead happy to be alive. And dead sad about Arete. Funny that. Even though I was to be sacrificed as soon as we reached Corinth, I still cared about Arete. *Arete* is the Greek word for *virtue*.

Chapter 34 - Paros/Antiparos, 24th of Boedromion, 378 BC

The twin islands were separated by a narrow channel, with the tiny islet half-way between them.

"Paros and Antiparos," Aesop said. "I can smell them. And that rocky little outcrop in the middle is Reumatonese."

"So we're on track?" I asked. "On schedule for my sacrifice, then?"

"On the button," Aesop confirmed.

And it's safe here, right?" Sukkot asked timidly. "I mean, no butch archers? No white trash Macedonian honkies? No cancellation pits?"

"Perfectly safe," reassured Aesop, "so long as we respect the local etiquette."

"Oh, for the love of crap! Now what?"

"Let me explain," said Aesop. We gathered around. "This tale begins two hundred years ago with old Archilochus, the High Priest of the twin islands which we are now approaching. Archilochus was dying. Every day his heartbeat was weaker. Every day his breathing was heavier. But the High Priest was determined to honour the Gods of Paros as long as he could. His twin sons, Alphos and Betos, on the other hand, were quarrelsome, drunken, sacrilegious louts and Archilochus knew that they would bring down the

415

wrath of the Gods and destroy the prosperity of the twin islands. One evening, Archilochus was taking his evening stroll when he spotted an ancient olive tree which had been struck by a thunderbolt. A branch had splintered, and one of the charred fragments caught the king's eye. 'I could use that to eat my porridge," he said to himself. And indeed, it had a long straight bit at one end and a concave elliptical bit at the other, just like a wooden spoon. He picked it up, laughed, and took it home.

"Pretty soon, High Priest Archilochus was in love with his new possession. He not only ate his breakfast porridge with it; he used it for his lunchtime broth, his afternoon herbal infusion and his dinnertime ragout. He kept it tucked up his sleeve. He took it to the temple rites, tucked into his belt. He carried it on his daily stroll. He took it to bed. All his subjects noticed the object's effect upon the High Priest. Whenever Archilochus looked upon it, he smiled. Whenever Archilochus was vexed or anxious, he only had to pull his beloved possession out of his sleeve and his face would light up with joy.

"But finally, Archilochus knew that the hour of his death was approaching. He called his twin sons, Alphos and Betos, and all the nobles and counsellors of the twin islands to the Temple of Apollo, the God of Truth. With gloomy, downturned faces the grey-bearded elders stood in a semi-circle in front of the altar, while Alphos and Betos knelt in front of their dying father. "For many a moon, my mind has been troubled by one question," said the old High Priest. "This question has kept me awake for many a long night, while the wolves howl in the forest and the moonlight brightens my chamber. This question has wearied my days, while the cicadas mock me with their song and the scornful sun beats mercilessly upon my bald pate. The question is this: to whom shall I leave my kingdom? Alphos and Betos, my sons, both of you have been disappointments to the Olympian Gods and to me. And yet I must choose between you. One moment ..." The king coughed into the back of his sleeve and drank water from the silver goblet brought to him by his acolyte *hebe*. "This is my final wish," said the High Priest. "Alphos and Betos, my twin regrets, I leave my wealth, the High Priesthood and the fate of the Twin Islands to whichever of you can name the thing that has brought me the greatest happiness."

""That's easy," said Alphos. "It's a piece of wood."

""No way," said Betos. "It's a spoon."

""Tell us the answer, great and holy Archilochus" cried all the nobles and counsellors, "so that the succession may be peaceful."

417

""It's ...," croaked the High Priest. "It's ..." And then he slumped back into his throne, and died without another word.

Aesop sighed. "Well, we all could have guessed the rest; The once-prosperous Twin Islands split into two warring factions. Alphos's supporters called themselves the Woodites. They set up their fortress on the eastern island: a single mound of rocks and earth surrounded by stakes. In the centre of their fort was a statue of Archilochus and a fox. On the plinth was inscribed, "No man ever steps in the same river twice." Alphos governed the island mercilessly according to a strict rule, which soon became known as the Strict Rule: on pain of death, all things were to be named without any human pre-conception or presumption. So, a wooden spoon was called 'piece of wood', because the very idea of a spoon is just a human notion. A horse was called a horse and leather was called leather, but a saddle was called 'horseback-shaped leather'. The Woodites' fortress was naturally named, "The Moundofrocksandearthsurroundedbysharpenedlogs."
The Strict Rule was enforced without mercy or exception, because the moment the east island accepted that leather could be called a saddle, it would have been as good as admitting that Archilochus had owned a wooden spoon - and that the kingdom therefore belonged rightly to Betos.

"Meanwhile, Betos's followers, the Spoonists, encamped on the western island, which they fortified with trenches, embankments and booby-traps. In the centre of their agora they erected a marble statue of Archilochus carrying a hedgehog, with the inscription "Opinion is the medium between knowledge and ignorance". The Spoonists' life was regulated by the Law of the Spoon, which required all things to be named exactly the way the speaker wanted; but the penalty for miscreants caught using the wrong words was to be cancelled, by being cast off the island's orygma, its highest clifftop. So every Spoonist had the right to choose whether to call the Woodites "foreigners", or whether to call Tiresias a 'woman'. But if six people decided that you had used the wrong word, you would be immediately cancelled to death, and, when you were properly dead, your brains smashed on the rocks of the orygma, you would be tried before a judge and jury for offences against the Law of the Spoon. And this arrangement was obviously necessary, because the moment you admitted that people couldn't choose to call a piece of wood 'a spoon', you were pretty much accepting that Alphos was the lawful king of the Twin Islands.

"Well," Aesop continued, "High Priest Archilochus died centuries ago, when Homer was still a beardless young man. But the Woodites and Spoonists are still at war. Both sides are trying to conquer Reumatonese, the little islet between the east and west islands. Can you see it yet?"

"I can see an uninhabited, scrappy little rock with a couple of dozen scrawny goats and a temple."

"Yup, that'll be Reumatonese," Aesop confirmed. "The most worthless piece of real estate in the central Aegean. And that's the Temple of Archilochus upon it. But you know, each side must have sent an invasion force to Reumatonese more than a hundred times, and neither the Woodites nor the Spoonists have been able to capture it, despite it being completely undefended. And you can guess why, can't you. The Woodites can't understand each other and the Spoonists can't stand each other. The Woodites row their ships with their spears, put wooden spoons in their quivers instead of arrows and use their helmets as soup tureens. The Spoonists, on the other hand, bicker endlessly about who is 'in charge', whether the Woodites are being 'othered' and whether Reumatonese has been fetishised, colonised or exploited. And the goats just watch the triremes coming and going, coming and going, from east and west, year after year.

"So," Aesop shrugged, "that's why I said we have to mind the local etiquette. East or west, either way, if one of us says a single wrong word, we're in deep doo-doo."

"Europe, bloody Europe," Sukkot muttered. "Straight out of their caves. Sometimes I wonder if we Africans shouldn't take Greece over - just to save these whites from themselves."

"Oh yes, massa!" Omphalos agreed. "We honkies jus' ain't fit to look afta o'selves."

The leader of the Buddhist holy men adjusted his orange robe and smiled as though he'd heard a joke that the rest of us had missed. To be honest, this Siddartha bloke had been getting on my tits the last couple of days. Even though he could speak Greek OK for a foreigner, the stuff he said still made no sense to me, and he always had this serene grin as though he'd just got away with letting out an undetected fart. "Both sides are right and both sides are wrong," he now said. "We bring the wood and the spoon into existence by perceiving them."

Now I was really losing my rag. "So - are we just going to hang around all day chatting?" I asked. "I mean, I'm not in a hurry to get to Corinth, obviously. But, as you may not have noticed, while we've been drifting into the danger zone between Paros and Antiparos, the Spoonists have seen us coming." A formation of 4 Spoonist triremes from the western island was rounding the rocky promontory on our port bow and heading towards us at full speed. They must have mistaken the Jolly Flogger for a Woodite warship making a surreptitious move on Reumatonese. We could hear the Spoonist hoplites singing heartily, as the foam from their triple-banked oars leapt and sparkled in the bright morning sun. I couldn't make out all the lyrics, but the refrain 'crush their brains and mince their guts' carried very clearly across the waves towards the Jolly Flogger.

"Hard a-starboard!" cried Sukkot, making a dash for the tiller. But I knew it was futile. There was no way our motley crew of philosophers, dotards, holy kids and superannuated storytellers could out-row a hundred and seventy battle-hardened heavy infantry.

Sukkot was crying in desperation, "There's no 'I' in 'team'. Teamwork makes the dream work. I want everyone giving a hundred and twenty percent," lashing us across our chests on every third stroke of the oars. I was rowing harder than I'd every rowed in my career as a slave. Every tendon in my arms and back was squealing in pain. Sweat was stinging my eyes. And still the lashes rained on our chests. We rowed faster. The blisters on my right hand split open and began to bleed onto the oar-handle. All around me, I could hear the groans and curses of my shipmates.

But suddenly Sukkot yelled, "Sto-o-o-op!" There was a look of raw terror in his huge eyes.

I turned around to see what had scared him. And there they were. Ahead of us, on the Woodite east island, a row of catapults was lined up on the clifftop. They were loaded with massive boulders and their arms were already drawn back and straining to fire. Did the Woodites think that the Jolly Flogger was the lead vessel of a Spoonist naval squadron?

The Spoonist triremes behind us had stopped rowing, and rested at ease, safely out of range of the catapults. The Spoonist hoplites had stopped singing and were leaning over their starboard gunwale to see where the Jolly Flogger would go next.

"I surmise," Aesop's flutey voice sang out, "that we are between a rock and a hard place."

Suddenly there was a volley of loud cracks, followed by a chorus of whistles and whizzes, and three boulders the size of Samian cattle were arching from the Woodite clifftops through the cerulean Hellenic sky and towards our frail little craft. The first flew overhead. The second fell just short of the Jolly Flogger and crashed into the sea, soaking us in fountain of foam. The third whizzed on a flat trajectory across our stern, knocking the heads of half a dozen galley slaves, including Omphalos's shrivelled and warty noggin, cleanly off their shoulders, before plopping into the sea on our port side.

"There goes my working capital buffer!" Sukkot groaned. He raised his plate-like hands to the skies. "Oh, thou great god Poseidon," he roared, "master of the ocean's fathomless depths, lord of the ocean's raging storms, if you bring us safely to Corinth, not only shall I sacrifice Diogenes of Sinope, but, in your honour, I shall also make Diogenes's death especially and exquisitely painful. I shall pull out his teeth and fingernails, and I shall crush his balls between two terracotta bricks while he is still fully conscious, just as a proof of my humble devotion to your majestic divinity. This I most solemnly swear. And, when his testicles are a smooth pulp, the texture of Cretan taramasalata, I shall..."

But before Sukkot could finish elaborating the details of my death, another three shrieking rocks were tracing a Menaechmic parabola from the Woodite catapults towards us. This second volley fell far out on our starboard side, causing the Spoonist hoplites to let out a mocking chorus of whoops and wolf whistles. While the holy men chanted prayers and arranged the headless corpses in neat rows, the rest of us watched the Woodite artillery captain haranguing his catapult team, and his soldiers running back to their machines and then adjusting their aim.

"Where was I?" Sukkot muttered. "Bugger. This artillery made me lose my train of thought. Oh, yes. Cretan taramasalata." He raised his arms skyward again. "Great Poseidon, and after that, I shall pierce

Diogenes's nipples with fishhooks, tie them to an ox cart and pull him through the..."

Suddenly they were screeching towards us again. Three rocks. Six rocks. Nine rocks. Twelve rocks. I could see them getting bigger. The screech becoming a roar. Bigger and louder...

Chapter 35 - Tiraspol, 23 February 2020

Tiraspol is a special city, Mikhail thought. It is in a country whose name depends on which way you're facing. If you are looking from the east, from Ukraine or Russia, then Tiraspol is the capital of *Pridnestrovie*, which means *"The land on this side of the River Dniester"*. If you are looking from the west, from Italy or Germany, for example, then Tiraspol is the capital of *Transnistria*, which means "The land on the other side of the River *Nistru*."

Even better, there is no agreement about which tongues are spoken by Transnistria's half million inhabitants. Their main language is Russian; that much is clear. But is their second language Moldovan, or simply Romanian written in the cyrillic script? And why does the Transnistrian administration insist that the language is Moldovan and also insist Transnistria is independent from Moldova? As the Americans say, go figure!

Mikhail is walking up 25th of Oktober Street, a broad boulevard running parallel to Karl Marx Street and Lenin Street. In his shopping bag there are two loaves of borodinsky black rye bread, two hundred grams of Ukrainian doktorskaya sausage, sliced, six eggs wrapped in a page from the Dnestrovskaya Pravda, two hundred grams of Moldovan brinza cheese, a tin of Russian sprats and a block of Belarusian ice cream.

It's three o'clock on a Friday afternoon, but 25 Oktober Street is almost empty: just half a dozen rodent-like oldies shuffling around in their grey coats and knitted hats. As Mikhail passes Pridnistrovie's 'Government' Building and the 6 metre bust of Lenin on its forecourt, a purple-nosed babushka stares at him. The babushka's mouth gapes slackly at his egg-like face. She clutches a shopping trolley, her body frozen, only the slow swivel of her watery eyes proving that she is alive. (Mikhail thinks of his mother - but only briefly.) He reads the bronze plaque dedicated to the heroes of the Pridnestrovian 'army' who gave their lives in 1992 for the 'independence' of their 'motherland'. He notices how so many of them share the same surnames and wonders whether this is a statistically unrepresentative sample of the population or whether Transnistrians tend to be related to each other. He passes the T34 tank on its plinth - facing west, naturally. In the park next to the Dniester are the remnants of the New Year market: a pylon of rusting rebars crudely welded into the shape of a fir tree and a couple of stalls selling boiled sweets and plastic trumpets. The stall keepers shuffle their feet in the thin, dry snow and clap their mittened hands together. A little further up, he sees the 'embassies' of the 'states' of Ossetia and Abkhazia - a tiny shared terraced house with a padlocked front door and two dainty hand-sewn polyester flags flapping above the front door. Then a foreign exchange bureau where you can trade real dollars for mildewy Pridnestrovian 'rubles' dignified with a picture of General Suvarov, Pridnestrovia's George Washington. That is where Mikhail picks up his Western Union transfers from the USA.

Mikhail's new father, Senator Shaun Shaughnessy, gives his son $3250 per month, revised annually in line with the United States consumer price index. The condition was that Mikhail must not enter the USA or talk to the media for 10 years. Mikhail found his father's offer attractive. Not fair, but attractive. And necessary. Lacking a homeland, friends and family, he needed at least financial security. Imperial College would not let him work remotely for ever - who ever heard of such a thing in February 2020? The screeching cacophony of America was intolerable for his Antilochus-Hesburger's, especially since he became the Ground Zero of media attention. But where to go, if not America? Britain had said that Mikhail did not belong in Britain and Russia had refused him entry to Russia.

But his mother had been born in the Mother and Child Hospital in Tiraspol, Pridnestrovia. That entitled Mikhail to the black Pridnestrovian 'passport', on which he could travel to the 'Republics' of Ossetia, Abkhazia and Artsakh. Mikhail signed the contract with his father's lawyer, under the supervision of a friendly woman called Emily. He flew to Tiraspol via Vienna and Chisinau. His father arranged, through the American Embassy in Chisinau, for Mikhail to be driven directly from Chisinau Airport to the Pridnestrovian 'border' without clearing Moldovan immigration. The Mayor of Tiraspol found him a VIP apartment on 25 October Street: 'VIP' meaning that it was a solid Stalinka from the 1950s, not a shoddy, jerry-built Krushchovka from the 1960s; 'VIP' also meaning that it had been repainted and the toilet flushed.

But Mikhail wasn't feeling too good this February afternoon. He was going down with something. His joints were aching, he was sweating and it hurt to breathe. What's more, he was certain who he'd caught it from: that Milanese guy wheezing his lungs out in seat 13C on the WizzAir flight from Vien to Kishinev. Mikhail decided to skip his Russian language class. Skipping a class when infectious would be according to the rules, not against the rules.

Mikhail liked his apartment door: solid steel and two deadbolts. He put his groceries into the buzzing fridge. But the heat indoors was unbearable. Soviet radiators cannot be turned up or down. He opened the kitchen window to let in the -6 degrees February wind.

Pridnestrovie gets its gas from Russia via a pipeline which runs through Ukraine. Pridnestrovie, of course, cannot pay for the gas since it has nothing to sell except divin (the name of Moldovan cognac) and contraband cigarettes. Russia therefore bills the gas to the Moldovan Government in Chisinau and Chisinau refuses to pay. But Pridnestrovie uses most of the gas to supply 95% of Moldova's electricity. Moldova must pay for that. And then the hot water from the power stations' cooling towers is fed into Tiraspol's radiators. So, Mikhail's heating was free. And at least the tropical heat of Mikhail's apartment suited Humpty the African Grey parrot.

Mikhail sat down in front of the TV. CMM was playing. The chyron was scrolling something about Russian tanks and mobile howitzers massing on the Belarus-Ukraine border - but that wasn't the main story. More importantly, a mob was storming Shaun Shaughnessy's office in Columbus, Ohio. Some had flaming torches, some wore conical white hoods, some sported red Make America Great Again caps, and most were obese. There was teargas. There was smoke. There were flames. National Guardsmen protected themselves with Perspex shields from flying rocks. The CMM anchor was saying, "After setting the worldwide web on fire, the Krutoy affair has now spilled off the internet and is setting fire to the streets of America. Last night there was Krutoy-related violence in Washington DC and 16 state capitals. Twenty-one state governors have declared states of emergency. Fourteen have called out the National Guard. It looks as though the Mikhail Krutoy controversy has triggered a wave of extreme right-wing violence that threatens to engulf our democracy. We ask: did Russian internet trolls contribute to this crisis?"

"Bwaark! Plato is a tosser!" Humpty squawked.

Mikhail flipped channels to Tox News. A man in a suit was perorating. He had brown, preternaturally bouffant hair, a face like supermarket ham and a slack chin. "... and now so-called "Black Lives Matter demonstrations" in twenty American cities. They call it the 'Krutoy factor'. We call it rampant violence and destruction of property. Chicago. San Francisco. Cincinnati. Cities with great histories, cities that represent the dynamism of liberty and the free market, these cities are now aflame. But I ask you this: when mom and pop stores are looted and hard-working white Americans lose their livelihoods - is that a demonstration, or is it a riot against democracy? When

Koreans and Vietnamese don't dare to step out of their front doors - is that a demonstration, or is it a riot against democracy? When volunteer firefighters of all races are pelted with rocks as they try to protect state buildings from the flames, is that a demonstration, or is it a riot against democracy? And, of course, the liberals and the mainstream liberal media blame it all on "Russian internet trolls". Well, do the liberals think that we Americans are so dumb that we need Russians to tell them that America is messed up?" This man in a suit points at the camera. His ice-blue eyes sparkle. "I say this, Russia. We don't need you to teach us that our democracy is going up in flames. We can see it with our own eyes."

"Bwaark! Plato is a tosser!"

Mikhail turned to the BBC World News: "... and for the third consecutive day, traffic was at a standstill in London's West End, as Black Lives Matter supporters and anti-immigration protesters glued themselves to various segments of Trafalgar Square, Marble Arch and Oxford Street. The police advise people to stay at home." And on France 24, against the background of a burning car, a suave man with the top three buttons of his shirt open, crazy curly hair and little round glasses - a Gallic television philosopher - is saying, "...and, vonce again, ze yellow vests are asking ze people of France, 'Ow much do you value your

Republic? C'est le soi-disant effet Krutoy. Ow much do you value your liberty, your equality and your fraternity?'"

Mikhail zapped across to Rossiya-1. Vladimir Putin was pinning a medal onto the left breast of a young woman with long blonde hair. She was wearing the olive uniform of the FSB. "Anastasiya receives Medal 415 for services to the information security of the Russian Federation." The President of Russia leaned towards her and whispered into her ear. He had a cheeky grin, as though he was about to play a practical joke or invade a neighbouring country and was dying to share the secret.

Mikhail shrugged. Returning to the kitchen he made himself a cheese and rye sandwich. He capped the plate with a wire mesh cover to keep the cockroaches off. Back in the living room, he pushed his armchair against the wall to make more space for himself in the middle of the floor. Then he pulled his virtual reality goggles down from the ceiling.

"Bwaark! Plato is a tosser!"

Mikhail had found peace.

Chapter 36 – Reumatonese, 27th of Boedromion, 378 B.C.

I felt a sharp stab in my big toe. I opened my eyes. A nanny goat was nibbling my right foot. I sat up in alarm. The goat peered curiously into my eyes, and then sauntered indolently out of the door of the abandoned temple.

"You're alive!"

I turned towards the voice. Siddhartha, the leader of the Buddhist holy men was crouched in a corner of the temple. Beside him were a bowl of water and some bloody bandages. He was stroking my little dog, Chorismos. Chorismos broke free and ran towards me, wagging his tail.

"Where am I? What's happening?"

"Where are you?" replied the holy man. "Well, it depends from which direction you look at it. The easterners call it West Paros. The westerners call it East Anti-Paros. But we can call it Reumatonese, if you like. We are in the temple of Archilochus. You have been unconscious for three days and two nights."

"And the Jolly Flogger? What about Sukkot? What about Aesop and Omphalos.

"They are all happy."

"They're alive?"

"Alive? Possibly. Possibly not. That's up to you. But happy. When the rock landed, it split the boat in two, right down the middle. As it sank, I heard Omphalos call out his last words: "I am the great admiral Prince Kalamindar of Macedon." And Aesop called, "There are no mistakes - only lessons." And Sukkot called, "Nubia forever!" So I think they all drowned happily."

"Are there any other survivors?"

"Just two: you and your dog," said the holy man.

"Just *three*: me and Chorismos and *you*, you mean."

"No, Diogenes of Sinope, just two survivors." The holy man opened his saffron-coloured robes to show me his wounded chest. The deep gash was already gangrenous. The smell nearly made me puke. "This injury is putrid, and I am feverish. I only stayed alive this long to nurse you, feed you and wash you. Now you are awake, I am no longer needed." The holy man smiled. "You have a herd of 24 feral goats. You have goat's milk. You have wild herbs and berries. I found some fishing nets and rye seeds in this temple. You shall live in peace for as long as you want."

"Is that it?" I asked. "Is that all you have to say to me before you leave me? Goats and fishing nets?"

The holy man smiled. "Well, since you have asked me for more, I will give you three suggestions:

"First, there will always be people who use words in different ways, and they will often argue and fight. But in your long journey you have seen that the words have meaning and no meaning at the same time. So, please don't decide to live on one big island or the other big island. Please stay on this little island in the middle, where you can look both ways and see both sides. Your island is called Reumatonese - the Isle of Flow.

"Second, please remember that, when two things are the same, you naturally think the same of them. If two beans are identical, you don't make one bean your favourite bean. That would be ridiculous. If two spoons are the same, you don't make one spoon your favourite spoon. That would be ridiculous. And, since you are identical to most other human beings in all the ways that matter, don't make yourself your favourite person. That would also be ridiculous."

"And the third suggestion? Advice from holy men always comes in threes, no?"

"You have worked out the third suggestion for yourself."

Two days later, I cremated the holy man on a pyre of driftwood, as he had asked me. With the wind behind me, I threw his ashes into the sea. That was eight years ago. Now it's just me and Chorismos.

Chorismos is showing his age, but I'm doing fine. When I think of how I once lived in Athens, and how things might have turned out in Macedonia, Sinope, Lesbos, Corinth, Paros or Anti-Paros, I remember how fortunate I am.

Peace.

Fig. 2. *Statue of Athena as a xylinokolaphopolimistes (wooden spoon warrior), Akademie Museum, Berlin. Attributed to Phidias. c. 440 BCE*

Printed in Great Britain
by Amazon

59355800R00249